I'll
the
Monster

I'll Be the Monster

Sean Gilbert

DUCKWORTH

First published in the United Kingdom by Duckworth in 2026

Duckworth, an imprint of Duckworth Books Ltd
1 Golden Court, Richmond, TW9 1EU, United Kingdom
www.duckworthbooks.co.uk

A catalogue record for this book is available from the British Library

Book design by Danny Lyle

Printed and bound in Great Britain by Clays Ltd, Elcograf S.p.A.

The authorised representative in the EEA is Easy Access System
Europe, Mustamäe tee 50, 10621 Tallinn, Estonia.

Hardback ISBN: 9780715656006
eISBN: 9780715656020

For my mum, who taught me how to read

Part I
Enduring Triangles

1

You are watching pornography in the hotel lobby as I wait in line at the reception. You wear tangled headphones pilfered from the airline, even though my Sennheisers are stashed in the bag at your feet. I wonder, absently, how much sound is leaking from the cheap plastic. Though the seats surrounding you are empty, patrons drift through the space, close enough to overhear an errant moan. A woman is pacing back and forth, about a metre from you. An elderly couple walk out of the elevator and drift in your direction. Absorbed in your task, you do not notice any of them. You will not flaunt the movie but you will not disguise it either. A part of you wishes, desperately, to be discovered.

Your phone is enormous. The close-up shots will be rendered to scale. You bite your thumbnail and squint at the screen, studious and intent.

When it is my turn, the receptionist welcomes me, wishes me good evening, asks how he can help, in a monotonous, melodic voice, as if he memorised the sound of these sentences but not their meaning. His gaze has a strange, unfocused quality. I lie and say it is our anniversary, he nods vaguely and slides two key cards across the desk. I state that my wife and I have been married ten years to the day, hoping that this will pique his interest. He is unmoved. His boredom makes him remote, unamenable.

'I was wondering if we could get an upgrade,' I say.

'You're interested in upgrading your room?'

'I'm asking if *you're* interested in upgrading my room. You know, given the occasion.' Usually I am better at this. Usually you are standing next to me as we fabricate anniversaries and promotions and proposals.

Now, the receptionist only stares, perhaps waiting for me to say more. His irises are dark, his skin an even, honeyed tan. He looks at me the way a plumber would regard a rusted pipe: some unremarkable nuisance. He has seen my type before, people who price their dignity at a few square feet and a freestanding bath.

'We are fully booked,' he states. He glances behind me where another hotel guest waits.

'There's always something,' I insist. I hope my tone is jocular, not pleading.

'In this case there is not.'

'I'm quite a regular traveller...'

At this, he smiles slightly, and it feels like a small collapse.

'So we get nothing?' I say, too loudly There is an edge of desperation that I instantly regret.

'You get the room you booked,' he states. Waits. Then adds, 'And, of course, my congratulations.'

Even though he has little – a low-paid job, no prospects – I feel, suddenly, as if I have much less. Sometimes whole economies go bust overnight. My credit card is gold. I have access to the BA lounge. Yet this boy's amused, bankrupting smile renders these things meaningless, makes me feel like a hoarder of ruined currency.

With stiff, self-conscious movements, I begin to extricate myself and I think the receptionist is almost disappointed; my humiliation is likely the only interesting occurrence of tonight's shift. He is about ten years younger than me, but I'm sure he considers our differences fundamental. People in their early twenties see their youth as intrinsic, not circumstantial. He regards my age as something that will never happen to him.

I do not return to you immediately, instead I pause and consider how to frame this defeat. I could suggest that the receptionist was an idiot or that he spoke bad English or tested my patience causing me to storm indignantly away. I could simply say that they are full, even though, just standing here, you can feel an emptiness hanging in the air. This was once a famous hotel and now all that remains is an atmosphere of grand ruin: thick curtains, dated carpets, a name that people vaguely recognise. It seems the perfect setting for a melodrama on late night TV, replete with maudlin alcoholics, devastated actors, thieves.

Two businessmen sit down on the sofa to your left. They talk and laugh loudly. Men like this always presume an audience, they pitch their voices so that strangers can hear them clearly. I find that I want them to notice the film.

Of course, you do not see these men. I watch you and you are worlds away. Maybe you are in the back seat of a used car, your limbs bent, the air thick and humid with the smell of others. You are wandering a deserted stretch of woods, where birdsong blends with the sound of a nearby motorway. The trees reach high, the scrub seems endless, dimensions that make everything, you, even your act of submission, seem small and incidental. Tonight, perhaps, you are in a filthy dorm room, football posters tacked to the walls, EDM blasting from muffled speakers and a queue of naked performers lingering close. A boy with the face of a child and the body of a man volunteers to go first. Half drunk. Anxious. Ready to disguise his inexperience with a show of bravado and blunt force.

The phone lights your chin from beneath and the rest of your face is gaunt with shadow. I have watched you watch pornography in rooms all across the world, yet never so brazenly. It confirms my sense that you need this holiday, that it has already come, perhaps, a little too late.

You do not look up until I am standing directly over you. You remove your headphones but do not press pause.

'What are you doing?' I ask.

'You know what I'm doing.'

'It feels gratuitous,' I say. 'Anyway, I offered to help you with that stuff.'

'You're too squeamish,' you state.

This is true. I no longer check your search history because I cannot bear even this. I do not follow you on these expeditions. Instead, I wait for you on the surface, quietly, unobtrusively, making sure you don't stay submerged too long. Tonight, it has been ten minutes.

'Did you find her?' I ask.

'Not this time. Did you get the room?' you counter.

'No,' I confess. 'The man was fairly stubborn. He was also an idiot – I'm not sure he even understood what I was saying.'

You glance at me strangely. 'He understood,' you say.

Though I do not believe in omens, I have faith in signs. Once, we achieved upgrades on the strength of a smile, an expectation. Now, it seems the world is moving against us. We have slid.

For a moment we stay silent. I listen to disembodied voices groan and climax, quiet as a whisper, in the empty seat where your headphones have fallen. A few metres away, one of the middle-aged men loses focus as he converses with his friend. His head locks, he squints, as if struck by a bad memory, or a suspicious odour beneath the perfumed air, and then slowly, almost cautiously, he resumes his conversation. That is your effect. That moment of doubt.

Sometimes I think the way to know you best is to study your radius of influence, the way you step into a room and alter it, slightly. I look at you now and want to share this insight, or some version of it, but I worry I will sound too reverential. Recently, it's been difficult to compliment you.

Your glance slips from mine. Your eyes land on your screen where a public threesome, shot in low resolution, is fully underway. The performers have the bodies and grace of farmhands.

'Men,' you say vaguely and sigh. Your eyes stay on the screen. 'They don't seem to notice,' you add.

'Notice what?'

'This should be an insult. Millions of films and they all follow the same script, the same shots, the same words, even. It's stunningly basic.'

'You expect character development and story arcs.'

'I expect humanity. I expect to see humans performing for other humans. All I see is body parts and organs. An anatomy class.'

'We went to very different schools, perhaps.'

You consider this. 'My PSHE teacher was terrified of sex, or talking about it, at least. She could only get through the lesson by sticking to the script. I mean this literally: she had an actual script. Even her jokes were written down. I feel that's what men get from porn. They want to stop their minds from wandering, fend off any surprises. They're scared of what might come into their head if they simply unzipped their jeans and began to touch.'

On that thought, you lock your phone.

'I've read there's a growing movement for feminist porn,' I say.

'Yes, OK,' you answer, impatiently. I understand your disdain. Feminist porn: it's the type of topic someone raises at a party to sound provocative. A *Guardian* feature.

'It's not even that I find men disgusting,' you say. 'Just dull. Uninspired.'

'I feel I should take offence.'

'You know I don't see you that way. You're not... "*A Man*".'

I begin to parse this remark, which falls so strangely between insult and praise, but you interrupt my thoughts.

'So we're stuck with a shit room?' you ask.

'This is a five-star hotel. We're hardly slumming it.'

You consider this. 'I'll give it a go,' you offer. 'It's worth another shot.'

'I don't think there's much point...' I reply, but you are already standing, shaking your limbs loose like an athlete before a heat. Now you are rifling through your bag for your wallet and passport.

It's like witnessing some astonishing creature hatch. You stride and seem to grow taller, more statuesque as you move. Your maxi dress flows like liquid and one of the straps has slipped from your shoulder; an image of feckless glamour. To any onlooker you would appear sun-dazed, sleepy. Only I recognise the significant muscle control that is required for such casual motions.

You lean across the desk. The man who served me leans in. You huddle, conspiratorial, flirtatious.

An instrumental jazz version of a famous Ed Sheeran song is playing through the Tannoy. I realise that it has been playing for some time. Only now, at this moment, the sound becomes unbearable.

You tip your head back and laugh. You rest your open palm on the countertop, inches, I imagine, from his.

The saxophone reaches for a crescendo and I think I could murder the performers of this song. But then, I consider that to a musician, being compelled to perform asinine covers to score lobbies is its own form of torture. This is a comfort.

Your back tenses with laughter: negotiations are going your way. One track bleeds into the next.

You take your time returning to me, wait a long moment before showing me the two new key cards. I peer over your shoulder at the receptionist, but he refuses to look my way.

'We've been upgraded,' you announce.

As we make our way to the elevator, you remark, 'I think we really dodged a bullet.' You say this earnestly, as if some actual crisis has been averted.

I am tempted to speak about relativity. Your relief is real, palpable, but it is also purely hypothetical. On some level, we will never be able to know this upgrade. All we will ever know is the room we are now walking towards. Like life, like love, the experience is total. We will assume that the other room was smaller, shabbier, inconveniently placed and decide that we are lucky. It is a small leap of faith.

Then again, I look at you, and it seems to me that if you walked out, this entire hotel would implode and cease to exist. I make another leap.

So I smile, and accept your version. I accept that we will be happier now in room 633 and that we have already made some small advancement.

The elevator is lit amber. You inspect yourself in the mirror and like what you see: a woman who can charm her way into a mid-size suite. Unlike previous occasions, tonight the triumph is all yours, you did not need me as a prop or foil. If anything, I was a hindrance, you will tell yourself. I do not begrudge you this. Increasingly, I notice that your days are arranged around these set pieces; between them, you vanish and are reabsorbed into the ether. And I want you to stay, just a little bit longer, even if it is at my expense.

The door shuts behind us and a strange artificial hush descends, like that of a pressurised cabin. You examine the toiletries. I examine the cupboards, press my fingers against the white cotton robes, which feel reassuringly expensive. You test the firmness of the mattress and say that it's good. I roam to the balcony door; the glass is thick and soundproofed. Below, the traffic is reduced to abstract circuitry, small beads of light, silently pulsing. You continue to inspect, seeking that small crack, the hidden flaw.

'We're north-facing,' I announce. 'Lousy views.' There is relief in this discovery. It means we can stop looking.

'So...' you start, tentatively, your eyes roving the room as you speak. 'What are we celebrating?' The phrasing is particular. For now, you avoid the true question with its brutal wording: *why are we here?*

'We're celebrating each other. Life,' I answer.

'We're not in the habit of doing that.'

I shrug.

'Usually,' you continue, 'these extravagances mark something else entirely. The exact opposite, in fact.' Your words land slowly. You speak with the deliberate rhythm of a woman who wants to be understood, wants to make her meaning plain. Or perhaps it is the rhythm of a woman who wishes to be interrupted.

The AC unit hums. Channels of cool air circulate the space; for a second, it is the only thing that seems to move between us. You roll your neck backwards and I hear a crack.

I feel your eyes crawl the length of me. It lingers on my wrist and the skin grows clammy. I am wearing your first boyfriend's watch. Now, you wear your father's smile. Little tokens, little trophies, reminding us of all we have overcome.

'An Omega,' you remark, with feigned appreciation.

'It goes with my jacket,' I reply.

'Does it.'

Raph. He was not the first man to hurt you, but certainly the most creative. You mention his name constantly; yesterday, you said it three times at least. You invoke him so that you know where he is, so that he doesn't creep up on you. I stole his jewellery for reasons that I do not fully grasp. I do not know if you find this charming or faintly grotesque.

Your mouth is open but no words come out.

It is too late to go so deep into the past. We are too tired to embark on that particular journey. I am managing your ambivalence in bringing this conversation to a decisive close. You study your toenails, where the polish has begun to chip. I unzip my bag and begin hanging shirts. Perhaps a part of you wonders if we are even capable of that discussion, if we haven't lost the vocabulary for certain aspects of our history.

And then your voice rings out loud and fast. It startles me. 'A homicidal couple,' you say, 'checks into a luxury hotel to save their marriage.'

I stare at you. You stare back, with a lopsided smile. Your eyes narrow.

The sentence is all thorns. You want to know if I will touch it or if I will go back to my shirts.

I do neither. I hedge. 'What does that mean?'

'It sounds like the making of a great joke.'

'It isn't. It's a statement.' Or a proposition, I think.

'Not yet. But we only need a punch line.'

'And another person.'

'Explain,' you say, intrigued. We are feinting now and you like the exercise.

'Those jokes always involve groups of three. An Irishman, a Frenchman and a German. A priest, a rabbi and a nun.'

'So we need one more character?'

'At least. Maybe two. The couple effectively functions as a single character.'

I'm not sure if that's true, but the logic makes you flinch. And then your energy deserts you, you fall back onto the bed and look out beyond the balcony doors.

'So, our murderous couple are stranded,' you sigh. 'Incomplete.'

'Maybe they're happy where they are.'

'Or maybe they'll find the butt of their joke.'

'They're safely tucked away in their room...' I insist.

'The night's still young,' you counter, but without conviction.

I follow your eyes to the view outside. The neon from the hotel sign gives the darkness a sort of Incandesce. Beyond, the world is black and glowing.

Recently, you asked if I would ever consider a threesome. You had asked me before, but that first time it felt like a test, a measure of my devotion. When you questioned me the other night, there was something new in your voice. Curiosity. My answer was immediate. We didn't need another. Another would only spoil things.

Maybe I understood your question too concretely. I admit, we have, on occasion, required an interpreter. We have needed to do things to a different body in order to understand one another more clearly. These people always presented themselves when the time was right.

It is almost ten. There is still enough time to explore the city, grab a bite. We could also call it a night without reaching for excuses. As I weigh these options, you retrieve two diazepams from your toiletry bag, holding them in your mouth as you uncap a miniature vodka from the bar. You swallow and glance at your phone.

I remember when you first showed me your signature cocktail. Vodka, soda and crushed sleeping pills (or ketamine, at a pinch). You called it a Desperate Housewife. I used to worry you would die in your sleep. I researched resting pulse rates and watched YouTube videos showing how to check for breath. It took me years to accept that you have the constitution of a horse, that poisons affect you differently.

You wake me before sunrise. Face down, you are screaming and thrashing, your shins land hard on the mattress and your feet strike the bedpost. You twist, scratch your leg, kick harder while the marks turn red.

'Wake up!'

You make a sound. It comes from low in your throat, an angry and despairing noise. I have never heard you make a sound like this; even after all these years, there are still parts that you manage to hide.

I touch your arm. You jerk violently away.

'I said wake up!' I yell so frantically that it seems I am losing it too.

I lay my body on top of yours, absorbing the shocks, as I have done, increasingly, for you over the last few weeks. Your night terrors are getting worse. You toss and buck, a hand claws at the sheets, but gradually your energy drains, overwhelmed by my heaviness. Your head twists left and right. I press my hand against the base of your skull, hold you firmly in place, hoping you won't bite your tongue. Your right arm flaps. I grab and pin the wrist.

In the morning you will say you slept like a baby. When I inform you of what happened, you will remind me that you do not dream. You will say I'm exaggerating, deny my version of events. But you will feel the stiffness in your neck, notice the scratch on your arm and know I was there.

'What are you dreaming about?' I wonder. 'What', not 'who'. Despite the distance, I know who you return to each night.

2

Cambridge, 2010
A Spiteful Passage

The punt pushed east.

It began its course somewhere upstream, near Grantchester, and made slow progress towards Cambridge, moving gradually with the tide.

A Bluetooth speaker rested on the huff, blasting Shakespeare at eighty decibels. The recording was loud and crackly and it played on a loop: *Titus Andronicus*, Act V, Scene 1. People said it could be heard as far as Orchard Street. Baffling police complaints were recorded from 2.54 p.m.: some 'Shakespeare yob' was wreaking havoc on the water.

Lewis Barker, a bus driver, was the first to spot the punt. He was sitting by the River Cam, gathering his thoughts after a difficult shift. Six hours in traffic and four belligerent complaints; during working hours, he despised his passengers and after, he despised himself, for capitulating. These dark reflections were interrupted by the sound of a villain declaiming:

…kill a man or else devise his death,

Then Barker noticed the boat making its strange, wobbling passage towards the city. As it drew close, he saw that the punt was freighted with charcuterie and fruit, ripening quickly in the heat.

Plums rolled about beneath a grey aura of gadflies. The captain seemed untroubled. He was reclining at the rear, gripping a bottle of Veuve Clicquot firmly in one hand. Lewis was reminded of all the reasons he hated this place. He loathed the undergrads, how they constantly encroached on your line of vision, imperious, entitled, as if they already owned the ground beneath your feet. This one seemed worse than most. He wanted the air as well. Wanted all eyes and ears on him, made claim to every sense.

...Ravish a maid or plot the way to do it,

Lewis considered shouting an insult at the boy; he had lived in Cambridge his whole life and had several cherished slurs at the ready. Yet he worried he would not be heard over the booming poetry. He considered taking a photo, selling it to the papers – there was always a market for ponces making fools of themselves. But something stayed his hand. He could not say what exactly. Perhaps it was the expression of the captain's face, the set of his jaw, the subtle grimace. Lewis had the feeling that he was encountering the rare person whose bitterness outsized his own. Despite the captain's languor, Lewis noticed the occasional twitch, that pulse of rage, dangerous because it was kept hidden. The figure's right arm jerked suddenly, as if remembering some indignation. And so Lewis watched the boat pass, without any intervention. The captain did not even glance his way, his eyes trained on some distant target.

The tourists on Mathematical Bridge had fewer qualms about photos. They jostled for spots along the wooden frame and vigorously clicked. The captain was exactly what they had come to see. Frankly, for many in that group, the excursion had been a disappointment. Cambridge was no fun during Exam Term; the streets were mostly empty and the few students they encountered looked miserably oppressed. They had expected more. It was as if this boy had read those yearnings and answered with exaggerated panache.

13

Set fire on barns and haystacks in the night
And bid the owners quench them with their tears.

His head nodded slightly from side to side, as if attuned to private music beneath the verse. It was not yet three and he appeared a little drunk. A few noticed the grapes spoiling at his feet, the wine warming in his hand. So blessed and still so wanton. Though they disapproved, in theory, of all that privilege and waste, they experienced an odd instinct to applaud. He drifted and left them wistful for a life they would not know.

Only as the punt passed beneath Trinity Hall library was the captain finally identified. Those that knew him smiled. A stunt like this was perfectly in character: to renounce his studies at the very height of exam season, to turn their course material into a public nuisance. They felt excited, incited. They had been living in little caves all month and here was a blast of light.

Those that knew him better were apprehensive. They identified the tragedy booming from the boat and suspected some warning. *Why* Titus Andronicus? *Why now?* They knew, also, that the captain did not deal in gimmicks. This was only a prelude. He was surely planning something greater, more outrageous.

I have done a thousand dreadful things
As willingly as one would kill a fly,
And nothing grieves me heartily indeed
But that I cannot do ten thousand more.

Such preternatural focus; he was only that still when plotting violence. And how his fingers tightened, tightened, tightened around the neck of the bottle. The real trouble would start when he docked. Disaster was afoot. Havoc. Yet they watched as if bewitched, that strange captain, that rotten cargo.

3

I nudge open the balcony door and the sound of traffic pours in through the crack. The floor tiles are already uncomfortably hot, the sky above a sheet of blue acrylic. Inscrutable and flat, the city below has the quality of a simulation.

You are passed out on the bed, unlikely to rise for another hour, at least. I make the decision to tour the facilities because I do not want you to wake and see me waiting.

The buffet breakfast is unremarkable: sheets of fried egg sit beside mounds of dry pastries. I sip watery coffee at an empty table as an instrumental rendition of a popular Taylor Swift song tinkles in the background.

The gym looks nothing like the photos. Running machines are packed inches apart in an atmosphere thick with disinfectant and old sweat. A news broadcast flickers across the series of overhanging screens, depicting an environmental disaster off the Ivory Coast, as generic house music plays. Back home, I pay an extortionate amount in gym fees, though I have never been a fitness enthusiast. I go for the same reason that others attend church, seeking some vision of order. Every inch of the immaculate space, with its warm towels, its spotless machines, seems to make quiet assurances: it is a place where people sweat lightly, where miraculous bodies gather.

In the hotel, the adjoining pool is small but the surrounding decor is tasteful enough. Light reflects from the water's surface and marbles the pale walls. An empty jacuzzi froths and a withered towel lies abandoned at its base. I ease myself into a lounge chair.

The sudden hit of chlorine in the clammy air, the feel of damp plastic against my skin. Our first luxury hotel, The Shangri La, was like a small village, boasting five pools, a lazy river, six restaurants, shops and a sprawling spa. At night, we smoked shisha and ate until we were sick. Certain memories loom like tall buildings; one can journey and journey but they always feel close.

'I don't think I could ever get bored of this place,' you told me on the first night, perched above an unfinished plate of lobster.

'I think you underestimate yourself.'

'You make me seem like such a bitch, sometimes. I'm not that hard to please.'

And I chuckled, because you sounded sincere. 'You're the most fickle person I've ever met.'

You laughed, taking this as a compliment. I suppose it was.

A few tables down, an older, fatter woman sat with her husband. She glanced over at the sound of your laughter and beheld us, for a moment, with raw anguish. We locked eyes and she quickly turned away. The woman wore extravagant make-up, black pearls, a dress that seemed more suited to the opera than a humid, al fresco dinner. Her husband sat in a short-sleeved shirt and cargo shorts. He checked his phone and scrolled impatiently. Even though she averted her eyes, she could not hide it, the hope for a different sort of night. Sometimes when I see couples of a certain age, they seem like they have lost some tragic game of musical chairs.

The woman avoided glancing our way, which was how I knew she was thinking of us for the entire meal. I sipped my wine. It took on new depths of flavour.

Women noticed me when you were around. Men were always

watching you. They looked against their better instincts, because, really, they did not want to see us. Together, we were a punishing vision; young and happy and seemingly rich. We fed like vampires on all those looks.

The waiter came to ask if Madam was satisfied with her meal.

'She is,' you informed him. You swivelled your Chianti, inspected its tears with satisfaction. 'There are notes of tobacco in this,' you asserted.

'You have a good palate.'

'And bark. I can taste bark.'

'Impressive,' he smiled, bluffing as shamelessly as you yourself. Perhaps you enjoyed making him agree with such a ridiculous statement. That is how I'd see it now, though at the time, I was still fascinated by your motivations.

'I'll have another glass.' When he was gone, you turned to me and in an excited, guilty whisper said, 'We really look the part.'

I felt it too: the thrilling ease. We postured, and through these postures, we became.

'We will always look the part,' I promised.

'I just hope it doesn't come crashing down…'

'It's been six months. We're good.'

You became aware of the neighbouring couple. The husband was unhappy with his food. As he complained loudly, biliously, his wife stared at her plate and shrank. You couldn't take your eyes off him. Your expression grew inward.

'How would you do it?' I asked.

'Do what?' you replied, innocently.

'Do what?' I echoed in crude imitation, my tone like a small bite along your neck.

You began to smile. We had not played this game for a while. I was reminding you that everything is a choice: we could choose to have fun.

You glanced at the drunk man. 'A crowbar,' you said.

'Be serious.'

You drew back, felt your synapses flex, your knuckles crack, looked at the man again, concentrating, enjoying the sharp clarity of the exercise.

'He's heavy, so nothing too physical. If he fell on me, I'd be done for.'

'Something in his drink,' I said.

'He's twelve stone. It would have to be a lot of something.'

'Certain fungi could do the trick.'

When our waiter asked if we'd like another glass, we both said yes.

For some reason, I remember Muscat as our honeymoon. But now, on reflection, I realise our official honeymoon was in Spain, years later. Oman was in celebration of the other thing. Though at this point we were unmarried, it inaugurated our true beginning.

This is why we are here. Our itinerary is packed with subtle allusions to that first trip. Recently, you have grown fascinated with our lowest moments, but I want to remind you of our triumphs.

4

Each memory bids another.

You gave me a gift. A book, wrapped in sheet music left on my desk.

The first time you said 'I Love You' was on a Post-it note, tacked to the fridge. You wrote it in a messy hand, alongside a reminder to buy milk.

Warm currents in frigid waters. They help me weather you and make sense of what is happening.

I float up six floors and down the hall, feeling dreamy and nostalgic. My reverie is broken when I enter to the ecstatic cries of a performer screaming *slut! slut!* over a wet slapping sound. The phone is abandoned on your bed; clips will keep looping until the battery dies. I reach for the phone, catching sight of an innocuous bedroom; there is an NFL flag tacked to the wall, so this must be in America. I notice the setting first, not the actors, as if viewing it through your eyes. Two thirty-somethings posing as teenagers screw against an Ikea desk that can hardly take the weight. The woman jerks manically and the man declares *fuck yeah*, his voice tired, unconvincing. I lock the screen.

The balcony door is flung wide. Already, several flies carve dizzy halos beneath the ceiling light, which you have turned on for no clear reason.

Outside, your legs hang over the balcony edge. You write your daily affirmations on hotel stationery. As I approach, you take out a Bic lighter and set the paper aflame. It flares dramatically, as if cursed.

'Are you supposed to burn that?'

'Yes. The psychologist said you destroy the list when you're done.'

'Wasn't that the list of negative thoughts… The Worry List?'

'I can't remember.'

'This feels sort of satanic. Like you're condemning the best version of yourself.'

'I suppose I see what you mean,' you muse. The feathery ashes stir at your feet. 'Still, I think I prefer to do things this way. I can't explain it.'

'You should have been born a witch.'

'I was.'

The acrid smell of burnt paper follows us inside. It troubles the flies.

Almost eleven. I make a point of selecting clothes. I could be ready in an instant, but instead I carefully place my shirt and chinos on the bed, pinch my lips as I contemplate the outfit, the pale blue against the cream. You easily ignore this prompt, slumping into the bedside chair with a look of exultant exhaustion, as if you have been on your feet all day.

'Can I borrow your charger?' you ask.

'It won't do you any good. I have an Android.'

'I always forget. I wish you'd switch. Things would be so much easier.'

'There's an even easier solution: pack your charger.' I say this woodenly and you ignore me. We have had this conversation countless times before, in a myriad of cities and continents. The fact is, you prefer it this way. You enter rooms unsettled and distracted, you answer calls warning that any second, you might cut out. *I'm only on 5 per cent battery* is your mantra and your warrant. It means you always have a reason to exit. Sometimes, in a different mood, it gives you a reason to stare, flagrantly, at strangers, to approach them, uninvited, for a favour.

'We'll have to pick one up,' you say.

'First we'll have to leave the hotel room.'

You roll your eyes and rise wearily to your feet.

You flip open your suitcase and I try not to look, knowing that the disordered contents will only disturb me. Of course, I can't resist. I look.

As well as a charger, I can already tell that you have forgotten a variety of essentials. You have not brought enough clothes. For some reason, you have packed an impressive variety of hats. Of course, you have also brought several books you will never read but that will push you perilously close to the baggage limit, meaning you will have no space for souvenirs. Meaning I will carry them. I've only recently become aware of this petty tallying, but the ledger has always existed. It began the moment we met.

Perhaps you intend to remind me that you are only here out of a bored sense of duty. You toss a shrivelled T-shirt onto the bed. Then a black sweatshirt that will be useless in the heat. The autumnal clothing is a rejection of sorts.

Then I notice the paper bag.

'What's this?' I ask, reaching for it; you tense, resisting an instinct to block me. 'Coco de Mer...' I read. Inside is a red lace bra with matching panties. I look up at you, quiet for a moment and your hand flutters to your face, a faint blush settling on your neck.

'We're on holiday...' you say to the bedroom wall. 'I thought it would be a fun surprise,' you shrug.

I imagine you in the shop, browsing erotic lingerie. I imagine you trying to imagine what I would like, and you seem so guile-less, so naive, standing there, surrounded by corsets, strangely virginal, as if all of this were new.

I take you in my arms and kiss you on the head. Another

man's hand might drift and graze the small of your back. Another woman might look up, expectantly, make suggestions with her roving fingertips, her hips. Instead, we remain perfectly still.

Sex has always been incidental to what we have. We endured a long courtship. We were delicate with each other, sensitive, avoiding any definite steps.

It was you who finally initiated things. We had just eaten at your favourite restaurant, conversation was unusually stilted. I attributed some of this awkwardness to the restaurant itself. The place was overstaffed, its owners hopeful that Cambridge would finally hearken to its unique offering: a camp, backstreet bistro with a twenty-page menu. A listless waiter hovered close, eavesdropping on the conversation, refilling water glasses after a single sip.

'We don't have to be…' you began.

'What?' I asked too quickly. I had never had a girlfriend before, had barely had any romantic encounters at all. I was on high alert, policing myself for mistakes, indiscretions.

'So gradual.'

'Oh.' I considered this and said, 'I guess I was trying to be a gentleman.'

'You're being Victorian.' You pushed away your plate. 'Maybe we should just get it over with.'

'How romantic.'

'The fact that I'm using these stupid euphemisms is sort of romantic. "It." Next I'll be referring to your "privates".'

'I don't follow.'

'I'm saying I'm excited. And nervous. That doesn't always happen.'

I asked for the bill. With the exaggerated gallantry of a nineteen-year-old on his first true date, I tipped ten pounds. The meal itself had been terrible, but the place made you happy. You liked the absurdity of the restaurant, the rapidly defrosted mains posed on tarted-up plates, the rustic decor, the delusions of grandeur.

We walked back to your room in near silence, like third years marching towards a final exam. I tried to imitate the men I had seen in movies, confident, leisurely, presumptuous. But I walked quickly and my shoulders were hunched. If you noticed this, you chose not to say anything.

Then we were in your room. Our clothes began to pile on your floor. And you were loud, theatrical. I was tentatively assertive; I licked your neck, pushed you against the wall. Both of us performed as if there were a group of spectators watching, circling, inspecting the show for cracks, until finally we collapsed onto the bed, exhausted and convinced.

You lit a cigarette and stared into the middle distance, solemn in contemplation. Perhaps you were expecting a deeper sense of satisfaction or relief. But sex itself was never our object. Even then, practically children, we were after something grander, a life together, a partnership, sanctuary. When one's aims are so far reaching, things always feel unconsummated and out of reach.

Band posters were tacked to your wall like camouflage. You had no passion for their music. You had picked them up at some vintage shop, attracted by the design and keen to make a gesture towards the normal student experience. Your real passion was the books stacked along your windowsill – Schopenhauer, Sartre, Nietzsche – you had an interest in radical freedom.

'What are you thinking about?' you whisper now, into my shoulder.

'I was thinking about that Italian place we sometimes went to. The pasta would arrive cold, we'd ask for wine and they'd come with beers. But we always went back.'

It takes you a moment to place the memory. 'God, you catalogue everything,' you say. 'You're like a historian, except you're only concerned with the last fifteen years, the two of us.'

'It's the only thing I find interesting,' I say sincerely and feel your head draw away.

'It isn't the only thing I find interesting,' you tell me guiltily.

'That's OK.'

'I care about all sorts of—'

'I know.'

You relax again and murmur 'If you ever turned against me, you would destroy me, you know.'

'That would never happen.'

Over your shoulder, I glance again at the messy interior of your bag; it has a brief and surprising beauty. People would never guess it is yours. Only I am given permission to know the disorder within.

'I'll need to borrow a T-shirt,' you murmur into my neck.

And I say nothing at all. I simply savour the moment; I like you best in my clothes anyway.

5

My glance slides off the unintelligible signs and storefronts. The landscape feels pleasantly abstract and empty of threat.

We pass a green medical cross and only now do I quicken my pace. Pharmacies give you bad ideas. You look at me with vague irritation, and I can't tell if you suspect my motivation or if you simply resent walking quickly on such a hot day.

'Shouldn't we head towards Sultanahmet?' you ask.

'Eventually. I thought we could spend some time getting the lie of the land.'

'OK,' you say, and sink back into your thoughts. Then you resurface abruptly. 'I get the impression that Sultanahmet would be more interesting. People don't exactly come this far for high streets.'

'This isn't a high street.'

'How would you describe it?'

We turn a corner and enter a broad boulevard, before us a slew of those inescapable shops – McDonald's, Zara – their shopfronts large, bright and empty. I glance at you resentfully, as if I've been tricked. Sometimes it feels as if the world conspires to prove your points.

'Do you want to get a McFlurry?' you ask in a neutral voice.

'No.'

You shrug. 'It could be interesting. Sometimes foreign McDonalds have their own local twists. They have a Za'atar Big Mac in Dubai, I recall.'

'We can go to the Old City,' I say, trying to focus my memory on the Coco de Mer bag, the meaning of it.

'You sure?'

But before I can answer, your hand is already in the air and a white Mercedes is crawling towards the kerb.

The taxi whisks us down the road, turns a corner and finds its place in a traffic jam two hundred metres away. As we idle, I watch the meter climb and listen to you make small talk with the driver.

Yes, it's our first time... No, you don't have any family here. You've heard great things about the food. You love Middle Eastern cuisine. You love Fatih Tutak.

The driver chuckles and agrees. You often inspire paternal feelings in men of his age. In a sense, you are testing them for that capacity.

He says you could be mistaken for a local. You tell him that your mother was a diplomat; you spent your childhood travelling and adapting. It takes great restraint not to roll my eyes.

The two of you fall into a discussion of manti and lahmacun. Of course, you are familiar with all of these dishes, have even made many yourself. You possess forensic knowledge of London's food scene, keep track of all the hot new openings, know their specialities, their myths, before the first meal is served. As you charm this driver, for no discernible purpose, I do not picture the food itself; I think of you sharpening knives.

The AC is cranked to full, so the taxi is uncomfortably cold. Outside, strangers are dressed skimpily, their movements slow and languorous. From the frosty back seat of the car, they have an imagined quality.

None of this is going to plan. I had hoped to visit this neighbourhood at dusk, when the crowds would be beginning to thin, the streets draped in tall shadow. I imagine the hordes of tourists that currently await us, beneath the unforgiving glare of a high-noon sun. They are overweight, saddled with bags and cameras and fanny packs, plodding forth and staring from flat, gormless faces. There is no space for wonder among all those hordes. We will amble through irritable, congested alleys, pause as others take photos and ask ourselves if we wouldn't be happier in Sicily right now.

Our car lurches upwards and a mosque crests a sea of low, sand-coloured structures; the sun glances along its enamelled surface, making it briefly molten. We are deposited and I rifle through my wallet for liras to pay him.

'Enjoy,' he says merrily, to you, not to me. Indeed, he manages to take my money without making eye contact.

A few steps ahead, you glance over your shoulder to make sure that I am keeping up. And then you vanish inside.

Hours pass.

We wander crooked limestone alleys. We avoid direct sunlight, but still, I have the sensation of being slowly cooked, of my brain heating in its juices. My shirt is stiff, stained white with salt, and the air beneath my collar has a sharp, acidic scent. Mosquito bites emerge on my calf, like welts.

You guide with confidence. For a second, I wonder if you have been here before, then dismiss the thought. I know everywhere you've been, I was there for most of the journeys. Still, there is an impressive briskness to your pace, a sense of direction and purpose as you lead us into the Grand Bazaar. We join a queue. Everyone beeps as they file through the metal detector, but the guard only squints, his hand keeps waving. It's as if he doesn't hear the machine ring, or as if he's searching for some other threat, beneath the surface of things.

Inside, we are immediately outnumbered by merchants. Intricate rugs are strung above our heads, wares are piled onto the street:

T-shirts, wicker tote bags, coffee pots in imitation gold. The sweet aroma of spiced tobacco and the smell of unwashed bodies mingle confusingly.

You scan the crowds, pausing on a group of westerners, young men about our age. Your head flits, alert, birdlike, to a lonesome backpacker who ambles the stalls with stunned incomprehension.

'You expecting someone?' I ask.

'What?'

'You seem sort of…'

'I try to approach each day with zero expectations,' you reply vaguely, yet your eyes still rove.

An old woman in a thin head scarf presides over a tower of embroidered tablecloths. She sees us pass, but watches us the way one might a flock of birds descending on some bench, just a fragment of scenery in the day's long drift. I have a strange and paranoid urge to contend for my reality. To buy all of her scarves, to kick them over, to assert my existence somehow.

You roam the stalls, engrossed by their sheer variety. You contemplate the purchase of incense, lean in and sniff at the coils of dull grey smoke.

6

Instead of following you, I hold back, wait until you slip from earshot, and seize this moment to return Peter's call. This morning, I woke to six missed calls from Peter, all placed within minutes of each other and accompanied by a single text,

> Mate, will you pick up?! You're giving me serious blue balls.

From any other colleague, this might cause alarm. But I can almost see Peter, at the back of some club, or kettled in a smoking section, jabbing at his phone and ready to share a ludicrous new venture.

He answers on the third ring.

'Finally!' he exclaims. 'My God, mate, it's been bloody difficult pinning you down. Like trying to get through to Beyoncé. Except the end result is a bit less gratifying.'

I choose not to mention that Peter himself has a highly ambivalent attitude towards work, that he vanishes for weeks, sometimes whole months at a time, explaining his absences with cryptic simplicity. *I had to go to France*, he stated after disappearing for a fortnight. *Wedding season...* he said, returning from an unscheduled break lasting the entirety of June and July.

'At least I've got you now,' Peter continues, maintaining that tone of teacherly exasperation. 'There's been a development. I bumped into Suzie a few days ago in Soho. Now Suzie, you may recall, is very close to the Ayik family. She said she doesn't see Ria much any more – from the sounds of it, Ria has gone full-blown nutter, Cheltenham Ladies' answer to Courtney Love. But Suzie's still close to Ria's dad and was happy to make an introduction. Of course, Suzie tends to make a lot of promises after a line. Later that night she seemed to be proposing some sort of school reunion in Marseilles. Marseilles! It didn't make any sense at all.'

'Peter, I'm afraid we have to make this quick.'

'Of course. The long and short of it is, Suzie came through. Mr Ayik will be happy to meet you in his home on Wednesday. The chocolate pitch is on.'

I experience a queasy combination of elation and fear. This is the best news we've had in a long time, but of course, you will not see it that way.

In the distance, you are bartering with a man who sells spices. He gesticulates impatiently. You mirror him perfectly, but amplify his irritation. He jabs at the air with a stubby index finger. You fold your arms, cock your head to the right and wait. If it weren't for your expensive sunglasses, your pale skin, your painted nails, one would think that you had spent your life in such markets, a short-order cook procuring niche spices at low prices. I turn my back, cupping the phone with my free hand, the stooped, guilty posture of a man addressing his concubine.

'I assume that works for you?' Peter asks, annoyed that I'm not echoing his enthusiasm.

'Well—'

'Mate, this is quite a big opportunity.'

'I'm aware, it's just… we're on holiday.' Coming from me, these words sound counterfeit.

'Which is how I know you have no other commitments. Look, you can afford to forfeit a few hours of hotel sex, or cocktails, or whatever it is you two are getting up to, in order to land a contract. We have to make sacrifices, mate. It's not easy, but that's the cost of entrepreneurship. We have the talent, we've got the guts, now we just need the opportunity…' he pauses, then adds for good measure. 'The world does not invite innovation. It does not sit and wait for you to succeed.'

It comforts Peter to make these speeches. In the years I've known him, his emotional states have stayed binary, vacillating quickly between hubris and existential collapse. The fact is, his role in our business does not require work or sacrifice; all he is expected to do is generate leads.

The chocolate pitch was my idea. Even this little sermon is effectively mine; it's been cobbled together from prompts and admonishments that I've thrown at him over the years. But he enjoys playing the role and I am normally happy to indulge him.

Peter was your friend first. You met at Cambridge, where he read English, half-heartedly, and dedicated his time to performing in any student production that would have him. We all assumed he would be famous. Perhaps we were drawn by the riptide of his own confidence. In our insular world as undergraduates, he had always seemed successful. Even professors were amenable to his charms, his infectious affability, bestowing upon him essay extensions and unearned marks. He looked upon the world and expected kindness. And the world, perhaps flattered, responded simply: it was kind to him.

He later secured a place at RADA and it was only after drama school that he had his first, chilling taste of indifference. After years of fringe theatre – small productions that occasionally toured to Edinburgh but went unreviewed – he moved into commercial work. The money was good and the projects were fun: deodorants, sportswear, tech. But as he approached his late twenties the auditions changed. He found himself performing beleaguered dads, stressed husbands seeking home insurance; adverts that aired during daytime hours, partially noticed by the bored and unemployed, scored with infectious jingles. With increasing horror, he found he was playing the men of his future. Their concerns were strange, banal, terrifying. Each performance was a sort of warning. Eventually, even these dried up. Casting directors said he had an 'anxious face'; something about his bone structure suggested comedy, not romance, the way his eyes were set precluded leading roles. Their comments felt so definitive, yet always vague. Like magic, he became the thing they saw, developed a nervous tremor and was dropped by his agent.

Peter found himself out of step with the modern world. In another era, perhaps, he would have thrived. It is easy to imagine him at banquets, or lazing among minor nobles. He is fun at parties, begins misbehaving after a glass or two of wine, can make indiscretions that others would be condemned for. Friends with more taxing lives come to him like an exotic retreat. It took Peter years to accept that this was his real gift, and to embrace his true calling as a dilettante.

Now the parties have become an end in themselves. By day, he hobnobs among elderly alumni at Groucho's or Blacks. By night, he drinks with the young at Shoreditch House. Peter finds shopper marketing beneath him; he has described our industry as 'grubby'. Still, he values his role at the company. He treasures the title of 'co-founder', clings to it like an alibi. This fits our needs; my cold calls are unsuccessful and my emails often go unanswered. I am unpersonable, I have been told, and a nobody.

'She's not going to like this,' I say, referring to you.
'Well, it's bloody imperative that she goes with you.'
'I know.'
'Clients love her.'
'Yes, I'm aware.'
'They like you too…' he adds in a mollifying tone.
'You don't need to explain.'

'You're more of a behind-the-scenes sort of chap,' he explains anyway. 'I wouldn't have you front of house, let's put it that way. No offence. I'm not telling you anything you don't already know.'

I literally bite my tongue, study the pain and almost miss the next question.

'So, it's just the two of you?' his words seem to trip from him.

'Of course,' I reply.

'Amazing. That's what I thought.'

'Why the question?'

'It's just something you ask,' he replies vaguely.

'No it isn't.'

But before I can pursue the thought, he cuts me off. 'Wednesday at three? I can confirm with Mr Ayik?'

This meeting will enrage you; you will accuse me of placing work before our relationship, undermining our time alone, of being unfaithful, somehow. Really, I know you simply hate the idea of meeting with another client. Each pitch comes at a cost. They are small enough to go unnoticed but the losses accumulate. You hate shopper marketing, have a lordly disdain for your own talent at it. Entrepreneurship was my dream for us. If the business itself was dull, the symbolism felt rich: a shared creation that we could nurture and grow, and would one day take care of us. You pretended to be convinced, but really you only joined me because you felt indebted. Secretly, you still search for meaning beyond our day job, still dream of some task or calling that can be uniquely yours. To me, this is a sort of infidelity.

7

I have been watching your tortured negotiations with the spice man for quite a while. Finally, the bartering draws to a close. The man bows his head and makes some gesture of defeat. As I approach, you ask me for sixty liras. He accepts the money, head still lowered, as if we have just cajoled him into performing some cheap and degrading act.

I feel that I have seen too much today, that the Old City, and the new city, and all these people, and all these improbable objects have been accruing, weighing on me like luggage that I can't discard.

'I bought sumac,' you say, brightly.

Tightly packed like that, it is the colour of rust. But it is sheathed in a thin plastic that will inevitably split in our suitcase. Then it will dissipate and spill over my shirts, change to the colour of blood. Our luggage will arrive at Heathrow looking like a small crime scene.

'Why?' I ask, and my voice sounds leaden. 'We have sumac at home.'

'Because I wanted to feel what it was like.'

'To…'

'To buy spices in a local market. To be like them.'

For a moment, this assuages me. It is exactly what I love about you, your profound ability to feel, to inhabit another.

'What was it like?' I ask.

'Small. Still, I was good at it, wasn't I? I really hammered him.'

We pass a steel trash can and you absentmindedly toss the package. You seem surprised by your own action and freeze as if weighing the prospect of digging it out. I'm almost insulted, as if I were some stranger who might judge you.

'We have reservations at six,' I remind you.

'Of course we do,' you complain. We walk a few steps. 'I bet you've scheduled every second of this trip.'

'This part isn't scheduled,' I state. 'And, frankly, it's under-whelming. But I leave it to you. We could stay here and maybe you could get a great deal on some baharat, or we can revert to my plan and go to Demira at six.'

This changes things. The word 'Demira' has a simple power. We have been to its two sister restaurants in London, but the original is a thing of legend.

'We have to leave some things to chance,' you say, to save face. 'Life's no fun without a little spontaneity.'

'That's your job. You act spontaneously and I do the clean-up.'

You turn, a look in your eyes that is almost coquettish. 'Your rules are so unclear… I have no idea what we're allowed to say out loud.'

'You're *allowed* to say whatever you like,' I reply and narrow my eyes, a provocation that makes you smile.

'Tell me a story,' you ask, slurring.

Through the taxi's tinted windows the streets are bruised black and blue. The roads are empty, still unfamiliar, so I have a pleasant feeling of suspension as we coast.

'C'mon,' you say, teasingly.

Even when drunk, you look cinematic, artfully dishevelled. Your head rolls along the top of the seat and comes to a rest near mine. The last gasp of a citrus perfume fades from your neck, your warm breath is scented with mint and whiskey. I glance down and I cannot tell if your eyes are open or closed.

Was tonight a success?

You took photos of the menu before you placed an order; a simple, anxious deferment. You wanted evidence of the pleasure, insurance against your own nerves. Sometimes your thoughts render food tasteless. Periodically, I catch you staring at photos of old menus, reconstructing some bygone meal, trying to access an experience that evaded you at the time.

The music was loud and the staff raucous. Chefs fed you free shots and high-fived each other as they sautéed scallops and charred cauliflower steaks. They saw you sitting there, laughing loudly, hair wild, eyes roving, your half-smile an open proposition, and they sensed a kindred spirit. They did not know they were simply staring at a mirror. You are expert at this.

'Apparently it's like this every night,' I said.

'What?' you said.

'This energy… It's always—'

You shook your head, unable to hear, too uninterested to lip-read. I felt strangely old and out of place beside you. Sometimes you share your light and sometimes, you keep it all to yourself.

You uploaded three shots to Instagram. You relaxed, knowing that whatever happened next, those images, perfectly framed and filtered, would be the night's enduring testimony. You ordered a negroni. Then another. You said you felt like smoking.

Two seats down, to our left, a drunk patron lectured the barman. At first, it seemed pathetic. The man was too lonely, too socially inept to notice how the barman squirmed, his boredom resembling physical panic. Gradually, we realised that the drunkard noticed, he simply didn't care. He had paid for his drink: he would speak and be heard.

He grew louder, impassioned. You kept losing your train of thought.

'How would you do it?' I asked, in a low, suggestive murmur.

36

'What?' You could not hear me over the rabble.

'How would you do it?'

You pointed to your ears and shrugged. Only on the third attempt, you heard and caught my meaning. You answered with a pitying smile, as if I had repeated a joke so tired, it was now faintly depressing.

In the ensuing silence, I studied you like a contact sheet. I tried to find the very moment, the very frame in which the joy left your face, leaving us with only the pose.

'Are you disappointed?' you ask now in a voice so foggy, I'm not sure you are addressing me.

'No.'

'I drank too much,' you state, unapologetically. You are silent for a long moment, perhaps passed out. At last, you say, 'We spent so long worrying. And now we're fine.' This observation hangs in the air, unfurls strangely between us. 'I guess I can't get used to it,' you say. 'I still treat each night like it's our last.'

'We're free of all that,' I reply encouragingly, though freedom, as a concept, has never carried any particular meaning for me. 'If you're craving danger, you should look at our books. We could always face financial ruin, if nothing else.'

I am hoping, of course, to segue neatly into my discussion with Peter and the incipient pitch. I do not like keeping secrets from you. The ease of it makes me nervous; it sets a dangerous precedent.

You repeat 'ruin' almost uncomprehendingly, like a piece of slang picked up from the street. Then you murmur, 'That would never happen to me.'

And the 'me' stings. It feels threatening precisely because it is not intended as a threat. To you, the observation is elementary, obvious. You grew up around wealth and understand its limits. These days, you are incapable of enjoying money, but you are also incapable of worrying about it, it is simply there, like air.

But I know how quickly things can come undone. Circumstance has welded us together. We are wartime lovers, crisis is our common ground. Things can look so different in the shifting light of peacetime. It will not be adversity that breaks us, but ease.

8

The day that Raph sailed down the river, all those years ago, you received many concerned calls.

His friends reached out to you. They felt guilty, complicit, confused. They knew they had encouraged his worst instincts all along.

'He was always very... *extreme*,' one of them remarked. Even then, even after all that damage, there was still nagging admiration.

You let them off the hook. You told them you did not wish to talk about it, that you were fine; you let them forget their involvement.

Your supervisor weighed in. He was a PhD student in his twenties and an inveterate gossip. Before he critiqued your draft, he indulged in some armchair therapy.

'He saw you with someone new, saw you happy, and he chose to spoil it... It's up to you if he succeeds. You don't have to be defined by him.'

You agreed politely. You pointedly uncapped your pen.

Of course, behind the scenes you were quietly cracking up. You'd meet me for lunch, ecstatic, and grow morose by your first bite. You'd begun handing in your essays late, or at strange hours; the writing was unedited and pages over the word count.

I wanted, I expected closeness. You remained distant, secretive. *What if we were wrong?* you sometimes asked. *What if I'm wrong?* Questions so simple, they could not be manipulated or argued against.

You diagnosed yourself with restless leg syndrome and from that moment could never sit comfortably. If I was on the couch, you'd spread out on the wooden floor. At night, you would be jolted awake by a profound and sudden desire to run.

We were barely in our twenties. It seemed that, once again, you had taken me to the bleeding edge of experience. Uncharted terrain. To some extent, I stand by this. I surprised you with the rental car and told you we were leaving behind our books and lectures, any thoughts of finals. We would just drive until you were better.

For the first few hours, it seemed to work. We were both comforted by the car's vibrations, the feeling of propulsion. As we glided across the motorway at sixty miles an hour, it was easy to believe we were progressing in another, more meaningful sense. By nightfall, your apprehensions had caught up with us.

'Turn off the radio,' you said.

'I thought you liked this song.'

'It's making things worse.'

We crawled through Manchester's Northern Quarter, hemmed in on both sides by converted Victorian factories, their bricks stained black by centuries of soot. I switched stations. Freddie Mercury sang, ardent and loveless. With each verse, his loneliness seemed to expand, until it was as vast as a stadium. It occurred to me that I could not relate to the lyrics. With you by my side, I would never need somebody else; I was complete. One spends a lifetime waiting, hoping for it to happen. Then it simply occurs, without ceremony or warning, and everything is different.

'Please. No music,' you said.

'I'm just trying to help you relax.'

'I understand that. It's not working.'

'What about Magic FM, or—'

'Look, nobody is writing songs about people like us. All this stuff is about love, and heartache and Friday nights and summertime… We're past all that now. When I hear it, I think… Well, I feel…'

'What?' I demanded, harshly, warningly. If you'd said 'regret', I would have stopped the car. Even if you'd only said his name (which, by now, had become a sort of byword for regret).

'I'd just prefer the quiet,' you said.

'Fine.' I changed gears.

A beat or two of silence, only the rain pattering on the roof of our car, a faint popping sound. In the rear-view mirror, I glimpsed your misery by fragments; knitted brows, a tight frown that gave you wrinkles, the finger coiling a strand of hair, loose at your temple.

'I can't stand it,' you said. 'You look at me like I'm your fucking juror.'

'I don't,' I said, but I did. You were right. My fate was in your hands.

'It's oppressive,' you muttered.

More anxious silence. The rain picked up, sounding now like pellets against tin.

'You know,' I began, 'I threw away my life for you.' It was perhaps the most pathetic thing I'd ever said. Craven. Desperate. Pure adolescent melodrama. Still, you seemed grateful. Conflict is your native climate. It is familiar and navigable.

'I didn't ask you to do anything,' you replied, more animated than you'd been in weeks. 'I didn't want—'

'Please. Don't try to win this on a technicality. You made it very clear what you wanted. You didn't have to say anything. And I don't expect anything from you, or—'

'Ever the gent. Most men would insist on a blowjob, at least.'

'I don't even expect loyalty or commitment,' I persisted. My voice was thick and earnest. I had tethered myself to strange new worries and threats. I had started looking over my shoulder, scanning people's comments for hidden meaning. These tendencies were now a part of me, they would be with me forever. 'It was a gift. Everything I've done for you I did because I wanted to. I can drop you at the train station right now, if you'd like. You can just leave, make your own way back.'

'I assumed that was a given. Or am I supposed to be grateful this isn't a kidnapping?'

'But before I do, all I ask is that you consider one thing. Do you think there is anyone else out there who would do what I have done for you? Just think about it.' I stared dramatically at the road ahead.

Deep in your bones you knew there wasn't. The world had taught you to expect nothing.

'He wouldn't,' I muttered.

We left Manchester without further discussion. You shrank in your seat, looking suddenly, horribly, like a captive. You would have preferred to argue; it was the silence that was intolerable.

We pressed on to Haworth and spent a restless night in a dour B&B. Our landlady was unaccustomed to such young guests and she gave us no peace, interrogated us on our plans, made endless pub recommendations. In the morning, we continued north, stopping in villages that seemed to sit at the end of the earth. The low, slate bungalows filled you with disquiet. We hiked beneath a sky the colour of skimmed milk. From high peaks, we watched the mist shred over treetops. You saw a confirmation of my warning everywhere you turned: this world does not care if you live or die. Only I do.

By day three, our shoes were soaked and the air was so damp that they wouldn't dry. You caught a cold. Our accommodation grew worse as we ventured deeper into the country. Small, grey towns where generations lived and died with their cattle. I needed to show you these things. I thought it would help.

It seems strange to confess that these memories – even the

arguments – are a comfort, now. They encourage me not to fear the future, or to fear change. We warp with each experience. Our sense of the world, of ourselves, is constantly bending. By now, we are perfectly distorted to fit each other. Our trials make us uniquely compatible and ruin us for others.

'I love you,' you whispered on the way home, almost timidly, as if in surrender. We were pulling out of a service station. Your eyes stayed fixed on the red Texaco sign, bleeding light. I turned on the radio. Squeezed your knee encouragingly. You stared at your pale reflection in the passenger seat window, spectral as it floated there, surrounded by black.

9

We see Benny, by chance, on the steps of a once-famous cathedral, now a famous mosque. Neither of us particularly likes Benny. Neither of us particularly likes this city (it transpires), so we're in a sour, unreceptive mood. Yet the encounter seems so unlikely that we suspect the makings of a great anecdote, which proves difficult to resist.

I have harried you all morning. Propelled by an anxious desire to make up for lost time and by the apprehension that precedes a confession (I still have not told you about the meeting tomorrow), I tried to make myself useful. I charged your phone while you showered. I passed you your handbag before you even thought to reach for it. You glanced about for your shoes only to discover them neatly arranged at the foot of our bed.

'What's with you today? You're like a hyperactive genie.'

We spent the first few hours dutifully touring the sights. Though we fanned out over the Old City, we seemed to always discover ourselves outside the Bazaar, as if we had some unfinished business with it. It made me doubt myself; I had thought we were travelling in a straight line, but really we were walking in spirals.

It is here that we find Benny. He is stalking a flock of elderly nuns and I am already framing the story (*And there, lo and behold, was Benny, chasing skirt – chasing scapular, I should say!*) as you approach. Astonished, he throws his arms up and takes you in a bearlike hug. It looks uncomfortable; I imagine you wincing as air is pressed from your lungs. Maybe it's this, the sight of you so entangled, that creates the first bristle of anxiety.

We have not encountered Benny since graduation, nearly fifteen years ago. He is effectively a stranger now, a relic. But, despite all that, a part of me responds with instinctive familiarity. Other worries, long dead, long buried, are briefly felt; it is like the aching of a phantom limb. I also have a few slightly quotidian concerns. Benny really is annoying. Once we've made contact, he could prove difficult to shake.

In short: I am having second thoughts.

But contact has been made and now I'm being summoned. I linger briefly, then enter the conversation.

'I always thought you two would end up tying the knot,' Benny says.

'Everyone did,' I say.

'That's why we did it,' you say.

'That's not the only reason...' I say.

'No, it's not the only reason,' you concede, churlish.

'And what brings you to these parts?' he asks.

We are in here because you suggested that I was incapable of spontaneity. I booked and paid for the trip as if rising to a dare. I surprised you with the flight confirmations and you surprised me with your reaction, reviewing the itinerary suspiciously, as if you'd been wrong-footed.

'The architecture,' we say in unison.

'Have you been to the Grand Mosque?' Benny asks.

We had been there a few hours earlier, watching the congregants murmur in private rapture; a bewildering, craggy soundscape. I had wanted to leave.

'I liked it,' I say. 'So, what are you doing here?'

'I recorded an EP a few months back and... I guess I'm trying to take a break from it all. London is a bit much at the moment.'

'You're still pursuing music?' you ask.

'Yeah. "Pursuing" describes it perfectly…'

I notice now that his posture is slightly stooped, as if carrying the weight of a floundering career on his back. Benny has not changed much over the years, but he looks more haggard, a hand-me-down version of the boy we once knew. I feel a faint stirring of sympathy.

'It's brave,' you say, unexpectedly.

'Bravery doesn't come into it. It's my passion: I couldn't quit music even if I wanted to.'

I wonder how many times he's uttered those exact words. They have the quality of a press release, manufactured and broadly disseminated. My sympathy evaporates.

'Where are you guys off to next?' He is kicking dust from foot to foot, listless as a child. 'Gözyaşı denizi,' I reply. 'The Sea of Tears.'

'Oh yeah, I've heard of that. That sort of dead lake… way out in Cappadocia. I was thinking of heading there. But apparently it's really hot this time of year. It's in the desert, right?'

Technically, it's an oasis. We launch into a thorough explanation as to how he is misinformed. We have an intimate understanding of the landscape. On the flight, we pored over travel guides in studious silence. Upon descent, we compared notes.

'Sounds good,' Benny says. 'Maybe I'll check it out after all. If my schedule lets me.'

'Your schedule?' I ask.

'Yeah, I'm here volunteering. This is sort of a pit stop between assignments.'

He pauses slightly, as if anticipating applause.

'I'm teaching English at makeshift school,' he explains, unbidden. 'It's a collab between Save the Children and local authorities. You probably remember the earthquake last year? There are still a lot of displaced families, even if the media seem to have lost interest.'

'But why are you here? In the city?' Do I sound put out? I round off the comment with a disjointed smile. It confuses him.

'We're encouraged to take breaks, explore the country. Otherwise there's a high risk of burnout, given the nature of the work.'

We bow our heads in solemn deference.

'What are your plans for the day?' he asks.

'We're doing the Heinous History Tour at three,' I admit, grudgingly.

You say nothing. I stare into your aviator sunglasses and see two warped versions of myself distending in the lenses.

He glances at us queerly. 'Sounds dark,' he says.

'It's very popular,' I reply. My tone is priggish, defensive. I relax my shoulders.

'It basically covers the same ground as all the other walking tours,' you add. 'Just with a little more... *bite*.'

'See, I need to do more of that shit. I feel like I'm wasting my time off.'

I realise, too late, that I have acted against our interests. There is an uncomfortable, pleading silence. You cannot endure it; beneath your hard enamel, you are rather soft.

'You should join us,' you say.

'I don't want to cramp your style...' he replies, but he maintains eye contact, making rejection difficult.

'Nonsense! Come along!' I say, before the scene becomes piteous. The tour will be brief and it will be easy enough to lose him in the crowds.

'Is it... how much does it cost?' he asks.

'It's free,' you reply.

'Free is good. I'm down with free.'

'Well, they expect donations,' I add.

'Fuck it! I'm in. Have you guys had lunch yet?'

'Yes,' I say.

'No,' you say.

We look at each other.

'I know a great spot,' he says. 'My treat.'

He begins ushering us towards a throng of tourists.

'I actually had a place in mind...' I murmur, without conviction. He chooses not to hear me.

'Honestly, this came at just the right time,' he tells us. By 'this', he means us.

'Oh?' you say.

'Yeah, I was going a little stir crazy. Obviously, the whole experience has been mad fulfilling. But, fuck, it's draining. The other volunteers have already pissed off. I'm the only one in my group who's staying on for another few weeks.'

'You must have felt isolated,' you say, because this is what he wants from you. He wants you to deliver cues so he can continue talking.

You have a knack for deep, meaningful conversations, the sort that leave people feeling satisfied, understood, absolved. You pride yourself on forging connections with as few words as possible.

And when the tables are turned, you are just as comfortable, happy to confide as well as listen. You are happy to share seemingly sensitive stories of your life at the drop of a hat. I think of the way you used to refer to your father, so frankly, without much prompting. *My father was a terrible man who has done terrible things: the world is better off without him.* It took me a long time to understand that this was not intimacy, but its opposite. Your brutal candour fended off questions, closed discussions. Listeners would inevitably be shocked, sometimes even flattered, by your confidences. But you were not sharing anything. You spoke and you cauterised; you spoke so you would not feel.

'I value my alone time,' Benny states, seriously. 'In my line of work – the music, I mean – you have to be comfortable sitting with your own thoughts. Still, I won't deny, it's pretty nice seeing a couple of old, friendly faces.'

Of course, even the most rudimentary facial recognition software in the world would be able to determine that my face is not friendly. I catch myself in the fleeting reflections of shop windows. But he is not watching me, he is focused on you. Your face is upturned towards the light, so your skin seems to shimmer. Like a movie star, you absorb his attention without seeming to notice it.

He looks at you with meaning, with suggestion. Patiently, he waits to make eye contact. His gaze is almost proprietary, like that of an ex-lover.

This closeness is just circumstantial. Back at Cambridge, he was little more than scenery. Now, walking down the street, we appear as a single unit. In this new, broadened context, surrounded by truer strangers, we suddenly have more in common than not. His arm bumps yours as you walk. An amiable collision. From a certain perspective, you two could be mistaken as the couple and I the interloper.

I am struck by the bleak serendipity of it all. You wanted to dredge up the past and here we have an emissary from our darkest days. And he doesn't understand at all. He will never grasp the symbolism of his arrival, or why we must make sure our time together does not drag on. Yet you do not match my efforts to get rid of him. The object of this game escapes me. Perhaps there is no obvious point, just risk. You are the sort of gambler who does not play for money, but for excitement. You can stomach exorbitant loss.

We arrive at Benny's chosen restaurant. It is a restaurant in the same way that McDonald's is a restaurant: a title earned through self-appointment. Outside, clusters of aluminium tables sit beneath wonky umbrellas that bear the branding of a local beer. We take out seats and contemplate a menu that serves mujadara alongside fish and chips.

Benny, perhaps enjoying the role of patron, orders on our behalf and he orders copiously. Neither of us bother making any additions or corrections; the food is pre-prepared and waits tepidly on shelves to be reheated.

Soon, I am watching Benny eat, which is putting me off my food. It is not that he talks with his mouth open, causing projectiles of half-chewed pita, hummus and cucumber to fly across the small space separating us. It's not that he uses his hands where most would use utensils ('going native', he says). I think that I am disgusted by the sheer speed of his consumption. His hunger is so voracious that it seems indecent, as if we're observing some animal part of him. I worry he'll consume everything in sight, our entire meal, possibly our neighbour's meal.

He talks without pause, inhaling food and exhaling words in stunning synchronicity.

Benny does not like the situation here.

Benny feels the local government is asleep at the wheel.

Benny is disillusioned with aid work, generally.

He derides this country, to sound clever, yet remains proprietary nonetheless; he subtly insists on some deeper connection to the culture, pronouncing foreign words with campy flourish, referring to regional politicians by their nicknames.

I keep scanning your face for signs of irritation, but you appear to be daydreaming.

'So wait,' I interject, 'did you qualify as a teacher?'

'I did some training,' he replies, grudgingly. There is a wonderful note of resentment in his voice. 'I rely a lot on my intuition, rather than empty qualifications.'

'I see,' I reply. 'Still, they aren't mutually exclusive.'

You either cough or laugh; I cannot tell.

He returns to the topic of volunteering. As Benny lectures me on the fiscal irresponsibility of an NGO, I undergo a simple analysis. This six-day holiday will cost slightly over £2,000. Each day, therefore, costs roughly £333; each hour (discounting sleep) costs £20. The exact cost of Benny's speech, therefore, is £10: that is what he has taken from me, in monetary terms, while ranting about his personal involvement in enlightening displaced youth. This figure seems manageable, yet Benny shows no signs of abating so the meter continues to run. I grind my plastic chair into the concrete floor and feel the legs bend under my weight.

Benny confesses that he feels 'icky' about teaching English. He accepts the necessity of the skill but yearns for greater linguistic plurality; he feels he is participating in colonialist traditions. He is just trying his best.

What if there were glass in his throat? The thought lands before me, the way the flies land and scamper across the plastic cloth. I do not swat it away.

Coffee is served. It is infused with cardamom, is poured into small thimbles. As the caffeine hits my bloodstream, something inside unclenches, loosens, a just-perceptible leavening. The sugar from the coffee finds and fills some small gap in me…

… But Benny is using the word 'hegemony' relentlessly.

He refers to Oxfam as 'Oxy', an abbreviation which is, of course, unspeakably annoying.

Sensations tangle into a delicious repulsion.

Benny has made a joke and we pretend to laugh. I notice that the coffee grounds have settled in the gaps between our teeth and the corners of our mouths, giving us ugly smiles.

When the bill arrives, it transpires that Benny has no cash. In fact, he has no wallet. Staring at the chit, he produces a stack of cards bound by a rubber band. The cards are all damaged, a translucent skin of plastic peeling from their surfaces.

'I don't think they take cards here,' I inform him.

'Ah,' he replies. We sit in silence. 'I may have a little problemo,' he says, eventually.

'It's OK,' I reply. 'We have cash.'

'Thanks, mate. I can pay you back once I find an ATM.'

'How have you managed so far?'

'Most people have accepted cards.'

'That's interesting,' I say. 'I've found the exact opposite.'

10

Even though Benny does not know the meeting spot, he takes the lead, lurching a few steps ahead of us. He walks strangely. More precisely, he lollops, throwing his weight forward as if his centre of gravity is misplaced.

Again, an uncanny wave of recognition passes over me. How many times have I watched Benny walk through college grounds or loiter outside a lecture hall? I have absorbed so much of him, the way he moves and talks and laughs, without realising.

Benny pauses before a busker, listening to her sing in Arabic, with the respectful, appraising concentration of a fellow artist.

We walk past him and he seems to make a point of not following.

'He used to be a bit of a heart-throb,' you say. It is the first thing you have said to me since Benny joined us. The very sound of your voice steadies me.

'That surprises me,' I say.

'Yes. I think it's because he had such thick facial hair. It made him seem manly. Now he just seems unkempt.'

It's true. His features, though recognisable, seem slightly deflated. The dark loops beneath his eyes, which perhaps once gave him a Byronic intensity, now merely suggest exhaustion. He is at the start of a downward trajectory.

Benny is nodding to the music, his movements slightly off-beat. His face shines with sweat.

'Do you think you could enjoy having sex with him?' you ask philosophically.

A single hypothetical question and my mind is full of Benny. His skin is damp, a heat rash flares across his chest. He is heavy and soft and all over me. His dick, a wet stump, collides with my thigh, leaves a residual smear as it moves up my legs.

'Maybe,' I say. 'But it would be a cheap sort of thrill. The thrill of self-debasement.'

'So...'

'So it wouldn't really have anything to do with him. I'd probably have a similar sort of rush if I fucked a Great Dane.' I consider this. 'Actually that would feel different. There would be an element of fear in that encounter. And a greater sense of confusion. Sex with Benny would offer a more distilled experience of self-contempt. Still, the negatives would outweigh the benefits, for sure.'

'I know you're not joking.'

'Good. I wasn't.'

'You don't think it's odd to share these thoughts with your wife?'

'You asked.'

'Not for such detail.'

'You want me to pretend that I could never, under any circumstances, enjoy sex with a man. That I'm like one of those guys in your movies, simple as a circuit board, programmed for dominance. But we both know that's not true, and I respect you too much to lie so obviously.'

'Sometimes I worry we know too much of each other.'

'Impossible. Too much intimacy is never a bad thing.'

'There's a difference between intimacy and this. What we have can feel so... forensic.'

'Since when have you been squeamish about forensics?'

You smile slightly. Recently, so many of your smiles have a faint, unspecific quality. It is as if you are not here experiencing this, but remembering it.

You glance back at Benny, who has not taken the hint. It is ten to three.

'Do you remember those rumours about Benny?' you whisper.

'What rumours?'

'Didn't he rip off a bunch of freshers…'

'That was a long time ago,' I say diplomatically, but instinctively reach for my wallet.

'Not that long.'

We eye Benny warily.

'You think he's a conman?' I ask, half joking.

'No. Maybe. He's weird. He talks like he's creating a diversion. Or perhaps holding back.'

'He certainly talks a lot.'

All I truly recall is that Benny was often near, orbiting the more popular kids, basking in their shine. Yet your words stir me. There is something I'm not remembering and the feeling is deeply unpleasant. The suspicion of some hazard left unattended. It is as if I have left a hob burning, as if a naked flame hisses in the kitchen, poised to spread.

I attempt a wolf whistle to get his attention but remember too late that I have never been good at those; the sound is hoarse and reedy. I moisten my dry lips, then abruptly stop.

'Raph,' I say. 'He was Raph's best friend.'

Suddenly it all comes back. Benny dressed in black. Benny discreetly leaving the room when we entered together. His theatrical anguish.

It wasn't some half-remembered scam that niggled, it was the fact that he collected donations for the memorial plaque. I gave him five pounds, you gave ten. We worried we had donated too little. Then we worried it was too much. This was a decade ago. It's just a coincidence.

You smile without feigning surprise and I realise you knew all along.

'Raph didn't have friends,' you state. 'He had accomplices, maybe. And he had bloodhounds.'

11

Our guide, Frederick, is blond and has improbably fair skin in this sun that is baking the rest of us alive. His pupils dance along the tops of our heads, tallying our numbers.

Benny's presence is just a coincidence. Admittedly, it is strange, it is rare, but it is a coincidence nonetheless. Benny has not followed us here; he can hardly follow his own thoughts.

I watch as Benny works his way to the front and grills our guide on political matters. Benny's words glide past Frederick; he answers the interrogation with non-committal smiles, or generalised remarks.

We are about to pass a range of holy sites. Benny wonders if we can enjoy such spaces while still remaining critical of what they represent. He worries about complicity.

'That is an interesting question,' our guide states, simply, even though it is not.

The crowd contracts as the tour begins. We pass ancient streets, streets that have seen riots and inspired wars. I can feel it. The crumbling limestone bricks have absorbed centuries of sunlight and history and unrest; they seem to radiate this bloody past, releasing it slowly like heat. We move through a market. Gaudy fabrics flap in the breeze, someone tries to sell me a pashmina.

Frederick keeps his eyes on the group and on the path ahead, calling out notable sites as we speed through; the landmarks dissolve into meaningless abundance.

The Heinous History Tour delivers on its title. Frederick wanders the streets, cherry-picking atrocities from the last five centuries. He conjures famines, public hangings, outbreaks of cholera and plague. Now, we are on the topic of spies.

We reach a small piazza and Frederick stops, allowing the group to reassemble. Dogs lie. Their drooping eyes suggest an exhaustion so profound, it transcends the physical. It seems more like despair. More like a universal precept. They are in that abject place to which we are all heading. A few spry street cats prance about as if to taunt. Perhaps they will eat the dogs when the time is right. Frederick begins to detail the story of a woman accused of treason in the sixteenth century. After seven nights in custody, she made a daring escape, took to the streets, raving, pleading for help, only to be stoned to death by her neighbours.

'This is not the precise spot where it happened, but it's close enough,' Frederick tells us. 'The exact location is near the Bazaar and often very crowded. Many amateur photographers. It defeats the mood, I think.'

I wonder what sort of mood he is hoping to create. Frederick speaks in measured, Germanic sentences but there is a new, slightly wistful tone to his voice as he depicts her last moments. We hush, like children. He describes the woman glancing up at the familiar houses, faces she has known her whole life, as rocks fall towards her head. He uses the future tense, *She will stumble to her knees, her last words will not be caught*, as if all of this is still ahead of us. *They kill her because they are afraid. Afraid she is a spy, or worse, that she is not... They do not understand themselves. But they have begun. They have committed to a path and now they must honour that dreadful commitment.*

My glance drifts your way. You roll the neck of a Coke bottle along your bright red lips. The lipstick does not smear and it leaves no residue on the glass. I think of all the kisses we have shared, how they can feel, at times, strangely contractual. In these moments, your mouth works mechanically and leaves no aftertaste, like a sip of distilled water.

Benny's head is bowed; his eyes appear to be closed in solemn contemplation. Then he looks up and a darkness passes over his face. He is looking at my wrist. I want to put my hand in my pocket, I want to cut off my arm, anything to hide the ill-gotten watch. Instead, I remain perfectly still, and wait for him to turn his head.

'We must progress,' Frederick announces. Everyone hustles, groggily, as if awoken from a nap. I seem unable to rouse myself. My mind is full of blood. Broken bodies. Reckonings.

Our group thins and begins filing through an alley single file. My heart flutters ominously. I concentrate on breathing.

'Mate, you don't look so hot,' Benny remarks.

'I'm fine. Too much sun.'

I look to you, but you are concentrating on lighting a cigarette. My heart beats faster.

You shake your lighter. You flick it. You search your bag for another.

'Maybe it's sunstroke. You want my hat?'

The thought of wearing Benny's hat, of sharing his grease, spurs a new wave of revulsion.

'I just need a moment.'

'We should get you inside…'

'I'm just hot.'

'Then we should get you out of the sun…'

'What's going on?' You saunter over and cock your head to the left, inspecting me as if I were perpendicular to you.

Frederick has already vanished and the stragglers are receding from sight. The air I gulp feels empty and spent.

My thoughts are strange, metastatic. I imagine myself in a sickbed in some institution. I imagine everyone I have ever known queuing to say goodbye to me, feigning grief and eyeing the clock. I believe I am going mad.

'I think we should go back, rest for a bit,' Benny declares.

You shrug.

Benny insists on accompanying us to the apartment.

I sidle up to you and whisper, 'I think I'm having a panic attack,' hoping you will patch me up and make me war-ready once more.

You furrow your brows. 'Why would you be having a panic attack?' you ask loudly. Benny can hear. 'Maybe you're having a religious experience, a revelation,' you suggest. You consider this. 'Only a heathen would get the two confused – I worry about your soul, honey.'

We get lost in a labyrinth of backstreets. Benny clings close, steadying me like a wounded soldier. My left hand remains plunged in my pocket.

In an otherwise empty square, we discover three Asian teenagers. They are giggling and speaking in Japanese. One of them is dressed as a camel, another as a princess, inspired by *The Arabian Nights*, but reimagined as sluttier and with more chiffon. The princess attempts to ride her friend. The camel takes a few steps, pantomiming grief and affliction, her friend preens and blows kisses. Another takes photos. The girls swap positions, now the camel is riding the princess and the princess emotes despair. Now they are stripping and exchanging costumes, working through every possible arrangement with the materials at hand. Something about this strange tableau stuns me. The world is not so serious. This place is like all places, it is only a playground. My breathing begins to settle. If there were truly greater forces at play, they would have surely got me by now.

'I recognise this bit...' Benny says. 'We should be close to the spice market.'

'Wait!' I say. My heart still rattles, but it is imperative that I stop this plan and keep Benny away from our hotel room. 'I think I'm feeling better.'

'Mate, you're white as a sheet.'

'Yes but…' I begin, speaking on each ragged exhalation. 'I… would prefer… to go… for… a drink.'

Your eyebrows lift.

'A drink?' Benny asks, sceptically, and I sense that he would prefer to come home with us.

'Not up for the cab ride,' I gasp.

'That settles it,' you announce, decisively. 'Let's get plastered.'

'I'm not sure—' Benny attempts. 'He still seems a bit…'

'My husband would like a drink. This is a fairly rare occurrence and I intend to exploit it.'

12

Cambridge, 2010
Elle

She met Raph at a bake sale, of all places. Sometimes, this still brought a smile to her lips. The whole sordid affair, the blood, the humiliation, all began with the smell of pastry and a vague charitable endeavour. The setting was so perfectly wrong, it had a sort of elegance.

They were raising donations for victims of tropical illness. At least, this was what Elle assumed. The actual sign was grammatically ambiguous, simply reading, 'Malaria: Cake Sale', as if the Cambridge Pentecostals were somehow on the side of the disease.

In charge was a man in his late fifties, dressed in country tweeds and a red apron. He approached his job with zeal, greeting shoppers, insinuating himself into their deliberations and flirting, unbidden, with the female pensioners. He was a showman. He reminded her of a politician pulling pints before the waiting press, or a celebrity arriving in a high-vis jacket to surprise the factory workers, grinning with a presumptuous humility and excessive bonhomie. It was slightly oppressive; Elle noticed herself avoiding his eye, hoping she would not get drawn into the act.

When it was Elle's turn, he focused on her for a beat too long. He sensed her aversion, he seemed a little affronted by it.

'I'd like to pay,' she stated, eager to hurry things forward.

'Your card's been declined,' he informed her. He said it loudly; other shoppers pretended to inspect the Chelsea buns, but she sensed them listening. 'Try again,' he suggested.

She entered her pin and he held the reader aloft as it dialled her bank.

'No joy!' he announced. 'Declined again.'

'Must be a problem with my card,' she mumbled.

'Card looks OK to me. The issue is with the bank,' he said. 'Or, more specifically, your account,' he added darkly, as if privy to all her financial mishandlings, her feckless instincts. He raised his eyebrows expectantly, ready to receive confession. 'Dear oh dear,' he said, with exaggerated forbearance.

He glanced at another shopper and rolled his eyes. Then he drew a breath, taking a moment to gather himself before reengaging with the chaos that Elle had wrought.

'Let's see what we can do,' the man said, tipping the contents of her shopping bag. He started separating the items, his movements brusque, pointedly careless.

She began, quickly, to despise this person. In a moment of dark clairvoyance, she knew him entirely. A man who comes alive when others fail, who masks his excitement behind a compassionate grimace. He was ridiculous, absurd – this righteous defender of scones, this lord of small things – but he had her pinned. Yes, she had met his type before. She had lived under this man her entire life.

This led, ineluctably, to a second realisation: the funds had not been transferred. Once again, her father had hung her out to dry. She had already pleaded with him for the cash. Now, he wanted her to grovel.

'Right, the sourdough is four quid, so if we lose this, it will take you down to nine. Do you think you can afford that?' He emphasised the word 'afford', his tone arch and ironic.

'Maybe it's better if I just leave.'

'You've already pawed over this bunch, so I can't sell it any more.'

'I barely touched it!' she tried to disguise her shame behind a chuckle.

He frowned disbelievingly and glanced at her hands. They suddenly felt grubby.

You're managing a bake sale, she thought, not a fucking biolab. Nobody expects their bread to be sterile.

'I have money in my room,' she said out loud and smiled.

'Looks like you have some cash actually on you.'

His eyes lingered on the bill protruding from her wallet.

'I'm not letting you off the hook that easily,' he said, smiling thinly. With this revelation, she felt the crowd's mood turn against her, could have sworn she heard others whisper. She had to account for the cash.

'I do have a bit of money, but that's…' her voice cut. She did not know how to explain that there must always be a twenty-pound note in her wallet. Ostensibly, it was reserved for emergencies. Its true purpose, however, was to go unspent. This was a habit developed young and sustained through the darkest days of adolescence. Elle had once stood outside a shelter and desperately studied the women as they passed, struggling to find some defect, some critical weakness that accounted for their station in life. It had slowly dawned on her that the only divide between her and them was the fact that her wallet was not empty. So that note had to remain, a talisman against disaster.

'A fiver,' the man sighed. He waved his wrist at the bag. 'I can't let you take it for free. Five quid. Hardly covers the ingredients, but at least the foundation gets something…' he spoke with kingly indulgence, pardoning the thief before him.

She became abruptly aware that there was a biro in the bottom of her bag. The pen seemed to announce itself, the way stashed cigarettes announce themselves to jonesing smokers. She imagined gripping it. She imagined hammering it into the man's neck, just beneath the Adam's apple, the cartilage weakening with each thrust, until it began to tear and split like old fabric, until the warmth spurted down her wrist. To pluck out that useless jugular, to feel it hang from the pen's tip.

She buried the thought. These moments of rage were a sinkhole, they swallowed her completely. Elle glanced up and shook her head with a ditzy smile, became what he wanted her to be, a confused and stupid girl.

'If you want me to go lower than five, I can't,' he said. 'It's simply too disrespectful to the bakers. And anyway, the point of this is to raise money for victims, not to offer Cambridge students a bargain. I would hope—'

'Mate,' a voice interrupted. 'Don't you think you're labouring this somewhat?'

And there was Raph.

He had swooped in silently while the man spoke and now flanked Elle's right shoulder.

He was slim but muscular, medium height. His sandy blond hair flopped over his brow, so his eyes remained narrowed, as if the world were constantly disappointing. But if Raph was physically unremarkable, this somehow threw his one winning feature into startling relief. That voice. Only twenty years to Elle's nineteen and yet he spoke with the effortless hauteur of a seasoned patrician, with a sort of omnipotent disdain, reassuring and strangely exciting.

'Can I help you?' the man asked, flustered, embarrassed, as if he had been interrupted mid-sex.

'Perhaps you could actually sell some flapjacks or something,' Raph said. 'Rather than digging through this poor girl's shopping.'

'It isn't hers, her card was—'

'Declined. Yes, we all heard. You've been orating the whole bloody thing quite clearly. We're all abreast. How much does she owe?'

The man did not answer.

'I owe fourteen,' Elle said. Her own voice was strangely defiant, as if her debt had suddenly become a weapon.

'All this fuss for fourteen quid,' Raph remarked. 'And I thought Christians were supposed to be nice.' He produced a crisp fifty-pound note from a monogrammed wallet.

The man held the cash pinched between his fingers. 'This is too much,' he said at last. 'It'll clear out all my small change.'

'Keep the change.'

'No no,' he said. 'That isn't what we're about. We're not seeking handouts.'

'And yet your hand is out.'

'What I mean is… I'm not… a charity.'

Raph's eyes darted to the sign, lingered on the word 'Charity' for a long moment and then returned to the man.

'Perhaps I'm missing some subtlety,' he stated.

She could not say why the man resisted Raph's money, why he committed himself to such an absurd position. She sensed he needed to make a stand. It was punitive to be caught in Raph's gaze. The man surely felt it, his own dignity being flaked away like dry bark, and still Raph kept going, pushing towards the tender pulp beneath. He did not want to owe Raph anything, to be forced to appreciate his donation.

The man pushed a box of cupcakes towards Raph. 'Take that, it evens things out.'

Raph stared at the tray for a long time. 'I see,' he said. 'You don't want to leave me shortchanged, Honourable.' Raph plucked one of the cupcakes and took a small, obliging bite. He smiled tightly and chewed slowly. The man interpreted this as a rapprochement.

'Coconut and charcoal,' he said, his tone, like everything else, a dazed hypocrisy, both mocking and proud. 'One of our bakers fancies herself a bit of an Ottolenghi…'

Raph gripped the box and walked two steps, towards a collection of elaborate cinnamon rolls. The man began detailing the pistachio crust, the cardamom notes, still with an inexplicable note of sarcasm, as if such refinements were beneath him.

Raph tipped the cupcakes into the mouth of an empty bin. They fell slowly, as if travelling through water. One of the other shoppers gasped.

'Too sweet,' Raph said, finally.

Elle was not sure what she felt. She had an empty, reflexive instinct to catch the cupcakes, dig them out, salvage what she could. But that wasn't all. She also felt confused elation, a tidal swell of muddy water. She imagined the flies that would soon descend. She imagined the man smelling the cupcakes as they cooked with warm rubbish.

'You can't do that,' the man said, ridiculously.

'Of course I can,' he replied. 'They were mine. And I didn't want them any more. What else would I do?'

The man muttered a jumble of furious deprecations. Something about ponces and privilege. Something about youth and delusions, some promise of a rude awakening. Each remark vague and quiet as if he already feared the riposte. His outrage was just a thin and chipping veneer. In the space of five minutes, Raph had made him look cheap and pointless.

'Do you know what the difference is between you and me?' Raph asked.

'What's the difference?' the man replied, attempting condescension, but sounding fearfully invested.

'Everything,' Raph answered. 'Literally everything.'

She caught up with him on the corner of Jesus Lane. The streets were empty in a way that seemed particular to Cambridge, as if they would never fill again. She hated this town on the weekends, when the other students seemed to disappear, when she imagined them calling home, or cosily hiding away.

'Hello again,' Raph said, politely.

'I just wanted to thank you.'

'No need. Frankly, I enjoyed myself.'

She believed him. He had not shown pleasure, exactly, but

palpable satisfaction, like an athlete training and performing well, delighted in his body, reassured by his skill. It was a feeling Elle thought she understood. She experienced it during tutorials, when she outmanoeuvred a pompous supervisor, or when some drunk fool challenged her at formal hall, and she made him regret it. Increasingly, she seemed to live for these moments of sanctioned violence.

He cut her off as she tried to introduce herself. 'I know who you are,' he said. 'First year, Gonville and Caius.'

She paused.

'You're the girl who gets the boys running,' he added, by means of identification.

What was there to say to that? She had only been at Cambridge two terms. 'Care to elaborate?' she asked.

He considered for a moment. 'Apparently, you get some of the girls running too,' he added, with a smirk.

Recently, Elle had been haunted by feelings of old age. Not yet twenty, she was convinced that she had seen all there was to know of the world. What remained were iterations, diminishments. Perhaps this was a symptom of her upbringing; in her experience, people did not change, they only calcified.

Yet how her fingers twitched in that moment, pinching the fabric of her skirt, releasing it, pinching again. Her vocal chords felt tight and untested. For the first time in a long time, her own body grew foreign.

'Well, thanks for the bread,' she said, stupidly dangling the bag of goods.

He answered with a gradual smile; it seemed to mask some vague disappointment that he was too polite to name.

'Do you know,' he said, 'I actually think I did all that for the bloke's benefit, not yours.'

'Oh?'

'You looked like you were about to stab him in the throat.'

The image returned: the pen, the jugular. It was like

discovering herself undressed, a shock of shame that subsided into a sort of thrill, a desire to show more.

'Maybe I'll see you around?' she asked.

'Maybe,' he answered, distractedly, as if he already knew the answer.

13

It is Happy Hour at the rooftop bar. We take our seats around an impractically low table. We are surrounded by sweeping views of the city and sea.

'Are the Old Fashioneds in the two-for-one offer?' you ask and our waitress nods. 'Perfect, I'll have two of those.' You snap the menu shut.

'I don't really like whiskey,' I say.

'I was ordering for myself,' you reply. 'Benny, what can we get you?' you offer, forgetting that we already 'got' him lunch.

'I'll have what she's having.'

'I'll have an Efes,' I murmur and you glance at me with disappointment.

It is like a terrible drug has cleared my system, leaving my insides stripped raw. I am calm now, but worried it could happen again.

Both of you drink quickly. Somewhere between this and the second round, the conversation turns to work. Benny refers to other artists on a first-name basis, though it's unclear if he has ever met any of them. You ask if he's had any hits.

He replies coyly. 'Depends on what you characterise as a "hit".' But then, before the conversation can progress, he tells you that the royalties from one of his tracks has paid for a year or two of leisure. This has granted him the freedom to make art he really cares about, divorced from market considerations.

'I'm obviously not in it for the money,' he says. 'I mean, if I were fussed about money, I would do something easier like finance or whatever.'

'Finance isn't exactly an "easy" industry,' I remark.

'Headhunting, then. The point I'm trying to make is, it's easy to tell yourself that you don't give a fuck about money, that you just want "enough". But getting a wad of cash is amazingly satisfying... knowing that what you made is valuable in this real, tangible way.' And then, 'I seem to remember that you have an artistic background,' he says to you.

'My mother was a singer,' you confirm.

'So you get it. These things run in the blood; civilians can't understand.'

Maybe it's the exhaustion, but I sit, limp, as images flash before me. I see my hand reaching over and sealing Benny's mouth. His jaw works beneath it but my grip is firm and I keep it there, until the capillaries begin to burst, until the whites of his eyes turn the colour of rosé. I glance over and see you smiling, as if you have witnessed my vision and it amuses you.

He downs his glass.

You order more.

To the north, somewhere over the Bosphorus, I watch a seagull die mid-flight. Incredible: one moment, it is soaring, the next it plummets. I feel a kind of physical sympathy for the thing, my stomach lurching as its stiff body falls.

You are asking Benny about his plans.

You are saying ours have grown a little diffuse.

Just as the seagull is about to smash into the river, it pivots, it grazes the hard surface of the Bosphorus, it ascends. Not death but the opposite: the bird was only hunting.

Benny is speaking with a thicker tongue, slurring slightly, but you remain crisp. Alcohol is a lubricant that keeps you running smoothly. You do not lose clarity with each sip, only gain a deepening ease.

'So you guys run a business?' Benny asks.

'Yes, shopper marketing,' you inform him.

'So you create ads?'

'Oh no,' you say, 'we leave that to the creatives. We grapple with far more pivotal issues, such as optimising window displays, and floor displays, and point of purchase displays, and—'

'He gets the picture,' I cut in, bitterly. Though your tone is bright, the very rhythm of your words is sarcastic. Your point is clear, one cannot affect passion for our industry without seeming at least slightly unhinged.

'Believe me, it's as interesting as it sounds,' you add, unnecessarily.

We are a clump of tangled nerves: you cannot mock yourself or your livelihood, without insulting me. You strike yourself and I feel the impact.

'We're the puppet masters behind your weekly shop,' you say.

'I don't believe in that,' Benny replies, vaguely.

'In shopper marketing?' I clarify.

'Advertising, marketing, all that stuff.'

'You doubt its existence?' I ask. I glance down. Even the sodden coaster clinging to the bottom of my beer is branded.

'I just think, we don't need more shit. The problem with the modern world is that there are all these companies and corporations trying to convince us to fill that hole inside,' and here, he jabs at his chest cavity, 'with products.'

'Huh,' I reply. 'I don't believe I've ever heard that before.'

'I go to Westfields and I leave feeling excavated,' he replies.

'So, you're saying capitalism isn't all it's cracked up to be,' I say.

'You should *tell* people!' you exclaim.

You smile at me, as if to say, we could have fun with Benny. But I realise that now, while you are smiling and while we are in front of Benny discussing our jobs, I must finally break the news.

'As a matter of fact, I didn't, um get a chance to mention this before... but a prospective client offered to have us over for coffee tomorrow.'

Your expression stays very still. 'You arranged a pitch,' you state, sotto voce.

'Not a – actually, Peter arranged it.'

'Peter Guiles?' Benny asks. 'Shit, I haven't seen Petey for centuries. That guy is—'

'You didn't feel comfortable reminding Peter that we're on holiday.'

Benny glances at each of us in turn, clearly delighted with these developing hostilities. 'She's not happy, mate,' he gleefully informs me.

'You should have told him to fuck off,' you say.

'I couldn't do that.'

'Why? He's used to hearing it.' A quick shadow of regret passes along your face. Secretly, you root for his success, even at the expense of our own enterprise.

'These things always work better face to face and he's based right here. This is a good opportunity.'

'Sounds like a fucking splendid opportunity. Who doesn't dream of travelling across Europe to pitch a Tesco promotion.'

At this, Benny virtually squeals with laughter. His voice is high and pre-pubescent-sounding. When he laughs, he writhes slightly, as if squeezing the noise out.

'It's confirmed,' I assert. 'We're going, so can we just cut this shit out.'

You glare at me, unyielding.

'Look,' I hear myself say, 'we both know how this goes. I play the bad guy and you play the victim. We argue, or negotiate, or skirmish for hours until you grow bored. And in the end, what happens? We do what we were always going to do. We go to the fucking pitch.'

Benny flashes me a look of squinting judgement, but you meet my stare with some loose approximation of respect.

You roll your eyes, shrug and give me the one thing I have been pining for over the last few hours: you bring this day to an end.

'We'd better get out of here,' you say.

I bound to my feet.

'Oh, *what*?' Benny protests.

'Will you go settle the bill?' you ask me.

Benny fumbles, slowly, for his wallet.

'Don't worry, Benny,' you say. 'We've got this.' And you turn to me with guiltless defiance.

14

Cambridge, 2010
Elle

Her father had begun parcelling money out in small, unviable supplements. Eighty quid at random, sometimes fifty, useless benefactions that only made her life more unpredictable. Because he was technically rich, Elle did not qualify for a bursary. Because Cambridge presumed affluence, students were prohibited from working during term-time. They were discouraged from even cleaning their own room; bedders arrived on Tuesdays and Fridays to scrub and hoover and unburden the young scholars of all practical concerns.

Not for the first time, Elle had the sensation of leading a double life. By day, she considered Chaucer, historicism, semantics. By evening she lived off tins of food and discount sandwiches, lingering in the supermarket as staff marked down the stock.

Still, she did not give way to panic. Elle was a born survivor. There was no telling when the seasons might change, only that change they would. Particularly if her father sensed her slipping.

For now, she rationed. She studied. She hardly left her room. Her interests broadened during this period. Of course, she still slogged through arcane Middle English texts, their constant rotation of *wynsome lavedies* and *hardy knicts*. Yet a new object of fascination kept her pinned to her desk: Raph.

As president of the Student Union he was a legend, debating on Thursdays and always winning. Each debate was recorded and posted online; she began to work through the archive, from his very first clash. He picked contentious topics and argued the reactionary position. He was against positive discrimination, anti-big state, anti-tax. In short, he was her political antithesis. Yet, for a figure who was so public, so explicit in his views, there remained something truly evasive about Raph. Any one of his speeches was objectionable, but together, they were confounding. He contradicted himself over the course of the season, switched his stance with glib delight, depending on his opponent or his mood. There was no coherent position, just a mercenary intellect, a will to triumph.

It was exciting, that display of violent ambition. She even felt a vagrant rush in simply rooting for him, in shredding her own convictions and beliefs – was he really arguing against free school meals? – in favour of his conquest. It was a small act of sublimation, of sacrifice, every time she clicked play.

In fact, there was much about her attraction that felt compromising and new. He was a few degrees shy of handsome; in certain lighting, he was positively unattractive. Oddly, those flaws excited her in ways pretty boys could not. When she imagined sleeping with him, she focused on the bent nose, the thin lips, imagined the sour tang of hot breath. She did not want a cinematic love. She craved something raw and a little ugly. Whatever she'd felt on Jesus Lane, she wished to feel again.

Very few noticed her drift towards seclusion. If anything, her absence from weekly bops or trashy club nights at Vodka Revolution added to her mystique. Only Jennifer, her best friend, seemed to maintain tabs on her. She noticed Elle's parsimony and started preparing double portions when she cooked. *Babes, I've done it again: dinner party for one. Help me finish it or I'll be a whale by Easter.* Interpreting Elle's solitude as depression, she began suggesting exercise. *Fancy a jog?* Elle did not. Three days later: *Hun, I've booked tickets to a mindfulness session. Probably bollocks, but maybe we go for a laugh?* Her tone was always offhand, self-effacing, but her gaze lingered anxiously each time Elle declined.

Finally, one evening, the games ceased. Jen arrived at her door, unannounced and grimly determined.

'Something's going on,' she stated.

'Perhaps...' Elle replied. There was no point in lying.

'I feel like this situation requires tact,' Jen began. 'But I'm no fucking good at tact and you're even worse at sharing. So I bought a gram of MDMA instead. We're going to get mashed, dance a little, and talk this shit through.'

Jen dangled a baggy of pale yellow powder. If this didn't work, she probably had another ten tactics up her sleeve.

'I'm all yours,' Elle said, resigned.

It was synth night at Kambar. Jen and Elle stashed, smuggled and then administered the drugs with a near-silent professionalism. They were like colleagues, like comrades, or some hybrid of the two. These illicit rituals offered a closeness that Elle found difficult to achieve with words. Slipping into the disabled toilet, Elle carved lines and Jen rolled a note.

'Jesus fuck,' Jen exclaimed after her first line. Her left eye was streaming. 'I'll never get used to that.'

Elle did two lines. The powder seared a path up to the frontal lobe, then settled.

'It still fucking canes,' Jen complained.

'I like it,' Elle said.

Jen snorted. 'Yes,' she said, 'but you're wonky, my love,' and touched Elle affectionately on the cheek.

They sat quietly contemplating their own bodies, alert for the first signs of lift-off. Sometimes Elle liked this moment best, the period before the medicine took effect. Even the drip of the tap was oddly thrilling, measuring out the last seconds of sobriety.

'There has to be a simpler solution,' Jen said to the air. 'Sitting in a bog and sniffing Class As just to get a straight answer. I only wanted to know if you're OK.'

'I've been a little off this week,' Elle admitted.

'You've been off all month,' Jen answered.

'I think I have a glandular thing,' Elle offered, timidly. She had landed on the excuse at some point during their walk. 'I should see my GP.'

Jen simply stared, insulted. 'Babes, I already know what's going on.'

Elle glanced down. Perhaps Jen had caught a glimpse of Raph's face on Elle's laptop screen, or overheard her nonchalant, but increasingly frequent enquiries about the Union scene and its controversial leader. Jen was the sort of person Raph made fun of in his speeches, and his contempt for people like her was fully reciprocated.

'Your mum's birthday is coming up,' Jen stated.

Elle's shame gave way to blank confusion. 'How do you know that?' she asked.

'You told me the first night we met. You said things got tough for you between Guy Fawkes and Christmas. And we don't need to talk about it. But you need to know that I know, and I'm here, and thinking about it, even if it feels like you're there, on your own. Because you're not.' She blinked. She had confused herself. From the contorted syntax, Elle deduced that the drugs had taken grip.

'Oh, shit,' Jen said guiltily. 'I thought I had more time.'

Elle herself remained sober, so she was confident that the sudden swell of affection she felt was real. Everybody knew that Elle had been abandoned by her mother at sixteen. It was the age that stuck out, because to abandon a child is a meaningless cruelty, but to abandon a teenager felt personal, felt considered.

Elle had resolved to make a fresh start at university, to conceal this chapter of her past. But she would mention it after a few drinks. She would allude to it when people asked what was on her mind. Somehow, it always slipped out: one day, she had woken up to find that her mother had simply disappeared. It was a fairy tale with an inverted ending.

At school, she had been the object of breathless rumour and maudlin concern, *If you ever need to talk, I'm like literally a call away*, fatuous offers from girls she hardly knew. Now, her background carried a dark romance.

Jen had been the only person to look past the melodrama and sense the loss. When Elle had once joked, *I'm like a half-orphan*, Jen had not laughed. In fact, she'd appeared stricken. Elle had loved her for that. She had also learnt to be more guarded.

Elle's mind turned once more to Raph. *You looked like you were about to stab that guy in the throat.* If Jen sensed anguish beneath Elle's persona, he suspected a sham, perhaps, a subtle con. In this moment, she could not decide who was right.

Jen shut her eyes and shivered, drawn by a warm, narcotic eddy. Soon, she would gather herself and expect further discussion. Elle would have to give her something.

'I hate that bitch,' Jen said, her voice disconcertingly soft. 'Obviously, I'm fucked now, but I've thought about this a lot. I hate her because she left you to that man. And then I feel guilty, because I know it's complicated, and she had to survive too and I hate her even more for making me feel like a bad feminist.' She turned. 'But I'll never leave you,' she said. 'I'm a lifer.'

Elle felt it, that quick, wrenching tug, a hunger that overwhelmed thought or better judgement. The prospect of an unconditional love. Just the thought of it, just the invocation, levelled her. Then it was gone. Realism prevailed. Elle reminded herself that Jen was making promises she could not keep. Under certain circumstances, Jen would, of course, leave. Still, Elle could not quite relinquish the hope. Perhaps this was why she did not correct her friend or modify the account.

'I *have* been thinking about my mum,' Elle said, in a tone of confession.

'I know.'

'I still can't understand why she did it,' she lied, as she always lied.

Jen said nothing at all, just stared hard, trying to will her affection into Elle, to make it felt. She squinted slightly with the effort.

'I love you,' Elle laughed. 'You're a fucking mess, but I love you.'

Jen snorted. 'You love me *because* I'm a mess. I'm the only girl in this entire city that makes you look restrained.'

Elle worried she might ruin the moment through overstaying. 'Let's get out of here.'

15

Before returning to our hotel, I stop at a market stall freighted with knock-off Dior and Louis Vuitton. I select a fake Rolex from the glass cabinet – the closest match to my genuine Omega. The merchant retrieves the watch with a campy flourish; he cradles it in a satin cloth, holding it to the light as if amazed that such a piece had ever fallen into his possession. It is as light as balsa wood; the face is scratched and the second hand moves in dying shudders. The merchant attempts to charge me two grand: we settle on twenty euros.

I do this out of an excess of caution and an instinct for self-sacrifice. I will wear this thing for the duration of our trip, in case you wish to upload a photo of me to social media, in case we bump into Benny again. The crocodile pleather strap scratches my skin. I look absurd. Tasteless. You sense my discomfort.

'If it's any consolation,' you say, 'I think this one suits you better.'

I resist an urge to shove you.

I offer to find a taxi, but you insist on taking the bus. I warn you that the route will be circuitous and you say, *Good, we'll see more of the city that way.* Really, you opt for public transport for the same reason I wish to avoid it. At this hour it will be crowded, bodies packed around us. You want to avoid conversation, my attempts at reparation, my questions. I watch you watching a teenage couple flirt. You turn your head at the sound of an English sentence somewhere behind us. Right next me, you are alone. More than alone. You have dissolved into the lives of these strangers.

It is your fault that today was ruined by Benny. It is my fault that tomorrow will be ruined with work. We're even. I should leave it there. The bus curves onto a boulevard lined with tall cypress trees. It's as if we have not quite left him behind.

By the time we reach the hotel, the silence has gained density. Neither of us has the strength to shift it. Instead, we go about our routines independently. I shower and wash my face. You connect to the wi-fi and begin to browse.

A single scrap from your daily affirmations remains extant. It is pinned beneath the leg of our balcony chair. The paper is brittle and the edges are scorched black. I read its only legible sentence:

11: Others would have done worse.

I question what this affirms. I let the paper disintegrate in my hand.

Inside, dubstep plays from your phone, punctuated by the simpering whine of a woman bringing herself to climax. The advert cuts abruptly and another scene begins. It casts a spell over the room.

A bell.

A door opening.

I, um, have your package, a man says.

His voice is uncomfortable, wooden. In this moment of shoddy masquerade he is briefly, thrillingly, self-conscious. He is not a trained actor and has no gift for it. Perhaps, he worries how the others – the crew, the director, his co-star – will judge him.

Sweat collects along his hairline. His muscles are a sort of disguise. Naked he is formidable, his enormous pecs evoke gods and stallions and beasts. But he looks ridiculous in the fake uniform and he is anxious that others see it too. All those hours at the gym, the sessions, the steroids, cannot protect him from the terror of a woman's laugh or a cameraman's snigger.

Where, uh, do you want it?

He falters. He will spoil it all unless he can gather himself. Because his job is to be hard. His job is to grunt, not moan. To be granite, ungiving, a cruel fantasy of manliness.

Usually, you skip these preludes. You avoid anything scripted, deeming such scenes 'irrelevant'. You know you will not find her here but still you linger; maybe you are watching for pleasure.

Do you mind bringing it here? comes the woman's easy reply. She is comfortable, inhabits her role more easily. She even seems to enjoy this moment of relative power.

Are you sure it's for me?

The woman likely remembers that this is just a gig. She thinks of the money. She is not like the man, who has put his whole brittle self in the hands of another.

It's quite heavy, the man says, the first creep of excitement entering his voice.

I know, she says sympathetically, and I could almost believe her. *You look hot, why don't you just come inside for a minute.* For a moment, she sounds almost motherly in her concern.

Yeah? he asks

Then begins the inexorable journey to the couch or floor.

What do you think of when you watch pornography? Only yourself, I imagine.

You pointedly ignore me as I move around the room, keeping your eyes fastened to the screen. You used to have a face that only emerged during these viewings, a concentration so pure, you appeared almost angry. Or predatory. You were like the men you hated, you shared their rage, their dissatisfaction. These days, you only look confused and vaguely sad when you glance up from the screen. You sense your mission is nearing its conclusion. This is the bathos of success.

I want to ask but I flinch from these topics. As you've no doubt noticed, I do not like to discuss endings.

I roam to the bedside table, my movements slow and wading. You have switched movies, and now a cameraman is asking a young girl what she would do for a hundred dollars. You switch again.

I have nothing to read, nothing to do; I had not anticipated so much solitude on our trip. On a whim I reach for the Bible on my nightstand. Together, we lay, the Puritan and his harlot wife. I read the passage that has been gnawing on my mind all day about a valley of dry bones.

The man on your phone groans and says *good girl* again and again.

What do you think of when you watch pornography? Raph. Always Raph. Only him.

16

Cambridge, 2010
Elle

Kambar was decorated like a western saloon, except with dry ice, cyberpunk lasers and alternative DJs: a quixotic mash-up of bad ideas. They fumbled into the main room and were absorbed into the pulsing mass of bodies. The floor was wet and the walls were sweating; it felt like being digested. Jen's energy shifted as the music picked up.

'If I don't dance I'll burst,' she shouted.

'I just need a minute. I'll catch up.'

Elle glanced at the blinking lights hopefully, wishing they might trigger something from the still-nascent drugs. If anything, it seemed the MD had taken her in the wrong direction, propelling her into a kind of excessive sobriety. She felt guilty for having misled Jen. She felt lonely, because though moved by Jen's concern, a part of her had been absent for the entire exchange, watching, planning. Perhaps she would only ever watch, observe her life from a safe elevation.

Elle found an empty booth. Finally, as she sat down, she came up hard.

It was like a shoulder being popped back into place. All at once, she was right with herself. The lights blazed, faces softened; the happy world welcomed her home.

She began to think of her actual home, as she always did

whenever she was even slightly high. This may have been the true attraction of drugs, the moment of dreamy return. They stood before her, her mother, her father, like embers suspended on the breeze. Her mother, pretty, even in her tatty dress, even as she began to give up in the later days. Elle felt no guilt in this moment, just dumb fascination at the contours of her mother's bent lips. And she felt no rage as she contemplated those doleful eyes that seemed to demand so much, a duty of sadness, a share of the pain. Perhaps it was a face that could forgive her. Perhaps it was a face she could forgive.

These were not novel thoughts. Elle considered them daily, but usually fast and all at once in a loud and anxious cacophony: *she was a bitch, just a child, maybe there was still time, nothing but charred earth back there.* The Ecstasy was like a new conductor, coaxing something clear from the syncopated rhythms of that unruly orchestra. Soon, the inevitable crescendo: she would let herself remember the day her mother left.

'Of course you're here.' For the second time, Raph appeared.

He looked prim, almost formal. His shirt sleeves were rolled up and his tie was removed; such were the only concessions he made to the club or the hour. 'This place is cruel and unusual,' he stated. 'Feels like Guantanamo, except you pay seven quid at the door.'

'So why are you here?' she asked. Her jaw had locked shut. Through her gritted teeth, the question sounded like a snarl. He glanced at her, intrigued by the strange note of hostility.

'I'm canvassing.' He pointed to a group of young men in fleeces. They were varsity rowers, all hench and sober and ill at ease. They stared miserably as the DJ played deep cuts of warped electro.

'I'm running for a second term. That lot represent a powerful voting block. I have to convince them I'm human, I'm fun.'

'And how's that going?' Elle laughed.

'We all want to leave. Nobody wants to say it. It's a war of attrition.'

Her head dropped down abruptly as if a chunk of vertebrae had turned to smoke. It jerked back up. Awful. She had planned their second meeting: it was to take place on a blossoming lawn or humped bridge; she was to appear composed, charming, at home in the ornate landscape. Now her fingers tracing the ridges of the broken-pleather seat, her jaw gurning back and forth.

Later, of course, she would wonder if luck had played any role. Because rowers didn't vote in the Union elections – they had nothing to do with the Union at all. She had clicked 'Attend' on Facebook; anyone with a login could see where she was going that night.

'What did you mean?' she asked. 'That day. About the boys running?'

He appeared unsurprised, as if the conversation had occurred only seconds before. 'People think you're a bitch,' he answered.

She shrugged.

'Aloof,' he added.

'And what do you think?'

'I think your pupils are the size of pennies,' he said. 'If you weren't so hot, you'd look like a bag lady,' he remarked. She hated herself, a little, for focusing on the compliment. *He thinks I'm hot,* she heard herself think.

Elle needed to rouse herself, say something defiant, smart, political.

'The world hates intelligent women,' she announced, her voice rising grandly.

'Don't do that,' he said, with the first trace of impatience. 'Don't be a cliché. In this place, people hate intelligence, full stop. They fear it and so they hate it. It has nothing to do with sex.'

There was some truth to this. Here was a whole cohort of neurotics who had nothing to offer but their minds. To be less intelligent was to be obsolete. Anything short of superlative was useless. If you were not The One, you were just scene dressing, an attendant lord to another's ascent. Raph clearly believed he was The One, and Elle wondered. His confidence was infectious.

'How long will it take you to sober up?' he asked.

'Hopefully about a month,' she answered.

'Let's say Sunday.'

She looked at him, his face appeared recomposed, briefly heroic. 'We've had our "meet cute",' he said. 'Twice, as a matter of fact.'

'Both times I've been a mess.'

'I've noticed. You're a damsel chronically in distress. I like it. But let's proceed to Act Two. I need to ask you a question.'

It wasn't fair to compare him to Jen, and yet she couldn't help but notice. With her friend, she raced ahead, could gauge what was expected of her. With Raph, she entered a new wilderness; the path was dark.

'I'd love to go on a date,' she said. She smiled, giggled bashfully, performed all the little gimmicks refined for these moments. He watched without mirroring. She wondered if he had ever done this before. Perhaps he had only planned as far as the question and now was at a loss.

When he leaned over, slowly, cautiously, she assumed he was going to kiss her. But then he simply poked her cheek, once, twice, as if testing the elasticity of packaged meat. His fingers smelled sweet, like fresh tobacco; his breath like ash.

There were boys who had asked her if she was 'weird about' condoms, or if she was cool with choking, as well as boys who simply dared without checking. All of this was somehow less invasive, less shocking than that prod. Less exciting, too. He returned to his seat, his finger still extended as if there lingered some residue, some evidence.

She tried to interpret the gesture. He was telling her to stop performing; he was searching for something real, the flesh beneath the cheap flirtation. But Raph simply resumed talking. In the same tone as before he made a snide remark about a dancing couple, and it was as if nothing unusual had occurred. His words were a sort of lubricant, smoothing out, softening the unpredictability of his behaviour.

17

You take off your face, put on another.

Make-up cases and soiled tissues with fleshy stains clutter the countertop. You settle on a neutral palette with a smoky eye, applying the cosmetics with a surgical hand. We have hardly spoken since returning from Mr Ayik's.

The pitch was a disaster.

It had started so well. We met in Mr Ayik's home to discuss his new venture. After many successful decades in finance, he was now making the unlikely transition into snacks, launching a boutique chocolate brand. Though the product was bad and the route to market bafflingly haphazard, his proposed budget was lavish, enough to sustain us for months.

We had been invited for tea and were ushered into a massive living room where Mr Ayik awaited us. The furnishings were tasteful, expensive, but the room was set up as a shrine to his daughter Ria. Photographs of her from infancy to adolescence clustered on the walls. He had framed one of her GCSE oil works, a hideous still life of a living room. It clashed against the designer sofa beneath.

Before tea was served, he asked a few questions about your university days with Ria. It was quickly apparent that he and Ria were estranged and that they hadn't spoken in years. You sized up the situation immediately – a father pining for his prodigal daughter – and you sprang into action. You understood his hunger as if it were your own, and you delivered. More than delivered. You were masterful: insouciant without being rude, quick to laugh, open, optimistic and acerbic at just the right moments. I was in awe and Ayik was entranced. Except it was more than mere performance; I saw a part of you thaw and come to life, kindled in the rare warmth of a paternal gaze.

The meeting drew to a close and we began gathering our materials. As you two chatted, I noticed my hands shaking very slightly. Thanks to you, the contract was as good as signed, our most lucrative yet. It would buy us time and it would open doors. Perhaps I could hire an intern. Maybe we could move offices.

He gave you a present, a book of theoretical physics by Carlo Rovelli. I have spent thousands on you in gifts, countless hours contemplating shades of leather, subtle deviations between brands. Somehow, this used paperback touched you in a way that I cannot. Maybe because he said, *I look forward to hearing your thoughts*, as he passed it over. He not only invited more contact, but presumed it.

But then it happened: you let your guard down. You allowed yourself to believe that he would welcome your candour, that he truly wanted your opinion. We both knew the flaw in the project was the chocolate itself. In small doses, it was flavourless, claggy. In high doses, it would probably cause intestinal distress. You gently asserted that the recipe would have to be changed – it needed sugar, fat, *flavour*.

He smiled at you, but shook his head slowly. His features softened, tender with memory.

'Ria has a sweet tooth,' he stated. He explained how since girlhood, she had agonised over her weight. 'Absurd, of course, she's always been perfectly gorgeous. Still, she once told me she'd give the world to indulge in chocolate without the guilt.' He shrugged, glanced at the wall with a bashful smile as if to say, *I have made this gift for my girl.*

He did not notice the shift. You maintained eye contact, nodded politely, but beneath that hygienic smile, a part of you crumbled. He called us a car, waited with us at the door and in the awkward silence, you were deathly still.

Only as the cab pulled up, as he extended his hand, you decided to say one last thing.

'You know, I did see Ria, not so long ago. She was racking up lines in the bathroom of a Mayfair club. Thin as a rail. Really, vanishingly thin.' You paused, you let him imagine it. 'I doubt she has any interest in low-cal chocolate now. Frankly, I thought she could use a sandwich.'

You left before you could fully register the look on his face. But I saw it.

In the taxi back you were silent. But your hands shook like a junkie's and you clutched his book tight. Perhaps you thought that he might still solicit your thoughts one day. A moment of rare self-delusion.

We have to draft another proposal to salvage what we can. I begin copying and pasting information from the internet, which I will sift through and edit with meticulous care.

'Well,' you say, 'I wish you luck.'

'Us.'

'I'm afraid I won't be able to assist with this one.'

'Have you got plans?' I ask, assuming this is a joke.

'As a matter of fact, I arranged to meet Benny downtown.'

I stare.

'Maybe you've forgotten, but we're on holiday,' you say matter-of-factly. 'I intend to enjoy myself.'

'How does Benny figure into that?'

'He isn't so bad.'

'He's awful.'

'Well, what am I supposed to do? My husband has abandoned

me for dietetic chocolate.'

I glance down at the screen. 'I need you for the creative.'

You laugh once and turn to find your bag. Of course, I understand your disdain.

'Come meet us when you're done,' you say.

I plan to let you leave. 'Do you—' I hear myself blurt.

You look at me, an eyebrow cocked.

'Do you think this is a good idea?'

'I do,' you say simply, either misconstruing my concern or ignoring it.

'He's not on Instagram.'

'Good for him.'

'Or X, or Facebook, or TikTok.'

'I envy his restraint.'

'Isn't that strange? He's an aspiring artist, chasing fame. Why would he go dark like that?'

You consider. 'I think he mentioned something about being an MI6 operative, so maybe that explains it.'

I want to chase this further. I am sure Benny has scrubbed his online presence, and recently. Instead, I say, 'Please be careful.'

You pause at the door. 'You know, you can join me. Be bad.' Your eyes are warm, unruly. It is the expression you wear at the beginning of a night, just before things turn. Before a dealer is called. Before a cab is booked. *Be bad*. A mandate with such broad potential.

'I said I'd get this to him tonight,' I state.

'He's not going to hire us, either way.'

'And whose fault is that?' I snap.

'Suit yourself,' you reply, disengaging with a shrug. You are already contemplating travel options. It is clear that whatever you have planned for tonight, I am not a crucial component.

You leave without looking back.

18

Cambridge, 2010
Elle

They met on the steps of the Fitzwilliam Museum that Sunday afternoon. He had already bought the tickets and a programme. Most boys were reluctant to spring for a pint, so the gesture seemed oddly gallant. The exhibition presented Russian Modernists of the early twentieth century; six rooms covered in dark abstractions. Raph paced the galleries at a relentless clip.

At first, there was a small thrill to that, his speed reducing these priceless works to wallpaper, reducing the gazing spectators to dupes. But Elle found herself growing curious about some of the pieces and would have been frustrated at his pace if Raph weren't so intriguing himself.

'You said you had a question for me?' she began.

'Soon,' he replied, as if even this brief exchange interrupted their progress unnecessarily. They spent only a few minutes on the works of Olga Rozanova. 'I think we get the gist, mostly triangles, more lines,' he summarised.

In the penultimate room, he finally stopped. 'Here,' he said. 'That.'

They stood before a black square surrounded by a beige border. Roughly six metres high, it took up an entire wall. She traced the frantic brushstrokes, a moment of urgency frozen in glossy acrylic. It was starkly beautiful.

'On loan,' Raph said. 'Went for twenty million at a Christie's auction.'

She raised her eyebrows appreciatively.

'Twenty million for a fucking square,' he said. 'Now, what I want to know is why. Why the fuck would someone spend that much for a square?'

It was obviously a test, but perhaps it was also a trap. She did not know him well enough. Possibly he was playing devil's advocate, that this was in fact a cherished piece, why else would he pay the admission, or share it with her?

'Is there some reason you're asking me?' she said, stalling.

'Apparently you're good at this sort of thing.'

'Says who?'

'Your tutor. He pops into the Pitt Club occasionally. According to him, you have a *vast aesthetic sensibility*. He says you have *negative capacity*, whatever that is.' His voice was vaguely derisive, as if these attributes were either ridiculous, or a slight liability.

'You want me to tell you this painting is bad?' Elle said, sensing his intention without quite understanding it.

'Or prove to me that it's good.'

There was an edge to his voice. She did not wish to either deride the piece or decode its beauty. Both seemed a type of vanquishment, a consumption. Yet, this was apparently the point, he eyed the work as he would a sparring partner that would not yield to his acuity, that would not blush or turn away from his insults.

'I'll have to think about it,' she said.

'Just tell me your hunch.'

'My hunch is that I have to think about it.'

Clearly, she failed the test. He did not say another word until they left. Elle pretended to inspect the remaining canvases, but her eyes kept darting to him, trying to decipher his silence, which felt colder now and more definite. He left her standing by a triptych. She made herself wait a few minutes before following.

Outside he greeted her with a quick, automatic smile. It was the sort of smile that waiters flash when they are caught daydreaming on shift, designed to conceal. He said they had lunch reservations at The Chophouse, where they shared a bottle of Chianti and ate steaks. Whatever had occurred in the gallery, Raph now channelled his ire towards the food, which he considered too well done. *A fossil*, he said. *With a side of vinegar*, he added, sipping the wine. She agreed, cowed by his conviction; her own palate was too crude to know if the assessment was fair. They spoke blandly about summer plans, her module decisions. It felt like punishment, but there was no way of expressing this. The whole conversation was too congenial, too pointedly pleasant, to raise an objection. When he settled the bill, she sensed an ending.

Surely that should have been it. On the short walk home, Elle decided that she would not speak to him again. Only, the numbness from Friday's drugs gave way to a new sensation, a sort of bleeding. Her bedroom had a sudden inescapable quality. It was a Sunday feeling, except worse. It was every Sunday, every anticlimax, every resignation compressed into one moment of primal disappointment.

Before long, she found herself in the college library, researching Suprematism and Formalism. By Monday, she had neglected *Sir Gawain* for Berger's *Ways of Seeing*. By Tuesday, she was composing a five-page text, a small treatise. It explained all the ways in which the painting worked. The paradox of its form; its bid to escape the concrete belied by the very materials of its language. The sadness of that paradox, the implied futility. All this thought, all this ardour dedicated to the viscosity of paint.

Delivered.

Read.

He began composing a reply then stopped. Began again and stopped. Then exactly seven hours passed and nothing happened.

At midnight her phone vibrated and she knew it was him.

Interesting. A sparing reply if ever there was one.

Thanks, she wrote.

Maybe you should write a book. As if the thought had never occurred to her.

One day.

Three dots, she watched him compose and she watched him stop. She could feel his trepidation and perhaps he could feel her yearning because the next thing he wrote was so oblique that she had to read it twice.

I want to rest my balls on your chin.

It was the most cryptic sext she had ever received. Filthy and oddly bland. What did he desire? A sort of table, an erasure. Even sex objects had the gratification of being fucked. Yet she felt heat rising along her throat, her thighs, that strange insurgent pleasure.

You can rest them wherever you want. Shocking herself, losing herself, just a little.

19

message you at six:

Wrapping up. How's it going?

You reply with your location and nothing else.

The mirrored wall of the elevator shows a man older than his years. I have become a tired archetype: the beleaguered husband pursuing his wayward wife. You are fifteen miles away, probably a few drinks in. It occurs to me that, should you catch yourself on some mirrored surface, you will be pleased by your reflection. You will see a woman who is desired by men. Benny will be trying to charm you, perhaps telling you of some pseudo-celebrity he met at Shoreditch House, or sharing the details of some recording session. As you listen, you will know that I am racing towards you, that I abandoned the pitch prematurely.

I do not know why, exactly, but I turn left, towards the hotel restaurant, rather than right, towards the exit. I take a seat at the zinc bar and order a dirty martini. Because I have not eaten, even the first sip of gin has impact. I feel my mind unclench and by the end of the drink, it falls comfortably slack. As I let my gaze drift across the room, I entertain fanciful notions. Perhaps I could stay here. Let Benny bore you to death. Pursue my own adventure...

The thought embarrasses me, it is such a small and petulant rebellion and, even this, I will not commit to. I glance around. Hotel bars never change. The young couples, the solitary traveller, the good-looking staff, the same scenes repeating themselves again and again, the same details painstakingly reenacted each night, as if the bar were trying to understand itself.

Before the hour is through, I will be hastening towards the Old City.

The woman who takes the seat to my left is not like the others. She wears an I♥NY T-shirt and khaki shorts, her boots are streaked with dry mud. I can tell by the way she examines the damp coaster by her elbow that she does not like it here. I know instantly that her hotel room is dark and empty, that she is in this city alone; her silence has a settled quality. She orders a pint, takes a sip, then gazes at her phone. She shakes her head, sips, composes a reply, her face tightens as she suppresses a smile. She receives an alert and, though she is in her fifties, flushes with girlish pleasure, her eyes widen, her body rocks forward; some friend, somewhere, has scandalised her. Now, the woman seems to have forgotten her surroundings completely. I find myself wondering if I could ever sit like that, with such muscular self-sufficiency. The small of my back aches from stooping.

Suddenly she looks up, pins me in a stare. 'Can I help you?' she asks.

'A fan of the Big Apple?' I say, pathetically. I have never been good at small talk.

'Huh?'

'Your T-shirt.'

'What? Oh. It's not mine,' her accent is English, a Londoner. 'The airport lost my suitcase. A single piece of check-in luggage, and they are quite overcome.' She looks irritably into the distance. Then adds, 'Actually, I hate New York.'

'Oh?'

'People refer to the buzz, how you feel it the second, *the very second*, you step off the plane. Seems to me this is just a romantic way of describing congestion and poor crowd control.'

'I often dislike famous cities. I end up feeling like I've been brought there on false pretences.'

'How so?'

'Tourism traffics in nostalgia. They lure you there with a vision of a place that no longer exists, perhaps never existed.'

She takes this comment at face value and asks, 'Have you ever been to Vienna?'

'No.'

'Vienna is ghastly for that.'

'Have you been to Prague?' I ask.

'Yes,' she answers. 'Regrettably.'

She moves seats so that we can be closer and faces me directly. The woman has a lean, handsome face, and speaks with curt authority. We fall easily into a conversation of cities we despise. She dislikes those that she feels are, 'self-conscious', notably the big three: London, Paris, New York. Places where people make smug self-referential remarks about their status as residents or where fellow tourists compete over their knowledge.

'...I just find myself thinking, if you know this place so well, why don't you try somewhere else... And they talk incessantly of food. Have you noticed that?' she asks. 'You can't even mention lunch without being barraged with recommendations. You like bread? You must go to this bakery, it's very old. You drink coffee? You must visit this café, it's very new.'

I hate modern cities, I tell her, places like Dubai. I describe the journey down Sheikh Zayed Road, malls and sand and billboards that stretch for acres.

'I haven't been,' she says. 'Though I transferred at their airport once and I didn't like what I saw.' I'm oddly touched by the comment, the implied solidarity.

We journey to Asia. I am not fond of Hong Kong.

'It's a very masculine city' she says in a contemplative voice. 'Even topographically. It has an incredibly male topography.'

I could keep going. I realise, I could loop the world again and again and still find fresh disappointments. As we continue our misanthropic tour, my energy builds. A truant thrill, because I am travelling without you and I am enjoying it.

We do not exchange names, so remain poised as strangers, our intimacy collapsible. She makes documentaries that explore weighty topics: FGM, death-row inmates. She is factual about her achievements. She knows too much of the world to be senti-mental, and she has been working for too long to emotionally invest. I like that. I can understand that. A vision of morality that is based on actions, your net balance at time of death. I may not put good things into the world, but I have taken some nasty elements out.

'Do you know,' she says after ordering another drink, 'this is the first time I've really spoken today. I don't normally travel on my own, I thought it might be difficult. Actually, it's rather easy; you just get on with it.'

'How are you finding it here?'

She considers for a moment. 'I like the cats,' she remarks. It is the first silly thing she has said since we began and she feels my disappointment. 'I enjoy their effect. You see these great burly men stop in the middle of a street to cuddle a kitten. Or shop workers who lay out saucers of milk. They're touching, those moments of spontaneous affection.' This is slightly better, but I'm still irritated by the soppy note. Personally, I hate the cats, I find their presence in the cafés and bars and shops a little grotesque. Anything in such abundance begins to resemble vermin.

'I suppose I'm not in a position to judge this place,' she says. 'Not objectively, at least. I was supposed to come here with my partner. She always...' her voice trails off. 'Suffice to say, we never got round to it. It taints things slightly. I find myself getting so *reflective*.'

'I'm the same,' I exclaim.

She is bemused by my enthusiasm. She cannot know that I am normally so inept at conversations with strangers, terrified by the very randomness, the twists and dead ends.

'To be honest, I'm not sure why I came,' she confesses. 'I suppose I just hate to leave things unfinished.'

'Maybe you were trying to finish her off,' I gambit.

She glances at me quickly. 'I'm quite sure that's not the case,' she says definitively.

'I just meant, perhaps you are trying to close that chapter.'

'Ah. I'm afraid it's been closed for quite some time.' Her tone is cryptic and I know I should not pry for details.

'And how has it been? Day to day, I mean,' I ask.

I realise I have inched forward, am literally on the edge of my seat. It seems, right now, that this woman's journey has profound implications for mine. I have you. I enjoy having you. Yet the thought of losing you always shadows the contentment.

'It hasn't been *sad* exactly. Really, I spend much of the day in a state of bafflement. I see the monuments, buy souvenirs, walk and walk and walk… but I'm not sure what I'm supposed to feel about any of it.' She pauses. 'I suppose she was my Rosetta Stone. Without her, this whole city is just a jumble of shapes and symbols.'

'I know exactly what you mean,' I say. 'I really do. Without my wife, I wonder if I would feel much at all. I sense everything through her. She's like my nerve endings. I don't think many people experience that sort of love. That closeness.'

It is true. There are moments when I see you and am stunned by your body, which is so distinct, so oddly separate.

'That's not what I meant at all,' she says and sips her drink more quickly than before.

'I think it is. Perhaps I didn't express myself perfectly. What I mean is, whenever I hear or read about "love" I feel everyone gets it completely wrong. They always focus on the difference. The

100

strangeness of their partner. How love requires accommodation or compromise, or... To me, love is about closeness, that sense of merging.'

'Sounds like eating.'

'It's connection,' I assert, perhaps too forcefully. 'When I met my wife, I felt like she'd been missing my entire life. Like I had some part of me back.'

The woman grimaces slightly and kills her drink. It sticks with me, that gesture. I feel like I have seen it before. The moment when the other realises I am not what they expected or want. You are the only person who has ever managed to hold my gaze. You know exactly what I am, and it suits you.

'I'd be curious to know how *she* feels,' the woman says, in an irritating academic tone.

'She feels the same,' I reply coldly. 'And don't do that.'

'Do what?'

'That knee-jerk feminism thing.'

She raises her eyebrows, as if to say my complaint warrants no response. And then I add, 'We're inseparable. In fact, this is the first moment I've been alone for this entire trip. I suppose I still have my "Rosetta Stone",' and I ape her accent slightly.

We should have left the conversation in Dubai.

'Does she make you feel clever?' the woman asks. 'Does she make you feel safe?'

'Yes.'

The woman's chin dips down, brushing her collarbone. She glances up, flirtatiously, and giggles, a simpering Lady Di, it as if she has been possessed. 'I'll bet,' she says, her finger roams the rim of her glass. 'I'll bet a lot of women are drawn to you. I might not agree with everything you say, but you have a magnetism...'

I have no idea what is going on. I feel I should reach for her hand. I bite my lip, prudish, indecisive, while her whole body blazes with suggestion.

Then the warmth leaves her face. 'See. We all know how to do it. We have to learn. We have to learn because of men like you. Charm, charm, charm while you're eyeing the door and planning your escape.' Her face is stiff and closed. 'Have a nice evening.'

She gestures for the bill and the barman goes to print it off. As she grabs for her jacket, I do something that scares us both. I lunge. I kiss the woman because if I do not, I fear I might hurt her. I kiss her because it does hurt her, our foreheads collide and she takes the brunt of the impact. My tongue darts into her mouth just long enough to sense the shape of it, the taste, to steal some basic knowledge of her, to prove that I can. And then I withdraw. The barman turns. The music plays. For a moment, she must wonder if any of it was real.

She signs the bill, charging the drinks to her room. Her hands are shaking. She is furious and she is afraid.

'Your wife is a lucky lady,' she says.

I sit for a long time, wondering how much the barman overheard. I wonder how long until the woman's shock wanes and what she will do when that happens. She will want to respond. Her vanity demands some retaliation. Beyond these practical concerns, I wonder if I am now, technically, a cheater. I think not: somehow the kiss had felt like self-defence. Still, you cannot know about it, this goes without saying.

The woman is in room 521; she wrote it quite clearly when signing the bill.

The woman has had two drinks, her reflexes will be slow. She is staying alone.

I mention this not because I intend to harm the woman, but because it proves something. She is critical of men, of the dangers they pose. Yet what has she done to protect herself? What responsibility does she take?

Outside, the veranda is empty. The iron railing is wreathed in bougainvillea that grows as thick as weeds.

She is still only metres away, in a room not far from ours. At some point, as she scrubs her teeth and tongue, her rage will overtake her fear. I have only alarmed her; half-measures are as dangerous as excess.

I hear a mewling sound and then something soft collides with my calf. The kitten hardly resists as I scoop it from the floor. I take off my jacket and cradle the thing in my right hand.

The woman likes cats.

I sense she is not a fighter, that beneath her bravado, she is delicate. But delicacy only exists in hindsight. It can only be known briefly, at the moment of collapse, when you apply a little force, feel a thing crush beneath your hand. Only as you tighten your grip, feel it shatter, only then do you know its fragility.

20

Cambridge, 2010
Elle

Raph did not like the word 'girlfriend', finding it puerile, infantilising. Elle did not much care for the word either, but she felt that some sort of term would be useful, because terms stabilise and fix. Without them, every night, each date was an act of reinvention.

Was the flower left in her pigeonhole intended as courtship, because he wanted more, or did it express gratitude for what she had given already? Or was it nothing, just a dead plant destined for the bin? He yawned as she described her day. Was this contented domesticity, or the beginning of the end?

It took her weeks to finally address the situation. Raph showed up at one in the morning. She was happy to see him, then just as quickly, resentful, even ashamed. She realised she had been waiting for him all night, hopeful that he might arrive.

'You're making me be someone that I'm not,' she said, as he undressed.

His fingers slowed. 'I'm not making you anything,' he replied, smiling inexplicably. Merlot had stained his lips and teeth, leaving his expression bloodied, as if he'd been feasting on rare meat. 'I've never once told you what to do.'

This was true, but only in a very technical sense. The act of withholding felt like an act of control. She had been backfooted into becoming some whining supplicant begging for a kiss, begging for a promise.

'What are we? I don't care what the answer is, I just need guidelines. Are we exclusive? Am I allowed to sleep with someone else?'

Perhaps she was hoping that he would blanch at the prospect, but his smile remained. 'You're allowed to do what you want,' he said. 'But I wouldn't, if I were you.'

The quick escalation, the rising note of threat: she told herself it was because he'd been debating and was still thinking like a predator. Yet she could not resist taking the bait.

'Or what?' she asked, dreading the answer.

'Every action has a reaction. You fuck a bloke from seminar, perhaps I fuck a girl from committee.' He watched her, decided he could push further. 'Or perhaps a new sort. One of your friends. I could finally throw Jennifer a bone...'

It took her a moment even to realise he was referring to her best friend. The suggestion was ridiculous: Jen loathed him. For a long time, Elle inferred this from her absolute silence on all matters Raph. But Jen was not great at reticence, and recently, over an awkward lunch, the dam had burst at last. She began listing his flaws: his selfishness, his politics, even his looks.

'All this for an absolute minger!' Jen exclaimed. 'And he's mean, at the end of the day, he's just mean. Even when you try to big him up, all I hear is prick, prick, prick.' She stared, trying to gauge if she'd gone too far; Elle simply waited for her to subside. 'He's a prick,' Jen added at last, for clarity.

Jen could not win this argument, even if she was largely right. When she spoke, her words had a faint, faraway quality. When Raph spoke, his words stayed in Elle's mind for days. Simply put, Jen wrote in pencil, Raph chiselled in stone.

'Let's have another night. Kambar, just the two of us,' Elle had offered.

'He'll show up. Like last time.'

'I'll tell him not to.'

'Then he'll definitely show,' she answered.

'Jen hates you,' Elle stated now. She had never revealed this, hoping at some point they could be reconciled.

Raph raised a patronising eyebrow.

'She told me,' Elle insisted.

'When we hug, her hungry little hands grip me through my clothes. I have to pry her off. Don't tell me you haven't noticed? I'm not sure if that's adorable or concerning.'

'She said you're ugly.' This landed like a child's soft fists.

'And you believed her,' he stated, without so much as a flinch.

Something was being ruined. Already the image of Jen hugging Raph filled her with revulsion. Before morning, she would have to decide who to believe, who to lose. She could only save one.

'I think I love you,' he said abruptly, as if privy to her deliberations. It was almost uncanny, he sensed threats so quickly. '*Think* being the operative word,' he hastened.

'What's there to think about?' she asked and there she was again; needling him for love as if hers had already been offered.

'I hardly fucking know you. That's the issue. You're all hooks,' he accused. 'You're like a trailer for a movie.'

'I'm trying to be open with you.'

'What happened to your mother?' he demanded.

'She left me.'

'No,' he stated. 'What really happened?'

Weeks ago, her mother had sent a card with a message so spare it seemed to physically strip something from her. Two years of silence and then: *Congratulations on Cambridge. I'm truly glad it worked out for you.*

It was the paucity. It was the past tense.

Elle had thrown the card away. Then, feeling it was somehow unsafe in the bin, dug it out and hid it in the leaves of a book.

Clearly Raph had noticed. Maybe he had found the note, deduced that there was a story, an angle.

'I'm not hiding anything,' she exclaimed. 'I'm trying. I keep fucking trying.'

Her voice frayed and there were tears in her eyes. She was on the edge, her fist clenched so tight, her nails might draw blood. Assuaged, he softened.

'I know,' he said. 'I know you think you are. All I'm saying is that you're holding back. It's a compliment, if anything. There's this piece of you that you won't share, and I rather suspect that's your most interesting part.'

He took her in his arms, held the base of her skull in his warm palm. She was exhausted, empty.

'Even when we shag, it's like you're somewhere else…' he said, tentatively, a little foot probing the soft earth beneath. She glanced up. 'Don't look at me like that,' he said. 'Sex isn't everything, but it's a thing. It's part of a broader picture.'

'When have I ever said no to you?'

'It's not about yes or no. It's about what. How far you're willing to explore… There's a world beyond missionary, you know.'

So began the period in which Elle attempted openness, in which she practised vulnerability. She never fully understood what he meant by these terms, only that she never quite provided enough. Sex played a vital role in the constant barter. She appeased him with new positions. *No, she did not wish to discuss her father… Yes, perhaps she was open to rope.*

She began attending Union functions. At first, she was touched by Raph's insistence. It was a progression, of sorts, to be seen with him, to be stood beside him as he paced the Keynes Library, preparing arguments. But, as always, it came with an unexpected levy. The girls did not like her, glancing through her during the long dinners. Conversely, the boys were too familiar. *Very nice,* they might say, eyeing the cut of her dress. They would scoot their chair a little too close, maintain eye contact for a fraction too long. It was not the intrusions themselves that bothered her, but the nature of their audacity. These boys respected Raph, even feared him. Surely they would not be so bold unless they sensed his tacit permission.

Lent term passed in a blur of drinks receptions and five-course meals. She met writers, politicians, activists, a glamour model. She pretended to remember names and to recognise faces, wore a beige smile that blended with whatever conversation she was hurled into. It was a time of sherry and cigars, gowns and black ties, yet these pretty vestments hardly concealed the Union's true function. It was a bear pit of ambition. The guest speakers wanted prestige. The members wanted contacts and clout. Even the blandest conversation was viewed through a narrow lens of triumph and defeat.

This was never clearer than at debate night. Like the actual Houses of Parliament, the Cambridge Union was raucous by design. The bar ran cheap drinks, booing was encouraged, as were heckling, grunting, banging. The sounds of the gallery rose up in one belligerent swell. She had witnessed inflatable sex dolls bounce across the stalls during a debate on pornography, one of the speaker's faces taped over the gaping, plastic mouth. She had seen a snowfall of black confetti flutter from the gallery as the speakers argued over an end to positive discrimination. Raph seemed truly at peace amid this chaos, watching with tired amusement. During his tenure as president, the misbehaviour only intensified.

He carefully restricted his own participation, debating three times a term at most. It was almost uncouth for the president to debate at all and he needed to protect his legacy. Raph held a fragile bond with his spectators. They enjoyed his savagery, as well as the romance of an undefeated record. They would protect his winning streak as long as he didn't push his luck, as long as he never bored them or took their loyalty for granted.

Of course, Elle had seen him debate in videos online, captured in low resolution from dodgy phones. But watching him spar there in the room, the air thick with cortisol, the abrupt thunderclap of boos or applause, was a visceral experience. The clips had only focused on his triumphant face. Here, you could see the damage he inflicted along the way. He debated until his opponents flushed, then went pale; until they sank their heads in submission.

It's almost tactile, he once told her. You're separated by five metres, but you can actually feel the energy leave their bodies.

Then, when victory was assured, he made sport with their corpse.

'We've learnt a lot about your so-called lived experience.'

'Yes, because—'

'In fact, that's all I've learnt. I came here to debate. This isn't debate. It's showboating.'

'Now, I—'

'I recant! The metaphor does a disservice to boats. You're not a boat. You're less; a barnacle, a parasite; you attach yourself to a cause and suck it dry.'

Raph often targeted progressives. Here, Elle believed he was misunderstood. He did not take aim at their ideas, but their worthiness. It was their pride that he enjoyed breaking. He liked the ones who really believed.

'You say you're doing this for the gays, but what do you actually do? You spend all your time trolling, calling out, shaming. Your principles of inclusion are expressed only through cruel exclusions. Hypocrisy in the name of equal rights.'

He studied his opponents for weeks, trawled their social media, spoke to former school friends, gathered intel anywhere he could. He would open his argument with a sharp ad hominem attack or with some artefact from the past repurposed into a knife. It would leave them flustered, unable to articulate, too distracted by their own bleeding.

'Tonight you're in support of free speech. Yet in the past you have petitioned to de-platform Dr Guildstone.'

'Well—'

'I have the petition right here, with your strange, squiggly little signature.'

'That was at secondary school... It was over a year ago.'

'It was eleven months. Your morals appear to be having an identity crisis.'

'I can have competing...'

'Why are you even here? You stand before me in a Paul Smith suit, at one of the most elite unis in the world, yet you sound like the very voice of the proletariat. You renounce privilege and yet you embody it. You denounce this university and yet you climb its ranks.'

'I worked my way up.'

'In which case, there's no problem. Others can do as you did: work and prevail.'

'Well, obviously, I had help. Not everyone is as lucky.'

'In which case you are the problem, as nepotistic as the rest of us. Just more hypocritical.'

His opponent kept tugging at his tie. In this moment, he would escape his own skin if he could.

'And you're always so angry,' Raph persisted. 'So petulant. Bitching on Twitter, whining to *The Tab*. Is there anything that you actually like? Let me guess. You. You like you. You enjoy being the one who says things.'

The laughter was always louder than the quips deserved. But Elle understood it. He offered a kind of freedom. Raph championed all the instincts they were taught to suppress. He was the nasty voice in your head, gratuitous and cruel. What a pleasure to clap for that voice, rather than resist it. What a thrill to watch it being unleashed on someone else.

Raph understood that even vegans crave red meat.

As term drew to a close, Raph began preparing for his final performance. He grew broody and short-tempered. When Elle suggested a dinner date, he glanced at her with confused resentment, as though she'd asked to borrow money. If she expressed disappointment, he bit his lip with theatrical restraint, as if weighing some devastating ultimatum.

She knew it was only a matter of time before the big and final argument. She spent her days in a state of preparedness, wondering what form it might take. But then Raph would come and blast away her misgivings as convincingly as he sowed them.

He was in unusually high spirits the night before the debate, but complained that he was struggling to unwind. Then his hand landed on her hip and she knew what he was asking for.

'I can't tonight.'

'Why?'

'I'm on my period,' she said, hiding her embarrassment with an exaggerated frown.

'I know,' he said. 'I can smell.'

She kept her head high, but her thighs tightened in shame.

'Why should that stop us?' he asked.

'We can do other stuff...' she offered.

'We talked about this,' he said. 'Openness. Vulnerability.'

'We didn't say anything about gore.'

He rolled his eyes. 'I'm not a little boy,' he insisted. 'It's natural. Periods are natural.'

He looked oddly childlike in that moment, his face a mixture of mischief and want. She said yes because she wished to make him happy, wished to keep this version of Raph a little bit longer. She agreed because beneath it all, she wanted to believe him, that he was capable of loving her, blood and all. At any rate, she said yes.

At first, Raph undressed her carefully, with near-reverence. But then, when she was fully naked and he was still partially clothed, his face locked shut. He was rough. He had been rough before, but always with some pretence of a game or a role. Somehow, that element of fantasy softened things, padded each thrust.

Now, his dick was like a blunt force. At first, she did not know what he was looking at. His eyes glazed with private recollection, another woman maybe, some studied porno flickered before his sight, a hatred that he could not share.

She yelped in pain. He noticed. He liked that. He liked that she had made an ugly sound, that he was turning her into a broken instrument. When she glanced down, it was as if she had been sawn open. He liked that too. He was clearly trying to make a mess.

'Careful,' she gasped.

He ignored.

'The sheets,' she said.

'They're fucking sheets,' he hissed, and sped up defiantly.

When it was over, he seemed to marvel at the scene, his gaze travelled the ruined linen, her blood-streaked thighs, his own body stained from the navel down, with fascinated contempt.

'You said you didn't mind,' she murmured, reading his repulsion.

'I said it was natural,' he replied. 'Disgust is natural too.'

In the morning, there was coffee waiting for her on the table. He sat in the window nook making notes, his features bathed in soft light.

'Morning, darling,' he said. It was as if the night before had not occurred. Or perhaps, she reasoned, it had achieved its desired effect. Maybe she had finally been sufficiently vulnerable, sated him for a time. She began to collude with his good cheer; she would not bring it up.

'You seem happy,' she offered.

'I am happy,' he confirmed. 'It's the last debate of the season and I plan to end on a high. Frankly, I feel like we both need the break.'

She was not exactly sure what he meant by that, perhaps a small acknowledgement that the Union was taking a toll on them both.

'This is your first Last Night,' he said brightly. 'There's a fancy dinner—'

'There's always a fancy dinner.'

'Fancier,' he assured her. 'Then the debate, then the afterparty, which is always delightfully bonkers.'

She started to prepare her outfit, laying a simple black dress on the bed.

'No,' Raph said, without looking up from his notes. 'This is a big night and that makes you look like you sell insurance.'

She selected a mauve gown with a dramatic slit and asked if that was any better.

'I like the colour,' he said. 'But I've seen you in that before and it fits like a monk's robe. You've got a good figure: be bold.'

He nudged her towards a little red dress that she was saving for an end of year ball. It was short and tight, the silk fabric slightly iridescent.

'Seems a bit much,' she said, examining herself sceptically in the mirror.

'It's just enough,' he said.

'I don't want to upstage you...'

'You were born to upstage me! You know, you make yourself too small. Since the day I met you with that pathetic baker. You must learn to stand proud. At this rate you'll leave uni with a crook in your neck.'

They left to attend their respective lectures. She convinced herself that the night would be fine, perhaps fun. Her body ached each time she moved, as she discovered a bruise, a tear. It was a sudden, unwelcome reminder of the night before, of how easily he had slept afterwards.

It was obvious that something was wrong from the moment she entered the dining room. As she drifted towards the table, the conversation died and the boys stared.

She was overdressed. She looked absurd.

'My God, Elle, you're a bloody vision!' announced Peter Fox, a ruddy-faced third-year who seemed always to be in a state of sensuous overexcitement. The boys sniggered. She knew that he was performing for them, not for her, that there was menace beneath his flattery.

Raph smiled innocently and drew out her seat.

'You really are a rare beauty,' Charles Bollinger said. He leaned forward and added in a stage whisper, 'A very rare beauty.'

Now the sniggers became laughter. The girls glanced at her, confused and resentful, as if it were her fault. Maybe it was. Because they had arrived in simple little frocks and she had come dressed as a gaudy harlot.

The first course arrived: charred cauliflower on a beetroot reduction.

'It matches your dress!' Peter exclaimed. 'Does it look appetising?'

'I sense Elle's a steak tartare sort of girl,' Charles ventured.

'Right, what the fuck is going on?' Darcey demanded. She was a second-year vet and could be relied upon to bring a fraught, maternal energy to all proceedings; she had a natural instinct to badger and admonish. She glanced at each of the boys in turn. 'You're all acting like idiots. What's so bloody funny?'

At the word 'bloody' the boys began to cackle. Finally, the penny dropped. Raph had told them. Peter held up his hand and shook his head with mock innocence and this only incensed Darcey further. 'Come on, Peter. Out with it. What are you nattering about?'

There she was, dangling above a foregone conclusion: this would be one of the worst dinners of her life. She looked down at her plate, the vegetable lying on a bloody clump. She wondered if he had picked that course specially for the occasion, just as he had picked the dress. She wanted to take her knife and draw it across her throat. It would feel like a letting. There was too much blood in her, flaming against her skin, pounding in her ears, leaking, disgustingly. And still Darcey would not shut the fuck up, still she was refusing to let the conversation progress, and the girls were nodding, they wanted to know just as much, and the boys were practically choking on their giggles, coughing on them, she hoped that one actually did choke, keel over and—

'It's Elle's time of the month.' Everyone turned to Benny. He blurted it, quick and artless. 'Apparently,' he said, glancing at Raph and smiling.

'Oh my God,' Darcey said, with directionless horror. 'Guys, that is so disgusting,' she said, her head pointed towards Raph in vague repudiation, but then turning involuntarily to Elle, the real source of contamination. She wanted to reprove the boys, but she could not help it: Elle disgusted her.

Elle stared at Raph, absurdly hoping for something, an apology or intervention. Instead, he watched with mild amusement, the etching of a smile on his lips. She realised then that it was over. She was being discarded.

When Elle launched to her feet nobody asked her to stay. Instead, she felt their eyes inspecting her as if she might still be dripping.

Outside, she stood in the front garden trying to light a cigarette as members ambled past. She remained like that, too dazed to leave, perhaps too unwilling. She could not end things on such an ugly note, she could not accept that Raph was truly so cruel, or that she, in turn, had been quite so stupid. When she sensed a presence behind her Elle assumed that he had finally followed her out. If he said the right word, even now, she would likely forgive him.

Instead, Benny approached her cautiously.

'You OK?' he mumbled.

'Fantastic,' she hissed. 'Pleasure to be of service.'

'They're bullies,' he said. 'What happened in there was wrong.'

'Didn't stop you from having a go.'

He looked surprised, flustered by the accusation. 'I was trying to help...' he sputtered. 'They would have gone on all night, dragged it out. I was trying end it.'

Perhaps he was telling the truth. It had seemed like excitement, a desperation to land a kick. Maybe it was more like a mercy kill. Raph had appeared somewhat annoyed, as if Benny had overstepped the punchline, ruined the fun.

'They're all brutes,' he said. 'Cads.' His face was earnest but she noticed an embellishment in his accent, a note of counterfeit. He was not like them. He had not grown up saying words like 'cad'. He stressed it, as if unentitled to its use. Even now, as he refuted them, he aped their style.

'You sound like someone from *Downton Abbey*,' she spat.

'Posh?' he asked, confused.

'A bad actor,' she said. 'A fraud.' She could tell from the way he glanced away that she'd struck a nerve. It was gratifying.

'He will never end up with someone like you,' Benny stated.

'What does that mean? "Someone like me"?' she said, trying to coax some spark of indignation, anything to combat the sinking feeling.

Benny continued as if he had not heard. 'He might end up with someone like Darcey. He'll spend his life hating her and most nights cheating on her. So maybe you've dodged a bullet. But for better or worse, it won't be you.'

'How the fuck do you know so much about him?' she demanded.

'I don't know,' Benny confessed. 'I just know this. In his eyes, you're an escape, a hotel room that he can trash and then leave. And you aren't the first.'

She could not accept it. His pity was as mortifying as the dinner itself. Worse, because it encompassed more, stretched into her future. She needed to prove him wrong. In many ways, it was Benny, not Raph, that spurred her forth, back into the Union, where the chamber was now full, back into the dining room, where Raph skimmed his flashcards.

'Not now,' he said without looking up. 'It's starting.'

'This will take less than a second,' she answered.

'I haven't got less than a second.'

Before any more words could be wasted, she scooped an abandoned glass of Syrah from the table, held it aloft, as if in salute, then emptied it down the front of his shirt. Even she was shocked by the sight. There had only been a few sips, less, yet he seemed drenched in it. The first splash landed against his chest, then it continued in streams and rivulets. She glanced down at the small glass, amazed, a line of Shakespeare surfacing: *Who would have thought the old man to have had so much blood in him?*

Somebody called his name. They were waiting.

The injury outpaced his anger. He simply stared.

'Good luck tonight,' she whispered. 'Just be yourself.'

Elle heard the heckles while she exited the building, as well as the laughter. Perhaps, for a moment, Raph told himself it would be a noble challenge. He probably thought, for a brief instant, that he could still win, that he could make some witty remark, turn his humiliation into an advantage, that through the force of his intellect, the machine-gun rattle of words, he could convince them all that his shirt was still white, that he was in control. What he misunderstood was that the audience only ever wanted blood and that he had shown up injured. They had enjoyed him as a gladiator, a prodigy; they liked him as a fool just as much.

The student papers reported the event in florid detail. There was a moment of disbelief as the illustrious and undefeated president approached the lectern like some bumbling wino pleading for loose change, said Varsity. The Tab took a more oblique approach. It launched a Kickstarter page to raise money for a new shirt, exceeding its target five times over. All this existed on the internet, a stain that Raph would never scrub clean.

Elle drew little satisfaction from the victory. If anything, the coverage unsettled her. He had not reached out or confronted her; in that silence, she began to contemplate the reprisal. He still had friends in the student press, perhaps he would do it that way. Or maybe he would email her tutors with some bald accusation. If she knew Raph, it would be big, baroque, executed with a cool head and dark pleasure. Soon, the anticipation bit so deep it felt like craving.

A full week passed before he appeared at her door wielding a pink box. She eyed it suspiciously and he flashed her a sheepish smile.

'Cupcakes,' he said, opening the lid. 'I thought... you know... um...' She had never seen him lost for words before. 'A little reminder of our glory days,' he said. 'I thought maybe we could start from square one.'

Still she was waiting for the trap, and he could tell.

'I was an arse,' he said simply.

She hesitated. She doubted. But she desperately wanted to believe.

21

The dot on my phone indicates that you and Benny have not moved for hours. I discover you both under a patchwork canopy, purple and green cloths stitched together and draped over an alley café, near Gülhane Park. You sit on cushions, a shisha pipe between you, voices bouncing between the narrow walls.

Benny glances up, sees straight through me, looks down then glances up again. There is a flicker of disappointment.

'Finally,' you say, unconvincingly. Your voice drops an octave as you release a cloud of smoke. 'I was starting to worry you'd run off with another woman.'

'Mate,' Benny says. 'You're bleeding.'

I realise there is a scratch along my right hand, shallow but gushing. I bury my hand in my pocket, feel the damp seep into the lining.

'It's nothing,' I say.

'Looks nasty.'

'What were you two talking about?' I ask.

'Past lives,' you reply.

The tip of the shisha nozzle is slick with your saliva. You hold it erect, then swing it towards Benny so abruptly he startles. He accepts it, glances at me, then takes a self-conscious drag, tasting you beneath the tobacco.

'Uni,' Benny says. 'We were talking about the good old days.'

'Raph,' you say. 'Specifically, we were discussing Raph. Benny was incredibly close to him.'

'Your ex,' I say tonelessly. My eyes are stuck on Benny; he thinks I'm addressing this to him.

'I suppose he's everyone's ex now,' Benny says, flustered. 'We were very tight,' he adds with practised melancholy. 'Strange that we didn't see more of each other,' he says to you. 'We only really spoke that one time... you know, before your... um... stunt.'

'I don't recall,' you say quickly. Before he can clarify, because it seems Benny has something specific in mind, you change the subject. 'Raph had a girlfriend for every mood. He had the posh girl he showed to his parents. He had the smart girl he took to his debates. The party girl—'

'Which one were you?' I ask. I know which one you were. We will discuss him, if that's what you want, but we will discuss him honestly.

'I was the girl he called late at night,' you reply unflinchingly. 'His experiment.'

Benny seems genuinely upset by this. Embarrassed, of course, but also hurt. He reaches for his mint tea. It is hot, and he replaces it too heavily, allowing some to spill over the side. He finds a paper napkin to mop it up.

'He was a prick,' Benny says. It is like watching a child swear, the word comes out odd and slightly misshapen. 'He had a lot of secrets. I didn't even know about all the drugs.'

'How could you not notice?' I blurt, incredulously.

'It seems crazy in hindsight. We were close, but our friendship was very controlled, regulated. I can't explain it.'

'I understand,' you say. There is a curious sincerity, even a softness, in your voice.

'But I sort of envy you,' Benny says. 'I mean, it seems like you've digested it, you seem at peace. When it happened, I just froze. For a long time, I assumed it was the shock and I'd eventually have an epiphany. But the shock never wore off.'

'I've experienced a lot of death,' you say. 'So maybe I'm just more used to it. To you, Raph was a life-changing event, but really his story is very ordinary. Predictable, almost. Raph was always selfish: it makes sense that he was greedy when he took drugs, too. Drugs are dangerous: he paid the price for that.'

I feel profound relief. You have quoted me verbatim, it is a lecture that I have delivered to you countless times and which you never quite seemed to hear.

I see myself pacing the narrow space between your bed and desk in uni halls, the speed of my steps betraying my own nerves, but my voice calm as a tutor's. *Everybody knows he was greedy above all else. They won't even be surprised.* I see you simply staring straight ahead, your doubts louder than my reassurances.

You sip your tea. Then you continue to speak, adding a new and unfamiliar appendix to the speech.

'The fact is, Raph always *seemed* devastatingly special and I'm sure he would have liked his death to seem special too. But, with age, you realise he was just a garden-variety narcissist. He is everywhere, one replaces another. There is always a Raph offering to buy you a drink. There is always a Raph waiting for you at the bottom of the stairs.'

You shrug, resignedly. Benny glances at me. The murmur from neighbouring tables rises up and, for a moment, we are adrift in other people's conversations and our own thoughts.

'Still, quite a nasty way to go,' Benny says. 'He'd been drifting on that punt for hours. His skin was burnt.'

You shrug. You watch him. I wish I could read you more clearly.

I am not sure what Benny wants either. Simply to go there, perhaps, to revisit the day.

'If I'd known at the time…' he blurts, very quietly.

'Known what?' you ask, your voice loud. 'What was there to know?'

'No,' he says. 'Nothing,' he says. 'I guess there's always an element of "what if?"' Now his voice is like a setting pole landing against the riverbed, guiding us gently, gently away from the edge, into some parallel current. He is holding back. We both feel it. You watch him.

'He was spotted by dozens of witnesses. Nobody tried to help,' I offer, in case it is guilt that is propelling him along.

'Well, they didn't realise,' Benny says. 'He appeared to be moving…'

'I've heard that,' you say, your gaze steady. 'People thought he was coming to cause trouble, mistook his *rigor mortis* for rage. I always thought that was perfect. In death as in life: he was always just an absence.'

'All the food had spoiled,' Benny says, his voice faraway. 'He would have hated that too,' Benny says. 'So undignified.' There is a slight twitch in the corner of his mouth, the beginnings of a smile.

'Karma's a bitch,' you say.

He laughs, guiltily, uncertainly, but laughs all the same.

We smoke until we are giddy and then we smoke until we are slightly nauseous. My eyes twitch from left to right, seemingly of their own volition. Discreetly, I inspect my injury. The blood is dry but there was more than I'd imagined. The skin beneath my fake Rolex has begun to itch.

Benny has moved hostels. He says he never stays in one for more than a few nights – three, max. He strikes me as the sort of person who has many rules and mantras, who is comfortable offering advice. In a way, we share this. Except my rules have arisen from necessity and I sense that his are an attempt to give his identity some arbitrary shape.

'Apparently this place is, like, five hundred years old,' he says as we drop him at his doorstep. 'I suppose that's not too impressive, given the neighbourhood. Still, I'm pumped. I got a space on the roof.'

'The roof?' I clarify.

'Yeah. Don't look so surprised. The roof is the best spot in the house. Amenities include: stars, the sunrise and open air.'

'I suppose I'd prefer a mattress and air con. But then, I'm no artist.'

'That you are not,' he confirms. I could shove him. Instead, I resolve to leave him to his shallow, stock-image wonders. I have my wife again and Benny is finally, almost, gone.

'Early start tomorrow?' he asks. 'Or what are you guys thinking? I'm easy.'

'Probably around ten,' you say. 'But I'll text you if we're running late.'

I wait for him to disappear inside. The doors click shut and I wait a few seconds more before I turn and say, 'Fuck you.'

'What?' You look happy, mischievous; a child about to be caught and tickled.

'You made more plans with him.'

'You left me alone for almost three hours. All that time, he kept grilling me about our schedule.'

'Why didn't you lie?'

'I didn't think to! You might find this difficult to believe, but I'm naturally very honest. With a few key exceptions.'

'Those aren't exceptions. Those are everything.'

'Anyway, it was only when he started inviting himself along that I realised I'd made a mistake.'

'Tomorrow, text him and say our plans have changed,' I say, my voice striking a strange note between an assertion and a plea.

'And what am I supposed to say when we bump into him? We still share friends. He knows Pete and basically everyone in the alumni network.'

I want to state that this doesn't matter, but of course it does. So instead I demand, 'What was all that shit about Raph?'

'I had to know if he knew anything... If he was aware at the time.'

'No. You *wanted* him to know.'

'Why would I want that?'

'Search me! Bloodlust. Revenge. You're still angry.'

You do not dignify this with a response.

The human desire to be seen and known is ubiquitous. I do not feel it in the same way. Perhaps this makes me sub-human. Or, perhaps, my needs are more modest: I am known by you and that is enough.

But it concerns me. Adulterers confess, criminals let themselves be caught, people will throw away everything simply to be understood, even by a stranger. What would you wreck for the thrill of the announcement?

'We can't let him come between us,' you say and I soften, instinctively, at your words.

'I have no interest in joining a throuple,' I remark sullenly.

'Ha! My God. A throuple with Benny…' you chuckle at the thought.

This is a joke to you. But you underestimate his stickiness, how he clings like wet dough.

'One more day,' you say, soothingly.

'I feel like you're keeping something from me.'

'What?'

'I don't know. It's just a feeling.'

You sigh. 'You're just tired. You do this when you're tired, you find paranoid connections between then and now.' You pause.

'Are you ever going to leave him?' I ask.

'Who?'

'Raph. You're utterly devoted.'

'I see. You're being poetic,' you state. 'I don't have the head for poetry right now.'

It is late. We are crossing Galata Bridge. Old men stand at regular intervals, fishing, their faces pointed towards the black water beneath. It could almost be beautiful, except I know that the river contains nothing but old bones, filth; I have seen it with my own eyes by light of day, seen the jellyfish blooming on the tide like spent prophylactics. Let it pass. Let it all flow beneath our feet. There is nothing to be salvaged from those depths.

You stop walking. You have been continuing the conversation in your head. 'If I can't be straight with you, then there's no hope at all. Who else have I got?' you ask, reflective, slightly sad. You seem to be hoping, almost, that I could have an answer, as if there might be someone you've overlooked.

22

You cannot find the lighter, so, this morning, you shred your affirmations to a mound of confetti, let the breeze lift and scatter them on the city below. The plaza is empty and the palms hang limp, their fronds beginning to brown. It is as if this hotel has grown taller overnight; the city itself, its restaurants, its people, has never felt so far away. A strange sensation.

You have been messaging your friend Jen since last night. Jen loathes me, but I don't allow myself to worry about it. Over the past four years, your friendship has fallen into a predictable orbit. Sometimes, in certain moods, you send each other ardent texts, affectionate notes, apologies or resolutions. You write to each other late at night and make plans that wither and die by morning. Sometimes Jen promises to send you an email that will lay it all out, things that cannot be said over WhatsApp. You are always relieved when this doesn't come.

The cleaners arrive early. Today, they travel in pairs. When they spot us in the hallway, they freeze, for just a beat, and then look to their feet in frightened deference. You do not seem to notice, just as you do not notice that this morning the air vibrates a little differently. Something must have happened last night. To a guest, perhaps. Not an attack – there are no police, as far as I can tell – but perhaps something stranger, a warning.

'You seem chipper,' you say.

'I'm looking forward to breakfast,' I reply.

In the lobby I spot the receptionist from the first night and we link eyes. He has lost his smirk, his insouciance. Somehow, I know that if I were to ask for an upgrade now, he would give me the penthouse, he would give me the jacket off his back.

'Are the hash browns topped with caviar or something?' you ask. 'You're grinning from ear to ear.'

At first, we do not discuss Benny as we travel towards him. That would only make it worse, prolong the exposure. We do not complain or betray our misgivings. We remind ourselves that we are adults and act as if we are visiting the dentist: the event will occur, we won't like it, but then it will be over.

As the taxi veers onto Bagdat Avenue, I realise I can antici-pate the driver's route. I no longer glance out of the window with curiosity. Instead, the streets have the grey, translucent quality that comes with bored familiarity. This is a problem. Without distraction my mind begins to drift.

I take out my phone, ostensibly to email Mr Ayik: a link to a *MarketWatch* article, perhaps, anything to keep the dialogue open. If we land this contract, you will never have to know how deep into the red we have forged, how fragile things have become.

Instead I google Benny. He is a shallow itch, sitting somewhere beneath the epidermis, the space where infections often thrive. I can't resist sinking my nails into him.

The last gig of Benny's that I can find was nine months ago at the Troubadour in Earl's Court. He comments on their Facebook announcement, stating that he is honoured to grace the same stage that once hosted Hendrix, Dylan and the Rolling Stones. Of course, anyone who knows the Troubadour knows that, these days, it is simply a coffee shop, a quaint relic from the sixties. Flicking through the photos, it is easy to discern that this 'gig' is little more than an open-mic night. Most of the other performers are ageing poets. Most of the audience seats are empty.

From here, I learn that he has changed his name to BB. There are several locked accounts associated with the initials. I still cannot understand why an artist would keep their presence so hidden.

Emboldened, I try to track down the successful track he kept alluding to, but the title evades me. 'The Smell'? 'The Odour'?

Then I see it.

I stumble across an archived press release from a toilet hygiene company on page two of Google. It mentions licensing 'The Stink', by Benedict Berkowitz, for their new online campaign. Slowly, it dawns on me: Benny is the voice of poo drops. There is a poetic truth to this discovery that is deeply confirming.

But there is more. He is hiding something. I know it. I feel it. I keep digging.

'Can you... Can you stop doing that?'

In my excitement I have been nudging you.

The press release is a few years old, but there are new comments. Strange comments. A girl called Petra accuses Benny of being a fascist.

...He is literally everything that is wrong with the world. I love your product but I will personally boycott Mountain Drops until you publicly disavow this artist.

It is impassioned and it is oblique. Beneath, a middle-aged woman called Kate signals her solidarity with a fist emoji. I cannot make sense of it.

I click through to his SoundCloud page, and this is my first mistake. Without warning, the app launches and the first few bars of his song play automatically.

Yo... Yo... Blud, bear tings sitting—

I kill the app but it is too late; his voice is too distinctive. Even in this autotuned recording, where he tries to fill his rather nasal delivery with bass and depth and adopts an exaggerated

South London accent, you recognise the sound. And you turn to me, fix me in a stare. Your expression has an almost feline quality, as if you are gauging the distance between you and your prey.

'What's that?' you ask, knowing exactly what it is.

'I was just fact-checking—'

'Stalking.'

'What?'

'You were clearly stalking Benny.'

'Yes, yes…' I say. I do not let your tone dampen my mood. Poo drops. A giggle rises in my throat. 'You know that song he kept hinting at? His big, financial—'

'I know,' you say blankly.

'It wasn't a single, it—'

'I said, I'm aware. The "Just a Drop" ad. I got all that.'

I turn away to hide my dejection. I open the taxi window a crack, just to occupy my hands. The breeze enters with a chopping sound.

'It doesn't suit you,' you remark.

'What?'

'That pettiness. It makes you seem small.'

You say this as if to be helpful. I glare at you, then correct my expression and proceed in an academic tone. 'We all do it. We see the mistakes of others and feel…'

You watch me, curious, expectant, 'We feel…?'

'Safer,' I say. You look mildly disgusted at that. I push on. 'Anyway, he ruined our day. He's about to ruin another. Forgive me for wanting a harmless moment of schadenfreude.'

'You seem to think about him a lot.'

'Hardly!'

You raise your eyebrows disbelievingly.

'How did *you* know?' I ask suddenly.

'What?'

'About the song. You must have "stalked" him too.'

'We used to follow each other, when he still had an account,' you reply, and I hear the false note, the strained nonchalance. I pursue the thread.

'When was that?' I ask. 'Did you know he was here? Before we bumped into him?'

You move your shoulders in a way that signifies neither assent nor disagreement. Ariana Grande begins to play on the radio; her ecstatic falsetto seems to make a pronouncement on the acrimony creeping between us.

'You kept leading us back to the Bazaar, where he was staying,' I say.

'It's the Grand Bazaar,' you state.

'So?'

'So, it's hard to miss.'

'Yes, but right outside his hostel…'

'OK, you caught me. I conspired to ambush Benny so I could have the pleasure of an awkward lunch. Christ. You're paranoid.'

'I'm right though.'

'You sound like a flat-earther.'

The driver sniggers and I could murder him. I could clamber over the seat and grab him by the throat and choke him to death. He leans back and cocks his head, anticipating my retort. Both of us notice. For a moment, we see ourselves through his eyes and are repulsed.

Benny meets us outside, his skin incandescent with sunburn. His sallow complexion is violently red.

'Benny,' you say. 'You look terrible.'

'I feel worse,' he replies. He smiles and winces.

'The roof didn't work out, I take it,' I state.

'It would have been nice if they'd have warned me… The sun is incredibly intense up there.'

'I suppose they considered it self-evident,' I reply. You glance at me. I reign myself in and try to frown sympathetically.

For a moment, the atmosphere is tense with things still

unsaid. It makes you uncomfortable. You open your mouth, about to speak, then close your mouth. *Good*, I think. *Do not fall into the trap.*

'What are you going to do now?' you ask, and I feel a stab of panic.

'That's the million-dollar question,' he replies, with self-pity.

'Just ask them to move you inside,' I say.

'Can't. No room at the inn. The guys at reception say they're fully booked.'

'Well... go back to the last place then. Break your three-night rule.' One would think, from the nervous energy in my voice, that I am the one sequestered on the roof.

'They're booked too. Apparently there's been an influx of Americans.'

'So I suppose you'll have to find some hotel...' I say.

You are silent. We are sentences away from disaster and you are calculating, trying to find some means of changing course. Or perhaps you are assessing risk. I have tried to remain nonchalant, tried to treat Benny as an inconvenience and nothing more. But when we were bickering in the car, I accidentally showed you my hand. How easy it would be to weaponise our interloper. He could be deployed to terrify, or frustrate, or subdue. Granted, he would be a weapon of self-destruction but, still, you must be intrigued by the variety of his uses.

'Everything within my budget is taken,' Benny says, almost lachrymose. 'Last-minute hotel rooms are sort of mind-blowingly expensive. I'm basically fucked. Honestly, I've tried everything, even reactivated my Couchsurfing profile, sent out an SOS... nothing.'

I glance off into the distance. You glance at me. Neither of us look directly at him.

'I mean...' he shyly begins, 'what's your situation?'

'We have a small couch...' you say in a quiet voice. I seize on that. I seize on that first hint of discomfort, the first suggestion that you are out of your depth. It reassures me that we are still on the same side. And there is justice in it too. You were hoping to dangle him in front of me, but now he has attached himself to your fingers.

'Minuscule,' I add. 'It's more of a chaise longue.'

'That's sounding pretty lush right about now...' Benny says.

Again, we fall silent.

'Well, of course, you're welcome to it,' you say, putting us all out of our misery or, at least, deferring the misery until later.

'I'd love to be able to be polite and turn you down,' Benny says. 'But I guess I don't really have that luxury. You two are basically saving me from homelessness. My Good Samaritans.'

'Don't mention it.'

'Also, if I'm honest, I'm a bit excited to check out your hotel. I've been slumming it for so long.'

For some reason, this last comment annoys me the most. Perhaps because his gain is directly proportional to my loss. He has taken something from me. Not just the afternoon, or the tranquillity of the room, but a quality more difficult to quantify.

You and I have not yet had sex and this unnerves me. The act itself is fairly inconsequential. We are not lustful in the same way as other couples our age; our carnal instincts are more complicated. However, with each day, the absence grows conspicuous. Sex is an agreement of terms, a confirmation that we remain husband and wife, have not drifted into a new configuration. I crave the emotional gratification. Now, for another night, we will remain chaste and unsettled.

He returns inside to retrieve his luggage and the two of us stand there, quiet and with a creeping sense of loss.

'He's like an albatross,' you eventually say.

'At least the albatross was dead. It didn't talk incessantly. I'd happily carry Benny around my neck if he would just shut up.'

'He's got under your skin,' you remark.

'I don't think we'll ever get rid of him.'

'Tomorrow we head towards the desert and he goes away.' You state this, but your voice lacks conviction.

'It doesn't seem to bother you at all,' I say, suddenly rueful.

'Maybe I have a higher pain threshold,' you shrug.

'It's not that. You think pain is normal. You're used to it.'

You give me a sharp look. We both know you grew up crooked.

'He wants something from you,' I say.

'Room and board.'

'No. More. I think he's in love with you.'

'You think everyone's in love with me.'

'They often are.'

'He isn't.'

Clouds skim the sky, their movement brisk and disjointed. I have the vaguest sense that all of this has already happened, that we are living through a memory.

'He isn't even attracted to me – I can tell,' you add.

'He wants something.'

Benny emerges strapped into an enormous backpack. Within its mildewed interior is a fortnight's worth of dirty clothes, probably as damp and stained as the T-shirt he is wearing, hosting colonies of bacteria on sweaty fabrics. And soon it will be at the foot of my bed.

We begin to walk.

'Guys.'

I think my mind is shrinking. Somehow, all I can picture is Benny's filthy clothes mixing with yours on the floor.

'Guys? Woah, not so fast.'

We slow.

I imagine him following us everywhere. He will follow us home. He will be at our rented office when we arrive for work. He will be waiting for us in bed at the end of the night. Others will expect him too. We will arrive at dinner parties to discover an extra chair. *Where's Benny?* our hosts will ask.

'Guys!'

We stop. We turn to face Benny, who is several feet behind.

'Sorry to be a pain in the arse, but I'm a little weighed down. Anyway, what's the rush?'

'This is just how we walk,' I say.

'Yeah, well, if you're tearing through the city at sixty miles an hour, you'll end up missing the whole experience.'

'What experience? We're on a street. The street's purpose, its raison d'être, is to be walked through.'

'You sound stressed,' he observes, and I am too galled to reply. 'OK, I'm setting myself a goal. Today, my aim is to teach you two how to relax.'

'How altruistic,' I say.

'To be honest,' you say, 'I find walking slowly rather stressful.'

'That's because you're not used to it,' Benny assures you 'Let me be your Sherpa.'

A man has set up shop on the kerb; he is preparing falafel in a makeshift fryer. The bubbling brown oil catches your eye.

'We have reservations at half one,' I warn. 'At Yeni Lokanta.'

'Yeni's?' Benny asks.

You grow uncomfortable. 'How many did you book for?'

'Two, of course,' I reply. 'I made the reservation over a month ago. I couldn't have foretold that Benny would be here.'

Benny frowns. 'If the worst comes to the worst, we could pull up another chair, I suppose.'

'Yes, or perhaps we could just sit in each other's laps. Then we'd only need one chair,' I snap.

'OK, OK,' you say, quelling the mood before it ignites. 'We'll just have to go somewhere else. No big deal.'

In whose interests are you acting? You do not like to see me lose control. Perhaps you are stopping me from humiliating myself. Or, maybe, it's possible that beneath the toying you have actually developed an affection for our intrusive freeloader and are trying to spare him the embarrassment.

Benny frowns pensively. 'I have an idea,' he announces, as if it's his first. 'Apparently Isotope Five has a new piece near the New Station.'

Neither of us respond. Personally, I've only understood a fraction of the proposal.

'The New Station is this gorgeous Ottoman railway station that's been rescued... reimagined, basically.'

'Reimagined,' I repeat. 'So what is it now? A launchpad?'

'It's full of these cool boutiques and cafés, that sort of thing. You guys will love it, it's right up your street. The setting is just... seeing all these new initiatives in those crumbling bricks, it's...'

And Benny struggles to find the word that will capture the beauty, the charm, of this fusion between old and new. The word that comes to my mind is 'ordinary'. There are New Stations everywhere: Mackie Mayor in Manchester, Market Hall in London, Time Out Markets in Lisbon, Chicago, New York. This trend for elevated food halls in decrepit environs has been going strong for the most part of a decade. Benny is simply describing gentrification.

He keeps talking. Now he is midway through a monologue about Isotope Five, a graffiti artist. Benny is describing the new work as combining 'golden-era Banksy' with the playfulness of 'any era, Dave the Chimp'.

'Benny, you want us to go look at some street art,' I summarise. 'And perhaps pop into a hipster café en route. Is that about right?'

'It isn't just street art. It's an event,' he says to you.

'Sounds like a Google job to me. I'm sure there are images of it online...' I reach for my phone to illustrate the point.

It's a mistake. Benny doubles down on you, speaking with intensity about dissidence and art. Is his boyish enthusiasm endearing? Perhaps it would be, if he were about half his age, an actual boy.

You are beginning to weaken. I realise that the forces of democracy are moving against me.

'I could call the restaurant,' I say. 'It's possible they can amend the booking.'

Benny frowns and weighs the option. 'Sounds sort of pricey,' is his final culinary verdict.

'I'd be happy to treat you,' I offer, through a clenched jaw.

'To be honest, I have a whole thing against expensive restaurants when travelling. Think about it, you get fancy restaurants in every city in the world, so ironically, they're not very special. If you want to really experience a place, you need to go to its dive bars, the little hole in the walls where locals eat.'

'You have dive bars in every city too,' I state. My voice is hollow. Resistance won't work. Benny's plans will simply happen, descending on us with the inevitability of nightfall.

'What do you say?' he asks you, who will now cast the deciding vote.

'Whatever,' you reply. Then consent with a shrug.

'Great! It's a bit of a schlepp, but trust me it will be worth it.'

And just like that we leave the Old City. Benny lumbers beneath his enormous backpack. You drift between us, sometimes talking, often content in the company of your own thoughts.

Occasionally, strangers glance at Benny, whose burns seem more garish as we step into the light. He is oblivious.

I make a point of relaxing my shoulders, my facial muscles, my pace. I do this to punish you. Because it occurs to me that I am holding all the tension and discomfort for both of us, that I am carrying twice my load. So, for now, I let go.

We board a tram, disembark and wander the little shops and cafés with ruthless expediency. Though Benny has brought us here, he has scant interest in the quarter, dismissing it with a single remark, *It's better at night.* It is mostly empty, and vividly Caucasian. In fact, the few patrons all appear to be European expats, bunkering with their laptops and attaching to the free wi-fi. We order overpriced cortados in a café. As it brews, I listen to a man in his mid-thirties conduct a Zoom interview. He speaks in pure, unbroken jargon, quotes Jeff Bezos and Larry Page and Elon Musk intermittently. He tells his listener, *You should love your co-founder more than your wife.*

How did we get here? The path seems to disappear behind us. Benny trips and he fumbles, but somehow, he always manoeuvres us. I glance at you. You are watching Benny. His hands shake as he pours brown sugar into his coffee. The way he stares at his little cup makes him appear secretive. I feel a frisson of intrigue.

We move through the downtown area, where the crowds are dense, and wade through thick and motionless heat. Petrol fumes settle on our skin as Benny navigates with growing confusion. He says we're close. You complain that your feet are beginning to hurt. Benny says it isn't far. I realise I'm smiling.

He takes us north and with every passing block, the neighbourhood seems to worsen. He stares at his tattered espadrilles.

The road slopes down, so the buildings seem to grow taller. Above, the air is webbed with power lines. We pass an abandoned car, its windows smashed, its interior gutted. We pass a group of children who stop playing and follow us with a burnt-out gaze. *Why here?* they seem to ask. They cannot compass our need for The Real. Our craven want for an Authentic Encounter.

The mural is, of course, a disappointment. Four by five metres, rendered in the faded pigments of a tattoo, it depicts a scene that loosely resembles *The Last Supper*. Except, of course, the main protagonists are corporate mascots.

'Right,' you say, your voice a low simmer. 'Very clever.'

Above us, TVs are blaring. Music is playing. A woman argues with her partner in guttural tones. The streets pump with spite. We sense a tremendous volume of bodies, just out of sight.

'I like it,' Benny replies, with forced cheer. He too is faking it.

'Seems pretty indistinguishable,' you say.

'From…'

'From anything you'd find on Brick Lane,' you snap. 'Or anywhere else. A sixth-form art class.'

'You have to see it in situ… Contextualise it, view it through the lens—'

'I *am* seeing it in situ, Benny. I'm standing right next to you.'

He doesn't see the danger. You are a powerful engine slowly revving. Your only function is the thresh, to violently separate good from bad.

'Maybe we should head for lunch,' I volunteer. 'Benny, you said you knew a place?'

Both of you glance at me with surprise; I haven't sounded this jolly in days.

'Yeah,' he begins. 'The uh…'

'The shithole,' I remind him.

The falafel shop looks no different from a generic chippy back home. You look at him with pure resentment. I try not to smile. There is no indoor seating, so we eat sitting on the kerb of the road. Inevitably, the food is strictly mediocre.

'We've earned this,' Benny declares, biting into his pita and causing a jet of garlic tahini sauce to spill over his fingers.

'Do you need a napkin?' I ask.

'Mate, it's designed to be messy. That's part of the fun.'

To prove a point, I eat with almost prissy delicacy, folding the foil wrapper neatly when I'm done.

It takes me a while to notice that Benny is not speaking. Things are so much better when he doesn't. I'm unable to fully enjoy the respite, however, because I notice his eyes have a quick, furtive quality; the silence is only provisional. He glances at you, at the mess in his hands, at you again; there is a coiled tension which you try to ignore.

'Last night was fun,' he finally remarks.

'Yes,' you agree. 'The shisha is strong here; better than the stuff on Edgware Road.'

'If you fancy anything stronger, I have some treats in my bag...'

And for the first time since we embarked on this expedition, you seem genuinely happy.

'Treats?' you ask. In your voice, a readiness to forgive. My heart sinks.

'Just some hash I picked up at the hostel.'

Cannabis. It is less than you desire but more than expected. You'll take what you can get. But this is not what Benny wishes to discuss, it is only a preamble.

'I keep thinking about Raph,' he says. He clears his throat. 'That conversation shook me up a bit, truth be told.'

You say nothing. You take a bite of your food and chew self-consciously.

'I wish,' Benny says, 'that we'd known each other better when it happened. We could have helped each other.'

'I didn't need help.'

'I didn't think I needed help either.' His voice has the consistency of spilled honey, stretching slowly, inexorably towards you. 'Look, I totally get it: he was terrible. But it's not about that. That isn't how trauma works—'

'I'm not traumatised, Benny,' you say, your voice severe; a warning.

'It isn't a sign of weakness. We all—'

'You're being—' you interrupt him.

'What?'

'You sound like a fucking podcast,' you say, and your tone is pure bitterness and contempt. 'All this touchy-feely shit. All these second-hand emotions, feelings that you've learnt from Twitter.' You shake your head, dizzy and exasperated. 'Everything is a *trauma*. Everything is *complicated* and needs *unpacking*... Raph's death is one of the least complicated things that's ever happened to me.' Benny looks at his feet as you continue. 'Maybe it's gratifying for you, I really don't know.

Maybe you find it interesting but, personally, I'd rather forget the whole thing.'

'And how is that working out?' Benny asks.

'Wonderfully.'

He pauses for a long while before remarking in a very quiet voice, 'He fucked me over too, you know.'

'Sorry?'

'I'm just saying my relationship with him was also complicated. I can probably relate—'

'Did he ever rape you?' you ask.

'No.'

'Then I don't suppose you can relate.'

Just like that, he's out of his depth. He opens his mouth to speak. No words come out. He is confused, he thinks you're angry at him and doesn't understand why. He knows that there is a certain protocol for discussing abuse, but then, you defy all protocol.

Normally, I would intercede. Your blood is up: you may prove reckless. Really, you've already said too much.

And yet I'm torn. It's so satisfying to watch Benny scramble. My fingers rub against each other as if I'm casting some sort of hex. Privately, I urge you to cross a line.

Instead, you groan with frustration and self-contempt, grimace slightly as a memory, like a tiny pointed object, works its way through your brain's soft tissue.

'Forget I said that.' And then, 'Honestly, ignore it. That isn't what I meant and I'm not one of those people.'

'What people?'

'People who cling to victimhood. Besides, it's not what you're thinking. I'm just saying that not all of what we did was consensual.'

'Fuck,' he says, lost for a moment and caught off guard. 'I'm so, so sorry.'

'Benny, what are you talking about? What are you apologising for?'

140

'Whatever happened to you.'

'Come on,' you say. 'As if you didn't know.'

He shrugs and shakes his head frantically.

'I had a reputation. You knew that.'

'I can't recall anything specific…'

'*All* the guys knew specifics.'

'Not this one. I wasn't like them. I wasn't looking for the same things…' He holds his palms up as if you were pointing a weapon at him. 'You know, I had a rep myself and it couldn't have been further from the truth.'

You squint, disbelieving, perhaps even a little disappointed.

You wore that reputation like armour. It was your most daring disguise, never to refute their gossip, their insults, but to embrace it all. To be the girl who dances on bar tops and passes out in disabled toilets. The girl who can drink the boys under the table, who will take dabs from any soiled wrap being passed around, no questions asked. A tactical loss for a strategic victory: they never saw you hurt, could never guess what you were thinking.

'Look, Benny, take it from me, these feelings that you want to talk about… They're not inevitable. You don't need to feel anything at all. It's a choice. You can close the valve.'

'If you ever do decide to open it, I'm here. That's all I'm trying to say.'

The gift is useless but it makes you smile.

You glance around the street and are struck by its strangeness, as if it manifested all at once, or as if we've been teleported here.

The food and the heat hit me in a sudden enervating wave.

A greengrocers' across the road catches your attention. Your eyes fix on a cart of red apples.

'The fruit seems brighter here,' you say, vaguely. 'Compared to back home.'

'It's inspiring, isn't it?' he asks.

'What's inspiring?'

'All these independent retailers, in charge of their own destiny…'

You groan. 'There you go again.'

'What?'

'Sounding like a fucking millennial.'

The two of you laugh, and I have a sudden feeling of translucence, as if I'm only partially perceptible. He is lying. I just don't know why or what about. I have the inviolable belief that none of this would have happened in the Old City. He moves towards you. Through a warren of alleys and dead turns, he is guiding us back towards ground zero. Now we are on the topic of university, we are discussing pain and regret. I have let him.

'I understand more than you realise,' he says. 'Believe me.'

And suddenly I do.

23

London, 2024
Benny

The rise and fall of Benny Berkowitz was short and unceremonious. Six days. In the space of six short days, he came within inches of achieving recognition, even fame, before torching his reputation completely. Now, his name was reduced to a warning, his career a case study in self-sabotage. Benny would have years to contemplate the particulars, to trace the quick genealogy of his downfall. But, for a time, he was simply stunned by the finality of his loss.

It seemed somehow inevitable, even perversely just, that his career should die in March, days before the memorial. The month began, as always, with a call from Beatrice Weston, Raph's mother. Usually, this conversation lasted no more than five minutes and followed a strict regimen of questions and answers. She was brisk, allotting him just enough space to reply with a few syllables. How was he keeping? Fine. And his family? Also fine. And his career, was he still singing? Rapping. And, yes, yes he was.

She made the same enquiries and the same errors each time: Bea had been referring to him as a singer for ten years straight. On some level, he presumed, these remarks were intended as ice-breakers. But her disinterest was so palpable, they had the opposite effect; she grew colder, more remote as she spoke, as if even this, the most rudimentary of catch-ups, was a baffling exertion. She made him feel inexplicable and uninteresting. There was no commonality, she seemed to say. They were merely stakeholders in a shared tragedy. Their bond began and ended with death.

He believed this was how Beatrice preferred to keep things. If he ventured beyond the practicalities of dates and times, her voice would tighten.

'How have you been managing?' he had asked her once, in the early years.

'You're sweet,' she stated, without answering.

By the time she reached her actual purpose, *I was wondering if you'd say a few remarks at my son's remembrance service*, they were both usually equally desperate to terminate the conversation.

This time, they were about to wrap up when her voice caught. It was a small sound, but in the context of this quiet call, and from Beatrice, whose manner was brutally intentional, it had the effect of whiplash.

'Benny, I'm sure you're aware that this is his tenth anniversary.'

'I suppose you're right,' he hedged. 'It's so easy to lose track of time.' Benny never lost track. He could tally the days, the hours. Raph had died and formed a new calendar of loss.

'I wondered if this year, you could perhaps offer a little more...' she asked. Her pacing, her perfectly neutral tone, suggested she was holding back, that her pleasantries masked calculations. Benny, who had been holding something back since the day they met, grew anxious.

'As in, speak for a little longer?' he clarified, hopefully.

'Gosh, no!' she said quickly and with noticeable emphasis. 'Not longer, I certainly find your speeches sufficiently *long*...' He ignored the slight just as he ignored her subtext.

Beneath her frigid civility, Benny occasionally detected the presence of something else, a creep of resentment or mistrust. She had never heard of Benny until her boy was discovered dead. After nearly a decade, she still could not quite place him.

Partly, no doubt, because he was so different from Raph's other friends. They were well-heeled Etonites who drawled while Benny sputtered, who emoted with thoughtless ease, performing sadness, joy, or whatever emotion the situation required, while Benny squirmed and searched for words. Maybe her doubts ran deeper. Perhaps, she noticed how vague he could be when discussing Raph's final hours, or how he always delivered his words to the middle distance, then avoided her eye as he returned to his seat.

'So much of that day remains foggy to me,' she persisted. 'I believe, perhaps, you felt the need to shield us from the details. A valiant instinct, but an unnecessary one. I appreciate that my son was no saint. I understand that he had a talent for causing trouble...'

Benny chuckled politely, then, fearing that this seemed callous, sighed extravagantly. He was not sure how to behave. He felt exposed and feared further exposure.

The voice that was always waiting began its snide attack. *She knows*, it said, *she knows*. Of course, this was impossible: the woman hardly knew his surname. Yet he could not dismiss his sense of being ambushed.

'Over the years, you've offered us so many... *insights* on how to grieve, how to contemplate loss. I wonder, perhaps, if you could offer some insight into my son.'

'You'd like me to make the speech a little more personal?'

'That's exactly right! More honest.'

It was as close as she had ever come to an accusation. He realised that she had been watching him all along, noticing each prevarication. In the past, he had tried to ignore how her eyes stayed pinned on him long after he finished speaking, even though her expression always remained politely impassive. It was not that she smelled a rat, exactly. It was simply that she smelled nothing at all. His eulogy was odourless, his prose so anodyne; he could have been discussing anyone.

For nearly a decade, Benny had been delivering speeches of pure, calculated banality. He expressed sentiments plagiarised from condolence cards and inspirational memes. His words were so generic that they flirted with incoherence, euthanising all curiosity until everyone was quietly praying for him to stop. As an artist it was humiliating, but as a survivor, he deemed it necessary. He could not risk their interest; he had a secret to keep.

'I'll do my best,' he offered. There was a slight tremor in his voice. 'Of course, I'll still try to strike a balance, out of respect for Raph.'

'I'm quite sure Raph won't mind what you say, given the circumstances.'

'I also need to consider the audience, make sure the content is appropriate…'

'Oh, Benny, you are kind. But let me worry about the audience. Besides, I'm confident that they would prefer your candour to your…' She trailed off.

Benny felt convinced that this polite skirmish was only the start.

The call left him in a disastrous frame of mind. It was as if the atmospheric pressure shifted, a sudden compression of air. For a long time he sat limp and heavy, staring at nothing in particular. Beyond his shabby room, with its balsa-wood partitions, others began to wake. He heard the syncopated rhythms of the warehouse as it rose for another night. The murmur of small talk and laughter drifted through the halls, garage and hard tech played from competing speakers. He listened to this as an inmate might, with a mixture of envy and incomprehension. All that levity and brightness seemed unreachably far. His mind was back in Cambridge.

It began with an omission, rather than a lie. DC Foster was a few years shy of retirement and visibly weathered from a life of shiftwork. Other officers danced out of her way as she passed, their tone dropping to a deferential murmur. But then, alone in the interview room, she opened her mouth and spoke in gentle caveats, her eyes soft. She extended such patience, it was as if she wanted to be misled.

I know this is difficult... take as long as you need... we're in no rush here, you set the pace...

DC Foster explained how phone records indicated that Raph had called him around the time of death. His nerves trilled with panic. The call: it sat in his mind, unpacked, unprocessed, a suitcase full of guts.

There's no suspicion of foul play, she added quickly. We're just trying to gain a picture of those last moments. Blood work suggests he was intoxicated... Did he sound intoxicated to you? Benny made a movement with his head; she interpreted this as a nod. Did anything in that conversation stand out? Anything you think we should know about?

There was. Of course there was. He opened his mouth and no words came out. Instead, a little air escaped his throat; a squeaking sound, wet and achingly vulnerable.

The officer, mistaking his fear for grief, glanced down. I'd like to say this gets easier, but really you're at the start of it, she sighed. It won't make sense for a while yet and even then... She paused. Benny, this isn't on you. I hope somebody else is telling you that, but I want to say it as well. This isn't your fault. When she glanced up again, her eyes glinted very slightly. She spoke as if reciting an article of faith. He sensed that she had been preparing for this meeting all morning, perhaps longer. It was a strange sort of intimacy, because in her need to reassure, to do the right thing, she lost sight of Benny. Failed to notice the way he wrestled with something unsaid. That he brought himself to the brink of articulation, before swallowing the words.

It was like falling, like letting go. He hardly spoke at all, simply allowed himself to be conveyed by her assumptions and her sympathy. *Raph had been more stressed than anyone could have imagined. He kept his habit concealed even from Benny, his closest friend. When he called he was incoherent. Benny reasonably assumed that he was only drunk. Raph hung up and the fentanyl took effect: a simple overdose.* Over the course of the hour, a story was formed and ratified. The investigation was concluded before the end of the week.

Then, suddenly, Benny, who had been largely invisible throughout his degree, became a known figure. His pigeonhole was stuffed with condolences, baked gifts were left at his door. He was proclaimed Raph's Best Friend, recipient of his final message: the stuff of lore.

It was a time of profound confusion. He accepted kindness the way an alcoholic accepts drink: ashamed and unsurprised. Every evening, as he struggled to sleep, he forged countless resolutions; he would stand aside and process his grief alone, let others who were more worthy, more entitled to comfort, drift to the fore. And yet, inevitably, he would find himself in some friend's bedroom late at night, crying real tears, as they prepared another round of tea.

Crucially, nobody asked about the call itself. Maybe it was considered too crass, or their curiosity was considered too compromising. Or perhaps Benny's absolute silence on the matter was too difficult to breach. At any rate, nobody clearly and explicitly demanded to know what was actually said, or why Raph had called him in the first place.

The remembrance service was a yearly penance. Every ounce of stolen sympathy was paid back in full as he stood in his cheap suit and stewed in his own cowardice. For the first few years, it had been a grand, maudlin spectacle. The invitations even came with a certain social cachet. Over time, attendance dwindled and the tenor shifted. Raph seemed less like a person, more a historic fact; sadness gave way to sombre respect. It was like watching him die all over again, just more slowly.

Only Raph's mother Beatrice remained defiantly unchanged. Each year, she returned, dressed in black, her grief evergreen. She always introduced him with the same epithet, *Now we'll hear a few words from Benny, my son's closest friend and the last to speak to him.* Sometimes she said this with a shade of envy or bitterness. Strangely, Benny interpreted this as a good sign; he sensed a dilation of sorts, her heart opening to a broader range of feeling. More often than not, she simply said it, and all he could detect was a grief that was black and dense and inscrutable. As others all around began to forget Raph, Benny and Beatrice remembered.

For several days, Benny contemplated the speech obsessively but achieved nothing. He could not write about Raph without conjuring him. In fact, Benny could do very little without summoning him. Raph had been deceased nearly ten years, but his voice carved the air like a dart.

Mumsy won't let this go, mate. She's like a dog with a stick, Raph insisted.

He was somewhere inside, still alive and criticising. The rhythm of his sarcasm as close as breath.

Everyone thinks you're some kind of hero.

'I never claimed to be a hero,' Benny protested, feebly.

You've certainly been loath to set the record straight.

Benny continued to write. With each sentence, he heard Raph's easy critique.

You're mixing metaphors... Why are you even using metaphors? You don't have a knack for them... laboured... verbose. Look, mate, there are a thousand things wrong with this speech, but more than anything, it's just boring. Grief is still preferable to tedium; you're only making things worse for everyone.

He had written and rewritten the opening paragraph five times at least.

Ben, just tell them what happened. That will make them sit up in their seats.

He watched the cursor blink, felt the seconds loop.

You're a pussy, Raph said at last. A pretender.

But Raph had already known this. He knew it at the time, better than anyone. Still, he had chosen to call Benny. Why? Why pick the one candidate who was certain to disappoint? Why entrust your fate to a coward? Raph, who existed in the synaptic fuzz between these thoughts, answered without hesitation.

Because I thought you were my friend. I thought, in a matter of life and death, you might actually do something. But why break a lifetime of sloth…

24

London, 2023
Benny

Benny had friends, of course, peers, but Raph was his true companion. Raph spoke in a subtle register that made other voices muffled and vague. And Raph was always speaking.

Part of the issue was that Benny lacked distractions; the day spread out before him, a shapeless, grey expanse. There was simply too much time to contemplate his joblessness. His CV was like a beautiful corpse: so many industries and false starts, a dozen origin stories implausibly smashed together. He proofread essays during exam season, was the door-bitch at a dive club in Camden, contributed to a zine and had worked the tills at a violin shop. He had sacrificed everything for music; and music, like a teasing lover, had offered just enough in return to keep him hoping.

Recently, Mitch, his manager, had secured him a residency at Hootananny's. Benny performed there every Sunday between midday and three, the graveyard slot. Often, he stood on the main stage spitting bars to an empty room, little more than an elevated busker. Occasionally, it heaved with the overflow from some other event. This could be even worse. On those days, he performed before packs of white men in collared shirts. Men who said *wablow* and *bumbaclot* in plummy West London accents, who danced with their arms distended, flashing gangsta signs and broad, toothy grins. Their applause was loud and impersonal; Benny suspected they would derive the same ironic joy from an Abba tribute band. How degrading, therefore, that he still warmed to their claps, still savoured them. He even lingered afterwards so he could receive their plaudits and fist bumps. It left him feeling grubby and confused.

As he collected his envelope of cash and prepared for the circuitous journey home, Raph stood waiting at the door. Of course, Benny did not believe in curses or ghosts. And yet, he did believe in Raph. He trusted that dyspeptic voice, always quick to remind him that cowards do not deserve the stage. That this lifestyle, this death by a thousand cuts, was rightful punishment.

It was in this bleak context that the miracle occurred. Benny had spent another morning attempting to compose the speech when his manager Mitch called. This was an unusual but often insignificant event.

Mitch was nice enough. He remained sanguine in the face of failure. When Benny's first EP didn't sell, Mitch replied shruggingly, 'Label execs are idiots. They'll be begging you for the next one.'

When Benny self-released the EP and it received no reviews and few streams, Mitch remained unperturbed.

'This could be a good thing. I've seen countless artists drown in overexposure. Slow and steady. Build that cult following.'

This unflappable ease had been a comfort once. Benny had interpreted it as confidence in the broader mission. Now he wondered if it was simply indifference.

He had imagined ending things countless times, except these daydreams always ended in reconciliation. Even in his wildest fantasies, Benny could not imagine leaving Mitch. He needed him. Partly for financial reasons, because Mitch very occasionally delivered the goods. Yet the reliance had an existential quality too. Mitch was the single thin filament connecting Benny to the industry at large. Without Mitch, he was merely a fantasist. Without Mitch, he had no answer to Raph's excoriations.

'You're welcome,' Mitch said.

'For…'

'Benny, I'm about to deliver some news that will change your life.'

Mitch waited. So did Benny. Today, he was in no mood to indulge dramatics. It was ten in the morning. and Mitch had probably been pounding espressos for the past three hours. Or perhaps fasting, or microdosing psilocybin, or wild swimming in the Thames Estuary: Mitch was a man of promiscuous fixations.

'Maybe I should take a guess,' Benny muttered. 'Hootananny's wants me to double up and cover Saturday Brunch? Or perhaps Bella Italia needs someone for aperitivo hour… You've scored a licensing deal with Superdrug, so now my songs will play as people stock up on Rennies.' That last one was so close to an actual deal that Mitch had negotiated, it hardly scanned as a joke, more as a hopeful plea.

'Fuck Hootananny's,' Mitch said. 'We're way past that now. Benny: Luke Tha OG is sick.'

This was cryptic to the point of meaninglessness, yet Benny felt his fingers tighten around the phone. Maybe it was simply the invocation of the revered grime artist; sometimes, just the sound of a famous name affected Benny like the smell of fresh bread. Or maybe Benny, who kept a forensic account of other people's careers, of where and when they were performing, already had an inkling of what Mitch was about to say next.

'Which means…' Mitch continued, 'Simon needs a new support act for his UK debut.'

'Simon,' Benny stated flatly and with disbelief.

'Simon,' Mitch affirmed. 'This Friday, Brixton Academy.'

For a long moment, Benny said nothing.

'Benny, this is big league. Permission to freak the fuck out.'

It occurred to Benny, as his heart began to pound with chemicals, as his imagination began to swim with colour, that it had been years, literally years, since he had received good news. He did not know what to say or do. Losing had become fundamental to his way of life, his only constant. Success was akin to a small identity crisis.

'*Scheisse!*' he screamed. He did not know why. He had never used that word before. But nothing in English seemed suitable. '*Scheisse!*' he said again.

'That's right!' Mitch laughed. 'Fucking *scheisse*.'

'Simon knows who I am?'

'Kind of!' Mitch answered. If his words were equivocal, his tone was joyously affirmative; Benny focused on the latter.

'Wait...' a moment of guilt. 'Is Luke Tha OG going to be OK?'

'Don't look at it like that,' Mitch answered easily. 'One man's acoustic neuroma is another man's big break. That's simply the way these things always work.'

And the world was altered.

Benny had been following Simon since his first hit. He was part of a new vanguard of Queer Hop, which took the beats and production aesthetics of noughties Gangsta Rap and blended it with Gen Z's embrace of progressive ideology. Simon was a Democrat, gay, politically engaged. He was righteous without seeming worthy, an ideologue with a sense of fun. Simon wanted change and he wanted head; he rapped about dick the way his precursors had rapped about money. *Pitchfork* described him as a 'necessary corrective, an unassuming radical'. *Complex* described him as a fashion god.

Simon's fame had a frightening depth. It was the sort of career that could swallow lesser artists whole, that could render them an afterthought. Benny felt an emotion deeper than envy when he listened to Simon's music. It felt more like longing, or fear.

Benny walked to Brixton Market and continued north

towards Waterloo through Oval and Kennington. He passed the skaters beneath Queen Elizabeth Hall, who smoked weed and undertook backsides with lazy panache. He crossed the river and pushed west, his energy outsizing London itself. He wandered the narrow streets of Soho, noticed the men clustering outside pubs, a guy in a gimp suit, tourists gawping. It all seemed different, somehow, like a river at low tide. The weather was good, and the streets were fuller than they'd been in weeks. That was when he noticed it: the quiet. Beyond the sirens and traffic, the rabble, the pop music leaking from vast shopfronts, there was a deeper silence he had not experienced for years. He did not hear Raph. Raph's endless baying had been stunned into submission. Benny was alone, finally, blissfully, alone.

In the new quiet, Benny slept deeper and for longer. He was more present in conversations, more prone to laughter and quick ripostes. His thoughts grew spacious. He marvelled at how cramped his imagination had become, how little room there had been for possibility and play. Before, he had considered more social media followers the epitome of success. Now, he was entertaining grand prospects: tours, LPs, a collab with Simon himself. He thought of Simon an awful lot.

Even the remembrance speech flowed differently. Benny found himself expressing new sentiments, glimpsing his dead friend from untested angles. *Raph was a complicated man. It's like there were two versions of him. One that was very easy to love and one that was not…* He jotted this idea down and was struck by the truth of it. *He was generous. Notoriously generous. During my first Michaelmas, he gifted me half a wardrobe of his old clothes. When I tried to thank him, he told me he did this not out of kindness, but out of hatred. He said he loathed polyester.* For a long time, Benny had buried this memory; it had occurred thirteen years prior and still caused a small reflux of shame. Yet he felt the audience would appreciate the anecdote and, from this new vantage point, he could as well.

Of course, Raph placed you in bad situations, sometimes. Dangerous situations. On the day he died, he called me with a message that I wasn't willing to hear... No, Benny would never say that in public. Up until now, he had hardly said it to himself. He shut his eyes and pictured Beatrice's garden with rows of vacant seats. Somewhere at the side, Simon stood watching, a sympathetic frown on his face.

As the gig drew near, Benny drafted and he practised and he worked. Mostly, however, he trawled the internet for videos of Simon. He watched Simon from the back of a Brooklyn club, the footage shaky, the audio clipped. He watched Simon bathe himself, languid in a freestanding tub, his tanned skin wreathed in bubbles. 'Soaking with Simon' had become a small viral sensation. It was his attempt to connect with fans in the most intimate of settings. The comments were endless: a hieroglyph of emojis, fires and hearts and eyes. Yet Benny saw something that the masses did not: when he looked at Simon, he was looking at his own future.

25

London, 2023
Benny

Nobody had warned Benny that he was one of three support acts and, worst of all, that he was billed to go on first. Benny had performed to empty rooms before, but never an emptiness of that magnitude. The DJ glanced down, his eyes hidden by the visor of his Nike cap. Guests streamed into the vast hall as Benny was trying to introduce his song, his voice echoing pathetically across the vast space. He could not corral a pulse from all that diffusion. It was like marshalling gas. When he asked a question, *How are you lot doing tonight?* the crowd did not answer. When he gave a command, *Let's make some fucking noise,* the crowd did not obey. He had not experienced chemistry quite so bad in all his years of performing. Soon, he abandoned banter altogether. He was starting to panic, rushing from song to song like a shift-worker joylessly working down the clock.

Somewhere between a chorus and bridge he thought he saw Raph, staring blankly at him from the pit. The lights shifted from amber to red and when his eyes adjusted, Raph was gone. It spooked Benny so profoundly that he stopped completely in the middle of the track. Suddenly, his own beat trundled past him, and Benny simply stood there, the mic pressed to his lips, drowning in dead air. Now, the crowd noticed him. People turned away from the bar to squint. Phones were appearing. He could see the captions already. Death on stage. Choke.

And then Simon appeared off stage to the left. He glanced up from his phone and met Benny's eye for the briefest instant. That was all it took. Benny remembered that tonight he was performing to one person. That all those below were merely bystanders to this moment of immaculate connection. He cleared his throat and launched into 'Dear Mariam', his magnum opus.

'Dear Mariam' had been written during the austerity years of the Tory–Lib Dem coalition under David Cameron. Structurally complex, it took the form of a series of emails attempting to console Mariam, a struggling mother, who had fallen behind on her bills. It was a biting indictment of political complacency, full of pathos and rage. By the end of the track, destitute and defenceless, Mariam overdoses on the streets of Peckham. Mitch had asked him to stick to the easy bops, and this crowd seemed more receptive to that sort of material. But he needed Simon to hear it. He threw his heart into the rendition, rocking from side to side, riding the rhythm, gesticulating with his left hand and clasping the mic with his right, describing the pitiful plight of Mariam in the impassioned spirit of a serenade.

He ended his set to stunned applause, the clapping sporadic and confused. He did not mind, nor did he try to interpret it. This was merely the penalty of the avant garde and really, there was a romance in being misunderstood. As long as his material resonated with his fellow artist, he could work on the masses later. So he exited the stage panting, his muscles hopping, beset by a feeling of noble exhaustion.

Benny waited. He waited through the two other supports who rapped blandly about selling drugs and crashing Aston Martins. He waited as the DJ mashed together a medley of trap, enduring the chants and long delays until finally the moment arrived.

Simon slinked onto the stage at half-nine wearing carpenter jeans and an old leather jacket. He appeared strangely waifish against the backdrop of his own success. His hair was cut short, dyed a noxious shade of green. As the lights came up, he drew back, let his gaze coast the sea of faces. He appeared coy and unconvinced, measuring the room as he might a would-be lover.

'OK then,' he said in greeting. 'I guess we better get going.' He launched into his first track, 'Nine Inches', a humid club anthem about riding dick. Of course, the room went wild. It did not sound like applause. It was more like a rupture.

Simon had it. He had it in such abundance that he seemed vaguely bored by it. His delivery was effortless, his posture almost limp. Benny had spent nearly a decade fruitlessly chasing that level of charisma and presence, that heady entitlement.

This close, Benny could study every little movement, how Simon kept track of the beat with his hips. How they ticked like a metronome from left to right. Benny felt the stirrings of some new emotion as he watched the subtle dance, a sad fascination that he struggled to explain. He thought of his own tortured posturing.

He considered the time that had passed since he was Simon's age, and it felt, just then, like something tangible had been lost, though he could not name it.

The audience knew every word. They sang along with aggression, almost shouting Simon down, and together became something strange and hybrid. Benny witnessed gym bros twerking with a stripper's finesse, young girls brapping, flexing their biceps, yard boys lip-synching to the joys of anal sex.

'A bottom in the morning and a top after lunch.

Love riding dick but can't forego the munch.'

Benny was euphoric. It was a dark high, like the buzz from a strong but dodgy pill. Because, for all of his political engagement, his erudition, his noble intent, Benny was in the presence of his better. By the encore, his own voice was hoarse and there were confused tears in his eyes.

If he had left then, simply collected his fee and posted a few perfunctory words on social media, his career would still be intact. But Benny could not leave. He knew the etiquette; he should not harass the headliner after the show. Still, there he was, standing outside Simon's door as the venue emptied, without a plan or purpose, just a shapeless need, an itch.

Simon sat topless before the mirror, slightly dazed and breathing hard. He was surrounded by several others from his entourage, the oldest looked no more than twenty. Their faces lit up for a moment as Benny entered, then abruptly fell once they recognised him. He stood before them, stooped and teacherly, as they waited for him to explain himself.

'Simon,' Benny said. 'I came to pay my respects.' His nerves had made his tone sombre and his words were all wrong. 'Sorry,' Benny added. 'That makes it sound like you died or something. You didn't die out there. You fucking killed it.'

The girl to Benny's right opened her mouth slightly, then closed it. She fidgeted with her phone, maybe wrestling with an instinct to film the slow disaster unfolding before her.

'I appreciate you,' Simon said and flashed a smile so obsequious, it appeared faintly menacing.

Silence. Benny realised he was staring at Simon's torso, the soft geometry of perfect abs. Simon followed his eyes and looked briefly troubled. A memory flashed across Benny's mind of a school locker room, an older, stronger boy emerging from the showers, a moment of indecision, of guarded negotiation. Like that boy, Simon turned definitively away, with the hint of a shudder. When he spoke again, his voice was cold.

'Honey, we're sort of in a rush. We've got a thing in Soho…'

'I just wanted to say again, I really fucking loved that set.'

'Thank you.'

It was time to go. Yet his feet remained fixed.

'I don't know if you caught any of my set…'

'Some of it,' Simon replied, factually. There was a warning in voice, in his clipped response. *Don't push it*, he seemed to say.

'I thought, maybe, my last track was sort of your vibe. I thought you might dig it.'

Someone in the room snorted. Nobody said 'dig it'. Even Benny didn't say 'dig it'.

Simon, who had been coolly polite up to this point, now smiled just enough to show his canines. 'I'm not sure I "dug it" exactly.' He glanced at his friends and then back at Benny. 'From what I could tell, you were rapping about taxes.'

'Well, austerity. But you know, the human face of it. The victims…'

'Right.'

'And I was sort of alluding to "Stan" you know, through use of a structural conceit, but subverting it by—'

'Honey, you get an A,' Simon cut in. 'Full marks.'

There was laughter, anxious and relieved and loud, because it had been repressed from the moment Benny entered. A blush began to burn.

'Look, I'm just a basic bitch,' Simon said, conciliatory. 'I don't know shit about structured conceits. To me, a song is simple. If it bumps, it bumps; if it don't, it don't.'

Benny glanced down. His hands were clasped together.

He stood by his music. He believed in his lyrics. Yet, before this new artist Benny felt incredibly old. While he had been sculpting his identity, altering his accent to sound more street, curating his clothing to seem on-trend, there had been a sea change. The new generation had no respect for contrivances. They did not want a persona. They did not want abstract ideas. They wanted something authentic, crude and real. Perhaps there had been a time for Benny, a window of opportunity, but the moment had come and gone. He suddenly saw himself as they might: a shabby salesman hawking VCRs.

'Look I hate to be rude…' Simon began. 'But like I said… we gotta bounce. I've got about twenty minutes before my molly kicks in and I don't want to come up in traffic.'

That was it. The beginning and end of Benny's big shot. He lingered beyond the changing room door and listened to them discuss him.

'You just lost a fan,' somebody said.

'I don't need more fans,' Simon replied. And then, compulsively, 'Fuck it, I don't want to jinx myself. Obviously I want more fans... I just don't want that one. Dude gave me the creeps...' Soon, conversation turned to drugs and cabs and Benny could hear them forget his existence entirely.

Outside, a crazy woman was yelling at the Sainsbury's security guard. She was calling him a monster and a rapist and the guard was so bored that he hardly met her eye. A man was selling mixtapes while blasting dancehall from cheap speakers. And harried locals were being belched from the yellow mouth of the tube and they all looked miserable, faintly soiled, as if they carried the tunnels with them on their skin. And the streets smelled of popcorn and weed and petrol and the cracked pavement was so narrow that Benny had to sidestep onto the road where crisp bags scuttled and empty tins danced on the breeze. Once Benny had loved this neighbourhood, its madness, but that was when he had stood apart from it. Now, it seemed close and inescapable. He felt like the litter blowing through the streets.

Still, Benny had his career, he had not yet done the Terrible Thing. But the germs of a great resentment had taken root. Because as Benny travelled south, he began to reconsider all that he had seen. Sure, Simon had shown strong stage presence, but confidence came cheap when you had a whole industry rooting for your success. A gay rapper was something of a novelty. But then again, it was 2023, everyone was gay. Really, Simon was simply reading the room, not a radical, but a marketeer.

Benny took out his phone and scrolled. Clips of the performance were surfacing with breathless testimonials. A journo from *Dazed* announced that the rap game had just changed. Cora, a friend of a friend, deemed the gig 'iconique' and claimed that Simon had given her 'Bob Dillan vibes'. But what the fuck did Cora know about Bob Dylan? And who made her the arbiter of icons? He kept scrolling. Two other rappers had uploaded a freestyle to YouTube. He kept scrolling. A drill artist from Streatham fawned over Simon before plugging his own gig three days hence. What was social media but a vast dinner party in which there was not enough food?

He kept scrolling.

Probably, Benny would have passively scrolled for the rest of the night, felt terrible about himself and then gone to bed, had he not come across the post comparing Simon to Biggie. Of all the indignities, this was intolerable. Because Biggie was a genius, a god, and there was only one Biggie in a lifetime. Because if Simon was Biggie, Benny was truly nothing.

Benny hit reply.

> Fun show. But do not get the hype for @TheRealSimon... Seems like this year's diversity hire?

Benny hit send.

At that very instant, a tree branch smacked against the window with an explosive crack. Other travellers on the top deck gasped and then giggled when they realised what it was. Only Benny's pulse did not steady; the real disaster was occurring out of sight.

All across the city, fingers double-clicked and screenshots were captured. Outrage was expressed (both real and feigned), disappointment, fury. People who had never heard of Benny resolved to avoid him. Fans unsubscribed. It was homophobic. Probably racist. It was pathetic, bitter, weak. His phone began to fit. Benny put it in his bag and let it spasm.

The post went against everything Benny believed. It defied his entire oeuvre, his artistic mission. And yet, a part of him had meant it, had felt it profoundly. This was only the beginning, before the private messages, blog posts, the trolling. Even as the first blast of rage subsided, he knew that his career was over.

Oh... My... God... Raph spoke again in his ear, his voice slow and delighted. It was the sound he made when eating delicacies, as if contemplating the pleasure rather than experiencing it. *Ben, mate... why the fuck did you do that?*

He could not explain himself.

Maybe you missed me? Raph suggested.

Somehow, this was the most frightening prospect of all. Perhaps it was the only explanation that made sense.

Well, here I am, Raph murmured.

At first, he set his profiles to private. But even this proved insufficient, because acquaintances and old friends got in touch to express their disapproval. Benny drafted long replies, apologising, explaining himself; the messages always remained unsent. He needed something fuller. He would have to block people, switch to private, fortify his online presence. Instagram was an easy sacrifice, but Facebook he found harder, its bank of old photos and old thoughts, the rambling messages sent to Raph and Raph's ever-brief replies. It still meant something to him, a great house that was never completed. He allowed himself one last voyage through the memories before he dismantled the edifice.

He saw the moment Raph disappeared from the photos, the moment he transformed from a subject to a ghost, haunting the frame. There were still parties and reunions but the grief was like a filter over the lens; all smiles appeared strained, muscular.

Benny observed the period in which people were beginning to heal. Years later, the ombre shifted towards lighter gradients. Now, the photos became blurrier, the scenes more raucous. Only Benny remained unchanged, meeting the camera with a staged grin and worried eyes. He remained perfectly still while everyone else vibrated.

He wondered what his life would have been like if he had missed the call. He wondered if he would have grieved and healed like all the others.

Then, as if in answer, a photo of an old friend entered his feed.

And then a photo of Elle. Her.

He had avoided looking at her all these years. Now, with nothing left to lose, he couldn't stop.

She had married him. They had hardly aged. Whenever he photographed her she was looking away, as if unaware, but she posed artfully: her posture straight, her chin tipped towards the sun. When she did meet the camera, her smile had a sleepy ease, as if her head were full of dreams, as if she had nothing in the world to hide.

26

I have heard that hotels manufacture customised scents to trigger primitive responses when guests enter. As the three of us step through the sliding doors I draw a deep breath, savouring subtle notes of English pear and spice, and feel a brief and ineffable sense of ease.

'This is fucking sweet,' Benny declares and my relief is short-lived.

'Right,' you announce, 'I'm going up to the room. Shall we reconvene in an hour or so?'

'Sure. Until then,' Benny replies.

You glance at me expectantly and it is only then that I realise you are dismissing me as well.

'I have to make a call,' you explain. 'I'd prefer to do it in the room, but if you need to rest, I can go for a walk or something.'

'A call?'

'I told you this. Jen and I arranged to speak.'

'What exactly do you need to speak about?'

'What?'

'You've been doing a lot of talking recently.' I sound like a schlocky TV detective.

'So?'

'It's causing me discomfort,' my voice is quiet but loaded.

'Oh no,' you reply. 'Not discomfort.' You even sound a bit like Jen when you say it, the way Jen might address some pestering fuckboy trying to buy her a drink.

'You can take the room,' I reply, tiredly.

I want to return to our holiday, and yet it dawns on me that this is the holiday now; a game has been started and you will see it through.

I amble through the crooked, fairytale streets of Balat trying to find a distraction. The road is narrow, clad on both sides by wooden houses in pastel hues. They pivot slightly from left to right, as if this entire neighbourhood has been sketched by a shaky hand. In a brightly coloured ice-cream parlour, next to a brightly coloured sweet shop, I buy a frozen yoghurt topped with pomegranate and taro. The dessert becomes flavourless after a few bites and my mouth goes numb.

You are talking to Jen. We rarely discuss Jen. I used to assume that you blamed me for the failure of that friendship. Now I think you just struggled with its loss and preferred not to think about it at all. Jennifer responded to me equivocally when we first met. *He seems nice,* she told you. *He certainly won't break your heart.* She liked the fact that your taste in men was evolving, but she assumed it would continue to evolve.

After university, many of your friends lost interest in you. There you were, a young wife, settled in a leafy suburb of West London. Ironically, you served as a sort of vanguard. Because at twenty-five they were still fanning out over the city, bars in Peckham, clubs in Lewisham, and you were running a business. People often assumed you were pregnant. You made your friends feel diffuse, directionless. They made you feel staid, forgotten. As I told you then, these were necessary sacrifices. Our circle of friends could be broad but never tight.

Only Jen remained doggedly loyal. She didn't understand

why you eloped so quickly after your father's death. She didn't understand why you failed to invite her to the wedding. But she reconciled herself to these facts as best she could. She would journey west to have dinner with us even when she was in the depths of a break-up. She suffered the awkwardness of a three-person meal, in which I always hovered close. You thought it sweet, assuming I took an interest in your friend. Really, I was trying to ward her off, slowing the conversation down, constantly clarifying names and asking for jokes to be explained. Jen was determined. She endured all this because she, like me, had a vision for you, so she was willing to sacrifice, to play the long game.

Jen wanted to be a ceramicist, but by day she worked in PR. This was the story of many of your friends, but while they described their lives shruggingly, Jen could be so theatrical about her failures. She hated everything about her job, from the cheeriness of her colleagues, to the temperature of the office: *Honestly, it's like a bloody spa in there. I half expect the intern to bring me cucumber slices and a warm towel.* She hated her clients and begrudged their success. *Fuckers. They're getting the best of me and they don't deserve it at all.*

Still, she ascended the ranks of the agency, using her salary to pay for materials and studio space, tapping up her media contacts to subtly promote her work. I found this troubling, this ability to live among the enemy and extract what was needed. I considered this as she sat in my house, sipping whatever cheap wine I'd opened – always the cheapest for Jen. Whenever you floated an aspiration for the future, she was emphatically encouraging. A nose-piercing, a new hair colour, a night class: in Jen's view, these were all inspired ideas. Only I saw past the thin veneer of positivity. She wanted change, whatever form it took. She hoped that all these minor alterations might reach a critical mass, then perhaps you would be moved to fundamentally change your life. And I would be out.

The last time she visited, I finally noticed the fissures emerge between you both. She came to our flat that Friday evening, hungover from the night before, nerves frayed from an ongoing work crisis.

Dumping her wet raincoat on an upholstered chair, she asked you, 'Can you make your Instagram less…'

'What?'

'Punishing.'

It took you aback.

'You're out there, living your bougie best life and I'm here, getting wankered at Spoons on blue cocktails.'

'That isn't true. At least, it isn't true any more.'

'No, maybe not. Now I get wankered on clear cocktails in bars with pretentious names. And I don't vom at the end of the night, I just cry instead. Progress.'

'You're being tough on yourself.' You rolled your eyes, trying to play the whole thing off as a joke. But Jen was insistent.

'Sometimes I think my only purpose is to make others feel more secure about their own life decisions. They should wheel me out in front of kids as a sort of warning.'

'What's got into you today?'

'I've got the AFD.'

You froze. Like a powerful, forgotten taste, the acronym sent you wholly backwards through time to university days. Amorphous Feelings of Dread; an ailment that afflicted you both after every night out. Back then, the only known antidote was each other's company.

'How's work?' you asked, hurrying the conversation along, resisting, at least for now, the seduction of her nostalgia.

'Today, a journalist replied to my press release with two words: please stop.'

'Yikes.'

'That isn't even the bad part. I actually replied to his email.'

'Saying what?'

'I thanked him for getting in touch (I got in touch, not him) and said maybe we could discuss his concern over a quick coffee.'

I took a seat on the arm of your chair. 'What about your pottery? How is that coming along?' I asked.

She seemed to notice me only then and betrayed a mere flicker of irritation, glancing at me briefly, before composing her face and responding to my question.

'I do have some news on that front, but...' she restrained herself. Maybe she sensed that I was not rooting for her, that her success would validate something dangerous. It would prove the necessity of certain risks. 'It's still early days. Actually, mate, I was hoping to get your other half alone...'

'Oh... Well, I...'

'You know,' Jen said. 'Girl talk,' she explained. It was just an excuse, Jen never used phrases like that. But I was powerless to refuse and so let myself be banished in my own home.

For the next hour or so, I manufactured reasons to enter the adjoining kitchen, allowing me to eavesdrop on what was being said. Soon, she was so engrossed in the conversation that she stopped glancing up as I moved food about in the fridge. She sounded worn. She returned to the first topic of the night, but less jokily.

'You wouldn't understand,' she said. 'Your idea of a fuck-up is skipping leg day,' she tried to laugh.

'I've done plenty of fucked-up things. You know that.'

I felt my throat tighten and stood very still and quiet.

'Nothing that really mattered...' Her voice was inviting.

There was a long pause and you must have been weighing up the options. Your friend, who had given you so much time and loyalty and consideration, was finally asking for reciprocity. She wanted contact. She wanted to know that she was not alone in those feelings of failure and doubt.

Of course, you could have given it to her. You could have made a chilling confession. Or simply alluded to the bad times, of which there were plenty. Could have given her something, at least. But you didn't correct her. You chose silence instead. You chose me.

Would you make that sacrifice again, now that you have a clearer sense of its cost?

I wonder what you are saying now.

You laughed modestly, 'I'm sure there's something... Though I can't think of it off the top of my head...'

To be famished and offered nothing more than a dried crust. She didn't even respond. I left the kitchen, feeling secure.

From that night on, a distance crept in between the two of you. Each interaction felt more like a performance. You spoke to her the way she spoke to journalists she was trying to seduce. Your phone conversations grew formal and flat; soon she stopped calling altogether. At a certain point, a friendship becomes defined by its omissions.

Jen once bought you a vibrator for your birthday. Wrapped in an ornate box, she presented it to you in a fancy restaurant, to see if she could make you blush. You inspected it in front of everyone, the veined rubber wobbling grotesquely in your hand. You switched it on, tested the pulsations. Finally, in a loud, clear voice, you concluded it looked rather small. And she laughed in a way that she only did around you. That was at the height of your friendship, your love reaffirmed through licensed humiliations, the sort we save for those we truly trust. Now, every year, she sends flowers by post.

I find myself back in the hotel lobby, the frozen yoghurt has melted to a slurry in the base of the cup. I scan the room and find Benny, and he is not where he should be. He is standing by reception, chatting to my nemesis in front of house. The sudden spike of fury I feel towards Benny is rivalled only by the fury I feel towards myself. I should never have left him alone. Not here. The receptionist is speaking. He falters, unsure. He leans in towards Benny, begins to slip, to divulge. Then he catches sight of me and his whole demeanour shifts. Benny gestures but the boy does not respond, simply stares at me. I hope, for all our sakes, that he has not already said too much.

Slowly, Benny turns. I correct my face, wipe the death from my expression. Benny peers at me. I smile and wave strangely with my fingers, like a coy admirer. It confuses him. Confusion alloyed with something else. Finally, he forces himself to return my smile.

'Why were you talking to the staff?' I ask.

'You mean Ali,' Benny corrects. 'I always talk to the workers. They have the most interesting stories.'

'You're a man of the people.'

'I am, actually. You say that like it's a bad thing.'

I should stop talking. These are untested grounds. Instead, I hear my own needling voice. 'So… Anything interesting? Any gossip?'

Benny regards me for a long moment. 'This place isn't as nice as it looks,' he says, his tone deliberate. 'Weird shit happens at night. Dark shit.'

Perhaps he is referring to the type of shit that could make a lonely old bitch panic. Or maybe he is bluffing.

'I have to deal with this,' I say, referring to the cup of froyo still in my hand.

27

Cambridge, 2010
Elle

People said that Cambridge was dreary outside of term. In fact, that summer was the happiest of Elle's life. She wandered the vacated colleges, the deserted libraries and found a home within that emptiness. The faculty noticeboard was plastered with outdated flyers, concluded lecture series, performances that had come and gone. It gave the lobby an air of vanquishment. She sat and read through them, like the lone survivor in a disaster film. The thought gave her an eerie sense of relief.

Raph sacrificed a trip to Cannes to be with her for the three-month break. He was entering his final year and suggested it would be a good opportunity to read for his dissertation, *You know, finally give studying a go*. He was vague when he discussed his research topic – something to do with postmodernism and the short story. Elle suspected that he did not go to the university library as frequently as he claimed. This made his presence more touching; he was there simply to keep her company. They learnt to leave things undiscussed. She did not ask him where he went in the afternoon. He did not ask her why she refused to return home. They learnt to live alongside these ambiguities.

Later, when she recalled this time, the scenes were rendered in pastel hues and soft edges; a lens smeared with Vaseline.

Elle could not remember who first brought up the poem. They had started drinking early and now she was tipsy. Somehow the conversation turned to mourning and then it turned to verse. Before long, they were both trying to recall the phrasing of a few lines from Tennyson. Raph kept insisting that she was wrong. It was strange, because she loved that poem and could recite whole cantos by heart. Finally, Elle reached for the volume on her shelf, flicking towards *In Memoriam*. When the letter from her mother fluttered to the floor, she felt as if she had been tricked. Maybe it was the way his eyes followed the letter, pointedly, while his body remained still. It struck her as suspicious; Raph always reached, grabbing impulsively at anything that piqued his curiosity. But he was not interested in the letter, he was studying her reaction to it.

She snatched it as she might a piece of soiled laundry. 'It's stupid,' she said. 'From my mum.'

He did not feign confusion. Clearly, he had already read it. But there seemed to be genuine sadness in his eyes. 'When was the last time you saw her?' he asked.

My mother left me when I was sixteen years old. She had said it so many times, the words had lost their meaning. That was the point.

Yet his expression, just then. It affected her. A sudden warmth, a thickening of the blood; his compassion was narcotic.

So Elle began detailing the last night she saw her mother. At first, she spoke falteringly, skirting the edges of a walled city. Then, a passageway opened and suddenly she was inside.

She explained how she knew that a fight was coming from the moment her father opened the door. Elle could read the signs the way fishermen read the sky. He swore a little too loudly, tripping over his shoes. He grew fixated with a broken lightbulb. *It's been dead all week*, he muttered. He ostentatiously flicked the switch again and again, as if this proved something.

She stayed quiet while her mother tried to calm him.

'I can run to the shop tomorrow,' she heard her mother promise.

'You said that yesterday. Story of my life. You can't do anything. I ask one thing.'

Elle retreated to her room, but left her door slightly ajar; a little crack of solidarity. She told herself she had not fully abandoned her mum to the wolf. She was still monitoring the situation; if things turned bad, she could emerge in a flash.

By now, fights were commonplace. They could be lurid and long, operatic in tone, but always meaningless. The neighbours wouldn't look her in the eye any more.

Tonight was different. Her mother was not backing away. She stood her ground. Her father was patrolling the hall, counting every extinguished bulb: there were four.

'We're hardly down to candlelight,' she snapped.

'That isn't the point.'

'There's a point? We've been talking about this for nearly half an hour and I'm yet to hear a point.'

'This flat is a fucking dump. I can't see.'

At this, her mother only chuckled, a cold and mirthless sound. 'You're a fool,' she stated, a simple, insoluble fact.

Elle heard an ironing board clatter to the floor, the metal legs snapping explosively against the base. It was happening. There was an animal response as the adrenaline hit. It felt almost like excitement. This confused Elle, frightened her.

'You're not going to fucking touch me,' her mother hissed. Beneath the rage, there was terror.

'I'm not?' her father answered, with a menacing sneer.

She heard her mother stumble as she was backed into the corner. And then her mother called her name, twice. A third time. Elle stood, paralysed. She advanced a few steps.

'Elle,' her mother screamed, more desperate now.

But her phone was in the living room. She had seconds, maybe less. She reached for the door. And then she watched it click shut, observed her own cowardice as a shocked bystander.

'Call the police!'

Elle forced herself to get as far as the hallway, witnessed her mother on the floor. At first her mother screamed for him to stop, but then fell silent as she curled into a protective ball.

'You bully. You fucking bully,' her father snarled, growing breathless between kicks.

'He crippled her?' Raph exclaimed, with slightly too much excitement, as if she were detailing the plot points of a salacious thriller.

'No, but he could have. He was drunk, and he's a big man.'

'So, you were complicit,' Raph said. 'You didn't help.' She detected impatience in his voice, as if he had endured a long riddle with an unsatisfying solution. But then he quickly added, 'I can't imagine what that would feel like…' and she worried she was being too sensitive.

Elle attempted a sardonic laugh. 'It gets worse.'

The next day, Elle opened her eyes and was awake. The room was bright, the morning already underway. She had spent the night on the surface of sleep. Every time she began to dip, an upthrust of panic forced her back up.

She could tell that her father had left early for work and she lay there, studying the mouldings along the ceilings. She hated the pattern, its endless ambulations, eating itself in infinite loop. She wondered if her mother had seen her in the hall. She remained focused on this one point. She stared over her mother's head, losing herself in the cornice.

Eventually, the smell of food wafted in. She realised her mum was cooking her breakfast, a gesture so inexplicable, so absurd, she felt a small twist of fury. She walked into the dining room.

'I thought you could do with something more substantial than coffee,' her mother said. A plate of scrambled eggs was placed before her, flecked with black pepper and chilli oil. Beside

176

it, two rashers of bacon. Elle's stomach lurched as she glanced from the meat to her mum. She was wearing a nightgown with very short sleeves. The bruises were already beginning to form along the length of her arms.

'Have you got lessons today?' her mother asked, absurdly. She was playing the hero, perhaps, the stoic; a brave soul who rallies after disaster.

'At school?' Elle asked, her voice cold. Elle could not explain her rage, but she could not resist it either.

'I guess,' her mother replied, laughing self-consciously.

'Yes. I have lessons at school.'

'I meant, which classes...' She lifted her teaspoon; having no use for it, she put it back down, with a loud, ringing sound. Elle hated that. She hated that her mum grew clumsy, that all it took was a shift in tone, a sarcastic remark.

The smell of animal fat hung heavy in the air. Her mother folded her mottled arms. They brought to mind discount poultry, raw purple flesh squeezed beneath a cellophane wrapper.

'Do you not have anything with sleeves?' Elle blurted.

Her mother stared, uncomprehending.

'It's just that I'm trying to eat,' Elle said, with contempt.

At that moment, something seemed to flatten between them. Her mother slumped in her chair and exhaled.

'You've always been a survivor,' her mother said, with a hint of bitterness. 'I used to say you didn't cry when you were born, just looked sort of pissed off.'

'Sounds apocryphal,' Elle said.

'I used to think so too.'

They stared at each other for a long moment. The sun was rising, the cold light revealing stubby yellow marks along her neck; she looked more ghastly by the second.

'You goad him,' Elle stated.

'He doesn't need goading.'

'Yes, but if you know he's drunk—'

'He's always drunk.'

'I can't sort out your marriage!' She brought her fist down against the table and all the cutlery rattled.

'You could have called the police,' her mother replied, quietly, as if to herself.

'I am not your sister,' Elle hissed. 'I am not your fucking girlfriend. I am not your social worker. It isn't my role. Do you understand that? You put us in this situation. You.'

Her mother rose from the chair, slowly. 'You're right,' she said, eventually. 'It's up to me,' she said. 'I've spoken to Kate. She has space for us… while I figure out next steps.'

Kate was her mother's oldest friend. She lived in a miserable one-bedroom flat above an off-licence, somewhere on the edge of Zone 4. The night before had been dire. Yet when she pictured Kate's home, the image was filtered through frigid blue light. It seemed like death itself.

'Where exactly would we sleep?' Elle asked, incredulous.

'She has a sofa bed. It isn't perfect…'

Elle snorted. 'Homeless. You're right, it's a little shy of perfect.'

She realised it wasn't the flat that frightened her, but the closeness. It was the prospect of sharing a bed with her mother. Would Elle be woken late at night, the mattress shaking, to her mother's choked sobs? And would she watch as her mother rubbed lotion into her bruises, and smell the lotion and watch the colours deepen. It scared her, that proximity to damage.

'Impossible,' Elle said.

'I was going to wait until the weekend—'

'Just get a divorce,' Elle cut in.

'Divorces take years. He could have killed me last night.'

'I have to go to school,' Elle said, rising to her feet.

'Elle, I'm going. I can help you pack—'

And then, somehow, she was on the Hammersmith line, heading west, staring out of the window, watching the graffiti blur as the train sped by. And then she was at school, late, and

Mrs Engels intercepted her in the hallway. Elle looked a mess; she might have been muttering to herself. She expected her teacher to pull her aside. Instead, she received a vague reprimand and was sent to First Period.

The day kept accelerating. Yet, whenever she was singled out in class, she always had an answer to hand. People just require eye contact and a plausible response. Elle was smart enough, quick enough, good at performing. She could hide entire worlds while still receiving the teacher's accolades.

Over lunch, her friends talked at her and formed weekend plans. Elle agreed, smiled, even laughed when necessary. All the while, her mind crunched possibilities, made involuntary calculations.

Premise One: Her father had never hit Elle; he was unlikely to start now. He had come close once, then spent the night weeping in her arms, begging forgiveness. It was an arbitrary line in the sand, but one he lived by.

Premise Two: If her mother left, he would need her more. Need her like an alibi. With her, he was a man spurned. Without her, his friends would guess the truth. Perhaps he would finally have to face the truth.

Premise Three: Her father paid for things he needed.

'Do you think Jacob is a player?' Maria asked, staring at her phone with a pursed expression. Her eyeshadow and blush had been applied with a heavy hand, her lips were wet with cherry gloss; she looked like a painted doll.

'Yes,' Elle answered. 'He's obviously a player.'

'Do you think that's a problem?'

Premise Four: To move to Kate's would be the beginning of the end. Her father would stop paying tuition, freeze the accounts. A financial siege that would make even Tube travel feel like an extravagance. Marooned, she would be swamped by her mother's grief. Her mother and Kate, the three of them trapped together like weird sisters, declaiming the world's cruelties over cups of watery tea.

Premise Five: It was all bullshit. Her mother had threatened to leave before. She would not go without Elle. Elle determined the next move.

'You're not eating your lunch?'

She glanced up. Maria was eyeing her chips. Her friends were debating whether the art teacher was a perv or just a loner. They flickered like shadows on the wall.

'It'd be a shame for it to go to waste,' Maria prompted.

'Help yourself,' Elle answered, shoving the food towards her.

On the journey home, Elle planned the conversation with her mother. She would be kind but practical. They would strategise together, Elle sharing her gift for disciplined logic, her muscular pragmatism. She imagined her mother thanking her, weeping a little, trying to hug her. Perhaps in that outpouring, she would recognise her daughter. Understand that surviving was not a moral failure. That Elle's instincts could save them both.

She knew at once that nobody was home. The silence was thick, definite. In her parents' bedroom, she flung open her mother's wardrobe and found it empty. In her bedroom, Elle discovered Kate's address, scrawled on an envelope stuffed with cash.

Elle stood staring at the money, her severance package. Unconditional Love. She had never realised she believed in it until that moment, as she experienced the first wrench of absence.

'I have been disabused,' she said to the empty room. She marvelled at the sound of her own voice, so level, so flat.

'And then you never spoke again?' Raph asked.

Outside, the sky was a deep indigo, somewhere between light and dark, one of those stranded summer hours when time forgets itself.

'She reached out, but I couldn't talk.'

'And your dad?'

'We came to an understanding...' Her mind trailed back to the year of pretending, the insipid cosplay in which he aped sadness and confusion, bravery and disbelief before friends and colleagues. Women from his office appeared. They came to offer consolation and support, but arrived perfumed, in expensive, date-night dresses, blowing through the house like gorgeous feathers. Sometimes they would pull her aside, *At least you lucked out with one of them*, they might say, glancing at her father. She never agreed, but her silence became a sort of testimony, something that he could work with. She was the troubled adolescent, he the abandoned husband. Long-suffering, forbearing nonetheless.

'That's behind you now,' Raph said. His hand landed on her knee; a warm, solid weight.

She believed him. For the first time in her life, she realised she could describe that episode without feeling engulfed. Maybe it was possible that it was in the past, that something new could happen.

The sex felt different that night. Until now, a part of her had remained distant. There had always been a voice of quiet narration, buffering her from the reality of his touch. She entered the role of the exciting and excited succubus, or seductress, enflaming his desire. That night, she surrendered to something instinctive and inchoate.

Raph noticed the difference too. After, he stared wide-eyed, catching his breath.

'I take it you had fun,' Elle said.

'You've been fucking holding out on me,' he gasped.

They did not refer to Elle's past again. Though the revelations stopped, the sex only intensified. In Elle's mind, she believed this was how they chose to continue the conversation.

And then one night, they ventured further.

There is a sort of vulnerability that is rarely glimpsed. Even between loved ones and partners. We hide it even from ourselves.

'I want to film you,' he said. 'We should record something for a rainy day; we're not always going to look this good.'

He said 'we', but the camera was pointed at her.

'This goes against all my instincts,' she answered, but felt herself smiling.

He smiled too. 'Exactly.'

Everyone celebrates vulnerability. It is demanded in artists, encouraged in friends, lauded in love. But there is always a bit of artifice, always a thin, protective skin remains. Real vulnerability is visceral, faintly grotesque. It is like staring at an organ. It makes people want to look away, even if they can't.

'I want you to call me daddy,' he said.

She recoiled slightly and he noticed; she could almost hear his pulse quicken.

A moment of stand-off.

'You'll have fun,' he stated, his voice had a new timbre. 'Trust me.'

She tried to pass it off with a laugh, but he did not respond. Raph simply waited, patient, confident, as if he knew something that she did not, as if even this hesitation, the way she stole a glance at the door, were little more than delicious prelude. Still he waited.

'OK...' She was on her knees. Something opened inside.

'OK, what?'

'OK, Daddy.' She felt the syllables crack through her.

Raph could sense those wells of shame the way certain animals smell water. To submit. To submit while saying that word. It felt like obliteration.

'What did he used to call you?' Raph asked.

'Pet.'

'Good, pet.'

There was a bag at his feet containing a school uniform, many sizes too small. She wondered how long he had been planning this. It was almost comical, the image of him studiously browsing

182

polyester skirts amid some Back to School display. And then her mind went dark, he was standing over her and telling her to change.

Elle would watch the video countless times. At the start, she remains recognisable. There is still a thin veil of irony, a sense that she is indulging the camera. But then it slips away and the viewer witnesses something more startling than tits. Her face is lit with fear and excitement; a moment of true, frightened self-discovery.

A thumb appears and pushes her lips apart.

Some air escapes her throat in a whimper. She hears that too, hears what is happening to her, it speeds her fears. Her enormous eyes stare up, needful, childlike, ablaze with lust. The thoughts, the resistance, the surrender rippling across her face as inconclusive as verse.

A thousand search terms, countless hours, and one will not strike upon a moment as raw as this. A true loss of innocence, porn at its most beatific and vile.

'Look into the lens,' he commands. 'Say it again.'

28

We find you reclining on the bed, reading Carlo Rovelli. Swedish synthpop is playing, the vocals are distorted and the beat has a thick, unctuous quality. Surrounded by decorative pillows.

Benny makes himself at home, dumping his bag on the floor, glancing with interest at the snacks above the mini bar. He helps himself to a tube of overpriced Pringles. His eyebrows are knitted in consternation as if there were something wrong with the food that he is stealing.

'Did you boys have fun?' you ask. Your voice has an unfamiliar levity.

'How was your call with Jen?' I ask in return.

'It was good. Really good, actually. We both agreed that we've been a bit shit and we want to fix things. Get back on track. Her business seems to be doing incredibly well.'

'Business,' I repeat, coolly.

'Yes. Her ceramics.'

I make an expression.

'I'm sorry, am I missing something?' you ask.

'Just seems a grandiose description for what's effectively an Etsy page.'

'She sells in galleries too. And museum gift shops.'

'Still, it's all very *craftsy*. Not exactly high-volume turnover.'

'You know there's a world beyond the Tesco discount aisles. I'm sure you find that difficult to conceive of.'

Benny sighs.

You wait a beat.

'Benny... did you mention that you had some weed stashed away?'

'Hash,' he corrects.

'I love hash,' you say brightly.

'This is a no smoking room,' I caution.

Both of you roll your eyes at the same time, catch each other doing it, smile complicitly.

'We'll open the balcony door,' you say.

'It could still set off the smoke detector. These sorts of hotels are just itching for an excuse to fine guests at checkout.'

'Got a condom?' Benny asks.

You glance at him with curiosity.

'It's the simplest way to disable the detector.'

'Can't help you,' I say.

'You two didn't bring condoms?' he asks, a very slight note of judgement in his voice.

'We're married,' I state.

'Oh yeah, I forget. Strange, my mind still resets to university, sometimes. It's been happening a lot recently.'

I open my mouth but no words come out. Any response would be some sort of concession.

Soon, Benny is rummaging in his bag for his own prophylactics and then he is tearing the foil with his teeth and stretching the damp latex around the sensor.

'You've done this before,' you say, raising your eyebrows provocatively.

'I love this shit. Makes me feel like a teenager again.'

And I think, surely Benny always feels like a teenager. My eyes fall on the pack of Durex and I notice the label, XTRA SAFE. For some reason, this strikes me, though I can't say why. Benny covers the box with his hand, protectively, and stashes it in his bag.

'I miss being naughty,' he says. 'You know what I mean? Harmless misbehaviour. Challenging authority and getting a slap on the wrist... When you get older, you basically *are* the authority. You can't be naughty any more, you can only be...'

'Criminal,' you finish.

Benny discovers that his pipe has been lost and so begins a protracted experiment. He warms the hash in his hand, tears off a piece and heats it on a teaspoon, using a powerful, double jet lighter. We sit in anticipation as the blue flame hisses, then, after a moment a thread of pale grey smoke escapes the lump. He hoovers up the vapour but seems dissatisfied with the results. He tries to light it again but burns himself on the spoon. On his third attempt, the lighter jams and he clicks and clicks but nothing comes out.

Occasionally he provides commentary, Fuck, I know what I've done wrong... I swear this should work... I've done this before, promise... And you are growing impatient.

My head throbs. With each failed attempt, the space grows smaller. I retreat to the bathroom to take a shower, simply to escape the flinty sound of Benny's lighter and his self-reproaches. His words pierce and become intertwined with my own thoughts.

The copper in my knock-off Rolex has dyed my skin green; I appear to be moulding. There are a few dried scabs where I've picked beneath the pleather strap and scratched and scratched, often to the rhythm of Benny's voice. Now I cannot tell which is uglier, the fake jewellery or the zombie flesh.

Our cleaner has not refilled our toiletries, so I take the last of the Ortigia shower gel and wash in a thin lather. Towelling myself, I still feel unclean, a filmy layer of sweat dried on my skin.

When I return, I notice that Benny has helped himself to our wine and is wearing my linen blazer. It is drooped over his shoulders like a shawl. He distractedly lectures you on foreign literature, seeming to forget the task at hand. Your eyes stay locked on the hash, as if willing it to combust.

I tell you both that I'll be back shortly, saying that I need to stretch my legs. As I shut the door behind me, you flash me a look of pure despair. I cannot spare you this. If anything, you have brought it on yourself; Benny is more your doing than mine.

The hallway's austere symmetry unnerves me for a moment. I am flanked on both sides by identical doors and it is easy to imagine that behind each, the same scene waits for me. It is a sensation I sometimes have while dreaming, a sense that all my actions and decisions will lead to the same inexorable outcome, the same point. The point is suffering.

I take a few steps, then hear a door close. You appear behind me in the hallway. You lean in and speak in an excited whisper, your breath wet in my ear. It gives me pleasurable shivers.

'We need to get rid of him,' you say. 'He keeps talking about Herman Hesse.'

'Jesus.'

'And all this Buddhist shit... I can't make head or tail of it.'

'I thought he was an atheist.'

'He's unbearable.'

You look suddenly younger, more alive. The impression is so striking, that for a moment I forget myself: forget the year, where I am, my age.

'Why is he wearing my clothes?'

'I don't know! He said he was cold... how was I supposed to stop him?'

'It's weird.'

'You're telling me.' You pause. 'Listen, he's hiding something. Jen says he's obsessed with Raph, like fucking obsessed. He's been writing speeches about him for years.'

This is bad, but I do not fully process the threat, I catch myself smiling. You called Jen for reconnaissance, nothing more.

We remain aligned. I realise now that I would rather be dead than misaligned.

'Maybe we should ditch him,' you suggest. 'Yes! Let's just leave, let's leave tonight.'

'We've already paid for the room.'

'It's just money...'

I don't like the idea. I can't say why, exactly. 'He'd tell people that we abandoned him. They would look at us differently.'

It gives you pause. 'Maybe we should just kill him?' you volunteer.

'Here?'

'I don't see why not. He might even like it. His body will have to be shipped back by diplomatic convoy. It's suitably grandiose.'

Our eyes meet and something kindles. We see each other again.

'How would we do it?' I ask.

'Poison?'

'Crucifixion?'

'I'm being serious.'

'I know. It's scary.'

Short breaths. Enormous pupils. And something in your tone as well – it reaches me, goes straight to the brainstem. It is like I have spent years and years in exile, and now, suddenly, I catch the accent of a countryman. And I realise I have been aching for it for so long. That sense of a shared origin. That realisation that we have no loyalty to anyone but ourselves. We can do what we want to them.

'Anyway, I'm not done with him,' you whisper.

I kiss you. Your fingers trail my neck, then creep into my hair, then you grab my hair in a fist so tight that I open my eyes and make a noise.

'Will you two love-birds give it a rest?'

We disentangle instantly. Benny stands behind us, eyebrows up, like we owe him an explanation.

'Benny,' I say. I can think of no words to follow. He claps me on the shoulder and calls me 'freak', then beckons us to return.

I think of how my parents must have felt when I caught them in the act one Saturday morning in my youth. It had happened more than once. And I think how these secret intrusions were never an accident, but a revenge.

I look at you imploringly. The moment has passed.

Inside, Benny has transformed a water bottle into a crude bong. I place damp towels beneath the crack of the door, sealing us in and making the room feel yet smaller. I understand that despite my best efforts, today the roles have been cast; I'll carry the worry and you'll play bohemian.

What is Benny? Just a catalyst and nothing more. He is a clown, not an assassin. I must hold the line.

You inhale deeply and do not cough.

Benny takes a series of shallow drags.

I draw on the bong. A tickling in my chest grows into an insatiable itch and soon I am sputtering. When I recover, my lungs and throat feel raked. You both laugh, but your eyes stay glassy and uncomprehending.

Seconds dilate. The sentences feel interminable. I glance down at my watch and all three hands have completely ceased moving.

'God, it's been a while,' you say.

Benny glances at you and does not breathe out.

'I miss pills,' you say. 'I miss that uncertainty. You never knew what you were taking or who you would turn into.'

'I only stick to organic stuff now,' Benny says. 'I grow my own mushrooms back home.'

You laugh. 'Of course you do,' you say, not sarcastically, but with teasing affection. The hallways feels like it was years ago and miles away.

'They used to have a pill called a YoYo,' Benny recalls. 'It was cut with ketamine or something, so you were constantly coming up then crashing back down. You could come up three, four times in a night.'

'I want a YoYo,' you say.

He laughs. He narrows on you. 'I bet you were a real pillhead back in the day.'

'I was all sorts of things,' you answer in a low voice.

I have nothing to contribute. There are whole realms of experience that I cannot relate to at all.

The bottle circles the room. The mound of hash diminishes and turns to ash.

A second passes and then another. The silence is as thick as soup.

Undertows drag us apart into moments of silent reflection. I remember our chat outside with a prickle of anxiety. I wonder if I'm supposed to be doing something. Finding a hammer. Finding nails.

'How did Raph used to talk about me?' you ask, and I realise you are far away.

'He didn't,' Benny says. 'At least, he didn't to me.'

'You're being polite.'

'I'm telling you, our relationship had rules. I didn't understand half of them myself.'

More silence. I wonder if my limbs still function. They hang from me, leaden and insensate.

'The fact is, I was in love with him,' Benny says in a voice so neutral he could be ordering a coffee.

I blink. I become conscious of my blinking. I blink twice more.

'You mean, like…' you prompt.

'I mean like, I used to write poems about him. Well, raps. If he called, I would drop everything. And when he didn't call, I was forever checking my phone. My days were arranged around him for two and a half years. I barely remember anything from uni. But I could tell you what book he was reading, what music he was into, who he was seeing, where he went each summer, which modules he was taking, his grades, his dreams…'

'Is that love or worship?' you ask.

Benny proceeds as if he has not heard. 'I lived in hope that we would end up sitting next to each other at the pub. Sometimes he'd let his leg slip and rest against mine and then the entire night would be a blur. Just the warmth of his thigh would have me tripping over my words.'

'So he knew how you felt?'

'Must've. He fed me on breadcrumbs for three years. To this day, I don't know what he got out of it.'

'Control,' you say. 'I didn't realise you were gay.'

'Oh, I'm not,' he replies, quickly. You give him a look. 'Well... I've never felt like that again, so who knows what I am... For the longest time, it seemed like *Raph* had all the answers. I think lots of people had that view of him. He could make you feel like such an idiot, but by the same token, he could also make you feel like the you were the centre of the universe.'

You are quiet for a moment. You know exactly what he means.

Benny continues. 'I used to go watch him every Thursday night when he chaired the debates, and I'd wait for him in the college bar after. I hated those people, they weren't my crowd. A room full of Etonians with influential parents... I'd be there in a hoodie and they'd be wearing fucking jodhpurs, or dressed head to toe in Ralph Lauren. Raph would pop his head into the bar and see me waiting. And sometimes he would come over and sometimes he wouldn't. But he'd always check.'

'Why?' you ask. 'Why Raph?'

'Because when he came over, it felt incredible. The rush was ecstatic.'

'But did either of you ever—'

'Sometimes. We fooled around sometimes; it was always on his terms.'

Your face is slack, a neutral mask. He is asking you to relinquish something. Not Raph, exactly, but some share of the pain. It has been yours alone for so long.

'We'd be chatting and then it would become clear that I was heading back to his. I never knew why, or if we would do it again, or what it meant. *He wanted me tonight because I pretended not to notice him.* Or, *he is being cold tonight because of that redhead; she reminds him of what his parents want.*'

His voice sinks into a blander register. Are the narcotics taking effect or is this the very monotony of desire pulling him back into slow orbit? I can see it so perfectly, Benny returning to the Union each week, attending events, college swaps, birthdays, drawn only by the hope of some short encounter. The long, gruelling devotion for one brief flush of contact.

They met in secret late at night and I can see that, too. But it is a dim perception.

Pale bodies witnessed through foggy glass. And when Raph withdraws, he takes all the life and light with him. Each date ends with crushing finality. Leaves Benny stranded on cold, ashen planes. I look at you.

'Did anyone else know?' you ask.

'Only Raph. Which made everything more intense. He initiated things. I mean, I never looked at him that way until he made that first advance. Then it seemed that he was the only person in the world who truly saw me. When he rejected me, it felt like the very essence of me was deemed rubbish.

'I was completely in his hands. Sometimes at the Union he would look across the room and catch my eye... Then, at the bar, he would introduce me to some girl. And he would watch. Watch me fall over backwards trying to be polite and nonchalant.'

'He did that for sport.'

'I know.'

'I was probably there most of those nights, in that bar, being punished at the same time.'

'I know.'

Something dawns on you. 'That night we met. He was doing it then.'

'He always did it.'

'But you still think you had something special,' you state with a strange note of understanding. Benny looks away.

'G is a gay party drug,' he informs us. 'When he overdosed, I couldn't stop coming back to that. Maybe there was a clue there…'

'What do you mean "a clue"?' you ask, your voice sharp.

'Maybe it explains why he was so cruel. It's stupid, but I can't help thinking things could have been different, that's all.'

'It wouldn't have,' you say. 'People like Raph are black holes. They just distort. That's all they do.'

Benny says nothing to this. I glance at you and worry that you are knitting together a whole epistemology without me.

'Were there others?' you ask. 'Did you have any relationships after?'

'No. I mean, I didn't even…' his voice trails. 'He had some piece of me – I'd given it without realising. And when he died, he took that part of me with him.'

Benny shrugs.

He is just an echo of that boy, his own desires growing less resonant and less precise. Here he is, over thirty years old, mourning a non-occurrence from a decade ago. This is what others can do to us. You could do it to me, if you chose.

A wisp of smoke escapes your nostril, then curls back in. You open your mouth and release a thin cloud.

'You spoke to him as he was dying,' you state. I look at you with shock, because you haven't ever mentioned this. *No big deal*, you said. Benny simply looks at you. His face is still – relieved, perhaps – and strangely handsome. 'What did he say?' you ask.

'I trust you,' he says. 'But I'm not going there now.'

'I thought we were sharing.'

'I trust *you*,' he repeats, and this time he stresses the you, just a little, and he won't so much as glance my way. 'We'll talk about it, but not tonight.'

For a long moment neither of you say anything, but I have the sense that the conversation is somehow continuing, in another room, beyond my hearing. Your face wrinkles slightly, as if you are looking at a map, measuring the distance between two points, calculating routes. 'He made a video of me,' you say. 'He held that over me for a long time. Even after he died, I'd go home and search the internet for that girl he filmed. I hated her...'

It isn't panic or paranoia that I experience – though this will come later, no doubt. It is a wave of overwhelming loss. Benny has stolen something that was once only mine.

'Did you find the video?' Benny asks, his voice soft with concern.

'Never. I thought when he died that I would... I thought I could stop looking.'

You draw on the bong but it is empty, just ash and dirty water. You force a smile. 'There's a version of me trapped on a dead boy's hard drive. I have to let her go. You should try letting things go too.'

'But you're still looking.'

'I don't expect to find it. It's just a compulsion.' You shake your head. 'It's a doomed quest,' you say to end the conversation. Benny responds with a look of pained sympathy.

Moment pass. The drugs intensify.

Benny taps ash onto the floor, rolls heavily to his feet and stares, dazed by the empty room. He seems, for the briefest moment, to have forgotten why he is here. Then he remembers and moves towards his baggie of hash. You observe this patiently and do not raise an objection. You remember everything. You remember why we are here, the purpose behind this macabre series of confessions and regrets, but for the life of me, I can't understand it. My senses are seeped in THC. My thoughts are marshy and the room seems to pulse. My tongue explores the roof of my mouth and it is like cotton meeting dry birch.

I pick at my scabbed wrist, pluck away the crust, seeking the wet wound beneath.

Benny catches himself in the mirror and gasps. His sunburn

has progressed and in the muted hotel lights, his skin is the colour of oxblood.

'I'm a monster,' he declares.

'It isn't that bad,' you say, unconvincingly.

'I didn't see it before…'

'It's hard to see your own face,' you acknowledge.

'We need to fix this…' he says. Thoughts collide and merge. 'Will I get cancer?' he asks, with a strange and nervous titter.

'How could I possibly know?' you answer.

'We need to fix this,' he repeats, distractedly. 'We need oatmeal. It's a remedy…'

I fall onto my back. The rhythm of my thoughts distends, stretches out as the two of you call down to room service, speaking at once, repeating your order of dried oats again and again, giddy, breathless between the laughter.

Now that Benny has shared his story, maybe the curse will be lifted and he'll vanish, dissipate like a ghost. More likely, no. More likely, some transference has occurred, from Raph to you. He will doggedly stick by your side.

There is commotion. Do we need milk? What about cinnamon? Bananas?

There is giggling.

My mind stalls.

In the morning we will leave him behind, I tell myself.

I can hear the noises of the hotel, its steel guts churning. Industrial machines crank and hum and struggle through the night to maintain a fragile equilibrium, a sense of normality that is hardly noticed.

The plumbing gurgles and hacks. A bath is being drawn. The door clicks shut so your voices are muffled.

'Let me help,' I hear him say. 'I want to help.'

You answer strangely with a noise that could be a laugh or a sob.

Just moments ago we had plotted his death and now I lie like a victim, stretched out on the floor. I pass out as you bathe Benny and the two of you make plans.

29

It was not my intention to befriend Raph. Not at first. But Cambridge is small and insular, so these sorts of encounters are, to an extent, inevitable. Sometimes I question whether there were other forces at play. We met because you could not forget him. We met because you needed your pound of flesh, and I needed you.

By then I was a second year and you were a finalist. Your friends assumed we wouldn't survive the transitions ahead. Some had begun hitting on you, laying the groundwork for a campaign that would likely intensify in the coming year, when you would be in London, alone, bored, looking for distraction.

'I could travel down on weekends,' I told you.

'Maybe,' you replied.

'You're not keen?'

'I don't even know where I'll be living… It all feels a bit abstract.'

You were brushing your hair before the mirror, briskly preparing for a tutorial with an older supervisor that you found attractive. There was something disturbingly casual and light about your movements.

'You could travel up to me? Job hunt from Cambridge.'

'That isn't going to happen.'

'You might miss it here.'

'I won't.'

I tried not to take it personally. Raph had ruined this place for you long before I entered the picture. Now, the narrow medieval streets made you claustrophobic. The familiar faces appearing at every party, bop and ball made you paranoid. You were prepared to jettison it all. I would be collateral loss.

'You want me to reassure you,' you said.

'Yes,' I confirmed.

'But it wouldn't make you feel any better. It would ring false.' You paused and considered your next words carefully. 'Look, I don't *see* us breaking up.'

'Of course not. Obviously.'

'But then, when I try to imagine the future, I don't *see* anything at all. It's completely black.'

I fell quiet and you assumed I was simply upset. But it was more than this; I was also intent, the hint of a crisis focusing my thoughts.

Certain students shut their eyes and dream of exam questions. They erect essay structures, rearrange all the knowledge, quotations, arguments. They are preparing against the caprices of an examiner, a threat that could take endless forms. It is a type of devotion, to live in that state of alarm, to inhabit the stress until it shades one's reality, grows familiar, even hospitable. I would go to hell for you. I would stay there, to keep you company.

The problem was Raph. Perhaps Raph was also the solution. It was hard to gain a full sense of it. You had not spoken to him since the previous year, and had confronted him only once.

'I asked him to delete the file,' you told me. We were in the communal kitchen, you were staring at a pot of boiling water and I was staring at your back. You only ever mentioned this chapter of your life in public spaces, where there was always the chance of interruption, a possibility of escape.

'And…'

'He said it belonged to him.' You sounded defeated. He owned a piece of you; the worst piece of you.

'I don't think it will get out,' I tried to reassure you.

'He's vindictive.'

'Still…'

'It may be too late. His friends have said things… made references…'

And then the door swung open and your housemate came in, slinging bags of shopping onto the countertop, talking loudly to her friend who was close behind. I knew the conversation was over and you would not bring it up again.

Raph preferred to work from the Rare Books Room at the University Library. He attended daily but rarely worked beyond the early afternoon. He took a break every hour to smoke a Gauloise Light – a rare and pretentious brand of cigarette that was tricky to come by in the small city – and lunched from twelve to one.

In certain moods, he fancied himself a Renaissance man. In others, a decadent fop. In the dour canteen, often just seats away, I watched him perform each character with astonishing conviction. Sometimes, he would sit with professors, his demeanour solemn and propitiating, as they discussed Europe's intellectual climate, the fate of the arts in the UK, the decline of poetry. On other days, he'd lunch with his Union acolytes. With them, he'd roundly denounce academia, declare that his degree was merely a means to an end, or his goal to obtain a Gentleman's Third.

To be clear, I came upon all this by chance. The UL is a ten-minute walk from college; it was natural that I should choose to study there from time to time. But soon we fell into a pattern, the tug of an unconscious rhythm. For a few hours every day, without exchanging a word, we were in lockstep.

Before leaving for a smoke, Raph would drift towards the

canteen for a takeaway coffee. Then he would return to his desk and retrieve his jacket with the cigarettes inside.

I decided to extend my surveillance. As soon as he rose from his seat, I would race for the exit and be waiting on the steps outside.

On one occasion, he was particularly out of sorts. I watched him pat his trousers and coat pocket with growing desperation.

'You OK?' I enquired.

'I seem to have… I've lost my bloody cigarettes.'

'Have one of mine,' I said.

'Cheers,' and reaching for the freshly opened pack, he noticed the brand. 'A man after my own heart,' he said appreciatively.

An hour later, we met again. I had been waiting on the steps the entire time.

'Seems like you're here even more than me,' he remarked. 'I'm actually rather glad we bumped into each other,' he said.

'Still haven't found your cigarettes?'

'This never usually happens. I keep them safer than my laptop.'

He took another without thanking me, lit it with his own brass Zippo, then asked, 'Which college?'

'Robinson.'

'Interesting. You don't strike me as a typical Binsonite.'

'What is a typical Binsonite like?'

He thought about it. 'Chavvy,' he decided. Then he gave me a wry, sideways glance to see if I'd take offence.

An elitist, Raph understood the world through a series of intricate though dated prejudices. They had been passed down from his father, from his father's father: a moth-eaten heirloom. I didn't rise to it.

'It's all nonsense anyway,' he said.

'What is?'

'This.' He made an arc with his cigarette that seemed to enclose the entire city. 'The lot of it,' he added. 'I can't stand it here.' His voice softened as the nicotine hit.

'You know, it's funny,' he continued. 'I used to rather enjoy English. At school, I mean… Bit of a cliché, but I was totally obsessed with Christopher Isherwood.'

I was not aware of this cliché; it seemed so niche. We came from very different worlds. Or maybe his perception of the world was just off-kilter.

'I don't know much about him,' I confessed.

'Oh, mate!' he exclaimed with sudden enthusiasm. '*Goodbye to Berlin* is just incredible. You can read it again and again. The way he describes cities… This, I don't know, mixture of loneliness and excitement… Well, it's not just that, it's not about loneliness, exactly…'

I wasn't sure what to say. This felt different from the practised monologues he delivered to his friends. It was strange, listening to Raph fumble over his words. It felt like gaining access to a private room. I must admit, there was a certain joy in the discovery.

'I really thought I would pursue that passion here. I had this image of myself…' he dropped off.

'University is never quite what we imagine it will be,' I said, with as much empathy as I could force.

He flashed a look of quick irritation. I had been glib and he did not like being paraphrased or misunderstood. He spoke briefly about his disappointments in himself; he had achieved all of his objectives, but had still drifted askew. I was excited, tantalised. But I was uncertain if this was another move in the game.

He rolled the Zippo in his hand and I watched the light bend along its surface. It looked vaguely antique. I told myself that if I truly took up smoking, I would buy one just like it.

He chucked it at me. 'Have it,' he said.

'What?'

'You've been eyeing it up this entire time.'

'Yeah, but I can't—'

'It's just a bit of metal.'

'You might need it.'

'For what? I haven't got any cigarettes.'

He raised his eyebrows and left without saying goodbye.

I kept the Zippo in my front pocket, felt it pressing against my thigh. It was heavy and reassuringly solid. Did he make a habit of bequeathing gifts to strangers? I tried to consider it rationally, but I was swept up in the gesture, which was so glamorous and so profligate.

The hours melted away. I went to your house for dinner. There was an old conservatory attached to the back of your house. The windows were dirty and the space was stuffed with rusty lawn furniture and abandoned pots with petrified houseplants. We were the only ones who liked it out there.

'Where have you been?' you asked.

'Working,' I replied distractedly.

'Not in the college library. I looked for you.'

Raph had almost certainly told others about Isherwood, his disappointments, his doubts; he understood the seductive power of his melancholy. Still, maybe this didn't matter. Maybe the important part was that he wanted to seduce me, like he had seduced you.

'Your phone was off,' you said. The stuffy air made your skin bright and damp, but your hair was neat, your body relaxed.

'Oh?' I glanced away, evasive.

'All day.'

'What did I miss?' I said, with enough irritation to make you freeze, your fork mid-air. You were shocked, but perhaps slightly intrigued by my insurrection. I mumbled an apology before you could probe the moment any further. Silently, I cautioned myself; I was getting closer to Raph, but I couldn't let him get inside.

A routine developed. Monday to Saturday, he would step outside and find me waiting. Before ambling my way, Raph would make a point of switching on his phone; it vibrated in fits as the texts and missed calls came flooding in. Raph would glance at the notifications then slip his phone in his pocket without responding to a single one. Was this all theatre? Did he need me to be aware of the faceless hordes vying for his attention? Whether intentional or not, it was effective; when he ambled over, I felt I had been chosen.

I believe Raph liked me, in part, because he could not place me. I did not belong to the Pitt Club, or the Union. I did not play sports or audition for the Footlights; nobody in his broad network of acquaintances knew my name. My smartest move was my restraint. I never asked for his number or added him on Facebook or attempted to make plans anywhere beyond the steps of the library. I knew he revered indifference.

He had a quick judgement for anyone who crossed his line of vision.

'Bloody moron,' he said as an undergrad scuttled past.

'Him?'

'Head to toe in winter tweeds… Honestly, people show up here kitted up as if they're off to fancy dress.'

'He's young,' I said, as if I were not. I noticed my voice developed a plummy lilt that had not been there before.

'He looks ridiculous. You know, you're too generous.'

Flattery with an edge of warning. For now, he considered me a kindred spirit, but we both knew this was provisional; I accepted his respect like debt.

Mostly, Raph talked about his past. Sometimes he adopted a tone of mock heroics, at other times he spoke with boredom or contempt. Over the course of the weeks I listened and patched together a chronology of his early years. I was working my way towards you, impatient to learn of your first encounter.

Instead, he offered a directionless biography. People seemed to drift through his life like threads of pollen, rarely mentioned more than once. His family name was listed in the Domesday Book, yet he lived in a world without constants or continuity. It left him untethered, horribly light.

I was patient. Truly invested, at times. However, after one rambling story, in which Raph opined at length on the loss of his uncle and his own sense of finitude, I decided it was time to try a new approach.

'You've had a good innings,' I shrugged.

'Bastard. You're supposed to say something comforting.'

'Most people would trade places with you in a heartbeat.'

'Most people are bloody idiots. As we both know.'

He waited a moment.

'You think I'm a ponce,' he said.

'Sometimes.'

'You think I'm quite ridiculous, pontificating about the ephemeral nature of life.'

'Yes.'

'I like that.' He gave me an appreciative smile. He trusted harshness, perhaps because it confirmed his sense of things. Or maybe because it presented a challenge. 'Look, I've got to dash into town. Fancy a walk?'

We cut through the gardens of John's to avoid the cyclists. Every few minutes, he encountered someone he knew, strangers who would glance at me with curiosity and a tinge of envy. As I have said, I did not initially understand Raph's appeal to the opposite sex, but I was starting to.

His many failings, even his cruelties, were insured against his wealth and breeding, his aristocratic features, the very shape of his nose. Sometimes, I felt a sort of rush when he touched me, when he clapped me on the back or gripped my hand with a surprising virility that bordered on rough.

'Hello, Raph.'

'Hello.'

A girl intercepted us as her friends picnicked across the lawn. There was an awkward silence; she had entered our conversation without much of a plan and he did not know her name. She was a fresher, no older than eighteen.

'Are you going to the debate on Thursday?' she managed, feebly.

'Of course,' he answered. I could almost feel his irritation. Raph once confided that stupid questions made him feel lonely.

'What's the topic?' she asked, and reddened. She could hear herself and was beginning to panic. Perhaps next she would ask for directions.

I readied myself for Raph's reply, something of brutal economy. Perhaps he would say nothing at all, just stare and watch her wither. I'd seen him do it before.

Instead, he matched her blush. Glanced away, glanced back. 'You know, uh, I… actually, I've got no idea. Is that really bad?'

She laughed and assured him it was not: he had a lot on his mind. For a moment, he simply smiled and she, overwrought, giggled.

'It would be great if you made it. Whatever it happens to be about…' he said.

She promised that she'd be there and we watched her skip back to her friends, giddy from her small brush with fame, with the triumph of making a president blush. I must admit, it gave me pause. I thought I understood Raph by now, but I had never seen him like that. I wondered what it was about her that had so completely derailed him.

A few steps later he remarked, 'Two.'

'What?'

'That girl. She was a two.' His voice was cold and impartial.

I hated this type of conversation, it was like attempting a foreign language. I was not sure what other men saw when they looked at women, but I knew that my criteria were different. I tried nonetheless.

'She's attractive. I would have said an eight.'

'God, mate, I'm not talking about her looks. I was talking about the length of the chase.'

'I don't understand.'

'The number of hours it would take to seduce her. To make her give it up.'

'Give what up?'

'I don't know, whatever she's got. Anyway, she definitely is not an eight, by either standard of measurement.'

'Were you interested in her at all?' I asked. There was a crack of judgement in my voice, he seemed to hear it.

'I was curious. That's normal,' he insisted. 'One goes to the market, one checks the price. It's what makes us human.'

A beat of silence.

'You're quite the Lothario,' I said. 'I bet you've worked your way through every faculty...'

'If the question is: "Do I sleep around?", then: yes, I do. What else is one supposed to do here?' He was huffy. Somehow, I had put him in a bad mood. All it took was a sentence that didn't quite resonate, a misjudged comment, and he would abruptly withdraw.

For your sake, I had to go on. You believed he had the video and this was my opportunity to find out.

And yet my sight was clouded. Intrusive images of you lying on some bed, garish with desire. I witnessed you through his eyes. It was a horrid sight. Still, I let my mind flit over it. It was not lust in your expression, but raw need.

'A lot of girls,' I said. My heart was racing.

'Yes,' he confirmed.

'And I bet every last one regrets it.'

He looked at me then with a flash of rage. It was constrained to his eyes. 'Depends,' he said. 'They certainly remember. I stick with them.'

'Like an STI,' I offered.

'And what do you leave them with?' he said suddenly. 'What do they think after a night with you? Nothing. They probably don't even notice it happening. I bet it's like fucking a large sponge.'

We stood naked on King's Parade. Our masks had slipped and now we could not unsee each other's faces. It was over.

'This place is driving me round the bend,' he muttered, as if he were already alone.

'It's not so bad,' I said. I needed to recover something, I couldn't fail you. 'It's unlikely we would have crossed paths anywhere else.'

'Not in a *million years*,' he agreed.

'So, some good has come from it all,' I was embarrassing myself, exposing my belly, panting for a rub. 'Presumably at some point we'll both end up in London...'

He snorted. 'I'm running late,' he announced. 'I'll have to leave you here.'

On the long walk home, I let myself fantasise about his evening ahead. I imagined him at a formal hall, drunk and making a fool of himself. I imagined him choking.

I had finally met the boy who taped you. Up till now, we had been two chattering parrots, each giving the other what we thought he wanted.

You barely looked up when I entered your room that night. I kissed you on the cheek and you glanced out of the window as if you hadn't noticed.

'People say they hate the smell of tobacco on others. I've never understood it,' you commented.

'Nor have I.'

'I do now. It can be quite repulsive.'

I didn't know how to respond. I was jarred by the sheer hypocrisy. You opened the book of criticism on your desk.

'Nobody takes up smoking at twenty,' you said, eyes still on the book, as if this were an afterthought, rather than a planned assault. 'Start smoking at fifteen and you seem rebellious. Start in your twenties and you seem, I don't know… desperate. Like you're having an identity crisis.'

'I'm not having an identity crisis.'

'I'm not so sure. New habits. New friends. Clearly something's gone wrong.'

I should have anticipated that moment. This was a city of rumours and you had friends everywhere.

'It isn't what it seems.'

'It *seems* like you've been fawning on my ex-boyfriend, helping him to pick up girls. Even after everything you know about him.'

'He isn't—'

'What?'

'He isn't exactly your "ex".'

Eyes narrowed, your whole body seemed to vibrate with rage and humiliation. I reminded myself to be careful: I wanted a fight, but not with you.

'I'm going to London this weekend,' you said, darkly.

'You didn't mention—'

'I need to clear my head. Make plans.'

I would have laughed if the panic hadn't been so acute. It was absurd. We had never been so close, only, you didn't know. I had lived in your skin, had felt his hand on my arm, the thrill of contact, the glow of his celebrity. The more I knew of Raph, the more I understood you.

I stammered my explanation. 'I wanted to know…'

'What? What did you want to know?'

What it felt like. What you felt. 'I wanted to know if it was true. If he had the recording.' A partial truth, but the easiest to explain.

'Of course it is,' you said, but your demeanour shifted, loosened.

'Then I want to destroy it. And him.'

You were curious. More than curious. It was as if I'd whispered some exciting profanity in your ear.

'What exactly are you suggesting?' your shoulders slid back.

You lit a cigarette. Outside, the moon emerged, pale as a wafer, dissolving in an expanse of blue. The sun had not yet set so they stood side by side, sun and moon, and your whole room was absorbed in their strange, liminal glow.

I relayed the events from earlier, his defensiveness when I'd asked about his love life.

'So...' there, a new coyness in your voice. 'What next?'

'I'll continue to meet him.'

'Yes.'

'Win his trust.'

'But from now on, you report to me,' you said. 'We're in it together.'

Days passed. Then a week. Raph had vanished. Each night I came home to you and you grew impatient for news.

'Maybe he's moved on,' I suggested.

'He hasn't,' you said.

'How do you know...'

'Because Raph never moves on. He keeps people. That's his entire MO.'

How much of you had he kept? You were excited, agitated. By day, you plotted some violent confrontation. At night, you took substances to climb back down from the dizzy heights. I noticed, with slight alarm, that you were trying new drugs, which you bought from a teenage dealer on Mill Road.

'I've never known anyone who enjoys buying drugs as much as you,' I complained. 'And I'm not talking about having the drugs. I'm talking about the literal point of purchase, the transaction.'

'I like the drama,' you shrugged. 'The cryptic text messages, the weird meeting spots. And I like the certainty too. I know I'll never have buyer's remorse.'

I inspected a clear vial you had left on your bedside table. 'This looks like tap water.'

'Quite the opposite. That stuff is strong – apparently it's big on the chemsex scene.' I could hear the eagerness in your voice; I wondered if you'd already had a sample.

'Should you be messing around with it?'

'I only microdose. Only enough to feel relaxed… Anyway, the money goes to a good cause. Ricardo needs a new moped.'

'Put it somewhere safe.'

I admit that a part of me liked worrying about you. It kept you close, kept us connected. And I knew you would be careful with doses.

A drug called G. It was the first I'd ever heard of it. Odourless. Clear. I was fascinated by all those absences. In that void, a whole world of possibility. G was potent; it was killing young men across the country. And the game we were playing was intoxicating.

We planned 'to scare him straight'. What this meant, in any practical sense, depended on our mood. Sometimes it involved blackmail and sometimes brute force. We surprised each other. We shocked ourselves. We drew the curtains and let our voices float on the air.

If we buried him up to his neck…

He'd die of exposure.

How long would it take?

Our minds twisted around each other. We coiled. I'd hardly thought this type of closeness was possible.

I almost said something really fucking dark.

Say it.

There are still aspects of me you might find scary.

Show me.

Though I had not seen Raph in weeks, it felt as though he was always with us. He watched us as we made love; his presence energised our movements. He waited for us in your room while we studied or ran errands, a captive tied to your bedpost. When we were with others and could not mention his name, he sat beneath our sentences, the constant subtext.

It was two weeks before he appeared again. When he emerged from the library, I felt a flash of shame, but it passed. I suppose I worried he could somehow tell, intuit the grotesque things we'd imagined doing to him. I reminded myself that I had said those things to you alone: the fantasies were as safe as my own thoughts.

He looked disappointed to see me, joining me for a cigarette with palpable reluctance, as if he were obliging me somehow. He kept his phone in his hand as he spoke.

'So,' he began, 'how's life?' He offered a thin smile.

'Fine,' I replied. 'Exam Term is always worse than you remember.'

'I'm not exactly sure what you're so concerned about. You're only a second-year: Part I of the Tripos counts for fuck-all.'

'You sound like you've been stressed.'

'Yes,' he replied, 'I've been stressed.' His voice was contemptuous; I was making him state the obvious. The amber of his cigarette raced towards the filter, it measured out our time together like a speeded clock. This conversation wouldn't last long. 'You know, there are certain jobs that won't even consider you unless you have a 2:1.'

'Of course,' I replied. 'In fact, the best graduate schemes expect a first.'

'Yes, all right.'

I had pierced him, only slightly, but I enjoyed the sensation. I focused on his facial expressions so I could describe them to you later.

'You're worried you've wasted your time,' I said. He glanced at me strangely; my sentence had an unexpected depth. That was intentional.

'I'm a hedonist,' he replied. 'Take after Wilde. As long as I had fun, the time was well spent.'

'We both know that isn't true. Nobody wants to peak at twenty-one. And it isn't much fun being unemployed, even if you've got money.'

'You're in a queer mood today,' he said, narrowing his eyes.

I shrugged. He faltered. His cigarette done, Raph should have gone back inside. But instead, he remained for a moment longer. Something about my coldness intrigued him; Raph liked me best when I gave him something to chase.

I saw everything in sudden, vivid detail. His nails had been clipped unevenly. In places, the tips of his fingers looked red and exposed. I observed the tuft of hair along his jawline that he'd missed, the irritated bumps along his neck where he'd shaved too close. About ten metres away, two friends were leading their bikes along Burrell's Walk. Even closer, but out of sight, a car was being parked, the soporific tones of a radio presenter leaking from the open window. My heart beat fast.

'Elle hates you,' I said. I surprised myself.

It took him a moment to place you and then he laughed once, as one might at a dirty joke. In his mind, that was all you'd become.

'She has reason to,' he said with a hint of pride. 'I forgot you were both at Robinson.'

'She talks about you all the time.' And now he looked up sharply. I felt the first crackle of interest. 'She says she'd like to kill you. Says she'd be doing the world a service. Honestly, she's quite specific. Quite graphic.'

From the way he smiled just then, you would think I was relaying warm wishes from a distant relative, or reminding him of fond schoolyard antics. 'Sounds like her,' he said, with something close to affection.

'The thing is,' I continued, 'I think she's obsessed. If you offered to meet with her, you know, to talk things through, I know she'd say yes. She'll tell herself she wants closure, but, really, she just wants you.'

'Why the fuck would I want to do that?' he asked.

'To prove you can.'

'Proven. I've had her. The fact is well documented.'

'No, that time you tricked your girlfriend. Granted, you did it with some ingenuity, but it wasn't much of a challenge.' He took the point grudgingly, like an artist reviewing his earlier works. 'She's spent the entire term saying she wouldn't touch you with a stick, that she'd rather huff petrol than taste your breath. She's different now. She's a ten.'

A smile broke across his face. Exams were weeks away, an intractable problem he could not fix with bluffing or charm. He had probably spent the whole afternoon pondering the mediocrity of his work, the bland inevitability of a middling pass. His enemies would love that. When the grades were posted on the steps of Senate House, they would search out his name, so low on the list, and smirk.

This was what he needed at the moment. What outrageous sport, to make you come back and to do it again. What audacity, what power. Here was a final truly worthy of his stature.

'What's your angle? Do you like her or something?' he suddenly asked.

'I fucking hate her,' I said, and scared myself with my own performance.

Naked on your bed, we planned the encounter. He would arrive and we would scare him. We would hurt him. We would make him watch the video, watch him watch it. We would bring a knife. A sabre from the fencing club. Acid from a battery. We were like children dreaming of being a vet, a fireman, an astronaut, beguiled by a vision but lacking any sense of how to get there, or what it would truly mean to become something new.

Our chats grew more frenzied. They would come on rapidly, escalate quickly and end just as abruptly. Footsteps on the landing, the sound of your housemate watching TV. Suddenly, the bedroom would reassert itself. We would be back in Cambridge; a world that was so much duller than the one we had created.

'This is fucking stupid,' you told me one evening as the weekend drew close.

'It was your idea.'

'A love cruise with my ex?'

'The other stuff.'

'That was just a game,' you sighed. You held your hand out and inspected your body as if it were a foreign surface. 'My arms are so… *lissom*.' It was probably the first time you'd ever used that word, you uttered it with a tone of discovery. Yet the adjective fit. I had a brief image of what your life could have been. 'I'd look ridiculous holding a knife, like a displaced housewife.'

'I'll be there too.'

'Your arms aren't much better.'

You took a dab of G and I watched your eyes lose focus. Over the next ten years you would learn to calibrate your doses perfectly, to heighten our time together, to bear it.

'There are other ways to do this. Subtler,' I said.

'Call it off,' you said, and waited for me to disagree.

Our dance had begun. But who was the lead and who the follow? It would change over time. It would change day by day.

For a long while, so much of what happened seemed a symptom of the place. We were halfway through Exam Term. The city centre was drained of students. Instead of hitting the clubs, they now volleyed, miserably, between their studies and the canteen. College bars were closed. Parties were banned. Posters for sold-out balls were plastered over the faculties, but it felt as if this time of celebration, the yearned-for ending, would never come. It was a period of suicide watch, discreet patrols of libraries, experts scanning the room looking for signs of distress. But outside the air was sweet. Trees exploded in white and pink. Birds sang all through the long, pastel dusk. A heady and confusing mix. When I think of that time, I think of pale skin and outrageous blossoms. I think of choices.

30

One day Raph stopped appearing at the library. Then he was on the front page of every student newspaper and on the third page of the regional press. It probably would have been of little interest to the public had it been a conventional overdose, but some of the details were haunting. He was discovered with a picnic, his right hand gripping a sweating bottle of Puligny-Montrachet, the other folded delicately in his lap. His hair was coiffed and his head was bowed. It was estimated that he drifted for over an hour, claiming a mile-long stretch of river for his macabre pageant. Later, when the facts emerged, people wondered if the performance had been intentional, a last supper. Others said the food was hardly touched, and wondered if he had planned on meeting someone. The ambiguities kept the story alive in whispers.

Then, of course, there was the Shakespeare speech, playing on a loop until the speakers died. Such a strange reference, such an obscure play. It would inspire much speculation as people tried to understand his last moments. You were known to be a specialist in *Titus Andronicus*; your dissertation focused on the toxic love affair at the tragedy's core. People sought your opinion. One went so far as to suggest it could have been a sort of homage, that Raph was trying to get your attention, to honour you, perhaps.

You were quick to kill that theory. Don't romanticise him, you said. He wasn't hung up on me; he didn't have a heart to break.

The day he died we were seen all over town running errands, many remembered that. We visited Jen for dinner. I recall her hinting that we were late, her eyes drifting my way, as if I alone were responsible. Still, she didn't press the point. We'd brought champagne, an unusual extravagance. She asked what the occasion was and you simply said, 'Life.' All night, you spoke to her quickly, a disordered stream of thoughts, and she couldn't keep up.

'Babes... you're talking a mile a minute,' she complained, laughing.

'Too much library,' you said quickly.

'Too much something,' she replied, sceptical.

But you were sober and keenly alert. While you continued to rabbit at Jen in the kitchen, I fell into a deep repose, the sort of contented exhaustion of a man who has spent a day labouring in the sun. Outside, cottony tufts drifted through the air. My thoughts moved differently that day, with a deeper, slower rhythm.

You claimed you didn't feel anything until you saw his face on the front page of *Cambridge Student*. He looked like a child, impossibly young. Or maybe we were just viewing him through new, slightly aged, eyes. You clutched the paper without reading a word and claimed you might be sick. You didn't throw up, though. After an hour or so, you realised that you were in fact quite hungry and you worried what this said about you. I watched as you devoured two bowls of pasta, the bolognaise rich and meaty.

You eyed me warily, didn't want to talk. But then, with time, you realised I was your only confidant. Nobody else would understand. Your grisly twenties had just begun.

All that rage, where does it go? Like energy, it is neither created nor destroyed. It just circulates and changes shape. We took Raph with us.

31

'**M**akes you feel like a rock star, am I right?'

'It makes me feel like a pig,' I say.

Benny is surveying the room, the empty booze bottles, the overflowing bin. There's a smear of ash on the carpet beside the hard black stain that might be a burn. A flaccid condom still dangles overhead. Next door, oatmeal has congealed inside the bathtub.

'You should have seen yourself, last night,' Benny continues. 'Blissed out on the floor... you looked like Bob Sinclar.'

I glance up sharply. Benny meets my eye, smiles and winks. I want to tell him that I look nothing like Bob Sinclar, that nobody has ever wanted to look like Bob Sinclar. But Benny knows this. He is testing me, searching for a raw nerve.

'I better eat something before we hit the road,' he remarks.

Shocked, not surprised. It's what commentators say, unthinkingly, after every political scandal. Or when somebody discovers that their home is underwater, having built it on a flood plain. The phrase has cycled through my mind ever since I woke up to the news that Benny is to accompany us to the Sea of Tears. You hardly felt the need to explain yourself. You mentioned it in passing after he left to take our place at the breakfast service.

'What do you expect him to do?' you had said with a yawn.

I was holding a wooden-heeled brogue. I put it down with such force that you were startled and then frowned. I must have appeared childlike. Really, I did this for your benefit; had I held it for another second, I would surely have thrown it at your face.

'This isn't about Benny,' I hissed. 'You. You are driving this fucking bus.'

'He heard Raph's last words. Surely we should know what they were.' But I can tell you are fishing, appealing to my anxieties.

'It doesn't matter. It was ten years ago.'

'But aren't you curious?' It is the first honest thing you've said since waking. You want closure. Truth. Something that I have apparently failed to offer.

'You are frivolous,' I state. You only shrug. 'Whatever Benny thinks he knows, it's only the tip of the iceberg. You better pray he's as stupid as he appears.'

'He isn't stupid.'

'More's the pity. Because you're the sort of girl that tabloids love. The *Daily Mail* will eat you alive.'

You force yourself to roll your eyes.

'They'll wear your skin,' I whisper.

Benny knocks. He has returned with an excessive quantity of bread rolls and cheese, smuggled from the buffet in thin paper napkins. He glances about playfully as if he has wrought an act of subtle larceny. There is a new swagger in his step, something almost territorial as he moves about the room. You read about quantum gravity while I pack. You are missing some earrings. I look through our bags and clothes. I tell you they're gone. You inform me that you loved those earrings. I know, I say. You tell me they were expensive. I check under the bed.

Benny is singing to himself in the shower; I have an image of him cracking his head against the marble base, then drowning in tiny droplets.

I take out my Bally wallet and stand before the mirror. It is made from full-grain, beige leather. After years of ownership, it remains supple, buttery. Sometimes, I simply clutch at it in my pocket, the way different fingers might search out a rosary. It reminds me that I have made good decisions and will continue to make more. In this world, you do not achieve Bally wallets through chance or accident. Today, however, it feels light. I count the money. I'm sure I had three thousand yesterday. Either I have made some unlikely error, or somebody is robbing me. I glance at Benny's oversized backpack. I glance at you.

'All right kids, we ready?' He is happy and bright. I nod. You do not move, lost in the world of quantum physics; your eyes are wide, as if reading a thriller.

This troubles me.

'We have to go, darling.'

You continue to read, reluctant to tear away.

'This book explains a hell of a lot,' you say, eyes still on the page.

'About what?' I ask.

'Everything. Us.' You fold back the corner of a page. 'Did you know that electrons don't exist?'

'They do,' I assert, though I'm on shaky ground.

'They only exist during interactions, when they crash into something else. Imagine that. That limbo. Your whole existence depends on violent collision.'

'They're electrons,' I state. 'Not lonely hearts.'

You hardly respond. Perhaps I have not given you something to crash into, because your expression is frosty and remote.

Your tutors accused you of 'overreading'. You had a habit of twisting texts to fit your own view of things, could find a French existentialist thread in the plays of Sophocles. *She doesn't always*

218

get the right end of the stick, one supervisor commented, *but it's always an interesting one.*

Now, you read science as if it were poetry. In your hands, hard facts soften into malleable symbols. And your visions are frightening because they are convincing. My mind travels the ozone, cold lunar stretches where distances lose meaning and all scales collapse. Without you, everything is just outer space, structureless, vast and dark. I hardly exist at all.

'We're going to miss this cab!' Benny calls from the hallway. For once, I'm grateful for the interruption.

You rise. The corners of your mouth twitch into a perfectly symmetrical smile. Somewhere in your mind, my words echo. Fear creeps up on you, makes your pulse race. What would the world make of you? What would they do to you? Benny cuts me off at the door and I suppress an instinct to kick his heel.

We are in it now. Whether through rage, or fear, or some hybrid of the two, our hearts race together, our blood moves at the same speed.

Part II
Desert

32

I have never doubted that you are the love of my life. We were standing in the college smoking area when this revelation first struck. We'd met only minutes before. Many doubt the concept of love at first sight. To me, it has always seemed wholly rational. Dogs can do it; a single sniff and they know whether they should growl or bark. Babies do it too, you hold them and they know. It seems to me that we spend our adult lives unlearning our convictions, teaching ourselves to dither, to question the obvious.

We met at an end of term party. The dining hall had been converted into a dance floor, the Common Room transformed into a silent disco. I spent the evening wandering listlessly from group to group. As these strangers comfortably discussed music, drugs, politics or sex, I lingered close by. In the months preceding matriculation, I referred to Cambridge with defensive bravado. It was just a university. Just a famous brand. All of that evaporated upon arrival. I couldn't even make small talk. I couldn't bear the sound of my voice. I worried that others could hear it too, the insincerity, the strain. The fact was, I didn't relate to people my age, but had become so habituated to loneliness that the feeling hardly registered at all. My degree stood before me like a sprung trap. At midnight I gave up, and headed to my room.

In an empty passageway, sheltered from the noise, I saw the shoe. It sat in a pool of light. A single black stiletto, perfectly upright on the tiled floor. I bent to retrieve it and at the exact moment of contact, I heard someone retch violently, as if the two acts were inextricably linked. I was outside a disabled toilet and the door, which was slightly ajar, emitted a crack of light. I knocked gently. A series of wet coughs came as reply. I stepped inside.

You were on your knees, hunched over the toilet bowl. One foot was bare. You did not notice me at first, but when you finally looked up, regarding me through watery, red eyes, you seemed somehow unsurprised to discover me there. I stood, the stiletto poised delicately in my left hand, my right hand pressed flat against my thigh, an unwitting Prince Charming.

For a long moment, nothing was said.

'My shoe,' you stated simply.

'I found it outside,' I replied.

I felt a stab of paranoia. I worried, absurdly, that you might think I intended to steal it. I slowly laid it on the floor, and then stood up straight. Your eyes followed the shoe and then returned to me.

'I hadn't noticed it was gone,' you stated.

'Now it's back.'

The air freshener unit issued a sharp hiss. The smell of bile mixed strangely with the scent of artificial vanilla.

'I've been unwell,' you explained. Your wrist fluttered towards the toilet, the room.

'Do you need help?'

'It's just hay fever,' you said, your eyes narrowed, as if daring me to object.

'Strange time of year for hay fever,' I remarked.

'I suffer... chronically,' you said, and stifled a hiccup.

'I hope it didn't spoil the party.'

'Yes. Well. At least I didn't drink too much or embarrass myself.'

'At least you avoided that,' I agreed, trying not to glance at the empty wine bottle by the sanitary bin.

You ran your hand through your hair and regarded the shoe again, almost scowling at it, as if the item represented a problem that refused resolution.

Even in the harsh, unsparing fluorescence of that toilet, you were striking. You were so beautiful you appeared futuristic, like some improved specimen. Your hair was pristine and your limbs were boyishly thin. I noticed then what others would soon comment on: a distinct similarity between our features.

You took your shoe and held it to the light; from the way you narrowed your eyes, I inferred that you were seeing double. Of course, I did not know any of the rumours about you then. I didn't know that on this night you had been living up to your worst reputation, pointedly, boldly.

All I noticed was your impeccable self-control, that though your blood was flooded with alcohol, your voice remained so level and deliberate.

'Can I offer a hand?' I asked.

'I hardly think that's necessary,' you replied, somewhat officiously.

Levering yourself up against the handrail, you lurched unevenly to your feet. You attempted to insert your bare foot into the stiletto, once, twice. Instead, you kicked off the other shoe and stood barefoot.

'Thank you again,' you said with polite formality, as if discharging a member of staff.

'A pleasure,' I replied; even to my own ears, I sounded disappointed.

You offered a firm, close-lipped smile and I hesitated, but after another beat of silence, I understood that it was time to leave.

'I hope you recover from your hay fever,' I said, turning away.

'A Clarityn and a glass of water, and I'll be right as rain,' you replied. Then, as I nudged the door open, you blurted. 'Please don't tell my friends you found me like this.' It disconcerted me. A note of desperation made the request sound more like a confession. Your eyes were imploring, streaked with make-up.

The door drifted shut.

'I don't even know your name.'

You told me, though it was counter to your immediate interests.

'Well, I don't know theirs. You're still safe,' I said, with what I intended as a disarming laugh.

'What's *your* name?' you asked, ignoring my levity, my attempt at small talk. I had introduced myself countless times already, to students, to college aunts and uncles, to tutors and pastoral staff. But never like this. It is rare, in life, to experience something truly new, a paradigm shift. I told you my name. You repeated it; boring and Anglo-Saxon though it was, something appealed to you.

'That's good,' you said. 'I'm over boys with strange names.' You looked up. 'I'm not supposed to…' your voice trailed and you got lost following the thought. 'My friends worry,' you said. 'I don't want this to be misconstrued.'

I wondered if someone had spiked your drink. I felt I should offer to call a cab or even alert the medics parked outside college grounds, their job was to deal with situations like this. Instead, I said, with a sincerity I would come to reserve for you alone, 'I won't tell a soul.'

Your shoulders fell as if kneaded loose. It was exciting, to see my words affect you like that, so physically. My chest filled with air.

'I should go.'

'Walk me home?' you asked. 'It isn't far. I'm on Adams Road.'

'I suppose…' I faltered. Evidently, I had made a good first impression. Perversely, a part of me wanted to cut and run, pick over the conversation in the quiet of my room and regroup before I had a chance to botch things.

'There's a flasher about,' you stated. 'He's been working the neighbourhood since last summer. I don't think I should confront him in this state.'

I was so grateful, just then, to that criminal, for giving me an excuse to take you by the arm. We walked through the college, pausing at the smoking section where soon we would meet each night. I wanted to say something witty and scanned my surroundings for inspiration. Though I reached for insight, I could only produce blunt statements of fact: music was playing, the night was clement, the bins were overflowing. Everyone we passed looked so uninteresting compared to you.

I sat by the bench as you dug out your cigarettes. You were explaining your most recent essay; I frowned, struggling to keep up. Your thoughts were subtle and quick; I felt the need to prove myself. A rugby boy walked past, and perhaps surprised by my look of concern, or my tense, anxious posture, he said: *Cheer up mate, it might never happen*. I blushed. I was only eighteen: I entered every situation expecting the worst. The jock laughed, and as he walked away, while he remained in earshot, you said, in a low, clear voice: *Cunt*.

Together, we watched his pace slow, then quicken. It was the defining romantic moment of my youth. It set the tone.

You sensed my excitement. 'No good will come of this,' you told me, laughing. You've repeated this over the years, a refrain that takes on new layers with each iteration. You uttered it first as flirtation, but now it's become something else. An understatement, maybe.

We pressed on.

One side of Adams Road was lined with ornate Victorian houses, now occupied by students and faculty. The other side led onto a vast sports field; the night had rendered it two-dimensional, a single wall of black. Dead leaves had fallen everywhere and the air was sweet with decay.

'I know everything about this flasher,' you said. 'I read all the articles and reports and blog posts. I know what he wears:

grey joggers, black hoodie. And what his preferred victim looks like: brunette, like me. And what his penis looks like: stubby and uncut. I could probably pick it out in a line-up.'

'Sounds like you actually want to meet him.'

'Yes, maybe.'

'And do what exactly?'

'I'm not sure... just *get* him.' You said it slowly and with relish. It was only a fantasy. I would soon learn you had seen Raph that night. The two of you had argued and he had ended the conversation with a threat.

'You know, in the Czech Republic they practise castration in cases involving sexual violence.'

'Sounds harsh.'

'Yes, of course,' you agreed, checking yourself. We walked a few paces more before you added. 'Of course, in Saudi, I think they can actually behead sexual predators, so you might say, Czech sex offenders are getting off light.'

'Is that so?'

Something in my tone sped you forth. You told me that in North Korea they opt for the firing squad. As you spoke, quickening, breathless, your class slipped away. You didn't sound like a Cambridge student. You simply sounded hungry.

All across this dark city, students discussed their favourite writers, the modules they dreaded, ambitions for the term ahead, while we discussed the flasher. We speculated on his bleak urges. What drove him to this street. What made him strike. What punishment might possibly fit the crime. We didn't know it yet, but our whole crooked enterprise sprang from here.

'You think you could take this guy on?' I asked.

'No, not on my own,' you confessed. And then you looked up, so suddenly, so directly. 'But the two of us might.'

228

33

At the bus station we walk through metal detectors. I have pre-emptively removed all metallic objects, so I glide through without a problem; Benny, meanwhile, keeps discovering more shrapnel in his pockets. At first, the guards find this amusing, but he soon exhausts their patience.

Inside, we pass women in black shawls, children shrieking between their legs, backpackers, businessmen. A dog howls. I flinch.

'It's just a dog,' you say.

'I know,' I reply. 'It was loud.'

'I'm just saying... I don't want any repeats of the other day.'

You are referring to our coach journey from the airport. The man sitting in the row ahead of us had been muttering anxiously as we departed. I studied him through the gaps in the seats. His head darted to the baggage compartment as he chanted prayers. I alerted you, expecting you to calm me. Instead, you blanched and grew quiet. For the fifteen remaining minutes of our journey, we contemplated our deaths incessantly. I imagined my flesh turning into a pink spray, your teeth melting on the tarmac.

'It's just a man,' you say, because you've caught me eyeing a bearded traveller.

'I know!' I say. 'Christ, where am I supposed to look?'

'No repeats.'

You buy a bag of pistachios and then we take our seat at the twelfth bay. I watch you crack the nuts with one hand, scoop out their green, streaked innards with the edge of your nail, just like your father used to. Your book is open but I can tell you're not reading. Your eyes have a hazy quality as you savour the salt. Are you thinking of him? Surely. When you drink, do you think of your father? When you spend his money? Your acts of defiance just bring you closer.

Benny is blowing bubbles with his sugar-free chewing gum; they snap and crack between his lips.

Because it is August, very few people are travelling to the desert. The bus is mostly empty and we sit separately, spreading out over several seats. The driver is surrounded by mirrors; his face is disassembled into a series of separate features, each piece of him twitching and autonomous.

We pass the city limits and barrel downhill. Leaning my head against the window, I let the vibrations rattle through my skull. I hear the engine groan, steam hiss against the brake pads. I think of the hotel and its many straining machines, all there to keep the rooms cool, the air fresh, the lights on. So much industry and labour, just to maintain a baseline of normality, a modicum of comfort.

I remember our kiss in the corridor last night. It felt like finding you again, but just as quickly you disappeared. Now, your book shields your face like a visor and I cannot tell if you wish to be found at all.

A radio is playing through the PA system, a lugubrious Turkish folk song reaches a climax and melts away. Then 'The Shape of You' by Ed Sheeran begins to play. Those tentative opening chords fill me with dread. Escaping Ed Sheeran is like escaping your own thoughts. He seems to wait for me in taxis, cafés, lobbies, his message always unchanged. Maybe I just don't like contemporary music. There comes a time in life when the pleasure we derive from a familiar song, from familiarity itself, outweighs the joy of discovery. But there is something distinctly nightmarish about Sheeran in particular. It's like running without gaining distance. Wherever I go, he's already there, ready to remind me I have not gone far. You say you like the song. It reminds you of dancing with your friends, the pleasurable uncertainty of a cheesy club night. I hate that as well.

We travel for hours. The motorway is broad and empty. A craggy mountain range flits past like a memory. Rock formations the shape of tulip petals rise up from the ground and then disappear as we push east. We wind through a town built around a geothermal crack. There is a smell of rotten eggs as steam escapes through the broken earth. The whole place appears damned, caught in a moment of smouldering. Yet all these sights dissolve into rolling ubiquity, because you are not looking.

I glance at you. You are still reading about quantum gravity, and I wish you would stop.

Benny bops his head absently to the music. Occasionally, he peels dead skin from his arms in stretchy, translucent sheets. *A Brief History of Western Philosophy* wobbles on his lap; I want to inform him that he is essentially reading a reference book, but am wary of engaging him in conversation.

He calls across the aisle to you.

'Do you ever think you'll have kids?' he asks.

You glance up, bemused, and more patient than if I had interrupted you.

'I think not. I haven't got it in me.'

'The mothering instinct, you mean?'

'Any of it,' you laugh. 'I definitely don't have the internal clock that women talk about… I doubt if I have the other necessary parts. To be honest, I shudder to think what would come out of me. It would probably have fangs and tentacles.'

'I'm sure that's not true,' Benny says, with feeling.

'It'd probably have claws and horns… its first words would be in Latin.' And now you really get the giggles, imagining our monstrous progeny. 'I'd feed it fish heads and raw meat. Other mothers would recommend singing it lullabies. I'd explain to them how, actually, I get the local priest round to perform an exorcism every bedtime.'

Your eyes are shining. An uncomfortable smile remains frozen on Benny's face.

'That's funny,' he states, mirthlessly. 'I think you're being a bit hard on yourself.'

'It was a joke.'

'I know. But still.'

'Do you want children, Benny?'

'Once I get my money right.'

'Music is a fickle industry,' you concede. 'Of course, everyone loves a comeback.'

He looks at you, unable to gauge the remark. It's the first time you've indicated an awareness of his career. Like me, he can't decide if the comment is careless or cruel.

'It's sort of trickier in my situation… I haven't figured out all the practical aspects.'

'Ah, yes. You need a womb. Well, if you ever develop a taste for the macabre, I could be your surrogate.'

'You might live to regret that offer,' he says, and I believe him. There is a quality of hopeful restraint in his voice that makes me think you are teasing him about a topic he takes seriously.

Benny moves seats so he can be closer.

'We hardly know anything about each other,' you remark. 'Only the bad stuff.'

'I feel like I know you,' he says. 'I wouldn't have shared any of those things unless I trusted you.'

'Yes, of course,' you reply with a yawn. 'But for this leg of the journey, let's keep things light. Deal?'

'I'm not sure if I really do "light".'

'What's your star sign?' you ask. 'You seem like a cancer to me.'

'Aries.'

'What's your favourite colour?'

'Fuck, I don't know. Do adults have favourite colours?'

'Mine's red. What was the name of your first pet?'

'I've never owned a pet.'

'Then your favourite teacher.'

'Those things are pretty different.'

'Keep it light, Benny. Don't deconstruct the question.'

'Mrs Evans.'

I think I recognise these questions. I have heard you conduct this conversation before. You invited your first boss to dinner at our flat once without telling me. I was surprised to find him sitting there at our kitchen table. He was just as disappointed when I appeared; he'd thought he'd have you to himself. You had been warned never to dine alone with him. You had been warned to keep your wits about you. When he resigned a few weeks later, by email, people were more relieved than surprised. They thought it strange, abrupt, but nobody looks a gift horse in the mouth. They were glad he was gone. Glad they never had to see his face again. Nobody ever did.

'What was your first job? I mean, your first proper job,' you ask.

My heart beats fast. I turn in my seat and lean over the headrest, seeking confirmation. Your head is pointed my way, but you seem to be looking at nothing in particular. A frozen smile hovers on your face; it is the type of expression people wear in portraits, withholding as much as it offers.

You stop short of asking for his PIN. Frankly, you'll soon be able to guess.

You know I'm listening. I believe you are speaking to me.

Discreetly, I unfurl a scrap of paper. This morning, I salvaged three more of your affirmations.

7. It felt good.

8. I deserved to feel good.

9. I paid in advance and I paid after.

I read it as a confession and was afraid. Now I read it as a call to arms. Like you, I overreach. You study the stars, and I study you.

'Tell me about your mother,' you ask. 'What's her name?'

Benny, as if entranced, answers in full.

And then he jolts, a resistant spasm. 'What about yours? I don't want this to be all about me… You had an issue with your dad, I remember.'

'He's gone now.'

'As in…' His voice trails as he catches your meaning. 'I'm sorry.'

'Sometimes I am too,' you say. For a moment, like Benny, I'm mesmerised by the sparkle of your tears. I could almost believe you.

34

I used to envy your narrative. I imagined if Hollywood adapted your story, it would be sympathetic: a flawed woman, beset by adversity. The director would refrain from easy judgements; the audience might identify with your missteps. How would they portray me? An Iago, an absence. Sometimes, in the early days, you struggled with this too.

'We both know why *I'm* fucked up, but what's your excuse?' you asked me once, only partly in jest.

You had just met my parents. You didn't understand my contempt. It is difficult to grasp over coffee, while they are offering you cake, doling out cheap, easy compliments. It takes time to grasp what they do, which is as quiet and slow as asbestos. Both of them share a maddening, sunny disposition. You can tell them any manner of bad news and they will smile and nod and seem to forget. I brought them plenty of bad news before I met you. I saw it as a challenge. Even so, I could never penetrate their levelling optimism.

'I would have killed for your set-up,' you told me on the way home. 'As far as I can see, your chief complaint is that they tidied a lot.'

'It was their only passion.'

Of course, I didn't need you to understand. Your own family

life was floridly mad. Your father was an alcoholic; you rarely spoke about him in detail. For a long time, I had assumed this was an issue of trust, that I needed to win your confidence. But after the initial shocking statements, nothing followed. When you spoke about it, you were frank but also summary. I had no sense of it. Years passed and the revelations never came.

You arrived at university like the survivor of some war. You were impulsive. People liked that about you. They said you lived for the moment; they did not see that you were marooned there, unable to think about the past. Each day was like a miraculous conception.

Exams made you nervous. Despite being one of the strongest in your year, you assumed that you would fail each assessment and visualised the meeting in which your supervisor would send you home. Sometimes, you worried that you would die in your sleep, or that time did not truly exist and so, from certain perspectives, you were already dead. It was easy for others to laugh this off as symptoms of a neurotic overachiever. They never saw the fear, or the radical uncertainty. You lived in a world where B did not necessarily follow A, where two plus two could equal anything.

You could be so defensive, so quick to argue, even with strangers. You must have learnt something from your adolescence, the way the body learns to defend itself against a virus. It keeps traces of those disturbances deep in the marrow, deep in the cells, and rallies fast the moment intrusion is detected.

Once, we had been walking home from the library. You dropped your Diet Coke in the street and a stranger watched you stoop to pick it up as it spurted and foamed. I cannot recall if he laughed, or even smiled, but you seemed convinced.

'Did you enjoy that?' you demanded, rounding on him.

'Huh?'

You stared with the eerie focus of contempt. Then you muttered something that I didn't catch.

'You wanna say something?' he asked, chest inflating, shoulders cocked back.

'I said "You're a fucking psychopath".'

His mouth dropped open. Likely, he had never been insulted with such conviction. And you wanted him to meet your challenge. You craved altercation. For a long moment, it looked as though you might hurl the can. The young man, sensing danger, backed away.

That's when I knew for sure, you had something inside you. And we had to get it out, before it ate you alive.

We returned to London after graduation. By then you had been estranged from your father for a few years, but still flinched every time we found ourselves near the City. Just being in his neighbourhood was enough to make you shrink. It was my idea to end this separation. I wanted you to experience his impotence. You once lived with monsters. But that was before me. I would throw open the cupboard door. I would crouch with you, investigate the shadows beneath your bed. I would do anything to show you that the bogeyman was no more. There was just us.

Of course, you resisted.

'I don't want to give him a second chance. I don't even want him to be changed, or better.'

'He won't be changed,' I said confidently. In my own way, I felt I knew your father. Just as I knew Raph.

'Then what's the point?'

'The point is to show him how *you* have changed. You're powerful now, and he is not.'

You understood what I meant by this. We had graduated just after the recession; opportunities were scarce and money was tight. But we had a clear sense of our power. We could never explain our greatest feats to others, but I believe they could sense it. Raw power. Animal power. Power to do what others only dream of.

You made the arrangements. One night in late September, we agreed to visit him for dinner. Situated in an expensive development between the Barbican and Moorgate, his home seemed too young for him. The entrance was all glass and chrome, and the reception area was sparse aside from a few ferns spilling from concrete pots. If anything, these touches seemed to embellish the emptiness. The corridors smelled of new carpet and fresh paint. A cheap vision of luxury, one which offers gleaming surfaces but no style. The perfect pied-à-terre for a tasteless banker.

The man who greeted us had thin, grey hair. He wore old-fashioned spectacles and a treacle smile. That first impression was always going to be an anticlimax. Your father was no fool; he understood your expectations and he knew how to disappoint.

'This means a lot to me,' he said as we entered. 'I can't tell you how much I've been thinking about you. Every day, really.'

Yet there was no evidence of thought. He had not bought any food. His fridge was bare save for two cases of beer. He explained, vaguely, that some delivery had not come; he had developed a dangerous nut allergy and now only shopped at specialist retailers.

Nuts, I thought, and that was all.

Though muted, the TV was left playing. Before we arrived, he had been watching sports. His eyes darted to the screen and I could tell, from the way his face occasionally brightened, that his team was winning.

He drank six beers while we were there, often yanking his shirt dramatically and injecting himself. I had known he was diabetic. Insulin is very dangerous. I wondered how frequently he made mistakes.

By his fifth beer he grew lachrymose, talked about the difficulty of estrangement, at times abruptly stopping, as if to fight back tears. Still, we were witnessing the dress rehearsal, not the perfected act. There were moments when he did not know where to take his performance.

'How have you been keeping?' you asked.

'Well!' he replied automatically; he was a man of impulsive vanity. He always wanted to be considered 'well'. Then he seemed to remember. 'As good as can be,' he added. 'It's been lonely.' His mouth bent into a frown, which was to suggest forbearance, stoicism.

For most of the evening you were quiet. I saw you as you would have been all those years ago, before you'd learnt to fend for yourself: subdued, voiceless. Of course, your father was content to hold court. He spoke expansively, providing a driven monologue on any number of topic – the media, his allergies, politics, his diabetes, television. I struggled to keep my attention from drifting. From time to time, I cut in. He allowed this, but as he listened he had the anxious expression of someone holding their breath.

'I actually think young people are incredibly engaged, politically, that is…' I said. He had been giving a long and confusing speech about apathy. I was speaking simply to stay awake.

'Of course, obviously…' he said. 'But the problem is they've stopped giving a fuck. They've checked out. They'd sell their votes for clicks on social media… And it's a false economy. A complete fucking false economy.' He had a habit of this. Of agreeing with you, before saying something that absolutely refuted the substance of your argument.

Towards the end of the night you looked frail. It was time to leave.

'Thank you so much for having us,' I said on your behalf.

'Don't mention it! I hope I haven't bored you too much.'

'Not at all.'

'And I'll see you guys again? Next week maybe?'

'Well, it's pretty hectic next week,' I said. 'We'll have to check our schedule.'

'Your schedule,' he repeated coolly. And then he turned to you. 'I have to say, if this is all I get, I'm going to feel a little short-changed.' He forced a laugh. 'You know, I didn't send you to Cambridge for nothing. It wasn't cheap.'

The comment startled me, that swift elision of boundaries, as if Cambridge were his accomplishment. As he spoke, his voice altered, discovered some sinister new register. Then, just as quickly, he became genial once more. Your fingers tightened around your bag, then you made a conscious effort to loosen your grip, to appear relaxed.

'Thanks again,' I said. At this point, he'd made no indication of movement. It was as if the conversation had reset and we would never get out.

'No need for thanks,' he said. 'As my daughter will probably tell you, I'm always hungry for audience meat.'

An alarming turn of phrase, said with a chuckle and faux self-mockery, but apt. There was something about listening to your father that left me feeling exhausted and diminished, as if he'd taken chunks out of me.

'It was just so great to meet you,' he told me at the door. 'I've enjoyed it very much.'

Before I left, we shook hands. His was like a clamp and he watched me strangely as he gripped. At first, it seemed like he was focusing on my forehead, not my eyes. I assumed this was the effect of the booze. After a moment, I realised he was trying to determine which one of us was taller.

We walked a few blocks without speaking. I had talked with your father for hours, but it was so difficult to recall any of the specifics of what was said. Just the droning intensity, the elusive, desperate sense of being stuffed with something inimical.

'He charmed you,' you stated.

'What?'

'He charmed you with all of his flattery and his stupid spectacles and all that Mr Nice bullshit.'

'If anything, he bored me. And the way he invited us back… a bit like a threat. I think—'

'He's not a nice guy,' you interrupted. 'It's important that you understand that.'

'I know,' I said, quietly but with urgency. I realised now, seconds too late, that my tone had been too intellectual. I had treated your father as a theoretical problem; I wanted to understand how he operated to prove to you that I could figure him out. But this enquiry came at the expense of *feeling something*, the experience of seeing him again, the inarticulate dread. For you, this was the most important part.

'He's worse than anyone I've ever met. Worse than Raph.'

'I know that. Raph only happened because your father got there first.'

Something in my voice convinced you. You accepted that I understood, but seemed to suddenly deflate. Your shoulders sank.

'You must think I'm nuts,' you said, miserably.

'No more than me.'

'Just because he tells you that he votes Labour, and believes in a London Living Wage, none of that makes him human.'

'I know.'

We were no longer walking. Your eyes skimmed the darkened windows above, then fixed on one in particular. Its curtains were drawn and against the pane there was a clutter of empty planters and household flotsam. It was depressing to look at. I couldn't imagine someone living inside. But your eyes stayed locked there.

'It was like living two lives,' you said.

I watched you return home and you seemed to visibly shrink. I experienced a perverse, almost guilty satisfaction. You had never shared any of this with me before. It felt like an advancement. I loved you even more for it.

You remained quiet for a long time.

'Sometimes, when he was at his worst, I was almost relieved. Grateful. Things were so clear. He was a monster: I wasn't mad.'

'Let's keep visiting,' I said.

'Why are you doing this?' you asked, exhausted and already demoralised.

We were on one of those narrow and winding streets that gathers and holds shadows, and always remains slightly damp. The shops were shuttered, their steel surfaces marked with illegible graffiti tags and laughing-gas canisters lay discarded in the gutter. A few pubs glowed in the distance, but seemed briefly unreachable.

'Because...' I looked at the miserable street for inspiration; it seemed we were always ending up in these dire alleys, so far away from the normal pleasures that others took for granted. 'Look, I'm aware of my limitations. I'm not the guy who will charm your friends, or impress people at a dinner party or make your girlfriends jealous. You could have had that person, but you don't. I'm the guy who will always do anything for you. That's the person you chose.'

The roots of trees extend deep into the earth. There is evidence that, as they tangle with their neighbours, they exchange nutrients, messages, warnings. We too are capable of such subterranean dealings. Little more was said. But as we approached the Tube, I paused and whispered, 'We've seen off worse than him.'

You reached for my hand and I took this as confirmation.

Like the time before, we fell into a period of passivity. We went to meet your father again, and then again.

There was no routine, just that gravitational tug. We would both feel it. We might be in a pub, listening to the chatter. Perhaps some older, drunker man would catch our eye and we would say, *Tomorrow we'll visit.*

Sometimes, at night, you would sit up in bed and more memories would come. It was scary. Like vast chunks of an ice sheet breaking off, advancing towards you.

'He was always looking for that spot, you know? He was so focused...'

'What spot?'

'The bit of you that's most vulnerable.' You were quiet for a moment then smiled joylessly. 'When I was a little kid, I convinced myself it was proof he loved me. He knew just where

242

to stick the knife, where it would bleed the most. Nobody knew me like him.'

A fractured reality: his moods, his punishments were so random, in some essential way, they undermined your belief in cause and effect.

I wondered if he remembered those assaults. Did they play on his mind as he shook my hand? I doubted it. Your father still believed he was the author of truth; the past was his to amend and redraft.

By now we were living in a former council flat close to your first school, in Hammersmith. There was a brewery across the motorway. Every morning, the air would thicken with the scent of yeast; it would linger for hours. I never understood why you picked that neighbourhood, so overpriced and far from our friends. Only, on some abstract level, I intuited that you were looking for something, something that had been stashed there since your adolescence, waiting to be picked up and rediscovered.

'Did he ever... did your father ever physically assault you?'

'My mother had it worse.'

I have to admit, in your brokenness, in your damage, I saw an opportunity. We were not yet married at this point and I knew that sometimes you still harboured doubts. Perhaps this was why I could view your father so clearly; in a way we shared certain instincts.

'Let's go tomorrow,' I said.

By the third visit, he seemed to emerge. He tested you more often, judged you more overtly. It worried me that you never spoke back. You just seemed to absorb the poison instead.

On some level, you still feared him. Our memories do not age. People who are long gone linger like squatters in the recesses of our imagination, ready to pounce and assert their rights. So when he said, *That shirt's a little tight, sweetheart*, with a smile, he ruined it for you. You did not throw it away. That would have meant admitting defeat. But I never saw it again.

'My God, you *are* a little slob today, aren't you?' he said with a laugh after you spilled your tea. As you mopped it up, your hands grew clumsy.

Nervously, you began speaking of a disappointment from your day. Your internship was challenging. Your boss, quite charming during the interview, had seemed to change. His critiques were so unsparing and so public, they left you feeling raw and defeated. There were other doubts, not yet fully metabolised. The previous intern looked just like you. She had the same haircut, the same accent and style. You couldn't say why, exactly, but this gave you misgivings, made you question why you'd been hired, what exactly your boss had been searching for. Your colleagues hardly looked at you. It was as if they sensed that something bad was on its way. In fact, something truly awful was en route. That very boss did not survive the year, but of course, that's a separate story.

This was the most I had ever seen you say in your father's presence. I was taken aback. Despite all that history, there you were, still struggling to break through.

'Well, enough about me,' he said with a gleeful smirk. The look on your face – confused, humiliated, collapsed. He chuckled.

'It sounds horrible,' I said. 'But they're lucky to have you.'

'You've got this one well-trained,' he replied dismissively, disappointed.

I bit my tongue and offered a curt smile. It was difficult to dissociate like that, but people do it all the time. I imagined a surgeon's dispassion as they addressed some malignance. Emotions would only get in the way. I needed to proceed calmly, with still hands.

Each visit, he grew more confident. I was surprised he never seemed to question why we kept showing up, or what we wanted from him. Perhaps he simply attributed it to his charisma. Of course his daughter was drawn to him – this was only natural. And why wouldn't her partner wish to join? A young, hapless millennial like myself; perhaps he assumed I had come there to sit at the feet of a master and learn.

Whereas at first he'd embellished his difficulties, now he exaggerated his fortunes. He spoke about the holidays he planned to take. His favourite restaurants: Nobu and Hakkasan. *I don't care for the formality*, he'd say, affecting humility, *but the food is damn good*. He liked the fact that these places were out of our reach. He wanted to imagine us salivating as he elaborated on their signature black cod. Somehow, his dietary restrictions did not keep him from the finer things in life.

His fridge was always empty, save for a few ready meals and a stock of beer. We brought him treats – snacks and wine, antipasti we could hardly afford. We always made a point of bringing food. I'm not sure what he made of that. Perhaps he thought we were paying for his company.

35

The last time we visited, we opened the door and almost gagged. He had been burning citrus essential oils in concentrations so strong that it made our eyes water. A thick, lemony smell that suggested contamination, hinted at some industrial-scale clean-up. He was already half-cut, his senses dulled. He kept the heating absurdly high, even through it was unseasonably mild for October. We never asked him to turn it down, never let him see us sweat.

'You're later than usual,' he grumbled.

'We swung by the pub en route,' you said.

'Oh?'

'I've been promoted,' I informed him. 'Just a small pay bump,' I felt compelled to add this: he had looked at me with such sudden misery.

There was a period of rueful silence. He did nothing to conceal his discomfort. It was as if we had made a joke at his expense.

This gave you confidence. Drink made you bold.

'Aren't you going to congratulate my boyfriend?'

'Listen, sweetheart, let me tell you something. No man actually enjoys hearing about another guy's success.'

He glanced over as if expecting me to agree. I did not.

'Besides, at your age promotions *should* come thick and fast. I mean, you're supposed to be overqualified for your first job. The gap between junior and mid-level is minor, piece of piss. But there is a fucking gulf between mid-level and senior. And then to get to the board level… You'll live and die without scaling those heights.' He appeared to relax as he spoke. These words were a comfort to his own ears. 'You work in marketing?' he asked me.

'Shopper marketing,' I corrected.

'And you're content in that industry?'

'I like it, yeah.'

'Christ. Reach for the fucking grit.'

'You know,' you broke in, 'most people don't consider the life of an actuary all that exciting. Most people don't even know what an actuary is.'

'Of course they do,' he said.

'Actuary: they don't,' you replied with a slightly unhinged giggle.

'Watch it,' he said, and for a moment, I caught a glimpse of him, the man who would grab you by the hair.

'I'm just saying, you're not exactly James Bond. You've hardly lived a life of intrigue.' It hurt him. The insult and the inflection into past tense, as if he were already gone. The corners of your mouth began to twitch, the beginnings of a sudden, irrepressible smile. 'Growing up,' you continued, 'whenever people asked me what you did, I'd always say "businessman", you know, to save them the boredom.'

'You better be careful, because I can play this game too.'

'Look,' you said, with another barely suppressed giggle. It was infectious, I wanted to laugh as well. 'All I'm saying is, nobody will be lining up to read your memoir. Surely we can both agree on that?'

'I'm still relatively young.'

'By what criteria?'

He paused. And then, 'I don't want to say something I'm going to regret.'

'Like what?' The thrill of a looming crisis. We had been feinting for hours, days, months. Time for contact; it didn't matter who got hurt. We needed impact.

'Sweetheart,' he said glancing at you with pure contempt, like he could destroy you. 'Don't make me be mean.'

The injunction was saturated with threat. Just like that, you let it drop. All that momentum died in its tracks, as if an engine had failed.

You began plating up the takeaway we had brought.

'He's been at the whiskey,' you whispered when I went over to help.

'How do you know?'

'I just know,' you said. 'I knew the second we came in.'

I think I grasped it then. The stifling closeness of those early years. You could tell from a glance or a note in his voice which substances were coursing through his blood, the ominous gap between a beer or a whiskey buzz.

We were heading for trouble, but I wasn't worried. You spoke and moved so quickly and with such precision. You were seeking something. You would find it.

'How's your mother?' he asked later, helping himself to a plate of noodles.

Your body stiffened. 'She's fantastic,' you said.

A lie. You hardly spoke to your mother; you both survived your father but your relationship did not.

'I'm glad,' your father replied, clearly disappointed. 'Is she… seeing anyone?'

'Yes. This big American guy called Brad. He works in oil, I think. Of course, these days, he hardly works at all, he has other people to do that for him.'

Another lie: your mother had never remarried nor expressed an interest in dating. But he could never know. You were loyal, if nothing else.

'Sounds like she has it made.'

'She does.'

'Brad must be a real stand-up guy to get *your* approval.'

'He is.'

'Nothing like me,' he added, teasingly, but with a mawkish note of hope.

'No. He isn't. Brad is… gentle.'

He glanced at me just then. 'Huh! These days people talk about being gentle as if it's a great quality. But it's the lack of a quality, isn't it? The shadow where strength or will should be,' he caught himself. 'But then again, I'm just a jealous old fart.'

Beneath the thick citrus fumes, I could smell the blood.

You felt a brisk, clarifying rush of anger. The calm that accompanies pure rage. I had to push it further, bring the moment to a crisis.

'Let's play a game,' I said.

'What game?' he asked.

'I noticed that you have a Monopoly board on your bookshelf.'

'Oh, you noticed,' he replied, vaguely mimicking my accent.

'I think it could be fun,' I said.

He selected the dog, I the hat and you the car. Money was distributed. We played in virtual silence, beneath a mood of naked acrimony. You moved across the board, swiftly gathering property. He could not find his footing, he spent lavishly but without strategy. He poured himself tumblers of whiskey and made mistakes. His money dwindled as you built hotels, determinedly driving him towards ruin.

On the thirteenth lap, you turned to me with an audacious proposal. 'Give me your portfolio.'

'You mean team up?'

'I mean, give me your property.'

'That's cheating,' he exclaimed, in a thick boozy voice.

'It's business.'

'I said, you can't do it.'

'On what authority? You're just an old man with a dozen mortgages. Look around, I own this board. I own the park where your dog shits and sniffs arse. I own the water it drinks, the kennel where it will be put down. I own it all.'

Your voice was like a heavy freight train rolling slowly across the line.

'Do not give her your cards,' he said to me. It was a strange, growling noise.

'Give them to me.'

And, of course, I did. You are the only person I have ever feared.

'Miserable fuck,' he hollered, bringing his fist down on the board and making an earthquake in our little town. 'Putrid fucking garbage.' You smiled, because you saw him then as I did: a violent man, pathetically reduced.

Perhaps he knew, on some level, that this was the last full evening we'd spend together. When the game was cleared, when nightcaps were proposed, he changed his tack.

'There's a reason I don't play that game,' he chuckled, as if, a minute earlier he had not wished to throttle me. Once more he became the self-effacing, tentative man I'd first met. He spoke of his difficulties, as if we might be brought to pity. The real desperation was in the way he lurched from topic to topic. He was struggling with semi-retirement: he was used to being busy. He was struggling with his diet; bringing out some dry biscuits, he made a show of inspecting the label.

'I always get the sense that my dietician wants to write a paper about me,' he said, perhaps proudly. 'I respond to insulin differently than most type 1s. I'm more sensitive.'

'So you've said,' you replied in a bored voice. A voice that made him talk more quickly.

I suppose his only consolation was that he found himself profoundly interesting. His diabetes, his work, his restaurants, his loneliness: all of these things seemed to him quite exceptional.

'Have your drink,' I suggested.

'Tastes different,' he slurred.

'It tastes the same,' I stated.

He stood up and sat back down.

'Do you need help?' I asked. 'Shall I hold your glass?'

He should have heeded his own resolutions, listened to himself as he articulated the dangers he faced. His diabetes would prove fatal in the end. He died of an insulin overdose later that night. Perhaps if we'd stayed a little longer, we could have saved him. But I do not blame us. Diabetes is hard to manage, even when sober, and he had narcotics in his system as well as a bellyful of booze. In his final moments, the drugs would have hit, one last blush, one last giddy flight, before the undertow dragged him deep, deep, deep. At least he died doing what he loved.

You showed up to his funeral dressed for spring, having splurged on a white lace Chanel top that you bought on credit. Easy to justify the indulgence when you stood to inherit so much.

'I heard you get it all,' his brother said to you, his voice like an accusation.

'Yes. I do.'

Your father never took out life insurance. He hated the idea of anyone profiting from his death. For the same reason, he could never bear to write a will: you were the de facto heir.

'Pretty big break: he had a lot of cash socked away. And you barely had to talk to him. Shun him for years and you end up with a flat, the shares, the—'

'Mark, you're salivating,' you said.

He turned crimson. He was wearing such a cheap suit; it didn't quite fit.

You let him flounder for a moment, then began in an airy tone. 'Mark, I believe there's a longstanding rumour that I hate you. I don't. You were scared of your big brother. That's all. You were a scared, quiet little mouse. And I cannot hate a mouse. I can't feel anything much about a rodent.'

He didn't know what to say. Baffled, he decided to continue with his pre-prepared insult. 'I'm sure you've already got plenty of plans for his estate.'

'Yes. I plan to waste every penny of it.'

And you almost did. You spent the money with speed and contempt. I had to beg you to put just a tiny bit aside, just enough to pay our salary for a year. I only needed a year to start the business. The dream was that we could eventually work for ourselves, become totally self-sustaining.

I found a shared office space in Dalston and worked long hours. Shopper Marketing, of course, is not my passion – your father was right about that. But passion is finite and I've given all of mine to you.

36

The bus stops on a stretch of motorway. We are the only passengers to alight. Most of the original passengers got off miles ago; we have not passed a city for hours.

A sign in the middle of the road displays stats in blinking amber lights.

Forty-degree heat.

Thirty per cent humidity.

The fluid around my eyes dries so that when I blink, I have the strange sensation of skin meeting skin. Benny pours a splash of water onto the road with a flourish and watches it divide into little pebbles, hiss and turn to steam. It leaves behind no trace.

'Hot as a motherfucker,' he declares.

To our left, a beige mountain range, to our right, the Sea of Tears, the misty teal water is perfectly still. A few miles ahead, the dark silhouette of a factory. It is processing the minerals mined from the lake, churning through the landscape, emptying it. Heatwaves make the whole area wobble, as if nothing in this area has quite solidified.

We walk north, towards the hostel. Our long shadows form a broken triangle on the tarmac.

Low-flying fighter jets from a nearby compound shoot past at irregular intervals. The roar of their engines splits the air. It makes the ground shake, which makes us shriek and duck for cover. Then we laugh, relieved and slightly embarrassed.

As the jets disappear, I wonder where they are bound. For all we know, war broke out while we were on the bus. I entertain the possibility. I imagine the outside world burning while we walk along the motorway, oblivious. I imagine London, levelled. I imagine you wandering through mounds of rubble looking for food. Your skin is black with ash and filth; you are missing chunks of hair. The thought makes me so anxious I could vomit, here on the road. I look at you and you seem concerned. Possibly you are imagining me in a post-apocalyptic landscape as well. I'd like to ask, but Benny is between us and this is a conversation I'd prefer to have in private.

Along the banks of the Sea of Tears there are cautionary signs.

DANGER: PITS

They are illustrated by a drowning stick man with flailing limbs. But there are no pits to be seen, just sea and land. I imagine the ground crumbling beneath my feet and I imagine—

'This must be it,' you say, pointing to a sprawling two-storey compound.

'Huh,' Benny says. 'Bit of a downgrade.'

'I didn't book it,' you reply.

'It was the only place that was open,' I say. 'The region shuts down over summer.'

'Then why are we here?' you ask.

'Because it's a natural wonder,' I reply. My voice sounds stern, paternal; I do not like that.

'I think I prefer unnatural wonders,' you say. 'Freak shows.'

Inside, multiple fans are spinning, stirring the hot air ineffectually. The reception desk is empty but a man sits in the adjoining office studying a weighty hardback. His face is inches from the page and his leg bounces anxiously, with a rapid, canine energy. I clear my throat and he responds by moving his face closer to the text. He sighs and grips the edge of the page.

'Look at the way he's reading,' I murmur. 'It's like he's afraid the book will break up with him.'

You slap your hand against a bell on the desk; it rings so loudly that even I am startled.

He jumps from his seat. 'My Goodness! Sorry. Have you been there long?'

You answer with a thin smile.

'I get a little distracted.'

'All good,' Benny says. 'What were you reading?'

'*The Faerie Queene*. It's an epic Renaissance poem, by—'

'I fucking love *The Faerie Queene*,' Benny replies with unexpected vehemence.

'Really?' The man has thick eyebrows and enormous hazel eyes. It's the sort of face that children like, friendly, approachable. Though there is something disconcerting here; his expression lurches between distraction and abrupt, focused intensity.

'Absolutely,' Benny declares. 'I spent a whole term on it at uni. I haven't gotten round to re-reading it.'

'It's over a thousand pages. Hard for anyone with a life to find the time.'

'You seem to be making headway.' Benny leans, almost seductively, across the desk to take a look at the page.

'It's the subject of my PhD: I don't have a life.'

He introduces himself, Demir Küçük, speaking with quiet intensity. It is the type of voice forged in libraries and symposiums. He explains that he is on the seventh year of his PhD, with no end in sight. Originally, he had been studying at Anglia Ruskin University. Benny informs him that we also studied in Cambridge, that the three of us had met there, in fact.

'Really?' Demir exclaims. 'Are you guys ARU alumni as well?'

'No,' you cut in. 'We went to the actual University of Cambridge.'

Though Benny cuts you a death stare, Demir's smile does not waver. He is simply happy to meet people who understand where he has been.

'So what are you doing here?' Benny asks. 'You're a little far from England.'

'My family wanted me to come back. They thought I was… changing.' His tone is briefly dark, secretive. 'We kind of had a deal: study abroad but then return. I guess they considered an endless PhD something of a loophole.'

'You moved in with your parents?' Benny asks, concerned and empathetic towards this backward step.

'God, no!' Demir exclaims. 'My parents are a good twenty – maybe thirty – minutes up the road. I still have my independence.' It is such a paltry victory that even you glance away, embarrassed.

'And how is your research going?' Benny.

'I really don't know,' Demir replies. He sighs. 'I guess I'm having doubts. Sorry. You don't want to hear all this.'

You open your mouth to say 'No' but I reach for your wrist so you remain quiet. Benny frowns sympathetically.

'Sounds hard,' he says.

The muscles around your jaw stiffen; you stifle a yawn.

Demir looks down at the guest book and seems to remember the purpose of this interaction. But Benny is reluctant to move on. Benny likes talking about university. Just the mention of an esoteric poem and his features melt. He remembers Raph. Even if he hates Raph now, the excitement returns like a reflex.

But something else is happening too.

Demir smiles and leans in across the desk.

'What is it about *The Faerie Queen* that you like?' he asks. I'm astonished at how he manages to wrest some flirty subtext from this topic.

'I'm often looking at old texts for inspiration in my own work,' says Benny. 'I draw a lot on allegory and themes of quest.'

'You're a poet?'

'Close. I'm a musician.'

'A Spenser-inspired musician.' He glances at Benny's backpack. 'You packing a lute?'

Are they about to fuck?

'I hate to interrupt,' you break in, 'but would it be possible to expedite things?'

Demir jerks up. 'Of course. Yes. I don't even have your names...'

'We're going to need an extra room,' I say. 'Our friend here is a last-minute addition.'

'Ah. That's a little problematic. We have an excess of beds but not many rooms.'

'Like a prison,' you say.

'I don't understand,' I say.

'You've joined us at an interesting time. This place is being colonised at the moment. The Explorers are here.'

Your shoulders slump. You are familiar with the Explorers scheme, which involves young, posh people being spoon-fed a gap year and has recently become the subject of countless TikTok parodies and Substack critiques.

The programme has grown notorious due to the disjointed intentions of those involved: the organisers hoped the scheme would be the catalyst for introspection and societal change; the kids wished to party and get laid. Their 'explorations' remained strictly sexual.

Cash-rich, time-poor university students are offered an ultra-compressed spiritual journey. They are catapulted into impoverished towns or risk-assessed disaster zones, dumped there like expired aid packages, then whisked away for a week of reflection where they can meditate on their efforts. What had begun as a noble idea is now a wholly cynical enterprise. Admission to the scheme costs just shy of three grand; for every day of charity work, they spend another two on 'wellness' and 'recovery'.

This current group, Demir informs us, have been ambiguously facilitating Relief International with their irrigation efforts following last year's quake. After a week of being bussed back and forth, they've failed in their stated intention of building wells, but have managed to acquire a vast repertoire of photos documenting their attempt. Hopped-up on their own magnanimity, exhilarated from their brief frisson with disaster, they are now celebrating themselves. By day, they practise yoga and are chaperoned on hikes. By night, they party. They have learnt that life is brief.

'It's a bit manic,' Demir says. 'I imagine it's similar to one of those hotels where war correspondents convene... everyone's just sort of going for it. Except those are hotels. This is just a hostel,' he adds anxiously, compulsively, as if we might have glanced at the flaking paint, the dated posters, the industrially produced furniture, and mistaken this place for a Marriott.

'Don't they have handlers or something?' you ask.

'There should be a few Explorer reps floating around. I never seem to notice them though. I think they've largely given up.'

'So, we have no choice but to share a room?' I ask. Because Benny remains my main concern.

'Yes, but only in a semantic sense,' Demir replies.

'I don't follow.'

'We call it a "room", but it's more like a barracks. You'll see. It's a truly massive space.' He is apologetic. Of course, it's not his fault. The true cause of my problem is standing next to me and remains blithely unaware.

You don't react at all. Maybe you've achieved a saturation point and more time with Benny hardly makes a difference. Or maybe the boundaries between outrage and excitement have begun to blur. This has become a disaster. Perhaps we are a little enthralled by its scale and strangeness.

After taking our deposit, Demir turns and rifles through a cabinet to find keys.

'I didn't realise you specialised in Renaissance poetry,' you say to Benny. 'So did I.'

He grunts politely, feigns interest. His eyes are on Demir's back; he does not notice how closely you watch.

'Except I was a bit more predictable,' you continue. 'I did my dissertation on Shakespeare. *Titus Andronicus*.'

I look at you sharply and Benny freezes. Perhaps he can hear it, Aaron's last speech blasting across the River Cam.

We never mention your dissertation. We do not refer to that play.

You are watching him intently; I almost want to step between you, shield him from your gaze. There are other ways of doing this; you are testing him, but too obviously. You are picking at his brain with blunt instruments.

'I haven't thought about that play for a while...' Benny murmurs. He is certainly thinking about it now. He has a vaguely troubled look, as if performing complicated arithmetic.

'Oh?' you ask. 'But it's such a good one.' Now you have even stopped blinking.

'They're all good,' I blurt. 'It's Shakespeare.'

Demir turns back towards us, and the moment passes. Benny is able to shake off the thought. But perhaps he feels it, a lingering pressure.

We are given a tour of the facilities. The building had been constructed in the late eighties, he explains, and was originally intended to be a luxury conference centre. Sadly, the expected conference boom never came. Over the next few decades the space changed hands several times, falling into increasing disrepair with each transfer, until it was hastily sold once more, for next to nothing, to an enterprising developer with dreams of regeneration.

'Though things aren't going to plan,' Demir confides.

Demir opens the door to the communal area and we collide with a wall of sound. The whole space has been painted a shade of tangerine that is the colour of tinnitus. A game of beer pong is underway between a throng of raucous girls and shirtless teenage boys. One side has just scored, and yet everybody drinks. Dilapidated couches line the periphery of the room, on which smaller groups sit chatting at full volume. Several different songs are blasting from several different phones and a reality show is playing on the TV.

'They've only been here for a day,' Demir remarks. 'It feels longer.'

'It's like *Lord of the Flies*,' I mutter.

Benny surveys the space and replies, 'So who's Piggy?'

It gives me pause. Nobody else seems to hear.

A teenage girl knocks over a bottle of vodka. She points and laughs silently, letting the liquid spill out.

'That reminds me. You each get a free beer,' Demir cheerily announces.

More corridors. We are shown an old breakout room now used for storage. Demir wrestles with a fridge, prises out three bottles of Tuborg and passes them around. Propped against the wall is an abandoned flip chart brandishing an incomplete formula in faded brown ink,

PEOPLE = ??

You seem to consider this for a long time before roaming over. You pick up one of the markers and write 'RUIN' beneath the question marks. Behind me, Benny tells Demir that he would like to modernise the Petrarchan soliloquy.

In the far right corner, I notice a heavy metal box from which protrude a series of plastic, corrugated pipes. It looks both dated and futuristic, a 1970s sci-fi prop. Instinctively, I tap one of the pipes; it shivers.

This alarms Demir. 'Woah! Woah!' he exclaims. 'Careful, that's the boiler.'

I inspect the piping, which, in places, appears to be reinforced with duct tape.

'It's seen better days,' Demir confesses. 'It's perfectly safe, but no need to tempt fate.'

Above the boiler there is a carbon monoxide detector.

'We test it regularly,' Demir says. He assumes I am anxious. I am not anxious, I am curious. Conversely, Benny seems suddenly troubled.

'Do you lock this room at night?' he asks.

They do not. This room contains the fridge, which contains the beer, and the hostel runs an honour system. A vulnerability; one should never presume honour among strangers, or even friends.

Our bedroom is on the first floor, there are seven bunks, meaning fourteen beds in total.

'If you need anything, please don't hesitate to find me,' Demir says.

'I might grab you later,' Benny replies. 'I'd love to have a little Renaissance riff session.'

'I'd like that, too.'

They both look at each other but remain silent, tentative, hoping the other will say more.

Demir's demeanour shifts slightly. His head slides to the left. There is a fluidity of motion in his hips that seems childlike, or feminine, or perhaps just incredibly comfortable. Then it vanishes. His posture corrects itself, and he stiffens, as if his joints had been tightened with a screw. I wonder if he has spent his life like this. Caught between expectations and modes of being, enrolled and yet forgotten, his mind on Renaissance poetry, his body stranded on these arid soils. Like Benny, he inhabits himself for brief spells, then becomes someone else.

'Is there anything to do in the area?' you ask.

'There's a day spa, about twenty minutes north, where you can try out the local mud.'

Your eyes brighten.

'Maybe "spa" is overstating it,' he hastily corrects. 'The exact translation is more like "bathing facility". It's a public pool constructed over a small thermal spring. It's nice. Sweaty. But if you're expecting a proper beauty spot like Pammukale, don't, this is much more utilitarian. There is a lot of mud though, I can vouch for that.'

'A muddy, sweaty bathing pit,' you summarise. 'Do we need to pre-book?'

'You should be OK. And of course, there are some fantastic hikes through the nature reserve. But at this hour, your best option is to shelter in place.'

'It's only three.'

'Yes, but the sun is particularly intense here. From the look of it, some of you have already been pretty exposed.'

It is hard to tell if Benny is blushing because his skin is still scabrously pink, but he glances away at least.

'Ah,' you say. 'You're referring to our pet monster.'

Demir isn't sure how to respond, so he just smiles politely. It's a strange turn of phrase, but one that seems to capture Benny's new status in our lives; the intimate horror of a stranger who is always close.

After Demir leaves, you inspect the rows of lockers against the far wall. Their doors hang ajar and the locks look rusted.

'How the mighty have fallen,' you say.

'It isn't that bad,' Benny says.

'No,' I reply. 'It's only bad in a semantic sense.'

You snigger. 'I think that guy's been stranded here too long. Demir seemed *ravenous* for conversation.'

'He's cute,' Benny blurts in a strange, choked voice.

'What?'

'I said he's cool.' He turns, pretending to rummage for something in the locker behind him. I sense that there are many things he is yet to come to terms with.

'At least there are plenty of beds,' I say.

'Yes,' you say. 'If one of us gets dismembered, we could have a separate mattress for each body part.'

I look at you.

'Mattress,' you say. 'This is more like padding.'

'I think I'm going to go clear my head,' Benny says. 'If anybody needs me, I'll be on the roof.'

He leaves and we stay silent for a few moments.

'What is his obsession with roofs?' I ask.

'Sounded ominous…'

'Yes,' I reply, ignoring the fact that you are goading me. 'What's he got to think about?'

'I'm going to read.'

'Did you mention anything to him? Last night?'

'Lots of things.'

'You know what I mean.'

You collapse onto the bed and find your place in your book. You have made it clear: you do not wish to discuss Benny. My questions will be ignored or rebuffed. I ask myself what we would talk about if he were not here, but my mind stalls. Somehow, he has become enmeshed with everything, contaminating all areas of discourse.

At first, this feels like a failure, but then it is possible I have good reason to worry. He has grown bolder overnight. Somebody should be monitoring these developments and be willing to clip his wings when necessary.

You do not look up. The mattress springs articulate your every movement, each shift and adjustment. I know already that I will listen to you move all night, measure your discomfort by creaks.

I open Instagram and distractedly scroll your feed. For every photo we upload, dozens more are taken. I look at photos of you laughing; photos of brightly coloured food framed against a rustic wooden table, photos of me captured at such an angle that I appear modelesque. This version of our life feels like it is slipping. My sweaty hands leave smears against the screen.

Maybe it is not our money he is trying to thieve, but us, our lives entire.

Your breathing is deep and regular. I too should try to enjoy this respite; he will be back before long. But what is he thinking about?

'I'm going to find him,' I declare. 'Check what he's up to.'

There are moments in life that confuse the distinction between advance and retreat. I tell myself that I need to pursue Benny; I need to observe him, see if anything has altered since last night when you had him alone. Still, I notice that I move a bit too eagerly towards the door, that I even feel something close to relief as I leave you in the gloom of the bottom bunk.

You do not look up. You read your book with an expression of concern. You turn the page worriedly and chew your bottom lip.

A fire door is propped open at the end of the hall. The carpet underfoot is ratty and worn through. As I approach, I can hear muttering, faint and rhythmic. He is singing to himself. He is singing about himself.

'Born with nothing but my mother's regret.

My only purpose in life: to service a debt.'

I know for a fact that Benny grew up in Acton and was privately educated.

He is hunched and scribbling, facing the desert beyond, looking to the empty blue sky for inspiration. I watch, breathing softly, my cheek pressed against the warm metal of the door. His voice falters, fades away, then returns with vehemence.

'Nike, Reebok: brands keeping us so distracted,

Consumerist concerns: a plague we've all contracted,

Rappers banking mad bill, blow it all on a grill,

Their threads stay fresh but their spirit is ill.'

He loses a few syllables and tries the line again.

I sit down, lean lightly against the door and listen to Benny compose. He experiments with accents and emphasis. He walks through some of the lines slowly, discovering their shape. At times, he seems to take pleasure in his creation, his voice climbs a few triumphant decibels and his intonation is crisp. Later, it fades to a defeated whisper; I hear him grunt with frustration. I hear him admonish himself.

The track itself is strikingly tedious. Beneath its tone of righteous indignation, its message is so inoffensive that you could imagine it being played in cafés or waiting rooms.

'Feelin' so low, I just wanna have fun,

Keep it solo, just give up and run,

Something, something, gotta fight

And Heaney was right: this pen is my gun.'

The reference to Seamus Heaney is one of several literary allusions dotted throughout the verse. His approach is intellectualised without necessarily being intelligent.

There is a point in every horror when the beast is finally revealed, all costume and bad CGI, and we realise it was unworthy of our fear. And at that moment, we are awash with relief and disappointment. Perhaps there is trepidation too; we will have to find something else to be afraid of.

I listen for almost twenty minutes as the song takes shape. He guides me through a maze of conceits and extended metaphors that leave almost no impression at all. I forget the lines as he utters them; I forget them before he utters them. I begin to understand Benny's lack of success. He uses music not to express emotion, but to constrain it. His art is not an exposure, it's an elaborate disappearing act.

Quietly, I rise to my feet. The door creaks as I move away from it. Benny stops abruptly, but then resumes, perhaps imagining the sound to be nothing more than the breeze.

Our dorm smells of wet ash. You lie with a damp compress pressed to your forehead and your book folded over your stomach.

'I don't think we have to be worried,' I say.

'Oh?'

'I mean, Benny has no interest in using us for his music. His main target appears to be late-stage capitalism.'

Your lighter clicks.

'You shouldn't smoke so many of those.'

'Why not?'

'Your teeth will turn yellow and your lungs will turn black.'

'Good. I want to appear as my authentic self.'

I wait for more. Instead, you glance over, smile politely and let your eyelids droop.

I'm hungry and you have food. I want to surrender and I want to attack.

'I'm sorry,' I say.

'For what?'

'Whatever it is. Whatever I've done.'

'I'm not sure what you're talking about.'

'You've been punishing me. Since we arrived in this country.'

You pause and then answer carefully, 'Not everything is about you. When you live so closely with another person, it's easy to confuse things. But really, we're all on our own journey.'

'Yes…' I say, though I don't agree with it. We are on the same journey, marching in lockstep towards the same destination. 'I'd appreciate it if you tried a little harder to respect the rules.'

'Oh my God.'

'It's true. We have rules. We don't share certain things with others. We don't get that close.'

'You have a habit of writing these rules after the event. So they're not really rules; they're descriptions.'

I sit on a bunk facing away from you.

'Maybe I should bring Benny in here,' I say. 'Tell him you're keen to hear him perform. I can be cruel as well.'

'I'd be happy to listen to his new work.'

'You wouldn't last ten minutes. It's torture.'

'You exaggerate.'

'Death by a thousand pentameters.'

There is a silence so profound it feels architectural, as if this whole room were built around it. And then I break it.

'*I miss Raph's dick as if it were my own,*' I say, pastiching Benny's voice with eerie precision. You look at me.

'Damn, I'd give my right arm just to hear that boy groan.'

Even from this distance, I sense your pupils dilate. Ugliness, like violence, is thrilling.

'What a terrible sitch to be so alone.

But what have we here?

It's Raph's ex-bitch.'

Your lips part and I approach.

'She seems real nice, but her blood's real cold.

She acts like she's hot, but she looks kinda old.'

You flinch at that. Crow's feet form around your eyes as if I have aged you by magic. I feel possessed. I feel Benny's hunger in my teeth and tongue. I feel your rage in my throat, as tough and as definite as my own jugular.

'Hey! Maybe we can run away, live off payday loans.

Spend our days rememberin' his cum face, his moans.

Maybe there's some bit of him left, on her skin, her breath.

I'll take what I can get.

I'd fuck that dead boy's bones.'

Your eyes register true shock and I am on the brink of kissing them. You want me too. I have found an artery, nerves, something vital.

'Hey guys.'

I freeze. Benny is centimetres behind; I hear him rifling through his locker.

'Hello, Benny,' you say brightly. I look at you, not him. I watch as you try to ascertain how much has been overheard. You smile but your eyes are steady, assessing.

'I'm gonna head downstairs for a while, meet some of the others,' his voice is quiet, emptied of its bravado but also everything else.

'Sounds good. We might come and join you if that's all right,' the cheer in your voice scans like an admission of guilt.

You make a quick movement with your mouth, a sort of contraction, then nothing more is said. I realise you are telegraphing some apology, that you and Benny have entered into a brief, private covenant. For a moment, I feel I don't know you at all.

37

The Tangerine Room smells of hormones and fresh sweat. Some of the Explorers have retired to their beds for a nap; those that remain look as though they have been awake for weeks. Demir is making coffee in the kitchen. His edition of *The Faerie Queen* and a book of criticism take up a third of the countertop.

Benny is sitting in a circle of teenagers. They compare their humanitarian achievements. They tell him how they almost built a well. He tells them how he almost taught his students irregular conjugations. Everyone is satisfied with their efforts and humbled by the enormity of their mission. Somehow, in a short space of time, Benny has earned their reverence. They gear their comments towards him and he presides over the discussion like a sage.

Now they talk of travel. From time to time, Demir glances over, hoping to catch his eye. Benny looks at nobody in particular, but I feel he is watching me.

The boys in the group all profess an interest in Japan.

'Japan is cool,' Benny says.

'You've been?'

'Course. You need a lot of money to do it right. These days I think it's all about South Korea.'

A girl in the group begins a long and confusing anecdote about a K-Pop band. She laughs nervously at her own jokes; the story lacks any point or natural conclusion so her sentences alight but never seem to land. Benny stays patient, nodding at intervals, I have to admit, he is good with kids. But I can tell he's not fully listening.

I remain in his peripheral vision. I pluck a random book from the communal library and pretend to read.

Another says they are planning to go backpacking after university for an indefinite period of time.

'You have to be careful,' Benny warns, his voice oddly severe. 'You meet a lot of fucked-up people on the road.'

'You meet fucked-up people everywhere,' a girl rejoins.

'Yeah,' a boy adds, 'there's this psycho in my Econ class who actually—'

'I'm being serious,' Benny interrupts and the others fall quiet to let him speak. 'I'm not talking about "*psychos*" or creeps at a bar, I'm talking about people who are really, genuinely, fucked-up. The people who are wired differently.'

Demir is watching Benny with obvious curiosity. The others sit in anticipation, but Benny wavers, weighing whether to go on. Of course he will go on. He has a performer's instinct: makes them beg for it.

'Sounds like you have someone in mind...' the girl prompts.

'Maybe,' he says. He begins carefully, speaking the way a chess player moves. 'There was this guy in Budapest. Nobody really knew who he was, a friend of a friend of a friend, that sort of thing. Anyway, he gave me the creeps from the very start. He was always sort of uncomfortable, never drank with us, never wanted to go out clubbing. That said, he never broke off on his own. It was like he was taking notes, every time I looked up he seemed to be watching me.'

I quickly look down at my book. I stare at the meaningless pile of letters and try to appear intrigued. The hair at my temples is itchy and moist. Benny continues.

'A girl in our group got assaulted by a taxi driver. I did my best to help, but she was distraught, a total mess. While she was at the police station the creep made me a cup of coffee. He'd never done that before. And while I was drinking it, he kept asking me questions: what happened? How long did it last? How did our friend seem? What *exactly* did she say when she told me? I realised it was the first time I'd seen this guy smile, the first time he actually seemed like he was holiday.'

I keep my eyes trained on the page but the words are blurry and unfocused. It occurs to me that I'm yet to turn a page, but I don't want to do that now, in the silence that follows Benny's tale.

'Seems like you're being a little harsh,' a boy says. 'His crime is what? Smiling?'

'Smiling was his tell. People like that conceal themselves. It's all they do. They sit there, trying to blend in. They're just reading the room. Reading everything about it. They love to read.'

I shift my thumb and the cheap ink smears beneath it. I glance up, involuntarily, and Demir is looking at me. He glances away.

'At least you have good instincts,' a girl remarks. 'I always end up with such arseholes.'

Benny chuckles, a little sadly. 'I don't. I have made so many mistakes.' His voice carries a new quality I can't quite parse. 'I often get it wrong. Of course, there were rumours about this guy, I should have listened. Apparently he killed his own cat. Imagine that. Imagine killing an innocent animal, for no reason at all.'

I choke on my own spit and sputter so loudly the whole room turns.

Benny stops for a beat. And then he calls my name. 'You all right over there?' he asks.

'Quite.' My voice is stiff, I am catching my breath. I do not look up, but I know they are all paying attention. I feel their eyes.

'You're together?' a girl asks, incredulous. Benny is cool and I am not.

'Course. I'm lucky this time. I get to travel with friends.' He is genial and bright. If he has raised a threat, he's dismissed it

271

just as quickly. It is possible that I have underestimated him. He senses things.

'This conversation is a bit of a bum-out isn't it?' he says. 'Why don't we play a game?'

'Like what?' the girl asks.

'Never Have I Ever?' It's as if he's whispered it in my ear. Benny is onto me. Unrelentingly close. I urge myself to call his bluff, look up, and meet his gaze.

In this light, his skin looks like worn leather. Flanked by adolescents, he is briefly formidable. Now, this is his holiday, his rules. I hate him with impotent passion.

'I'd get in on that,' Demir says.

They link eyes. I seize the diversion, leap to my feet and retreat from the room.

'Where are you off to?' Benny calls.

A tactical withdrawal, I think. 'Back in a minute,' I say.

'I want you to play,' he says. 'I bet you could shock us. I'll bet you've done all sorts of stuff.'

38

In the reception I sit and wait, listening to the occasional clap of laughter from the adjoining dorms. Young people drift in and out, trailing deodorant and body spray. Girls criss-cross between the dorms and showers, hair wrapped in towels, their skin still damp. There is a pulse in the air. Evening approaches.

A girl sits at the foot of the stairs, positioning herself in such a way that others must squeeze past. Her flawless skin is glossy with serum, her dress very tight. She sighs; she is dramatically sad.

Her friend discovers her with alarm. 'There you are! Babes, what's the matter?'

'I'm thinking of Tarik,' she states in an almost-pout.

'Tarik?' the other says, her lips bend in reflexive sympathy. But she thinks and nothing comes. 'Wait, who is Tarik?'

'The little farmer boy,' she answers with a creep of irritation, as if her line partner has fluffed the scene. 'The one who lost his sister,' she prompts. 'In the earthquake.'

'That was Burak.'

'I just wish I could have done more,' she says, ignoring the correction. And who can blame her. The name is not important. The specifics are neither here nor there. Only the image. Only the ineluctable photo of her comforting a bewildered, still trauma-tised child, or playing a dazed game of catch, or embracing his friends with both arms, their little bodies scattered on either side of her like petals.

'You can't put that on yourself,' her friend states. 'You did literally everything you could.'

Oh, to exist among those two-dimensional planes, where a feeling is as brief as a hashtag, as transient as a morning scroll.

You roam down the stairs, head elsewhere, notice me and startle.

'What the fuck are you doing there?' you ask.

'Benny is acting up,' I say. 'He's plotting something.'

'Right. So you're cowering,' you reply with a faint note of contempt. 'Please, can we not be the creepy ones? I just want one night off. That's all.'

I begin to protest, 'We're not—'

'You look incredibly creepy,' you state.

'Pineapple,' I hiss. Your face clouds briefly, then you grasp my meaning. We do not have safe words: we are always relatively safe. But we have the opposite. We have codes that prompt incipient danger.

'No,' you say.

'It doesn't work like that.'

'Veto,' you reply. That has never happened before, so for a moment I'm at a loss as you wander into the main room.

Benny's circle has disbanded now. The young people have splintered into small groups of two or three, and talk to each other with drunk intensity. Jenga pieces are scattered on the floor, there are wet patches on the sofa from spillages, and a Nintendo game blasts from the TV.

'I guess I better get to work,' you mutter.

Benny and Demir sit at a small table piled with board games, they are drinking wine and Demir is mostly listening. His expression is mildly concerned.

You take a seat and glance around with impatience.

A boy of about nineteen strides into the room. He is

unnaturally thin, his face mottled with acne, but he has a hickey on his neck and the bearing of a young Caligula. He takes his place among two of his friends and describes a scene of astounding perversity. They gawp and celebrate and obscure my view of Benny.

Your eyes land on the girl. She sits on the floor assembling a puzzle. Everyone in this place wants to be seen, but she craves the opposite. She makes herself small. At first, she is easily overlooked, but once noticed, it is impossible to tear your eyes away.

She stares at the pieces of the puzzle with an expression of agonised absorption. The boys begin to yell and laugh, *You're fucking sick*, one of them happily exclaims. She does not look up. I realise that she, like me, like you, has practised this before. She is zoning them out, willing them into non-existence.

'You've made a lot of progress,' you say.

The girl does not reply.

'I've never really enjoyed puzzles,' you remark.

'Nor do I,' she says.

'Then why…'

'Because everyone here is disgusting.' The girl has a loud, factual voice.

'This is based on…'

'The number of times I've been invited to give a hand job.'

'That does sound rough.'

She snaps a small corner piece into place. The periphery is almost complete but the inside is a mess: a few shards of scenery, a glimpse of a tree or fern and nothing more.

'Aren't there any nice girls here?' you ask.

'The girls are even worse.'

'How old are you?'

'Nineteen.'

'A tough age.'

'They said that about eighteen.'

'Eighteen is tough too.'

'They said it throughout the entirety of my adolescence.'

'Look, it stays bad for a long time.'

From the way you look at her, I can sense that you are not motivated by boredom or idle interest.

'When does it get good?' she asks and is trying to be blasé, but there is a little note of longing that makes her sound her age.

'I'll tell you when they tell me.'

'If you're still waiting, then I'm in for a long ride.'

She has called you old and it has made you smile.

'The teens, the twenties, it's all a horror show. I can't say anything conclusive about the thirties, but the early forecasts are troubling,' you say. 'Sorry,' you add.

'It's OK. I appreciate your honesty.'

You like young people. You understand their problems in a way that other people our age cannot. Their terror makes sense to you. Their despair seems rational and coherent. Occasionally, you wonder if you should have become a teacher, but we both know that is impossible; you'd only encourage their worst instincts. You are incapable of the necessary hypocrisies for that sort of work. Still, you must be flirting with the idea even now as you watch this girl.

'Have I depressed you?' you ask. 'I just didn't want to give you false hope.'

'Don't worry about it. I've got a pharmacy's worth of Xanax in my room, so I'm prepared for hard truths.'

You say nothing to that. Xanax is hard to come by.

'My parents think I'm a delinquent,' she says after a moment.

You shrug. 'Maybe they're right.'

'They want me to be a lawyer.'

'Don't do that.'

'Sometimes I think it would be easier, having your whole life laid out for you in a long, flat path.' She stretches her hand over a plane of puzzle. 'Anyway, that ship has sailed.'

'You're still young enough, if that's what you really want.'

'Yes, but I have a record now. Petty theft. My parents can't understand it. They give me a generous allowance. Always have.' She squints at the broken image, then continues, imitating their voices. 'Why would *you* steal a sports bra? You don't even exercise.'

'Do *you* understand it?' you ask.

She pauses, 'I thought I did,' she answers in a considered tone. 'I kind of do it for the rush. And there *is* a rush, a kind of Ritalin focus. But now I think I do it for the relief. When you step out of the shop, the feeling is just... gorgeous. It's like, I got away with it. You know? for once I got away.'

You do know. You nod, almost sombre with understanding.

'And then there's just the simple relief of being a fuck-up, of letting yourself fall off the tightrope.'

'You're too young to be a fuck-up.'

'I'm growing into it nicely.'

You sit and regard her tenderly, the way a sister might. How do you find these people? Water seeks its own level. You too have a long history of petty theft. At supermarkets, you'd scan the wrong items at self-checkout, buying Pink Ladies at Braeburn prices. In coffee shops, you'd sometimes take a snack while the baristas were distracted, consuming it in front of them as they made your coffee. As if you wanted to get caught. It irritated me. Eventually I intervened.

You didn't do it for the thrill, but for a revenge of sorts. The world had taken so much and you were reclaiming its debt, pound by pound.

My hand drifts over my front pocket and I remember the cash that seemed to be missing this morning. For the first time, it occurs to me that you could be the culprit; that, in your eyes, I have blurred with the world at large, all those people who take.

'Why did you come on this trip?' you ask. 'You don't seem like the others.'

The girl glances up and smiles. The effect is powerful, a burst of unexpected sunshine. You have seen something about her, recognised her, and she is grateful.

'I thought it might be meaningful. They said it would be meaningful.'

You stiffen and become your age.

'Never, never make that mistake again,' you say and even I'm struck by the harshness in your voice.

'I'm not… Obviously I won't be coming back.'

'Never rely on someone else to provide you with meaning.'

'It's not exactly—'

'You'll be waiting your entire life.'

'OK.'

'And they'll sell you something you don't want anyway.'

'I said, OK.'

The suddenness of your conviction must confuse her. She rolls her eyes, trying to hide her embarrassment behind a surly gesture. But her face is downcast.

Two pieces click into place, but they do not, as yet, connect to the larger picture..

'Are the activities on this trip mandatory?' you ask. You connect a side piece to a corner piece.

'Not for this part. There's a hike tomorrow but I think I'll bail.'

'Good. We're going to that spa, we'll take a dip in the Sea of Tears, maybe try out the mud… Why don't you join us?'

'I'd like that,' she says.

'Good.'

'I'd actually really like that,' she says, her voice like a hiccup.

I glance over; Benny and Demir have snuck away. You are down on your knees, shuffling closer to your new friend, while I stay disconnected, floating between.

You talk to the girl, whose name is Stella, for at least an hour. She answers your questions candidly; she doesn't flinch at your prying. In fact, she seems as fascinated by her past as you are, and can describe it objectively. I find myself growing oddly jealous of the girl, who is able to discuss herself with such ease and can adapt so quickly to your way of thinking.

I wonder if I am supposed to be feeling envious, if that is precisely your point. I wonder if the girl, like Benny, has been carted out as a demonstration. You are frustrated, impatient. You talk to Benny because he knows how to talk to you. Granted, he speaks in a dialect you find grating, sentimental, indulgent, imprecise. But at least he speaks.

Only in certain moments do you let yourself remember. I have learnt a whole language for you. You remind yourself that I come from a place of deep silences.

39

We have walked nearly a mile to the petrol station. It is dusk and the whole landscape is painted in Martian hues of mulberry, salmon, streaks of fuchsia. Beside us, the vast body of water makes no sound or movement, just silently diminishes hour by hour.

'Demir's nice, isn't he?' Benny asks.

'He's nice,' you confirm.

'I never usually talk like this,' Benny says. 'Usually, I'm sort of on the down-low. When you're bi, you learn to keep things to yourself.'

'So what's changed?' Your tone is guarded.

'I'm not sure exactly. It's this trip. I feel like making a fresh start.'

Your voices sound far away, muffled by the wet air.

Darkness descends. The kiosk's neon lights switch on and each letter is surrounded by a halo, faint as an apparition, as if the sign were haunting itself.

'I'm having fun,' you state, objectively. 'This wasn't such a bad idea after all.'

'You should have seen your face,' Benny says to me. 'When we stepped into that hostel. You looked like you'd been dropped into a Third World slum.'

'It looked different in the photos,' I say.

'Things always do,' you say.

'This is real travelling,' Benny says.

Why is he here? Demir has offered to make him dinner, so he doesn't need the supplies. Not that there was much to be had at the shop; our meal consists of a box of dates and a few bags of ketchup-flavoured Lay's.

We found Benny on the roof, drinking beers with Demir, and felt as if we were interrupting. When you mentioned that we were going out, he froze, briefly torn, then decided to join us. Perhaps it's pure malignance. Maybe he can't bear to afford me a moment alone with my wife.

A bat appears overhead and dances madly in the emerald light, then merges with the darkness.

'I'm all dried out,' you say, reaching for the water bottle only to discover it empty. The long pauses between speaking make all of our comments feel loaded.

'He has such a creative approach to academia. You know? He's got an artist's mind.'

Or maybe Benny is simply parcelling out the pleasure of this new romance, subjecting himself to this brief separation so that he can dream about Demir and their imminent reunion.

'Perhaps you two will be a power couple,' I say.

'You might be jumping the gun a little…'

'A Spenser scholar and an aspiring musician. You'll be eyeing up mansions in no time.'

'And what's your talent?' Benny asks. 'Brooding?'

He despises me. So maybe he is here for your benefit, trying to spare you my company.

There is a beat of silence and then we both laugh to diffuse the tension.

'I have lots of discreet talents,' I say.

'Mate, take it from a gay dude; discreet is the last word I'd apply to you.'

The comment takes us both aback; just a moment ago he was bi. Things proliferate quickly in the heat. Benny blossoms. He flourishes. And I believe this has something to do with you. I also believe that it comes at my expense. But the night is warm and my thoughts are clumsy and I cannot gain a precise sense of things. What did he mean by calling me indiscreet?

You take a selfie and laugh. Your whole body is wilted across the picnic table. You manipulate your phone using your wrist and thumbs, the rest of you stays limp, your arms draped.

'My camera is so blurry,' you say. 'This looks like a still from a soft-porn film.'

'Let's see.'

You turn your screen to us and we view your face through a fleshy mist. Your collar bones are exposed, giving the illusion of nudity. Behind you, a wall of black.

'I want to try,' Benny says, yanking down his T-shirt.

You take the photo and cackle. 'What a stud.'

The humidity gives his skin a post-coital sheen; there is an intensity in his eyes that sits along the margins of curiosity and aggression.

'My turn,' I say.

'Take off your shirt,' you reply.

'What?'

'Your collar is too high. It ruins the impression.'

I take off my shirt and pose.

'Brilliant,' you say. You cackle again and take another shot.

'I would,' Benny says, in the voice of a lecherous construction worker.

He is joking. But the flattery makes me bold. I run my fingers through my hair, I glare, I caress my bottom lip.

'OK, now the cast photo...'

Our bodies press. A twist of limbs. Our eyes are primed on the screen, we pout, and pose, and make lewd suggestions with parted lips. I feel skin and I'm not sure to whom it belongs. Soft hairs move along my skin and tangle with my own.

'These are great,' Benny says.

The photos are confusing. Our bodies are arranged in such a way that Benny's arm appears to connect to my shoulder and your leg emerges from his waist. We have to stare at the image and reconstruct where one begins and the other ends.

'Let's go for the money shot,' you reply.

The bat appears again, then vanishes. I realise my arm is still resting on Benny's shoulder, my fingers skim his neck. He looks up with curiosity. His eyes are gentle and searching. Perhaps he's wondering if this touch was shy or accidental. For a moment, you too seem uncertain. You want something that you didn't expect. You crave a surprise, something new. You want to know it's possible. And Benny is malleable. He can be twisted just as our bodies now twist.

And I feel like the bat, suspended in the eerie glow. I wrench myself from Benny with such force that he startles, then seems to blush.

'I think we should head back,' I say, my voice granite.

40

> Hello mate. Hope the holiday is going well... Let me know when you have a few minutes. Would be good to catch up. Px

I read Peter's text several times with a growing sense of dread. He has never struck such a tone of polite restraint. In good moods, his texts are littered with brazen hyperbole and outlandish typos. In bad moods, he disappears, saying nothing at all.

Our dorm is musty and dark and I have hardly slept. Benny came in from his date with Demir some time around three, crashing across the room and muttering to himself. Then, at four, we woke again. It should have come as no surprise that Benny snores.

'It's like he's suffocating,' you whispered to me in the dark. Your eyes were white and imploring.

'If only.'

The Explorers are already up. Six are piled onto the sofa and the floor, staring blankly at a TV like a pack of resting lions. Somewhat inexplicably, they are totally engrossed by a programme in which middle-aged British couples plan and execute garden extensions. At the kitchen bar, Demir is explaining to two others that he intends to take some time off. They do not pretend to listen.

'...The fact is, I've been staring at this dissertation for so long, that I can't see it any more... I can't tell the wood from the trees. So, I'm giving myself a holiday. If anything, it will benefit the work,' he says this emphatically, as if expecting someone to protest. But the teenagers simply pour their sachets of instant coffee into mugs and shuffle along.

'What inspired this little holiday?' I ask.

Demir is surprised when he hears me.

'Academia is a creative discipline. And creativity requires moments of conscientious pause.'

'That phrase sounds familiar,' I reply, dimly recalling one of Benny's exhaustive accounts of his own process. 'I don't know if I would base my work ethic on the teachings of an aspiring rapper.' I'm not sure what I'm seeking here. A footing, maybe.

'I think Benny works incredibly hard,' Demir replies, curtly.

'Of course.'

'Artists are always honing their craft, always gathering material. Even if you can't see it.'

'You two were up late last night.'

'We had a lot to discuss.'

I have the distinct impression that they talked about me. I know better than to press the point. Just as I turn to leave, Demir blurts, 'In fact, we were thinking of heading up north tomorrow, a little camping trip.'

He watches me, his face a strange alloy of hope and defiance. I'm not sure why he has disclosed this information, but I imagine Demir has been in this desert too long, enduring endless, unpunctuated shifts with only a dead man's verse for company. He has had good news. He has an urge to share it, even if he does not like me, even if he does not care, actually, what I think.

I step outside, into the immense heat. The landscape smells faintly of sulphur. As we drink the water here, our skin will smell of it too; it will ooze from our pores, into our clothes, give us demonic auras.

You emerge with your friend from yesterday, both of you wearing shades. She is chewing gum and you are lighting a cigarette. Your skirt is pleated and your nails are bright red.

You blow smoke from the corner of your mouth. Benny is close behind; as he exits the building, I hear him call out farewells to the young people inside,

'Safe, safe. I'll catch you when I'm back, yeah? We can spit some bars...'

With every hour, his popularity seems to grow. It doesn't surprise me, exactly, but it confounds my sense of right and wrong: Benny should not be liked.

'Are we ready?' Stella asks.

'I'm staying here,' I say, surprising myself.

'What?' you ask. 'Why?'

'This place will be deserted,' the girl says. 'The others are going for a hike.'

'I'm counting on that. I've got a headache.'

Benny says nothing, he's probably resisting an urge to high-five you.

'We'll be gone all day,' you state.

'I need to speak to Peter anyway. I think he has an update on the pitch.'

Hidden behind your sunglasses, your eyes can't be seen, but I'm sure you have just rolled them. Without another word, you begin walking towards the motorway.

I wait for the Explorers to leave before helping myself to their food. I make an unsatisfying sandwich from cheap white bread and packaged meat. For much of the morning, I watch Demir try to occupy himself. He is fidgety and distracted. I can almost hear *The Faerie Queen* beckoning him from the office. He continues to busy himself, tidying areas that are already clean. I pretend to check the news on my phone and to enjoy this time alone.

The three of you return early. I hear you and Benny talking loudly in the hall.

'How much could it possibly be worth?' you ask.

'It's not about that, I have years of texts,' Benny replies. 'The texts are priceless.'

You both enter the room and Benny charges straight for the couches, tearing through the cushions and making a mess.

'What happened?' I ask.

'Benny lost his phone,' you reply.

'I didn't lose it.'

'Then I'm confused,' you state.

Stella follows sheepishly behind. Her hair has fallen over her face and she shuffles to your side, but seems uncertain what to do in the presence of two bickering adults.

'What I mean is, I've never lost my phone. I've had that thing for over six years.'

'Then it sounds like this could be a blessing in disguise. Time for an upgrade.'

'It had sentimental value.'

'It's a phone.'

'And a lot of fucking notes.'

Having searched the couch he stares up despairingly. The girl feebly glances about the room, to assist the recovery effort, but her heart's not in it, she's only trying to be polite.

'Someone jacked it,' Benny announces.

'Someone jacked your ancient phone?'

'Yeah. Maybe.'

'Benny, I have an iPhone 14. Stella, yourself?'

'15 Pro,' she answers immediately

'*Very* nice,' you say. 'So, Benny, they bypassed a couple of grand's worth of tech for a brick that barely has internet capability? It doesn't add up. Unless your thief is a fellow hipster looking for an ironic statement piece.'

'That isn't why I have it.'

'Or an antique dealer?' Stella volunteers. You laugh and her whole face brightens.

'Look,' you begin placatingly, 'the most likely option is that you dropped it somewhere in the spa or on the beach. It will show up.'

'Yes, but if it doesn't—'

'Benny, it'll show up. Nobody wants your shit phone.'

This reassures him. Demir can be heard in the laundry room struggling with the dryer and Benny goes to join him. Stella loiters between us.

'Do you uh… like, want it now?'

'Later,' you say. Still, she waits. 'Class dismissed,' you say, and she takes the cue to leave.

'What's up with her?' I ask.

'She's unloading some of her medication,' you say quickly.

'You're kidding me.'

'I offered to pay. And it's only Xanax.'

'You're buying drugs off a kid, then, presumably, trafficking it back to the UK.'

'Yes.'

'We go through five security checks at the airport.'

'They have bigger fish to fry. Anyway, anything to take the edge off. He's been going crazy about that bloody phone.'

I can't help it. It makes me smile and you notice.

'He's deeply sceptical about you,' you say.

'What do you mean?'

'Don't know,' you reply, suddenly coy. 'He asked a lot of questions.'

'Like…'

'It wasn't so much *what* he asked, as *how* he asked it. I felt like I was at the school counsellor's office. He was very delicate. *Is everything OK at home… Do I have people I can talk to…* that sort of thing.'

'And what did you tell him.'

'I wasn't sure what to tell him. They were interesting questions.'

I'm too tired to play.

'I have to call Peter.'

You raise your eyebrows. 'Still haven't got round to it?'

My skin barely registers a change as I step from the stuffy reception into the sulphury desert air: the boundaries between inside and outside grow blurry.

Peter answers on the second ring. 'Hello, mate,' he says.

'Hi. You, um…'

'I called about the Ayik pitch,' he states. There is a strange quality to his voice, 'Basically, it's not happening. Just wanted to let you know, so you don't have to constantly check your emails.'

Usually when I speak to Peter, I feel the strain almost immediately. But now he is quiet, waiting for me to respond. He had simply called to spare me uncertainty; an unusual act of thoughtfulness which adds to my confusion.

'That's awful,' I hear myself say. The truth of this dawns slowly. Despite its unlikelihood, I had counted on that money. I had needed a positive sign, an assurance from the external world.

'You all right?' Peter asks.

'Did he provide any feedback?'

'He thanked you for your time… I'll admit, it was unusually curt.' When he speaks again, there is a strange, tripping quality to his words. 'Look, mate, you're really good at this. This marketing stuff.'

'I know,' I answer, bracing myself for a rambling pep talk.

'And you'll be good at other things too,' he adds tentatively.

'What does that mean?'

'Just that there's a difference between failure and letting go. Letting go can be empowering, can feel good.'

'Peter, this is just a hiccup. One pitch, that's all.'

He sighs and I can tell he slightly pities me. There is something about his attempt at kindness that is unbearably depressing. For a moment, I feel so sad that I'm a little frightened.

'Peter,' I say, in a managerial tone. 'Trust me. I have a plan. I can see what we need to do.'

He makes no reply.

'Are you quitting?' I ask, incredulous.

'We can talk properly when you get back.'

'Because that would be the stupidest fucking move you could make.'

'C'mon mate, there's no need to get hostile.'

'I do beg your pardon, Peter, I'm just a little fucking surprised. You are one of the least employable people I've ever met. What next? All you know how to do is sit and eat and snort. Not exactly marketable skills, Peter, even a pig could do that. Or a mule, maybe you could work as a drug mule.'

He takes a moment to process my rage. So do I. He begins a sentence, then stops.

I realise that I cannot picture him at all. I shut my eyes and try to imagine his face. All I see is a jagged collage of my own features, and Benny's, and your own cool eyes, grey and staring.

'Mate, be kind to yourself. OK? Everything will be fine, we'll sort it when you're home.'

We hang up. The sun sinks low and bloodies the sky. It looks enormous along the horizon.

This vessel is taking water; even the rats are beginning to jump. Peter will not be with us for long. We've lost another pitch and we have lost a founder. None of this will surprise you. Nor will it disappoint you.

The air crackles. I have a sense that important things are happening just out of sight. Everyone is growing and becoming. I remain, waiting, as the light leaves the sky.

Yet we have come too far to give up now. Benny and Peter are weak men. They believe there is a grace in falling, in submitting, only because they can do nothing else. You too have entertained thoughts of submission. But I have cured you in the past.

41

Inside, you are explaining the concept of light years to Benny and a small group of Explorers. You sit on the couch, slightly elevated, talking quickly. They are cross-legged on the floor around you, in rapt silence.

'What I'm trying to say is that out there, in Andromeda, for instance, the past is not the past. The Holocaust could be happening right now. Or the Dark Ages, 9/11, your second birthday... These things may not have even occurred yet. Theoretically, our entire history is waiting to reoccur.'

Your audience nods. As I approach, you lose your train of thought, growing self-conscious, as if I've caught you in a compromising position.

'There is a corner of the universe where you haven't been born. Your slate is totally clean, you've never made a mistake.'

'But you will,' I state, my voice like a cold draught. 'Anyway, I'm not sure it works quite like that.' Of course, once again, I'm out on a limb: my knowledge of space–time is severely limited. But I sense that these concepts affect you negatively, and we have been here before. You have sought solace in tarot cards, star signs, counsellors, meditation, always turning back to me after these hopeless expeditions, disappointed.

I do not have to remind you of these failures; you read it in my face, you hear it in my voice. I am your partner but also your witness.

'Nobody quite knows how it works,' you say, 'this is all theoretical.'

'Yes, but even so, I don't think any theoretician is suggesting that the past is literally floating around in outer space,' I chuckle, politely, to close the discussion.

'But it feels... true, doesn't it? It makes emotional sense.'

'So does fiction,' I say.

'You haven't read the book,' you insist, but quietly.

'Darling, it's a bestseller. You can pick it up at airport bookshops, along with Dan Brown and that thing about how tidy homes create tidy thoughts.'

You don't say anything. The others expect a riposte; you are the resident cosmologist and they stay enchanted by your vision. Instead, you just watch me, sensing, perhaps, that I will not let the point go. I do this because we have spent our lives progressing, so I find your conception of a circular universe ridiculous and disturbing. History is a jaw beneath our feet and it stretches wider every day. The past is gone and digested. This is the only truth you need to know. Stay with me, in the here and now, where we are alive. Just stay.

'It makes sense to me,' Benny offers. 'Sometimes it's like you can almost feel the past, I can't explain it exactly...'

'I never said my idea or my interpretation was genius, just—'

'It's nonsensical,' I state. 'That's what I'm getting at: you aren't making any sense.'

If I am being cruel, it is a cruelty you understand, bound by rules, softened through repetition. It is unlike the cruelty of the outside world, which is lawless and unpredictable and which I shield you from.

Your cheeks redden and nobody looks at you. We let it drop.

But then, 'My husband, of course, is an expert in all things.'

I stare at you, surprised that this conversation is to continue.

'He spends his day writing and writing and writing notes. Have you noticed that, Benny?'

'Um, sort of.' Then he turns to me, apologetically, and says, 'You do have a habit of jotting things down.'

'I'd say it's an obsession,' you correct.

'They're not notes. They're letters.'

'To whom?'

'To you.'

'Maybe Benny was right, my love: it's time to take up a hobby.'

I open my mouth but before I have time to speak, you have spun round to address the others. They seem to be running on a delay, they laugh seconds after you land an insult, bewildered by this new direction.

'He used to write children's stories too, if you can imagine. Horrid little fables that would make the Brothers Grimm blanch, give grown men nightmares. Of course, publishers wouldn't touch them with a bargepole.'

'I didn't write those for publication… They were for you.'

'I didn't care for them much either.'

My fists clench. I am breathing very fast.

'Drinks,' Benny announces. 'I think everyone's getting a little bit cranky, which usually means it's time for a beer.'

'I don't want a beer,' you say.

'Then a nap,' he replies. He is worried for you.

You look at me and you look at him. Your blood is up. So is mine. You've torn strips from me and you want to keep going. So do I. I want you to say more and I want to retaliate. Yet neither of us speak. We know that if we go on, we will fight until there is nothing left.

You stand and leave without another word. I wait a moment and then rise to my feet, but before I leave, Benny catches me by the arm.

'Why don't we have that drink?' His voice is calm and patronising.

'I want to speak with my wife.'

'It might just be better to give her some time to cool off. You know, give her a bit of a break.'

'Her? You want to give *her* a break?'

'Yeah, I mean, don't take this the wrong way... but you were being a bit of a cunt just now.'

'You don't know us,' I say, my voice steady as a pendulum.

'Maybe I do,' he replies, his voice inscrutable.

I follow you.

Benny pauses in the middle of the room. He looks at me and he looks at his teenage fans, who have already begun heeding his advice and are retrieving the booze. Perhaps it's a difficult choice. He can remain and get drunk with adoring juveniles, or he can follow and meddle in a stranger's marriage.

As I mount the stairs, I hear his decision.

'Yeah, yeah... I'll be right back. Just going to make sure everything's cool.'

It is Benny, I think. It is the fact that you have spent the day with him. It is the fact that he never really leaves and even in your dreams, you can hear him, smashing through the room, snoring, gulping the air with laboured breaths. It is the fact that he only wants to discuss things that hurt, the worst people, the worst days of your life.

In the dormitory you are lying on your bunk, glaring at your book. As I approach, I can see that your eyes are not moving. Your fury is expressed through your perfect stillness.

Benny is close behind.

I make an offhand remark – to myself – about the state of the room, which has not been cleaned, and Benny replies. I lie on my bottom bunk and stare at the off-white mattress above. I focus on the large brown stain that spans several slats.

Benny is talking about music. An artist he likes has dropped a new mix. He is disappointed by it. He intends to listen again.

My resentment grows. I probe the feeling the way I would

explore a rotten tooth or bleeding gums, tentative, ambivalent, curious. Maybe the three of us will be buried together. Maybe we'll even share a headstone. People will visit our grave and read through our names. *How curious*, they'll say, *how sweet*. Beneath the ground, our bodies will disintegrate and combine.

A can of Coke rests precariously on your belly. You stick a cigarette in your mouth and light it.

'I don't think we can smoke in here,' Benny says. You don't respond. 'Naughty, naughty,' Benny adds, uncertainly. You blow a smoke ring in quiet defiance. He is embarrassed. 'She can't hear me,' Benny says. 'She's back in outer space...'

You reach out and snap the plastic No Smoking sign face down against the bedside table. You do this without looking. You do not need to look, your sixth sense has been activated.

I walk over and take the cigarette from your lips and drop it into your can of Coke.

'What did you do that for?' you demand.

'You'll get us in trouble,' I reply.

'So?'

'So, you smoke too much.'

'I married my mother,' you say.

I straddle you.

'Let go of me!' you exclaim.

'No.'

'I said, let go of me,' I feel your muscles pulse. I feel the trapped energy, seeking outlet.

'No, I need to tuck you in. Mummy has to tuck you in.'

Laughter starts to ripple through your body, your flesh vibrates.

'Don't make me hurt you,' you say between these sudden giggles. 'Don't make me be mean,' you say, quoting your father.

'You can't hurt Mummy,' I reply. My face is inches from your mouth.

'Yeah? Ask my actual mother.'

I pin your wrists behind your head and speak through my teeth. 'I'll ask her when I'm done with you.'

Benny chuckles uneasily. 'You two are mental,' he says.

I grip you. I feel your hips move between my thighs. Something is taking over. Some rhythm. We are notes of music in a dreadful tune.

'This is feeling a bit Amanda Knox, actually,' he says.

We turn to him in a synchronised motion.

'Do you like true crime?' you ask. I release you, you coil round, quick, and rest your head on my shoulder, next to mine. It's looks like we have two heads. To Benny, we must appear like a hydra.

'I saw something on Netflix...' Benny says, evasively.

'We love true crime,' you say.

Yes. When one of us can't sleep, we play podcasts documenting notorious murders. A third voice in our room, tonelessly explicating barbaric acts. The forensic minutiae is oddly calming. *At 3.45 a.m., he took the body of Jessica Cuttell to the basement of Grovemore Place and removed the teeth.*

'It's not my thing.'

'Your "thing"!' I laugh.

'We're obsessed,' you say. 'My favourite story is the Batman Prowler.'

'He was never caught,' I inform Benny.

'Not even a suspect. You know, he killed seven people? In their own homes.'

'He raped even more people... I think he raped over fifty.'

'And he's still out there! When I think about that, I get so... angry. I'm desperate to meet him. I'd love for him to break into our house.'

'She is. She's even considered ways of luring him in... You know, like leaving our door unlocked, sticking to predictable habits...'

'And we've blocked out what we'd do when he got there. First, he'd break in and probably creep up behind me – that's his

MO – and I'd turn and scream and scream. And I'd say, *Please!* I'd say, *Wait! How on earth will you rape me with that! Go fetch something bigger!* And he'd realise I wasn't screaming at all, but laughing.'

'And I'd come up behind him with a cattle prod…'

'…and he'd wake up in a soundproof room, tied to a chair with black wires.'

'With tools everywhere.'

'Horrible-looking tools, with thick drill bits.'

'Brown rust.'

'Yes.'

'And I'd have a phone in my hand and I would threaten to turn him in.'

'But that would just be a joke,' you say. 'We would have zero intention of letting him go.'

'No. Otherwise, we'd have no use for the tools.'

Your fingers play delicately along my neck, your index finger roams my jugular, the gesture lingering between caress and threat. Benny is finally quiet. We watch him very calmly.

'I feel like, um—' he loses the thread and falls silent. We are patient. We let him regain composure. 'I feel like you two are making fun of me.'

'Why would we be making fun of you?' you say in a sour, disappointed voice. You want to play with Benny, but he's mewling, pathetic. It's like taking a meat cleaver to a peach: no satisfying impact, just an oozing.

'If we were making fun of you, you'd know,' I say. 'We'd start with something more obvious.'

'There's no shortage of material.'

'Yes, I mean, your life? It sort of makes fun of itself.'

'That's mean,' you say.

'Sorry, Benny.'

'But it's kind of true,' you add.

'I take my apology back.'

'Now, Benny, tell us. What would you do if you had the Batman Prowler in your basement?'

'What?' he splutters.

'You could do anything to a pervert like that. You wouldn't have to feel guilty, you'd be doing God's work. Where would you start?'

'I don't know,' Benny murmurs.

'Have a think,' you insist.

'You don't have to be so...' he begins.

'So what?' you ask.

'Nothing. I don't know what I was going to say.'

'Say something,' you demand. 'We're waiting.'

You're on your feet and moving towards him.

He flinches.

'What are you doing?' you demand.

'What?' he asks.

'Were you going to hit me?'

'You're intimidating my wife, Benny,' I say. I'm on my feet too.

I take a step, and then another.

'This isn't you,' he murmurs.

'Is it not?' you answer. 'Who is it, then? Who am I?'

He glances at his feet. His body shrinks and you take another step.

'Who the fuck am I?' you ask. 'C'mon, let rip.'

I hold back. 'Benny,' I state. 'You appear to be in a situation. Now is not the time for reticence.'

You are sitting next to him. 'Answer,' you command.

'Answer what?' he exclaims. 'What the fuck are you talking about? Fucking Prowler. Fucking "who am I?" I don't understand what is happening.'

His face is red, the veins along his neck swell. Perhaps he will have an aneurism and leave us standing here, sweaty and unsatisfied. That would be just like him.

Yet, you pause. His alarm makes you falter. You shut your eyes so you do not have to look.

'Benny,' you say, your excitement ebbing, exhaustion creeping in. 'We cannot go on like this. What did he tell you?'

A moment of incomprehension, then a moment of abject panic as he catches your meaning.

'That's private,' he whispers, pleading.

'It's time to share,' you say, still not looking at him. 'It's time to be vulnerable.'

I hear your call and approach, there is a pillowcase in my hand.

'I can't,' he hisses. 'You have no right to ask,' and I am not sure what he means by this, but suddenly there is a knock at the door. Demir enters. He stops in his tracks when he sees us and his smile fades.

'Some of the kids were going to have a jam session on the roof,' he says. 'Benny, you've been requested.'

I am paralysed by sudden and instinctive shame, as if he's caught us naked and sprawled on the floor.

Benny darts to the hallway and is gone. We linger, so they leave without us. Of course, we weren't invited anyway.

We hear them shuffle down the hall, hear the fire door squeak open, the sound of chatter and the strumming of a guitar, and we hear the fire door clatter shut.

'You had no choice,' I say to the room, and the room does not answer. 'He knew all along,' I say.

'No,' you answer. 'It doesn't add up.'

'He knows now,' I say, and I hope that this is enough.

We are too exhausted to change, to shut the blinds or brush our teeth. Instead, we lie there as the light bleeds from the room. We do not stir for twelve hours straight. We sleep like athletes.

In the morning, we wake late and discover a note on Benny's pillow. He has absconded, and is travelling north. Demir plans to meet him there when he finishes his morning shift. Benny thanks us for having let him tag along thus far. He suggests we should catch up on the other side. I read it several times. Folded into the note, some cash. He owes us more, I believe, and I inform you that we were short-changed. You seem uninterested. I read the note again. He is still out there; I feel the threat, like distant heat, but we can deal with that when the time is right. For now, I cannot bring myself to panic.

Finally we are alone and I feel satisfied. I feel optimistic about the remainder of our time together. Yet I have to acknowledge that the energy has diminished. It's like the moment after hosting a long and arduous dinner party; even if you hate your guests, even if they have bored you and overstayed their welcome, they inevitably take some vitality with them when they leave. Quiet descends, it takes a moment to adjust to the emptiness of the rooms. We begin gathering the dishes and the glasses, inspecting the furniture for stains, dealing with the mess that has been left behind.

42

Cambridge, 2011
Benny

Benny was working from the basement of his college library, hoping to forget about Raph. He had been there since lunch, six hours in a still and dingy twilight. Somehow Raph had stamped his presence even here; he rose up from the desks like the smell of wood polish and old paper.

Benny was trying and failing to lose himself in airless theory. The article on semiotics was very dense; as he peered down at the cliff-face of words, he experienced a rising panic, as if he were holding his breath. He glanced towards the stairs at the sound of footsteps: *Perhaps...* He forced himself to look back down at the page: *Of course not, he never came here. That was the point.*

It had been a miserable summer. After the stunt at the Union, Benny had feigned outrage. Really, like everyone else, he had been secretly thrilled by Raph's downfall. Partly because Raph had deserved it. Partly because a humiliation of that magnitude would require a long and private rehabilitation, a closed circle, trusted friends only. Raph would need him for support. Even as the disaster unfolded, before the votes had been cast, Benny was phrasing his consolation and preparing soothing remarks.

His predictions had been partially correct. The debate had ushered in a new era of tenderness and intimacy, only Benny had not been the recipient: Elle had. For three long months Benny waited for Raph to call. Instead, he received the same updates as everyone else; a few photos appeared on Facebook, a couple of chipper dispatches posted on a group message.

He pretended to be happy for the couple. When people asked him about it, his tone was bemused and avuncular. *I didn't see it coming*, he might say, *but I think she's good for him. He's finally met his match!* He hoped he sounded wise and knowing, as if he too were no stranger to such affairs, as if he were quietly pleased that Raph was settling down, joining him on a more enlightened path. In fact, Benny was effectively a virgin. Raph's new relationship remained as mysterious to Benny as his previous flings.

It was confusing. For a long time, Benny had convinced himself that this was normal, that beneath the conspiracy of silence, all young men were equally anxiously uncertain. Now, he was not so sure. There were sporadic house parties throughout August, as parents went on holiday. Benny watched the way his schoolfriends pursued girls: with an ease of purpose, with clarity and intention. To Benny, flirting was a test; to them, it was a means to an end.

He did not consider himself gay, though the few fumbles with Raph, and the inordinate amount of time he spent thinking about Raph, and the frequent shameful dreams dedicated to Raph, did provide compelling evidence to the contrary. As final year loomed, Benny decided he needed answers. He forced himself to visit Heaven, a three-storey gay club near Embankment. It seemed like a new frontier. What instincts would wake, what dreadful thawing might begin in the clammy dark? He prepared himself for an unwanted epiphany.

Unfortunately, Benny remained unthawed. He shuffled awkwardly from floor to floor as if undertaking an inspection. Techno was playing upstairs, pop below. There were hundreds of bodies: muscled, skinny, fat, well-dressed or hardly clothed at all. Each was equally strange. His own body remained steadfast and inert.

302

For a long time, he stood at the bar. Eventually, he caught himself watching a man to his left. The guy was middle-aged, bald and wreathed in tattoos. He wore an oversized wifebeater, the gaping armholes offering fleeting glimpses of his lean torso, the occasional flash of a nipple ring.

'First time?' the man asked.

'Yes,' Benny murmured. 'Is it obvious?'

The man smiled. 'Call me Mystic Meg,' he said.

Benny feared entanglement. He worried that even this brief pleasantry offered the stranger false hope.

'You're watching me and shitting yourself,' the man observed.

'What?'

'You're thinking... I don't want to end up looking like that.'

It was exactly what Benny was thinking. There was something faintly grotesque about all the men he witnessed. It was as if their gayness had spread to every part of them, reducing them to caricatures. Even their joy aroused his suspicion; it seemed too overblown, exaggerated, some candied substitute for actual joy. Perhaps, on some level, he simply believed that these people could not truly be happy. Certainly, that was how Raph would see it.

'You think too much,' the man said. 'I used to think too much, too.'

'I'm just not very comfortable here.'

'Don't blame you. This place is a fucking dump.'

'No, as in, I don't think I'm gay,' Benny replied, half expecting the man to sneer, or roll his eyes. Instead, the man simply shrugged.

'Then I predict you're going to break some hearts tonight,' he said, and winked. He pushed a beer towards Benny. 'Drink it. You're shaking like a leaf.'

He watched the man disappear into the next room and sensed a small shoot of possibility. He was not attracted, exactly, and yet he could imagine talking to him for a little longer. He could imagine meeting the man's friends, perhaps straying to the smoking area, where warm bodies were pressed together. That they could touch without forfeiture, without becoming something new.

And then his mind went blank; he had no idea where such moments would lead. The night felt briefly mysterious, briefly ripe. But suddenly a Lady Gaga song started playing and there was a rush to the dancefloor and things became clear once more: he did not belong here.

He left the club feeling sober and relieved. Yet a deeper question remained. There had been women at the club and he had observed them as indifferently as he had their gay friends. Perhaps he possessed a sexuality so tragically niche it was restricted to a single living person: Raph.

Raph was a subtler flavour. With Raph, all the phases of romance were layered together in one delicious gulp: the longing, the surrender, the tragic separation. Even as their bodies tangled, they were preparing their alibis. Maybe Raph offered a closeness made possible by the certainty of its own collapse. As pathetic as it was, Benny liked the fact that Raph did not like him, that Benny's own ambivalence and misgivings were mirrored in Raph's downward sneer. He liked the fact that they remained unchanged after. That they could touch without forfeiture, without becoming something new, like the men in that club.

The new year began and Benny struggled to keep pace. The start of Michaelmas term was a time of ebullience, the whole city misted in promise. Afternoons were warm while the evenings had a thrilling bite; people moved quickly through the streets, huddled close. Everywhere, in the bars, the lecture halls, outrageous plans were being formed, buoyed by a spirit of enterprise and hope. Even seasoned professors seemed a little giddy those first few weeks.

Benny did not attend the opening sessions at the Union; nobody seemed to notice his absence. He experimented with new social groups and left with a sense of empty exertion, as if he had spent hours conversing in a foreign tongue.

And then Raph called. He said he needed to see Benny straight away, his voice sly but urgent. All the soul-searching, all the inconclusive enquiries, those miserable months were forgotten in a moment of exultant relapse. He would have Raph again. They would be together, for a night, at least.

It was not the reunion that he hoped for. Benny made *cacio e pepe*, but Raph, who lived less than five minutes away, showed up late, so the butter clarified and the pasta went cold. Raph glanced at the food with faint concern.

'Mate, do you eat like this all the time?' he asked.

It soon transpired that Raph required technical help. Specifically, he wanted to learn how to anonymise his web activity. Though the brief was clear, Raph kept his broader purpose veiled.

'What makes you think I know anything about that?' Benny asked.

'You're good at hiding things,' Raph replied, his voice serrated. And then he caught himself. 'Look, mate, you're a tech whizz. You do all that stuff with Torrent and Bitcoin. The boys at the Union are still getting their heads round email. Why haven't you been at the Union, by the way? Everyone's asking after you…'

And, of course, Benny relented, unfolding like a petal in temporary warmth. They crowded in front of his small desk, their thighs just grazing.

'Explain it to me like I'm an idiot,' Raph said.

'You are an idiot,' Benny replied, with a cautious note of flirtation. It made Raph visibly shudder. For the rest of the tutorial Benny controlled his tone, comporting himself with professionalism. He taught Raph how to delete his search history, deploy incognito mode, how to disguise himself further through use of a VPN, how to access the deep web via Tor. It was a sprawling tutorial of unnecessary depth. Benny found himself introducing superfluous information, hoping to extend their time together. Raph took notes, attending to the lesson with uncharacteristic focus.

'What's this about?' Benny asked at last, when it was clear that he had imparted everything he could.

'I'm thinking of becoming a porn star,' Raph answered. 'But I don't want my director of studies to find out.'

Benny didn't know how to reply. Of course, he had been thinking about sex since Raph had arrived. As they discussed privacy settings, a part of his mind had roamed, sniffing at the path ahead. Yet there was something so blunt about Raph's tone that Benny recoiled slightly, as if he'd been flashed.

'It was a joke, Benny,' Raph said, rising to his feet and reaching for his jacket.

'I know.'

'You can put your tongue back in your mouth.'

Everyone knows what happened next. Raph released the video on the night of Angie Scott's house party. He sent it via private message to a few friends and they forwarded it on, and it spread like bacteria across the network. Benny watched it happen without quite understanding. Suddenly, boys were whispering, reaching for their phones, guarding their screens. Elle wasn't there, but by midnight, the whole party was muttering her name.

Raph appeared in the early hours to perform a smirking victory lap. Benny found him in the kitchen mixing himself a drink, inspecting a whiskey bottle with disdain.

'What the fuck have you done?' Benny asked.

'Rescued my legacy,' Raph answered. That was all he had to say on the matter.

He had not published the video online, but this remained an option. Benny lectured and pleaded and appealed to his self-interest, *This could hurt you as much as her.* Raph simply regarded him with faint curiosity. Eventually, his patience ran out.

'Ben, stop it. You've never been a hypocrite, so please don't take it up now.'

'Hypocrite?'

'You wanted her gone as much as anyone. More than anyone, I imagine. That's why you helped. Now look, I'm single again: just how you like me.'

He knew he needed to cease contact completely. Benny blocked and then unblocked Raph. He deleted Raph's number, reaching for a more permanent solution. These little gestures did nothing but sharpen his craving. Abstinence was just a whetting stone. Now, when unknown callers flashed on his screen he grew frantic, a jumble of digits and Benny could practically smell Raph's cologne; he answered telemarketers with breathless anticipation.

Benny sat in the library, trying to remain true. When his phone rang, he resolved not to answer it.

Then it rang again and suddenly he felt warm metal against his cheek, cracked glass pressed against his ear.

'Hello?'

Raph whispered his name.

Benny felt his pulse hop beneath his skin. He noticed that Raph's breathing was laboured.

'What is it?' Benny asked.

Raph answered with a slow and luxurious exhalation.

My God... Benny thought, and his mind flicked back to the many times Raph had called and spoken only in rasping breaths.

'I'm not doing this now,' Benny insisted, but he was already hard.

Phone sex at random hours had been a staple of their friendship. As with all things, Raph always initiated. Once, Benny had assumed Raph did it out of fear, requiring the veil of anonymity to truly be himself. Gradually, he had understood that it was more about control. Raph liked the fact that Benny always answered, whether he called in the morning or at dead of night.

Would Benny skip a lecture? He would. Would Benny ditch a drinks party? Or a formal hall? Would he arrive late to a play? Of course. Raph didn't even have to ask. He simply had to pant. He had Benny by the throat, the balls, he always said yes.

'No,' Benny announced, but he was wet, his body awash with rage and dopamine, in mutiny, loyal to Raph. 'We aren't doing this,' he insisted, but his voice was defeated, and his eyes were already drifting to the door. When Raph moaned a little, Benny's nerves trilled in reply. Yes, even after all of this, they both remained in compulsive harmony.

Why fight it? Why try?

'One second,' Benny whispered, glancing furtively to the other desks. Then he was searching for his student ID. Then he was tapping out of the library and rushing towards the men's room, the phone pressed to his ear. Anyone that passed would have assumed he was learning of some tragedy, lurching forward with haunted eyes.

'OK,' he said. 'I'm alone.'

'Ben…' Raph gasped. By now, Benny was so lonely, so untouched, that even hearing his name whispered was like a wave breaking against his chest.

Benny's eyes slid shut. Darkness. A familiar darkness. Strange images emerged from the black. He saw their perfect bodies slammed together. Benny's leg spasmed and collided with damp ceramic of a toilet bowl. He shuddered as a cool bead of condensation travelled his calf. He imagined pushing his hand into Raph's face, watching his features smear beneath the pressure. He imagined Raph grabbing at his hair. His hand worked up and down. He could smell himself, mixed with the damp tiles, the piquant notes of urine and bleach blending with that squalor as Raph reclined somewhere on cotton sheets. He imagined Raph laughing at him, spitting.

Benny climaxed, crying out as if he had been kicked. The emptiness spread, he caught his breath, unsure which shade of degradation had pushed him over the edge. There was distant laughter coming from beyond the door.

'That was the last time,' he said emptily to the phone. Raph had stopped breathing. Benny imagined him sprawled across his bed, his phone dropped to the carpet.

Usually at this moment, Raph would say something cruelly innocuous, as if nothing had happened, or as if it were all so trivial as to warrant no further comment, *Mate, do you think I could borrow your lecture notes?*

Now, Raph did not even give him this. Benny waited and Raph said nothing; perhaps he was already asleep.

The mirror opposite revealed a pitiful sight. His trousers were bunched about his ankles, his boxers slung across his calves in a damp tangle. He was hunched, still clutching himself. His stomach was slightly exposed, thick black hairs curling from the feminine arc of flesh.

'You're pathetic,' Benny said into the receiver. No reply. His voice echoed slightly. 'You're fucking disgusting,' he said. 'You're going to die alone, you know that? Because your an animal, worse than an animal. You're—'

Then the line went dead.

What, exactly, was the last thing Raph heard? Did he survive to hear Benny groan? Did he make it to the insult? Which insult, the first, the second, the last? As his organs shut down one by one, did some part of Raph resist, prevail just long enough to hear Benny declare that he deserved what was happening to him?

Benny lost himself in these details. He forced himself to imagine Raph's last seconds from every angle. Over the weeks, the scene took on monstrous distortions. And then the scene lost meaning and reality, as if the whole episode were cut from the same fabric of a terrible dream. All that remained was a conviction in his own perversity. He was the boy who came as his best friend died. It would take a lifetime of work, an act of unimaginable self-sacrifice to expiate that.

43

It has been said that you and I look androgynous. For a man, I am rather skinny and have little body hair. You are flat-chested, with strong, masculine features, as if you decided to be a girl at the last moment. When we stand side by side, people mistake us for siblings. When we tell them we are man and wife, they pause. *So much for 'opposites attract'*, they sometimes murmur.

Now, our skin has tanned the same shade of brown. Your hair has lightened in the sun, so our resemblance grows uncanny. All this is to say, it can be easy to overlook the differences.

You will have noticed some omissions and distortions in this account. Of course, you'll understand why I've deemed it necessary to make certain amendments. I place your comfort, your safety, above everything, even my desire to be plainly understood. Still, I hope you can read between the lines, that the message therein is legible.

The things that we do to ourselves, to each other, in our minds often possess a greater reality than the things that come to pass. Do I suffer from too much imagination or too little? All I know is that the external world, the world we share with others, can feel so unsatisfying. The world we have created together is vibrant and frighteningly real.

Let's pause on one of the things that did not happen. I propose a thought experiment. Let's imagine that Benny did not pack his bags that night. Let's imagine that he stayed.

We wake at dawn feeling rested and focused: we have been dreaming of Benny all night. His lids slide open and he watches us dress through bleary, bloodshot eyes.

'What the fuck?' he asks. 'What time is it?'

'We're going for a hike,' you say. It is as if yesterday did not happen; your voice connotes sunshine and certainty. Your father taught you that. 'We have to start early before it gets too hot. Are you joining us, or what?'

He looks at me and then he looks at you. He waits a long moment before rising slowly to his feet.

'Come on, lazy bones,' you urge.

Even I'm convinced. For a moment, I'm able to forget that this is just a cover-up, that Benny has seen something about us which we regret showing.

'Everyone's still asleep,' you say. 'So we have to be quiet as mice.'

'I'll meet you two outside,' Benny replies, loudly.

'We can just wait for you—' I say.

'I need to shit, OK?' he snaps. There is vitriol in his voice. Nothing has changed; I believe he truly hates me. In fact, I have a sense that he is coming on this journey not in spite of me, but because of me.

'We'll be out front,' you tell him.

The burnt-orange sky hangs low and caps the earth strangely. Benny emerges, looking shiftless and uncomfortable. His enormous backpack is strapped to his shoulders, though he has emptied out most of its contents so that it sags and bounces limply as he walks.

He trips over a broken paving stone and swears.

'Quiet!' you hiss, glancing up at the still-sleeping hostel.

We turn left and walk along the motorway, ignoring the red signs warning us of invisible pitfalls. We find the trail of flattened grass, then veer right towards the mountainous nature reserve. Cicadas scream in the tall reeds.

'I just got déjà vu,' Benny remarks. His voice has softened. Perhaps the exercise, that first rush of endorphins, is helping him to relax.

'Careful,' you warn, 'you'll get me talking about outer space again. Then my husband will have another fit.'

Benny sniggers. We press on.

'Things got kind of heated last night,' he says. You shrug. 'The fact is, maybe you were right to be kind of pissed at me. I haven't been totally open with you.' You falter, just slightly, then regain your pace.

I am the phantom at your back. I watch. I listen. You do not know if you wish for him to continue. It doesn't matter any more. For the first time in a long time, the path ahead is clear.

'Let's just focus on having a good day,' you say.

The path climbs gently and the vegetation grows thicker. Branches tangle above our heads and reduce the light. The air tastes of hot, dry leaves.

You are reading from an A3 brochure you have borrowed from the hostel, and identifying rare plants as we pass. I am navigating from a hiker's map.

'Christ's thorn jujube,' you say, indicating a copse of bristled trees.

I hear the distant call of a raven.

'Sodom's apple,' you say, pointing to a tree bearing a green, waxy fruit, the size and heft of a baseball. Benny plucks one and pitches it into the overgrowth; we do not hear it land. You and I try the same, casting stones that make no echo.

We climb upwards. You are ahead of me, wearing a white

cotton dress hemmed in Grecian blue. Gladiator sandals. You look like a priestess come to preside over a blood offering.

The leafy plants give way to barbed cacti. At length, we reach a waterfall. Without speaking, the three of us strip to our underwear and wade into the emerald pool. You stand beneath the falling water and run your hands through your hair.

'You look like you're in a Herbal Essences advert,' Benny calls.

You begin moaning ecstatically and scrubbing at your scalp. Benny laughs, paddles your way and joins you beneath the pounding waters. His stomach is white, hair spreading like moss across his torso. His boxers have slipped low, revealing the plunging lines of pelvic bones. Do you notice these things? Do you notice the way his body pivots towards yours? Do you wonder if you wouldn't be happier with a man like this, light, silly and forgetful?

I sit on a rock and let the moisture evaporate from my skin.

You two swim into the waterfall and find a ledge within; I watch your bodies flicker in the refracting light. You remain there for a long time.

When you burst back through, you are ebullient, delighted.

You return to me breathing quickly, arms covered in goose-bumps and cheeks glowing.

'You didn't join us,' you say.

'No,' I confirm.

'You're not going to believe what he just told me.'

'No more,' I order. 'No more words.'

'You're going to want to hear this, trust me.'

Benny is about two metres away, watching us in the corner of his eye.

'I can't say now,' you continue. 'But he's not a threat. He's not anything, just... sad. Lost.'

I inadvertently shudder. In those words, you muster more compassion for our interloper than you have ever shown me.

'Abort,' you whisper. 'We can abort.'

You say Benny is not a threat. You are good at assessing risk. But only if it affects you directly, and our interests do not always align. This is something I have learnt these past few days.

'You looked very serious, sitting here on your own. Like a frustrated anthropologist.' Your voice is friendly but calculating. You sigh. 'Things don't have to be so serious,' you say. There is the faintest note of longing in your voice. You yearn for the inconsequential. But I cannot offer you this; I never could.

'We should press on,' I state.

'I've got to be back by noon,' Benny warns. 'I promised Demir I'd meet him for lunch.'

'Just a little further,' I say. 'We'll be back in time.'

'To be honest, I'm starting to feel a bit knackered myself,' you say, your voice careless but calculating. You are trying to broker a deal.

The path lurches upwards and contracts, forcing us to walk in single file. It narrows further, so that my feet no longer fit and I have to cling to the wall of rock to maintain balance. Now, the path is all precipice. Beneath us, a sheer drop.

'Did you say this was the gentle trail?' Benny asks.

'Yes, it's marked in black,' I say.

'Black means difficult!' he exclaims. 'It means experienced hikers only. Christ, we're not even in the right shoes. She's wearing bloody sandals.'

'I'm OK,' is your quick reply.

Dirt and dry twigs crunch beneath my feet. Pumice fragments crumble and fall over the edge. I listen to their whispery decline and imagine my own body falling until the backs of my knees feel like sponge. It is not the likelihood but the proximity to certain death that makes me dizzy. A single lapse of concentration, and my body would plummet. I realise that I do not fully trust myself. It is so tempting to fall, to let myself slip.

The path wraps the mountain like a vein. You round a corner and vanish.

'I really don't like this,' Benny says. 'I'm too hungover.'

'It gets easier up ahead,' you call out. And because we cannot see you, your voice sounds apparitional; the spirit of the land.

We find you waiting in a clearing. It fits the three of us, but forces us close together. Above my heavy breathing, I hear a flock of invisible birds sing to each other, their delirious voices overlapping.

'Benny, you look like you've seen a ghost,' you say.

'Funny you should mention death. This is fucking dangerous. Am I the only one picking up on that?'

'It seemed easier on the map.'

'We didn't even pack proper supplies…'

'Would you like some of my water?'

'I would like to be back at the hostel in time for lunch,' he snaps. 'I told you I had plans. And I'm only here because…' his voice trails as he senses my approach.

'I'm sorry,' you say. 'Do you want to turn back?'

'There's barely enough room to turn. Besides, there's no way we can take that route downhill.' He sounds angry and caged. 'We're fucked.'

'I said I'm sorry!' you repeat, sufficiently contrite to make him soften. 'Look, it was a mistake. I wasn't doing this to scare you.'

'Yes, well, I scare easily,' Benny states with a self-deprecating shrug. 'We both know I can be a bit of a coward.'

Again, you take the lead. Now the trail is broad but steep. A burn begins in my calves and travels up my legs.

'You're not, by the way,' you say.

'What?'

'A coward. I don't see you that way at all.'

Benny's voice soften. 'I know I am. Kind of you, but I don't need reassurance.'

He intuits something. Beneath the sounds of nature, the breeze in the trees, our shuffling feet, perhaps he hears the faint ticking of a clock. Benny quickens a few paces so he is at your elbow.

'We all make mistakes,' he says with intensity. 'I have made massive ones. We don't have to let them define us. We can change.'

With a jolt, I realise he actually wants to save you. He is trying to save you from me.

We have reached another clearing where the rock overhangs a valley, dramatically plunging in a near-vertical line. The birds are shrieking in my ears, crazed and gleeful. You walk right up to the edge. Benny follows.

'You have to move on from Raph,' Benny says. 'I know what it's like to be bound up in that sort of obsession. He made me forget who I was. After uni, I ran right back into the closet. I was too numb to notice what I'd become. It ruined my music, my lyrics were empty, fake…'

'Your music is unsuccessful because you lack talent, Benny,' I say.

He freezes. He meets my eye.

'You're just like him,' Benny murmurs. 'Beneath the charm…' He hesitates. He sees something.

'Go on,' I say, my voice is warm and inviting. But there is a rock in my hand. He notices it.

Benny looks quizzical and irritated for a moment, but then remembers himself. He remembers he is here for you.

'I have always been trying to kill Raph,' he says. 'He made you vulnerable to other men, never trusting your instincts. I could've killed him for what he did.'

'Yes, well, conveniently someone else did it for you,' I reply.

'What?'

'You don't get points for thinking about things,' I say.

You tense. We have crossed a line. I see you struggle to subvert the inevitable, a flash of panic on your face.

'And we're not like you,' I say. 'We don't harbour regrets. Raph was only the start.'

'The start,' he echoes, confused.

'Cut it out,' you hiss. 'He's joking, Benny. You know what he's like.'

'Benny, I'm not joking.'

'He is.'

'Benny, we murdered Raph and now we're going to murder you.'

We cannot go back. What's done is done.

Benny turns. He is backlit by the sun. A nimbus of flies is weaving behind him; they know what's coming. The birds sing madly.

Black dots glitter in my peripheral vision.

It's as if the oxygen is richer up here. I'm dizzy with it, I feel it in every cell.

There's a look in your eyes of frightened vertigo.

'Elle, you don't have to stay,' he blurts. 'You're better on your own.'

'We are always together,' I state, flatly.

'For now,' he says.

'Forever.'

You are staring at him, not at me. You are not reading my cues. You are failing to notice that I've advanced a pace. That my knees are slightly bent, my centre of gravity lowered.

'What's happening here, Elle?' Benny asks with panic. 'Elle—'

You reel towards me. 'Wait,' you say.

But the first stone is cast and cracks his nose. His bag slips from his shoulder. Blood flows over his mouth. Blood flows over his chin and onto his shirt. It drips into the porous rock below.

He looks at me, stunned. Two fingers up like a martyred saint. He observes that there is another rock in my hand. Behind him, there is a chasm. He sees that he has seconds left to live. Nothing. Measured against the scale of his life, against the hours and years, what is left is immeasurably small. He is already dead. From a certain perspective, it has already happened.

Yet here he is, still standing, still staring, still sentient enough to observe the curious spectacle of his own murder. He blinks twice, his sight is tinted red.

Perhaps he can live. He looks down at his bag.

Now, he no longer has thoughts, just images. Images of himself, diving for my legs. Images of his head split open. Images of his fingers round my throat. Primordial visions, conceived by his ancestors, passed through the bloodline. He must fight.

'Stop?' you say, you ask. Not a command but a question. You have never sounded quite so weak. But now I realise you are also holding a rock. Your gaze is focused on my neck.

You are not sure. I realise you are mentally flipping a coin. Heads: Benny. Tails: me. Heads for valour, tails for safety. Pick heads and you can live with yourself, pick tails and you will live long and luxuriously. You think you struggle. I watch the revelation dawn across your tortured features. You are no hero. You're not much of a wife either; a wife would never have flipped the coin.

Benny reaches for his bag, and my second rocks lands against his temple. A thin jet of blood slashes across my chin, marks my mouth.

He glances up, dazed and plaintive. This is how he will appear in my dreams.

He falls to the ground with the third rock. There is a dull cracking sound. I think of a spoon against a soft-boiled egg. I think of shell fragments biting into the flesh within.

I am standing over Benny. I shove him once with my heel. Then again. His body flops like used rubber and he is on his back. I shove him again. He tumbles over the edge and you scream, suddenly terrified, as if you are falling with him.

A series of dull thuds, snaps, and then nothing. For a moment, the birds have been stunned into silence. Then, tentatively, one by one, they begin their song again. How quickly nature resumes and forgets. Weeds will grow over him. His body will turn to soil. I cannot tell if this gives me comfort.

There are bloodstains on the ground. I kick at them until the dark patches fade and disappear. Dust, fine as smoke, rises and coats my shins. For a queasy second, I imagine some small part of Benny lingering in the air to be inhaled.

'We agreed not to,' you say, simply, as if I've just accepted some dinner invitation on your behalf.

For a second my mind is blank and stupid. Death leaves behind a rupture. Briefly, it untethers thought.

'We didn't agree to anything,' I say.

'It wasn't necessary this time.'

'He was a threat.'

You look at me, doubtful. 'A threat?'

'He knew.'

'He *suspected*.' Your fingers flutter to your cheekbone. They are searching for something – a smudge, a spray of blood – to wipe away, but there is nothing there. Your skin is perfect.

'He saw right through us,' I say.

'Yes,' you remark. 'He probably did.'

I rifle through his bag and retrieve a blunt bread knife, likely stolen from the communal kitchen. I push it against my hand; it creates a depression in the flesh, but draws no blood. Despite your mood, you laugh and it puts me at ease.

'What was he going to do with that?' you wonder.

'I don't know. Prod me to death.'

'That couldn't slice a sandwich.'

Right now, these are still just fragments, absurd and individual. There is no context so there is no meaning. But that will come, and it will land heavily.

I toss the bag over the edge, but stash the knife. If the body and the knife are found together, questions could be raised.

'I guess he knew something wasn't right,' you say.

'But why did he agree to come?'

'I think he wanted to give me a chance to escape.'

I stare into the distance. 'It had nothing to do with you,' I state, but my voice is vague and unconvincing.

We backtrack. We wash in the same waters where Benny frolicked only an hour before. We forge on. The sun is high, white-hot and unrelenting.

You say, 'It feels different this time.'

'Quiet,' I snap. My eyes dart reflexively. Our voices might carry on the wind.

'You have to be kidding me. You're worried someone's going to overhear? Look around, it's just you, me and our Maker. And He probably doesn't give a shit. That's become pretty obvious.'

'I don't know what's got into you.' My thoughts run clear but my heart is still pounding. I am racing ahead – what will we say to Demir – and scanning backwards – did anybody see us leave this morning?

'We left before the others were awake,' you say with a hint of frustration. You are grappling with issues of the soul; my concerns are practical.

'That's good,' I say.

'Doesn't it make you sick? How easy it becomes…'

'Stop.'

'Benny saw me differently,' you insist. 'I don't think anyone has seen me like that.'

'So?'

'I could have told him anything and he would have forgiven me. I think that's why he stuck around so long.' You sigh. 'It seems to me that if Benny had forgiven us, forgiven me, things would be different somehow.'

'That's the stupidest thing I've ever heard.'

'Why?'

'Because he's the stupidest person I've ever met.'

'You asked me,' you reply, quietly.

I think about the girl on Raph's hard drive. Then I think of Benny and his foolhardy bid to save you. He didn't understand. We transcend the grey and petty, the ordinary lives of others.

This is what I see for us. My vision is my charge.

'He was a decent man,' you say. 'He tried to put good things into the world.'

'And we take bad things out. That's just as useful.'

320

You rub your head and wince. We could debate all day but it wouldn't make a difference. For now, it's as if the world has been stretched past its elastic limits; it sags, it droops.

I notice that I am shivering. My skin is numb. All I know is that I would commit any atrocity for you. I would kill and maim and lay bloody offerings at your feet. Surely that counts for something.

44

We are descending the mountain. We are on the motorway. The hostel is in sight. A girl waves frantically from the beach. She hops over the steel guardrail and jogs towards us, meeting us in the middle of the road. It is your girl, Stella.

'What the fuck?' she demands.

'Sorry,' you say. 'We got distracted.'

'So I've been out here growing a melanoma because you were "distracted"?'

'Have you got it?'

She digs through her side bag and produces Benny's phone. She slaps it into your waiting hand indignantly.

'I could have given it to you in the hostel. I don't see why this had to be so cloak and dagger.'

You check to make sure the phone is off and say, 'I appreciate this.'

'Well, I don't get it. That thing is worth all of, what, ten dollars?'

She is trying to impress you. Even in her indignation, she flaunts. The girl has not looked at me once.

'I don't plan on hawking it,' you state. You switch on the phone. It is not pin protected. You switch it back off. 'And you can't tell anyone about this.'

'Obviously.'

'No. Not *obviously*, I need you to understand. If something happens to Benny – and, God willing, it won't – but if something did, they would blame you. And why wouldn't they? From their perspective, all they'll see is a dysfunctional dropout from a flyover state with a history of petty crime. They will see the CCTV at the spa, where you are flagrantly lifting this from Benny's bag—'

'Hold up. There—'

'There was CCTV at the spa. I didn't mention it because I didn't want to frighten you. They will also notice that you were missing and unaccountable for a good section of the morning.'

'So were you! What the fuck is going on here?'

'I was with my husband on the beach,' you calmly reply. 'And back home I'm an upstanding citizen, not an angry girl with a prescription for antidepressants.'

'I was doing you a favour,' she says. It is as if you've stolen her voice and left her with just a whisper. For a moment, everything about her – her cut-off shorts, her cheap, lime-green bag, her confusion – seems devastatingly young.

I avert my eyes.

'I trusted you,' she says, still in that quiet voice, more bewildered than angry.

Your face is granite. Your eyes hardly blink. But you make a slight movement. It begins in your stomach, a sort of contraction, as if you had just been punched and are trying to absorb the blow.

'I meant what I said to you on the first day,' you state. 'Don't trust anyone. And I'll add to that lesson now: give a wide berth to people who resonate. Maybe if you were happier you'd make better friends. But for now, don't rely on your gut.'

Stella shakes her head and timidly says, 'Fuck you.' She waits a beat longer, hoping, perhaps, that this is all a joke, that you will recant and make the unpleasantness disappear. But you give her nothing.

She turns and runs off, face lowered, looking much like a girl who has had her heart broken for the first time. Or perhaps like a girl who has had her heart broken too many times to count.

You stand there and watch.

'So, this was all part of your plan,' I say, surprised by the note of accusation in my voice.

'There was no plan.'

'And yet here we are. Benny's phone will not have pinged next to ours at the time of his disappearance. And he won't have been able to text anyone to say we were together. And, by now, you have access to his emails, no doubt. Or at least the answers to his security questions. I heard you on the bus. I knew—'

'There was no plan,' you say again. 'There were only provisions.' You begin walking towards the hostel. 'He could have been with us, right now, discovering his phone between the cushions in the common room. And I could have been with her, in a dorm, popping Xanax and gossiping. This is the outcome you chose, where everything and everyone is broken. But I agree, it does feel predictable. It does feel like we were always going to end up here.'

I seize your wrist. 'Bullshit,' I hiss. 'You've been planning this for days. I know you. You wanted it.'

'You forced my hand.'

'This is ridiculous,' I say.

'He brought a knife. You spend every waking hour staring, watching, but for some reason you assume that you yourself can't be seen. Benny understood the way you looked at him. The way you talked to him. He saw you.'

This catches me slightly off guard. The words coalesce strangely, another version of events begins to form. I keep talking, to chase the thought away. 'I'm sorry. I'm so bloody sorry that—'

'You don't know the meaning of the word.'

'So, what does it mean?'

'Maybe it doesn't mean anything. For me, it's just a way of life.'

And you stay resolutely silent for the rest of the walk, even though I desperately want to talk, or argue, rail at you, anything. It is a punishment. It is a familiar punishment, one that I deserve.

There is a new face at reception alongside the familiar one. Demir practically leaps at the sight of us. His face is clean-shaven and slick with moisturiser. Today, he is wearing a collared shirt and slim, expensive-looking jeans.

'Hey guys,' he exclaims, glancing past our shoulders; he is expecting Benny.

'Hello, Demir,' you reply. You take a moment, bracing yourself.

'This is Eva. She'll be running the place for the next two days,' he says, still watching the door.

'If you ever leave, that is,' Eva says. Her voice is warm and teasing, a smile plays on her lips. 'This guy has been bouncing off the walls all morning,' she tells us. 'He doesn't know how to relax, even on his day off.'

You remain tensely by my side.

Eva works her way across the room, then hefts a sack of linens. 'I'll be in the laundry room,' she says to nobody in particular.

When she is gone, you approach the desk. 'We are supposed to be checking out today, but I was wondering if it would be possible to stay another night?'

'Oh. Sure...' he replies, the first ripple of confusion crossing his face. 'When Eva gets back, I'm sure she can sort it.'

'Fantastic. I'll take it up with her then.'

'And that will be... the three of you?'

'What?'

'It's just, I thought... Benny and I had plans to travel a little, but maybe that's all changed. Is he—'

'Benny left this morning. At least, as far as I'm aware.'

'Left? As in, permanently? I don't get it'

'I think he made a little detour perhaps… He said he had a date with that girl. Stella? She came with us to the spa the other day and he's had designs on her ever since.'

'She just came back,' he states, tonelessly. 'She didn't look like she'd been on a date. She looked like she'd been crying…'

'I worried that would happen,' you reply with a frown. 'Benny's no gentleman.'

'Oh, come on! Benny? Benny is a geek. He reads Renaissance poetry… He's hardly some rabid frat boy.'

'We've known him a little longer than you, Demir.'

Though he seems to reject the information, some part of his mind is absorbing it. Doubts invade the most tender places of his imagination. There, they will metastasise. Wreak havoc on him for months to come. He will learn to question himself a little more.

'I don't get it,' you say, resting your arm against the front desk. 'I know this isn't very "PC" or whatever, and I adore Benny, but sometimes I think bisexuals are just sort of… greedy.'

You look to me for confirmation. I nod obediently. You are being deliberately ugly. You are exposing the world we inhabit together, the necessary evils that sustain us. The singularity of purpose. The vulgarity.

Demir's eyes are unfocused but his pupils contract. He is looking at something that is not observable to anyone else.

'We'll sort out the reservation later,' you say.

We go upstairs and scour the room for Benny's belongings. His clothes are absorbed into our own luggage, his diary is stashed in your purse. You look frail as you move about the room.

The adrenaline is finally wearing off, leaving me in a state of painful withdrawal. I glance about the room looking for a task, something to fix.

'You're always thinking,' you say. 'Sometimes when I sit close, I believe I can hear it.'

'Everyone's always thinking.'

'Not really,' you reply. 'The first time we kissed, I didn't think anything at all. My mind went completely blank. Totally empty. I'd never experienced that before. It's probably why I liked kissing you so much… I craved another hit of the void.'

I have not eaten for hours, but my stomach is somersaulting, I feel like I could retch. Black flies will hatch where his eyes should be. A rustle. A scavenger will pick up the scent of rot and approach him slowly, with interest.

I am standing. When I shut my eyes, I see bone pierce weathered skin, so I am trying not to blink.

'I need some air,' I say.

'So get some air,' you reply.

You retrieve your phone and in a moment or two pornography begins to play. A man is asking a girl if she has ever had sex on camera before.

'Do you have to do that now?' I ask, annoyed, incredulous.

You do not respond.

'Use headphones,' I say, but you do not even look up. 'I don't know why I bother saying this out loud. I should just get my dick out, upload it to an amateur channel. You'd be more likely to get the message.'

'That's really—'

'What?'

'Never mind.'

'Tell me,' I bate you with uncharacteristic vehemence. I can't tell if I'm angry that you're watching porn, or that you're not watching it enough. Your eyes are glazed, your movements strange and perfunctory. You stare at the screen the way a blind person might. 'Go on,' I say again.

Instead, you simply lock your phone and toss it aside. Something in this gesture tells me that we will not have this argument again. Even if the video finally surfaced, even if you found that girl now, you would have nothing in common with her.

'Why don't you get some air,' you say.

The low is part of the high. I will return, I tell myself. I will return to earth.

The building seems to rearrange around me and I discover myself in the empty common room. Demir stands at the kitchen counter; his copy of *The Faerie Queen* has resurfaced. He no longer has a reason to leave the hostel or to take a break from his work. Demir squints at the page. Leans in. His brows knit together; he has seen something in the page he does not like, perhaps a stray line whose significance he'd overlooked and which compromises his thesis.

The problem with living life in such tight focus is that any small disruption – the formulation of a paragraph, an internal contradiction – has a catastrophic register.

What did Benny tell him? Will he put it together? When they discover Benny's body, will he speak up? Or will he just retreat deeper into his book for meaning? Lacerate himself with trivialities and ignore the rest.

A solipsist builds his home on shifting sands. His materials are driftwood, twigs, leaves. But there is a terrible storm each night, whipping gales, floods, and his every thought, his every impulse, is devoted to maintenance, to saving the rickety structure from collapse.

'You making any progress with that?' I ask.

Demir starts and looks up. For a fraction of a second, he seems saddened by the interruption. I have invited him to pan out, to remember where he stands; he appears disappointed to find himself here. He remembers the world that awaits him, where all interactions are seen through a rubric of menial demands: sheets to be cleaned, deposits to be collected, payments to be processed. New faces every day and all the while, an aching desire to connect. It is like dying of thirst at sea. Better to work. Better to go deeper into the poem.

'I wouldn't say progress,' he replies. 'I only make progress occasionally. You work and work and work and then one day it sort of clicks into place,' he says emptily.

'When will you finally finish?'

'You never finish a PhD, you just publish or abandon it.'

'I don't think I'd have the patience for that sort of higher learning,' I say. I am still searching his face for a clue, for a trace of mistrust, a desire to challenge or attack.

'Oh, it's nothing to do with patience,' he says. 'I mean, yes, a lot of patience is involved... but really, academia is the only thing I know how to do. And it feels a bit late to try anything else.'

He will not be the man to defeat me. Perhaps he could have been, should Benny have lived; people spur changes in each other. But that possibility is gone.

I smile politely. 'My wife and I have had a lot of fun here. Much more than expected.'

'Yes,' he says, nothing more.

'I'm sorry my friend disappeared.'

'Oh,' he says, and looks down. 'I mean, I can't be too surprised about that. I work in a hostel. Besides, people disappear; it's what they do.'

'Yes,' I confirm. Except Benny doesn't. It was his only strength: he stuck. 'Well, either way, it was shitty. We were pissed off ourselves – he didn't even chip in for the room.'

And somehow it's like I've murdered Benny again. Only, this feels worse. Demir makes an excuse to leave. I think of Stella and Benny and you and Raph and Demir. I stay like this. Sometimes, alone, the dull monotony of my worries has a hypnotic effect, the pattern of each anxiety is so familiar that I'm lulled; my own thoughts feel like lithium.

You find me downstairs and invite me for an evening stroll. You take my hand and lead me to reception. I notice that your skin smells of clementine. You say your new moisturiser is too thick

329

to absorb properly. Eva overhears you and suggests you switch to aloe vera. You say maybe. You say you'll consider it.

The doors shut behind us; our hands separate and you fall silent. The chill is sudden and total; it is like a cloud passing over the sun.

Perhaps this is what would have occurred if Benny had stayed.

Then again, in terms of everything important, in terms of us, does it really make any difference whether it happened or not?

45

From: benny5000@gmail.com
To: Heather.Simpson@hotmail.co.uk
Subject: RE: Summer

Yo Heather,

Yes, I'm still alive. Sorry... I lost my phone and there's fuck-all reception out here anyway. All in all, a complete shitemare. On the bright side, I wanted to disconnect from London vibes, so maybe it was a blessing in disguise. You get it.

Obv will be back for Carnival, can't wait. Are you thinking of going on the Sunday? The Monday? Both? Lemme know.

Things have been OK. Working at the school was mad-fulfilling and put my own shit into perspective, I suppose. Since then, I've been hanging with this couple – those friends from uni who I mentioned last time. You know how some people come along at just the right moment? Well, I guess it follows that some people come along at precisely the wrong moment. I felt like the wife and I could have been friends if we'd met back in London. But ultimately she was just too much work. Sort of a wannabe Madame Bovary. Whenever she opened her mouth, I couldn't tell if she was going to laugh, or scream. I don't think she could tell either. I felt sorry for her, but then... some people just make shit decisions, then spend the rest of their life bitching about it. Ultimately, fuck them. Ultimately, all they do is take. Maybe she deserves what she's got. Anyway, if I ever had thoughts of marriage, I have been cured of them.

This morning I gave them the slip... didn't say goodbye. Does that make me a terrible person?

I can't wait to see you. I had a (very brief) romance and I want to share all the gory details. I've written some new songs; I think you'll like them.

I really do think I did good work with those kids. It's something.

Benny XX

From: Heather.Simpson@hotmail.co.uk
To: benny5000@gmail.com
Subject: RE: Summer</EML INFO>

Heather! So formal!

Shit, that sounds awful. How do you always end up meeting these people??? I finish at nine – want to FaceTime? You seem like you could use some contact.

Hetty X

From: Heather.Simpson@hotmail.co.uk
To: benny5000@gmail.com
Subject: RE: Summer

Hello??? Please don't disappear again.

Hetty X

46

On our last day, we wake late and wait for dusk before venturing to the Sea of Tears for a final time. We walk along the motorway, listening to our feet slap against tarmac. Within steps, it feels as if we've been walking for miles and our clothes are soiled.

'God, it's hot,' I state.

'Yes,' you answer politely.

'I don't know how the locals manage…'

'I suppose they acclimatise. You can acclimatise to anything.'

There are moments when we hear ourselves and are terrified. We exchange phrases that pre-date us, were minted by others, have been in circulation for generations. I listen to the way I talk to you, as if you are someone to be deceived or placated, and feel I am committing some violation. You hear it too, and respond with pointed pleasantries, as if to say: *this is all that remains.*

On a deserted stretch of beach, you sit against a rock, ready to finish your book. You are reading intently, but I can tell you are already taking less pleasure in the subject. You're reading now to get it done, to put it behind you. In the distance, I watch a busload of pensioners wobble into the water. As they enter, they shriek with alarm and flap about in pain. You don't notice them or me. You look up from your book and stare past it all. I feel shy, approach you like a penitent.

'Check out those geriatrics screaming in the water. It's Kafkaesque,' I say.

You say nothing. You are staring at the horizon as if conversing with it.

'Don't you think?' I ask.

'What?'

'Check out those—'

'That isn't what "Kafkaesque" means. Kafkaesque doesn't just mean "strange".'

I hug my knees. The sea is the colour of lapis and is glowing in the late sun. It quietly evaporates, filling the air with moisture as it shrivels. One day it will be a great sandy scar in the landscape. It is happening even now, at a rate just below visible perception. The sky above is as purple as a bruise.

'You bore me to tears,' I practically hiss. It is the cruellest thing I can think of. You roll your eyes as if I've confirmed some low expectation, but I know you're hurt. Becoming tedious is one of your deepest fears.

I get up and walk. It is important that we separate now, briefly, if we are to be civil by dinner. And I need you to be kind by dinner. It is no secret that you are the intended audience of all my actions. You are my only referent. Without you, my gestures are like prayers floating in outer space, clutter in the cosmos. Our thoughts find completion in each other. When we are not communing, sentences just echo in my skull.

Suddenly, the earth gives way. The ground swallows. In an instant, it consumes my ankles, my shins, my knees. I try to squirm free but slide deeper down, as if I'm working with the pit, coaxing my body into its throat. My thigh vanishes. I am seconds from disappearing and I can see it: the landscape will remain still and quiet as my lungs fill with mud. Instincts wake. My legs go rigid and my arms clutch the sides of the pit, I heave myself vertically then tip myself towards solid ground. As my leg swings forward, my swimming trunks shred and fall away. I emerge naked, my chest heaving, and covered in mud, like the first man.

The mud dries and cakes almost instantly. As I walk, it breaks from my body in clumps. I walk to the Sea of Tears, easing myself into the boiling waters.

The salt seeks out the most delicate parts – patches of skin that are grazed and raw, spaces inside that are moist and tender – and punishes them. I wince as the salt finds its way into discreet cuts, stabs at an abrasion along my thigh. I step forward and the water lurches up to my chest. It gets inside me. It slices.

All around, tendrils of steam unfurl and wave at the sky.

The salt stings with precision, as if it knows my body, its vulnerabilities, better than I know it myself. I flinch: a muscle tightens, its neighbour constricts; tension grinds up my torso. I think of the millions of nerve-endings packed within, dormant until they wake and scream. I think of the messages shooting through my flesh, the intricate networks now rallying. My body rages, my heart races. And I feel alive, even though I am jerking like a marionette. I fall backwards, and the water catches me, keeping me afloat.

My eyes fill with salt tears and everything shimmers. I grimace. My jaw clenches shut and my lips curl into a forbearing smile.

When I return, you are done reading. You toss me a towel from your bag without comment. It's time to go.

You leave your book on the beach for another traveller. Predictably, it has offered no answers. We are each other's universe, outer space is once again a tedious abstraction. I ask if you'd care for a dip and you say there's no need. I tell you that it's invigorating, that I feel alive, that the water feels alive. You say we have to make a move.

A memory crosses my mind. We went to South Korea in the

rainy season. Though neither of us admitted it, for the first time it seemed as though we had nothing to say to each other and the prospect was fairly terrifying. You kept complaining that it didn't feel real, that you didn't feel real. I couldn't understand.

'It just feels like we could be anywhere… I don't feel connected to this place. I can't explain it.'

'It's because we're stuck in the hotel. And we can't exactly see Seoul properly through all the storms.'

'No, it's not that. It's deeper than that. Something doesn't exist.'

I took you to a fish market on the outskirts of the city to eat live octopus; an authentic experience, something unique. We arrived late, after the vendors had packed up, and passed through the abandoned space, empty crates, streaks of blood, the smell of something rancid in the air.

The restaurant was little more than a hole in the wall. The only other patrons were drunk on soju and beginning to fall asleep. The chef brought out the octopus, sliced it before our very eyes and scooped the tentacles into a small bowl.

It was the most disgusting plate of food I will ever see. The bits of limb writhed and clutched and knotted together. Their suction cups slapped against the bowl and inched up, as if to make an escape. You plucked a piece from the bowl, dipped it in the chilli sauce and ate. You chewed for a long time and then ate some more.

'You look like you're going to faint,' you said.

'I think this is a bit much for me.'

'It's dead,' you said.

'Yes, but—'

'It's dead,' you affirmed again.

One stray tentacle broke from your mouth and grabbed at your lips. The electrical impulses continued to fire long after death. The nerves continued to shoot, as if its very agony were keeping it alive.

Acknowledgements

Thank you to Nuno L. Whether being ambushed with a literary reading at the end of the day, or a tirade or an inspiration, you have always responded with generosity and insight. It's impossible to define all the ways in which you've helped, both with this project and everything that surrounds it; suffice it to say, meeting you remains my luckiest break. Thank you to my mom for seriously applying her thoughts to countless edits of this book, overcoming the awkwardness of certain chapters and keeping the flame going during moments of extreme doubt. Thank you to my sister for always being my advocate. A special thank you to all the first readers whose support helped me weather uncertain times: Helen G (it's hard to believe it's been fifteen years since that chance encounter at the British Library, I truly cannot wait to get my hands on your own debut), Amy W (who battled a fever in Panama to get through an early draft and has read virtually everything I've done), Shama (who read the novel with such zeal that she managed to generate some early hype among the backpacking community in Mexico), Sophie W (your dreamy voice notes remain some of my most unique, if not surreal, feedback). I am grateful to the original pet monsters, Wam and Daisy I., two early readers who allowed me to reinterpret our actual holiday so strangely and still remained, as always, joyfully supportive. Thank you for this and for all of the adventures. A special thank you to Becca J, not only for her friendship and unwavering support, but for the gruelling job of performing the first scrupulous copy-edit on a very messy manuscript. It was no small task and just one of the many ways in which you've shown yourself forever willing to jump into the trenches for those you care about. A shout-out to the entire Mother May I group: Taz, Lora M, Haz, Abi M, Hoz, Henning GS, Ed K: you all know what you did. Life would be so much greyer without this gang. Thanks to Sas V, Rebecca H, Deli S, Rachel B and Niccy D for the afternoon calls.

Clare Bullock is the sort of editor that writers dream about. She has brought so much passion and sensitivity to this project; the experience of working together is something I will take with me for a long time. Thank you to the entire Duckworth team, a group of professionals who are unwaveringly industrious and delightful. A huge thank you to Genesis Foundation and Jewish Literary Foundation, it's hard to imagine that any of this would have happened without the support of their incredible Emerging Writers' Programme. I have been so lucky to be mentored by Sophie Mackintosh, a writer I deeply admire. Sophie's generosity with her time and thoughts is something I hope to pay forward one day. Equally, her injunction to go weirder is also just great advice, generally. Thank you to the Society of Authors and Arts Council England for offering funding at a vital stage of edits. Thank you to Cara Lee Simpson for her excitement about this novel.

I have had some great teachers and supervisors over the years who have all left an imprint. Thank you to Micheal H, Jeff M and Robin K for an incredible undergraduate education and lessons that I still remember. UEA was a life-changing experience and I was very fortunate to have two extraordinary workshop leaders. I am grateful to Naomi Wood, who fundamentally shifted my approach to line editing, bringing more accountability and control to the process. I am also thankful to Andrew Cowan, who read the early, amputated short story that this novel is based on and encouraged me to keep going. Thank you to my fellow workshoppers Niamh G and Louise L, both great writers who nudged this project in particular directions, perhaps without realising. Thank you to Arathi M for powering through an early draft and for generally being an iconic practitioner and devotee of the arts. Thank you to John T and Maddie M for colouring that entire period of my life. Thank you to Bonita M for all your help and clarity outside of the editorial process.

It has been incredibly fun writing this section of the book and there are others, less directly linked to this project, who have made just as much of an impact. Despite my interest in dissecting character flaws, I've been unusually blessed by the actual people who comprise my life.